WHITEOAK HARVEST

WHITEOAK HARVEST

MAZO DE LA ROCHE

DUNDURN PRESS
TORONTO

Project Editor: Michael Carroll
Copy Editor: Jennifer McKnight
Design: Jennifer Scott
Printer: Marquis

Library and Archives Canada Cataloguing in Publication

De la Roche, Mazo, 1879-1961
           Whiteoak harvest / Mazo de la Roche.

Originally publ.: Boston : Little Brown, 1936.
ISBN 978-1-55488-467-4

           I. Title.

PS8507.E43W45 2009   C813'.52   C2009-903248-1

1   2   3   4   5   14   13   12   11   10

Conseil des Arts   Canada Council   ONTARIO ARTS COUNCIL
du Canada   for the Arts   CONSEIL DES ARTS DE L'ONTARIO

Canada

We acknowledge the support of **The Canada Council for the Arts** and the **Ontario Arts Council** for our publishing program. We also acknowledge the financial support of the **Government of Canada** through the **Book Publishing Industry Development Program** and **The Association for the Export of Canadian Books**, and the **Government of Ontario** through the **Ontario Book Publishers Tax Credit** program, and the **Ontario Media Development Corporation**.

Care has been taken to trace the ownership of copyright material used in this book. The author and the publisher welcome any information enabling them to rectify any references or credits in subsequent editions.

J. Kirk Howard, President

Printed and bound in Canada.

www.dundurn.com

Dundurn Press	Gazelle Book Services Limited	Dundurn Press
3 Church Street, Suite 500	White Cross Mills	2250 Military Road
Toronto, Ontario, Canada	High Town, Lancaster, England	Tonawanda, NY
M5E 1M2	LA1 4XS	U.S.A. 14150

For Ted and Fritzi Weeks

CONTENTS

I

ADUMBRATIONS

THE OWNER OF the touring car was interested in the filling station from which he was getting a fresh supply of gasoline but his wife was more interested in the young man who was attending to their wants. She had studied art for a time and it seemed to her that she had never studied a model who had so stirred her imagination. She found herself wishing that she could see him on the models' stand in an attitude that would best display his slender yet vigorous body, his handsome head covered with dark waving hair. She nudged her husband and with a glance drew his attention from the filling station to its owner.

"Streamline," her husband said, out of the side of his mouth.

"Look at his hands," she murmured.

"Hm — hm," he grunted.

"And his eyelashes."

"Too long."

The youth turned off the fluid and addressed the driver of the car.

"That will be two dollars," he said pleasantly. He added, as the motorist produced his wallet: "You have come quite a distance; it's a Texas licence, isn't it?"

"Yes, we've had a long trip but we've enjoyed it. This is a pretty country around here."

The youth smiled as he pocketed the money. "I suppose it is," he said, "though I am no judge. I've never been anywhere else."

"Lived here all your life, eh?"

"All my life. I've always wanted to travel. But I have never been able to afford it."

"Oh, well, there's lots of time for you," said the motorist, with a rather envious glance at the boy's slender length.

His wife put in — "You ought to go on the films. You'd make lots of money there."

"On the contrary, I am about to be married."

"No!" she exclaimed. "You don't say so! You're certainly young."

"I feel that an early marriage will be best for me," he returned gravely.

"Well," said the motorist, starting his engine, "good luck to you!"

"I'll say she's a lucky girl!" added his wife.

The proprietor of the filling station made a little bow. "Thank you," he said.

"I like your place," said the motorist. "It looks as though it had once been a smithy."

"It was. An old fellow named Chalk kept it. As a small boy I used to come here to have my pony shod. His son works with me now."

"I guess this road has changed a good deal since then."

"Oh yes, it's improving. I get a lot of customers." His bright eyes looked confidentially into theirs.

At that moment a tall man came out of a nearby cottage, threw a long leg across a fence and, with an antagonistic glance at the motorists, approached the filling station. He was followed by two old spaniels and a very young Cairn terrier.

The motorist's wife looked up at the sign above the low stone doorway and repeated aloud:

"W. Whiteoak, Motor Repairs."

The youth gave another of his old-fashioned bows:

"I hope you'll come my way again."

"We certainly will, if we're in this direction. And take my advice, and go to Hollywood."

Just as the car started, one of the spaniels gave a self-assertive yet listless bark, and moved heavily in front of it. His master sprang to the rescue and it was only by a violent swerve that the motorist avoided an accident. He threw an accusing glare at dog and man as the car lurched on its way. This was returned by a sneering grin from the owner of the spaniel which stood pridefully waving its fringed tail aware, in its blindness, that it had been the centre of disturbance. It turned its head and licked the hand that now released it, listening, with apparent approval, to a well-chosen string of profanities.

Wakefield Whiteoak observed plaintively:

"If there's any swearing to be done, I think I should be the one to do it. I don't like my clients sent off in such a mood."

His elder brother's expression became somewhat apologetic but he exclaimed derisively:

"Your *clients*! I like that!"

"So do I," returned Wakefield tranquilly. "For they are really much more like clients than customers. There is a personal touch between us. I help them and give them good advice. I might sometimes almost call them patients for they come to me with their motors deranged or powerless for lack of petrol. They are like sick people, and I send them away healthy and in good spirits."

"You like the sound of your own voice, don't you? You should certainly have been a lawyer. Of course, I always wanted you to go into the Church. You'd have made a first-rate parson and had all the women chasing you in your surplice."

"That hardly sounds respectable," returned Wakefield, rather disapprovingly. He laid a restraining hand on the collar of the blind spaniel as a motor lorry sped past. "You ought to keep Merlin on the lead, Renny. He'll certainly be the cause of an accident one day."

Renny answered curtly — "Rot! He never leaves my heels. That idiot in the touring car was to blame. Heel, Merlin! Heel, Floss! Where the hell is that puppy?"

Both brothers began to search for him and discovered him investigating a pool of oil in the station. Tucking him under his arm Renny stared at the blackened ceiling where on a rafter were still fixed a couple of horseshoes.

"It seems only yesterday," he said, "when I used to bring you here for a treat, in front of my saddle, to see Chalk shoe my nag. I hate seeing the place turned into this."

"Changes will come," returned Wakefield. "There is Mrs. Brawn's sweet shop turned into a tea shop. I remember how I used to spend every penny I had at Mrs. Brawn's, and how once I got an awful licking for spending some ill-gotten gains there. But I don't trouble myself with such recollections. As Shakespeare says — 'Let us not burthen our remembrance with a heaviness that's gone.'"

His elder, as he had expected, was reduced to an embarrassed silence by the quotation. He had as a matter of fact got it only that morning from a Shakespeare calendar, given him by his sister last Christmas, and was anxious to use it before it was forgotten.

Now he said rather dictatorially — "But you really must do something about the eavestroughs on this place, Renny. The one at the back is quite gone and the ground is being completely washed away. Just come and see."

Renny Whiteoak's embarrassment turned to a taciturn aloofness at the mention of repairs. He followed his brother and examined the broken eave without interest. His dogs began digging in the cavity formed at the side of the building by the dripping eave. He remarked, abruptly:

"I have just promised Mrs. Wigle to shingle the roof of her cottage."

Wakefield shrugged despairingly. "I thought that, when I saw you coming from there. Poor Mrs. Wigle! You promise her a new roof regularly every spring."

"A few odd shingles will patch it up," answered Renny, easily.

"And what about my eavestrough?"

"I'll send a man around to look at it."

Wakefield was forced to accept this. He asked, "Are you going home?"

Renny looked at his wristwatch. "I must stop in at the tea shop. There are some repairs needed there, too. This springtime is the very devil for expense. Want to come?"

Wakefield did want to come. He always wanted to go where his eldest brother went. Renny had been a father to him and more indulgent than most fathers.

They set off along the path that led irregularly alongside the road. The grass was a young green and fresh dandelions pressed brightly against it. The sky looked inclined either to rain or shine, while a small-voiced bird alternately piped or flew from tree to tree, appearing to pursue the brothers on their walk.

They stopped for a moment in front of the church that had been built by their grandfather, Captain Philip Whiteoak, more than eighty years ago and stood listening a moment to the murmur of the stream that curved about the churchyard where their father, his two wives, two infant brothers and a sister, a grown-up brother, and their grandparents were buried. The church on its knoll looked as remote as in those early days when the primeval forest hedged it round and only a wavering path, made by the feet of the Whiteoaks, their neighbours, and the villagers, led to its door. It stood, in the strength of its stones, like an unconquered fort. Renny loved this building, but rather as the shrine of his family than as the temple of his God. It hurt him that Wakefield who was soon to marry Pauline Lebraux, a Catholic, had turned to that Faith. He had not opposed the change, because he was in favour of the marriage, but he seldom lost an opportunity of referring to it with dissatisfaction. Now he said:

"I'm sorry you've turned papist, Wake." He used the term he had always heard used by his grandmother whom, in many ways, both spiritual and physical, he resembled.

Wakefield felt no shrinking from discussing the subject, for he cherished a sanguine hope that he might himself be the instrument of converting the head of the house.

"I'm sure," he answered, "that you'll live to rejoice in it."

Renny felt what was coming and shied, interrupting Wakefield by shouting his dogs to heel. But Wakefield opened his argument and continued it undaunted even though Renny quickened his stride to one incompatible with conversation. Only when he said — "The trouble, the greatest trouble, with the Anglican Church is that She is not holy," did his elder turn to him and exclaim:

"She's holy enough for me and I wish you'd shut up about her."

"Very well," said Wakefield, resignedly, "but the day will come —"

"Here is the tea shop," interrupted Renny, and turned abruptly to its door.

Over the door was a gaily painted sign, with the words — DAFFODIL TEA SHOP — in gold and green, while a large bowl of daffodils stood in the small-paned window, on either side of which yellow curtains were drawn back by pale green ribbons. Inside, the tables and chairs were likewise painted green; yellow freshly laundered cloths set off the flowered china, and a vase holding a few daffodils stood in the centre of each. In a small glass case, boxes of sweets tied with bright ribbons were for sale. The shop was empty but for a yellow cat which arched itself against the oncoming of the dogs.

A bell had rung at the opening of the door and now a strong-looking woman, in her early forties, with short tow-coloured hair and a face in which fortitude and recklessness were rather attractively blended, appeared. She wore a fancy daffodil-strewn smock that badly became her, and, in spite of such flamboyant identification with the shop, she looked strangely out of place there. She was Clara Lebraux, Wakefield's future mother-in-law.

She gave him an affectionate smile, and he bent and kissed her on the cheek. Between her and Renny a look of intimate understanding was exchanged. In her glance there was an almost masculine ease, combined with a passionate appreciation of his hard, thin grace, the predatory chiselling of his features, beside which Wakefield's youthful good looks became insignificant.

The warmth in Renny's eyes turned to amusement as he exclaimed:

"You look like the devil in that pinafore, Clara."

"I know," she agreed, "but it becomes the shop, and no one will notice me."

"I like it," said Wakefield, "and I think it's becoming too."

"In short," added Clara Lebraux, "it was Wakefield's idea."

"Just like Wake's taste! You look much better in a man's overall, cleaning out your stable."

She shrugged. "And feel much better, too. But stables don't pay, and poultry doesn't pay, and fox farming doesn't pay. I'm willing to make myself into a figure of fun, if only I can make this tea shop pay."

He looked instantly serious. "It must pay," he said.

"It hasn't yet."

"You've only been open a month. The season has not begun."

"I've sent at least a dozen of my clients on to you," said Wakefield.

"And several of them arrived. They asked me questions about you and said it was a pity to see such an intellectual young man at your job."

"I think it pays to bring intellect to any job," returned Wakefield. "Even this tea shop, if run —"

Clara interrupted — "My goodness, I have no intellect to bring to it!"

Renny asked, "Have you had any customers this morning?"

"Not yet. But it's Saturday and a fine day. I should have plenty."

The cat now leaped in furry rage to the top of a table, overturning the flowers and spitting down at the dogs which surrounded her. Renny snatched up the vase, Wakefield put the spaniels outside the door, and the cat was hustled to the kitchen. Clara Lebraux laughed good-humouredly.

"Come now," she said. "You must sit down and have coffee. There is some freshly made."

"And I can vouch that it's good," said Wakefield. "I come in for a cup every morning, don't I, Mother-in-law?"

Renny said nothing but sat with crossed legs, fingering his puppy's ears. Clara went to the kitchen from where came the appetizing smell of fresh coffee.

Renny remarked:

"I must buy a box of Pauline's sweets."

"Do," said Wakefield. "She hasn't had much sale for them yet. It's discouraging. I give a box of them to every one of the family on their birthdays but they always look rather knowing, as though they thought I only put money into my own pocket when I buy Pauline's sweets. The almond creams are good."

"Yes, I'll try the almond creams."

The owner of the tea shop now returned with coffee and biscuits on a tray. There were three cups and she sat herself down by her guests.

The coffee was steaming hot and there was cream for it. The two older ones sipped theirs almost in silence while Wakefield talked animat-edly of his work and his approaching marriage. Occasionally the eyes of

Renny and Clara met, rested a moment, as though each drew a certain peace from the other's presence, then turned again to the youth, the man's with tolerant affection, the woman's with slight irritation.

The attention of all three was drawn to the door as Pauline Lebraux appeared at it.

"Don't let the dogs in," shouted Renny, as though to a child.

Wakefield went eagerly to the door to meet her. She stood smiling at them all, slender and dark, a complete contrast to her mother. She carried a package which Clara at once espied.

"More sweets, darling!" she exclaimed. "Why, I haven't sold the last lot yet."

Pauline looked worried. "Oh, haven't you, Mummie? But you told me it was going very well."

Renny broke in — "It is going well. It's very lucky that you have brought this fresh lot, for it happens that I am going to see a man who is likely to buy a horse from me. He has five kids and I must take them some sweets. Five girls" — his voice grew in heartiness — "they'd like a box apiece. It will help to put the deal through."

Pauline looked at him dubiously. "Are you *sure?*" she asked.

Wakefield put in — "It's absolutely true what he says. He was wondering, just before we came in, what he could take those girls."

Pauline's forehead was smoothed. "I'm so glad then that I made fresh sweets."

"No, no," interrupted Renny, "I'll take the old lot. They're only kids. They'll never know the difference."

Clara Lebraux rose and selected five boxes of sweets from the glass case. "They are quite fresh," she said, and handed them to Renny. She arranged the ones Pauline had just brought in the case. "Will you have some coffee, dear?" she asked.

"Thanks, Mummie." She sat down at the table, and Clara rapped on it for the maid.

Renny got up. "I must be getting on," he said. He remembered the repairs which Clara was asking for and thought that if he left now, on this note of generosity, she might feel reluctant to demand them.

"Whom shall I pay for the sweets?" he asked.

"Mummie, of course," answered Pauline in an aloof tone. She could not quite bring herself to believe in the five sweet-craving girls and, as for a long time, she felt no ease in his presence.

He drew out his worn wallet and handed Clara three dollars. She waved them mockingly:

"Look! Pauline makes more than I do!"

But if Renny thought he would escape her demands he was mistaken. She led him out through the kitchen to view a sagging corner of the back porch. At the same moment the front door opened and a well-dressed couple entered the tea shop. Wakefield at once began talking in a high-pitched tone to Pauline.

"Darling," he said, " isn't this the most marvellous find? To think that we have discovered a place where they make such coffee, such tea, and such scones! And I must buy you another box of those chocolates!"

Pauline bent her head, her cheeks reddening. Wake was pressing her foot under the table.

Outside Renny exclaimed — "He's a regular playboy, as Gran used to say."

"God! I hope that he and Pauline will be happy together!"

"Of course they will!" He said this more fervently as he was not at all sure of it. "Now what about the porch?"

It was a flimsy wooden addition and it threatened to fall at one corner. He eyed it speculatively.

"All it needs is propping up," he said, with the hearty ring in his voice that his tenants knew so well.

"Don't you think there should be a new porch?"

"I do," he said. Then he added, gravely — "But, Clara, if you knew how scarce money is with me, you would not ask even that. The interest on the mortgage fell due last month and I had the devil's own time scraping it together. I'm down to rock bottom and there are repairs to the stables and farm buildings that are absolutely necessary."

"I know, I know," she agreed. "It's awful. But, if you will just have the porch propped it is all I shall ask. It's positively dangerous as it is."

"I'll attend to it," he said. "I'll do it myself. No need to have workmen about. I can do it. It simply needs propping."

He espied a thick block of wood lying among wooden boxes in a corner of the yard. "We must have this rubbish cleared away and make a nice little garden here." He dragged out the block of wood and carried it to the porch. "Now I'll raise the porch and you roll the block under the corner." He pulled off his coat.

"You can't do it alone! You'll hurt yourself! Let me fetch Wake."

"No, no, he might strain his heart! Do what I tell you, woman."

The elemental tone of command which he introduced into his voice amused her but it had its effect. She removed her gay flowered apron, laid it beside his coat, and grasped the cobwebbed block in both hands. But she kept muttering to herself — "He can't do it! He can't — he's no right to try."

Bending his lean back, he gathered all his force and, in one muscle-straining heave, raised the corner of the porch, supporting it on his shoulder. "Now," he said, between his teeth, "shoot in the block, damn you!"

She thrust it under the porch which he cautiously lowered. He was panting as he straightened himself. A vertical vein in the middle of his forehead stood out like a whipcord. He grinned triumphantly at her but grasped one shoulder in his hand.

"What did I tell you?" he exclaimed. "It's as steady as a rock. All you need do now is to plant some nice vine or a rambler rose to climb over the corner."

"You've hurt yourself," she said sternly. "What is it?"

He made a rather shame-faced grimace. "It's nothing. Just a bit of a wrench. I'll rub it with liniment."

She put her short strong hand on his shoulder. She said — "Damn the porch! I wish I hadn't spoken of it."

Closing his eyes he stood motionless, as though from her touch he drew ease. Before his closed eyes rose a moonlit autumn wood, the figures of a man and woman in each other's arms. The magnetic attraction that had drawn them together was of the same quality. They were equal under its force, as two trees receive equally the magnetic current from the earth.

She removed her hand; he opened his eyes and saw the sadness in hers.

"It's a shame," she said, "the way Pauline and I have hung on to you — ever since my husband died. And before that — all through his sickness."

"You know," he returned, "what Pauline has been to me — like my own child. You know what you have been."

"Well, you have liked us, that's one thing," she returned, in her abrupt, rather sulky voice, and picked up her flowered smock as the bell of the shop sounded. "There — I must go in. They'll need me." Her eyes caught the five boxes which he had laid carefully by his coat. She asked — "What are you going to do with those? That story about the five girls was just bluff, wasn't it?"

He answered gravely — "No, they are absolutely real. I must have sweets for them."

She knew he lied, and loved him the better for it. She held his coat for him but he objected.

"No, no, I'm blazing hot. Throw it over my shoulders."

She exclaimed fiercely — "You can't put it on! You know you can't."

He gave her a mocking grimace, touched her lightly on the cheek with his fingers, and, taking the coat from her, turned away. The bell of the tea shop again sounded.

As he walked sharply along the road, with his spaniels padding at his heels and the Cairn puppy weaving a mad pattern among the ten legs that moved so enticingly in unison, his mind was busy with the varied problems of his life. He had a good many of them, he thought, a lot of responsibility, but he would not have minded them so much if money had been less scarce. As it was, the last payment of interest on the mortgage had left him feeling financially flattened, most dreadfully hard up, for the time being. Still — it was paid, and he had six months' freedom from worry on that score. A sense of pride deepened his inhalations of the spring air as he reflected that, through that mortgage, distasteful as it was to him and bitter to his family, he had been able to prevent the building of a row of bungalows on property adjoining his own. He had added that property, a lovely bit, to his estate. Only that morning he had walked over it just for the pleasure of seeing it free and undefiled, its trees spreading their new foliage in confidence. He had held his dogs back that they might not worry the rabbits he saw scampering there. Short shrift they would have had from the builders!

He thought of Clara and Pauline Lebraux and their venture of the tea shop. He hated that sort of thing for them, but fox farming had not paid and they must do something. Perhaps, if Wake did very well with the garage and petrol station, the tea shop might be discarded after a time. Lord, but it was disappointing to see clever young Wake turn to such a dirty job instead of to one of the professions or, better still, to farming and horse breeding! But Wake could not get on with Piers, the second brother, and there was no use in trying to make them. After the first few months on the farm when Wake had been willing to break his back and to obey Piers in everything, there had been rows. Besides that, Wake was not strong enough for the job. This new work just suited him. And he'd got religious! It was embarrassing the way he was always trying to convert one.

He thought of Meg, his sister, and what a stiff time she and her husband had been up against. They had taken in paying guests this spring and did not seem to mind it. Though it went against his grain to think of a Whiteoak doing such a thing and he believed it was enough to make his grandmother turn over in her grave.

He thought of his wife and his little daughter, but they had barely entered into his mind, taken privileged possession of it, when the hoot of a motor horn made him look to his dogs. His brother Piers was in the car. He stopped it and said:

"Hello! Want a lift?"

Piers's wire-haired terrier Biddy was on the seat with him. Beside herself with excitement at seeing the spaniels, who were old friends, and the Cairn, of whom she roundly disapproved, she leant over the seat and literally screamed as Renny and his dogs established themselves in the back of the car. Merlin raised his muzzle and gave a troubled bark.

Piers asked, over his shoulder — "Where do you want to go?"

"Where are you going?"

"Home. Then to the farm. I must see what the men are doing in the back fields. I've just sold those Jersey calves to Crockford."

"Good. Did he pay you?"

Piers grunted and took some notes from his pocket. He handed them over his shoulder to his brother. Renny pocketed them with satisfaction. Then, remembering that he owed Piers for hay and oats, he assumed a jocular air and began to tease Biddy, throwing her almost into hysteria. The car started with a jerk.

Though there was a considerable stretch of years between the brothers it appeared less than it was, for Piers, sitting solidly at the wheel, had a look of self-confident maturity, while Renny's vivid glance, his quick, wary movements, combined with his leanness, made him appear much younger than his years. Yet, in spite of Piers's sanguine masculinity, an observer would have felt that Renny, with his bony features, his sculptured head, and arrogant mouth, was the more formidable of the two.

It was but a short distance to Piers's house, set in an old-fashioned garden just coming into flower. The rough-cast walls had taken on a warm tone in the sunlight and all the windows were open. At one of them, holding her year-old baby, stood Piers's wife, Pheasant. She took the child's tiny hand in hers and waved it at the two men. She put on a small voice and called:

"Hello, Daddy. Hello, Uncle Renny!"

Piers gave Renny a sidelong glance of pride. "Not a bad-looking pair, eh," he muttered.

"Fine — both of them," said Renny. He called out — "Hello, young Philip. I've a present for your mother. Come and see!"

"A present!" cried Pheasant. "There's nothing so rare in these days. I'm mad to see it."

"Don't be excited," said Renny, as she ran along the flagged walk and opened the gate. "It's only sweets from The Daffodil."

But Pheasant had expected nothing more important. She took the box in one hand while with the other she clutched her child to her.

"Oh, thanks! How perfectly lovely! Pauline is a marvel at making sweets."

Piers asked — "How are they getting on with the tea shop?"

The line between Renny's brows deepened. "Well, the season has just opened. It's hard to say what it will be. Two people came while Wake and I were there."

There was something self-conscious in the way he mentioned the fact that Wakefield had been with him when he visited The Daffodil. His thick bronze lashes flickered over his eyes. Pheasant thought — "If I were Alayne, I'd see through all this. But she doesn't — she doesn't! She's never really understood him though she loves him terribly. I'm glad Piers isn't so attractive to women. And, even at that, he is handsomer." Her eyes flew to Piers's face.

"Coming in?" she asked.

"No. I've work to do. Where is Mooey?"

"He has a headache, Piers. I think he concentrates too much at school. He's *so* eager to learn!"

"Good Lord! Concentrates! An eight-year-old, at a little private day school!" His face darkened. "These Saturday headaches — they make me tired. What they mean is simply that he funks coming over to Jalna to ride. He funks it, just because he's had a fall or two. And here I am with a fine pair of ponies to show which must have a child rider."

Renny said — "Promise him a present if they win at the Show."

"I'll promise him a damned good hiding if he doesn't toe the scratch. Where is he?"

"I sent him out for a walk. I thought it would do him good."

Piers made a sound of disgust. "Upon my word, the only Whiteoak among my three is this one. No mistake about him." He tickled the baby whose resemblance to himself was remarkable. "And, in our family, I am the only one who takes after our father, and he was the spit of his dad. It's the authentic face for four generations straight."

Renny looked critically from father to son, then, cocking an eyebrow, he said:

"One like Piers is enough, eh, Pheasant?"

"Well, I do think," she returned, with her air of a sedate child, "that Piers might be more lenient with Mooey and Nook. It's not their fault if they don't take after him. Knowing what I do of horse breeding, I should say it is his own."

Renny grinned derisively at Piers. "A dud sire and no mistake."

Piers looked as nearly sheepish as was possible to him. He said gruffly — "Well, I can't waste any more time," and started the engine. The baby, at the same moment, tugged at the necklet of red beads that Pheasant was wearing and broke it. The beads flew in all directions.

"Oh, oh, my precious necklet!" cried Pheasant. She set her baby down and began a search for the beads. Suddenly Nook's voice called from an upper window — "Mummie, he's eating one!"

Pheasant snatched up the child, held him head downward and extracted the bead from his mouth, he immediately looking as though nothing had happened.

"A close shave!" ejaculated Renny.

But Piers had seen two heads at the window. His face flushed and he rapped out sharply:

"Mooey, come down here!" He stopped the engine.

"Now, Piers," implored Pheasant.

He turned on her. "What did you mean by telling me he was out?"

"I thought he was. He must have just come back. Don't be rough with him, please."

Young Maurice now appeared in the doorway and came slowly toward them, followed by his shadow, little Nook. It was true that neither boy showed any resemblance to Piers. Nor did they particularly favour their mother, though both had her quality of elusiveness, the look of sensitive woodland creatures, defensive yet vulnerable. Mooey was too tall for his age, thin, and rather pale. His brown hair fell in thick locks on his forehead, giving him a gypsy air. He was physically timid yet spiritually he could show great fortitude for his years. Nook had a look of real fragility, an exquisite skin, sleek fair hair, and hazel eyes, one of which showed a slight cast.

Piers stared at his first-born.

"Well," he said sarcastically, "I hope your headache is better."

Mooey answered, not without dignity, "Yes, thank you, Daddy."

"I hope you feel able to come to Jalna and help school the ponies."

"Yes." He stood hesitating as to whether he should get into the front seat with his father and Biddy or into the back with his uncle and the spaniels. Renny settled it by opening the door next him. "In you get," he said, "mind you let me have a good account of your riding."

Piers looked at his wristwatch and exclaimed at the hour. The car started with a jerk. Pheasant and Nook were left searching in the grass for red beads.

Renny, indicating the boxes of sweets, said, out of the side of his mouth — "Make a good showing with the ponies, Mooey, and I'll leave one of these in the saddle-room for you, on the shelf below the ribbons."

Mooey smiled soberly and nodded, then looked straight ahead of him at his father's stalwart back.

Piers stopped the car at the gate of their sister's low-set rambling house and Renny and his dogs alighted. The dogs were met by an Airedale who greeted them as friends. An elderly lady, sitting in a deck chair on the lawn, called out — "Good morning, Mr. Whiteoak! Won't you come and talk to me?"

He gave her a somewhat surly nod and strode quickly toward the front door. Here he had to make way for an incredibly sallow man coming out. The man stared at him almost aggressively.

Followed by the dogs he went straight to his sister's sitting room. He found her there alone.

The eldest of the family, she was now aged forty-nine, would be fifty before the year was out. Her complexion had the clear freshness of Piers's, only paler, her grey-blue eyes had an expression of innocent candour, and her pouting pink lips were girlish in their stubborn sweetness. Only greying hair, her thick waist, and over-plump neck showed her years. Her voice was caressing when she greeted him. She put both short arms round his neck and drew his hard-bitten, high-coloured face down to hers.

"Dearest, dearest boy — I haven't seen you for days and days! What have you been doing with yourself?"

"Who the devil are those people?" he growled against her cheek.

"My P.G.s! You've met the old lady before — Mrs. Binkley-Toogood. I hope you weren't as rude to her as you were the last time. The yellow gentleman is a newcomer."

He drew back and scowled at her. "Meggie, how can you take these people into your house?"

She folded her arms across her full bosom and said reproachfully — "What can I do? With Maurice's stocks going down and down — with my child growing older? I tell you, Renny, these paying guests are our salvation. And such nice people, too. I quite enjoy having them. Mrs. Binkley-Toogood has travelled in the East and the gentleman you met in the doorway has had the most interesting diseases. It's all very broadening. I do wish you and Alayne would try it at Jalna. I think you ought to when you have a mortgage on the place and need money so badly."

"Alayne and I — at *Jalna*!" His eyebrows, his nostrils, the lines from nostril to corner of mouth were bent to his horror at the idea.

"Surely," returned his sister, "surely Alayne does not consider herself so much better than I am —"

He interrupted — "It's not that. It's the thought of paying guests — or whatever you call them — at Jalna. I'd starve first."

"Well, I don't see any sense in it."

"Meggie — you do! You'd never ask me to do such a thing. Why, Gran would turn over in her grave!"

"I dare say she would. She's the sort of dead person who would turn over in their grave. But she'd just have to get used to the new order of things as we all do."

A retort was on his lips, but a shooting pain through his shoulder made him wince.

"What is it?" she asked.

"I heaved the porch at the tea shop and gave my shoulder a crick."

"Poor dear!"

"It's nothing serious."

"But I hate you to be hurt. How is Mrs. Lebraux getting on?"

"Not too badly. Everything looks nice."

"Doesn't it? And such good tea! I was passing the other day and she called me in to have a cup. She absolutely refused to let me pay for it."

"As though she'd let you pay for it! She likes you, Meg, and you've always been nice to her. She's had a hard time of it since Lebraux died — and before, God knows!"

"I *admire* her," said Meg fervently, all the more fervently because Renny's wife had always been very cool toward Clara Lebraux.

He produced the boxes of sweets. "I've brought you and the kid these. One each. The daffodils on the top are rather nice, aren't they?"

"Charming!" Meg's eyes glowed as she opened the box. She had no modern ideas about keeping slim. She bit eagerly into a piece of maple cream fudge. "I have never been without sweets since the tea-room opened and as I eat almost nothing at table they are really good for me…. Ah, there is Patience! Come, darling, and see what Uncle Renny has brought us."

Patience came in through the low open window, straddling the sill with her bare brown legs. She was a charming child with her father's wide grey eyes and her mother's sweet pouting smile. She knew exactly what she wanted and almost always managed to get it. Dimples dented her cheeks when her favourite uncle put his offering into her hands. She hugged the box to her.

"Oo," she exclaimed, "just what I love! And one for Mums too! You are a darling!"

"Be careful how you squeeze him!" warned Meg. "He's hurt his shoulder."

"How?"

"Lifting the side of a house," he grinned.

"You *are* a tease!" She threw herself on him.

With these two he was happy. He settled himself in a stuffed chintz chair and lighted a cigarette with Patience on his knee. He suddenly thought of himself as extraordinarily blessed. He thought of Clara and Pauline Lebraux, of his long friendship and protective care for them. He thought of young Wakefield, to whom he had been as a father and mother. Soon Wake's marriage to Pauline would weld the link stronger. He thought of Piers and Pheasant and their three boys. A vision of his two old uncles in their house in Devon hid all else for a moment from his eyes — dear old boys, he hoped they would come over for a visit this summer. He thought of his brother Finch, six months married, living with his bride in Paris, getting on well in concert work — a young fool in other ways, but most affectionate. His thoughts reached out to those distant parts drawing, in dark invisible strength, the images of his own flesh and blood nearer. Then his mind turned to Jalna and his own wife and child. He thought of Alayne and of their troubled, passionate life together, like a spring bubbling out of the dark earth, unable to give a tranquil reflection of its surroundings. Then the face of his child obtruded itself, vivid, dark-eyed, scarlet-lipped, and his own lips softened into tenderness.

Meg and Patience had been watching him.

"A penny for your thoughts," said Meg.

"You're such a dear old funny-face!" cried Patience.

He gathered her to him with his sound arm and hugged her. "I was thinking of my dinner," he said.

All the way home, across the fields and down through the ravine, his thoughts were on his wife and child. Like some primitive ancestor he quickened his steps, as though anxious lest some harm had befallen them in his absence. He paused just once to examine the trunk of a great pine tree from which a branch had been cut the autumn before. Over this scar the resinous lifeblood of the tree had collected in amber-coloured coagulations and, in one place, had formed into an elongated thread reaching almost to the ground. Renny bent his head and sniffed the pungent smell. He laid his hand on the trunk of the tree.

II

FATHER, MOTHER, AND CHILD

RENNY'S WIFE, ALAYNE, was arranging some sprays of wild cherry blossom in a black glass vase in the drawing room. To her they seemed the very soul of spring, flowering in exquisite whiteness after the long bitter winter. She touched them tenderly for fear one petal might be bruised, and when a flower did fall, she carefully laid it on the water where it floated, with upturned face, like a tiny water lily. She had charming hands. She handled the sprays of bloom capably and, when she had arranged them to her liking, she stepped back a pace to see the effect. She was not satisfied. This room, with its heavy damask hangings and richly toned carpet, was not one that showed flowers to their advantage, least of all the fragile blossoms of the wild cherry. She rejoiced in the delicate lines of the Chippendale furniture and sometimes amused herself by imagining the background she would create for it, if she were given a free hand. But Renny thought it perfect as it was. The point where their taste differed most was the wallpaper with its massive gilt scrolls that had decked those walls for eighty years, and looked good for another eighty.

Alayne shivered a little, for she had put on a thinner dress today and the room was cool. The dress was a flowered grey-and-blue foulard made with little ruchings. As she caught her reflection in a mirror she thought that both colour and style were kind to her.

She had put little Adeline also into a thinner frock and she wondered if she had perhaps been too precipitate. There might be a cool breeze on the porch where the child played. There was no need to wonder where she played, for every now and again she made a noisy outcry in one of her games. Alayne went to the door and looked down on her.

She had got a saddle that had belonged to her great-grandmother, a side saddle of old-fashioned design, and she was poised on it in an attitude both vigorous and graceful. She grasped a crop in her small hand and with it belaboured an imaginary mount which apparently shied at the jump at which she was putting him.

Alayne stood, unseen by her, delighting in her strength and vivacity. Yet this very strength and this very animation stood between her and her child. Adeline was so different from what she had been as a little girl. She could remember her early childhood better than most, for she had been much alone with her parents and all her little sayings had been treasured and repeated to her, as her baby clothes had been carefully laid away as she outgrew them. Almost once a year she had been taken to the photographer and a most satisfactory portrait made. There was little Alayne at two, wearing a heavy-looking hat tied with a huge bow under her chin and standing solemnly on the seat of a padded chair. There was little Alayne at four, standing in a doorway with a butterfly bow on her fair hair. There she was at seven, holding flowers and showing a profile that was beginning to be something more than childish. In all the series of photographs the keynote was a sweet gravity, an earnest eagerness to understand things. It was a pleasure, her parents had often told her, to take her to the photographer's and it had been difficult to select the best proofs, they were all so good.

How different when she and Renny had taken Adeline to be photographed, at the age of two! It had been literally impossible to keep her quiet long enough to pose her. She had struggled to investigate everything in the studio. When they had tried to restrain her she had screamed. When the distraught photographer had brought out his most amusing toy to please her, she had been all too pleased, laughing immoderately, so that her very palate showed. She had laughed till she had wetted herself and Alayne, humiliated, had to carry her to the dressing room.

There she had had an idea. Renny should hold the child on his knee to be photographed. He eagerly agreed to this, but Adeline was in a fever of excitement. She climbed all over him, hugging him, kissing him, shouting in glee. Of that lot of proofs not one had been worth finishing, though one pose had been so truly splendid of Renny that Alayne had felt a hot resentment at the grotesque little figure on his knee which, blurred and caricatured, had spoilt the picture. The one result from this terrible morning now stood in a silver frame on a table in the drawing room — an infant with a scowl, a too large nose, and an almost frightening resemblance to her great-grandmother.

Now looking at her Alayne felt that only a painter could do justice to her beauty, her creamy flower-petal skin, her hair of so rich and dark a red that its colour could only be compared to a rarely fine chestnut newly stripped of its sheath. This hair clustered in thick locks about her temples and nape, and seemed capable of expressing her very moods, seeming to rise and quiver when she was in a rage. Alayne remembered hearing Grandmother Whiteoak exclaim — "Eh, but my hair was my crowning glory when I was young!" She supposed it had been hair like this. She remembered the old lady showing a few rusty locks, whether of wig or dyed hair Alayne had never decided, beneath her impressive lace caps.

Adeline brandished the crop and shouted:

"Up, now — up, now, my pet! Over you go! Now — now — up!" She set her small mouth and stiffened her legs and back. Then, as once again the visionary steed balked, her face was contorted and she said, in a tense voice — "Damn you — you son of —"

Alayne did not let her complete the horrifying imprecation. She ran and snatched Adeline from the saddle and gave her a little shake.

"Baby, baby, you *must* not —" then she remembered that what she ought to do was to ignore the words, and faltered.

"Must not what?" asked Adeline inquisitively. There was an amused smile on her fine lips.

Alayne thought — "She sees through me. But I won't let her get the best of me." She answered — "You must not bounce and shout so. You will make yourself so hot. You will tire yourself out."

Adeline turned from her with a swagger and threw her leg over the saddle. She had the power of rousing antagonism in Alayne. With just such a gesture as this she could make Alayne's heart beat quicker, make her even desire a scene, but she spoke in a controlled voice.

"You must come now and have your hands washed. It is your dinnertime."

"No," returned Adeline curtly. She rose and sank now on her plump behind as though in a comfortable jog-trot. "Can't stop," she added.

Wragge, the houseman, now appeared and presented an evil-looking piece of paper on a silver plate. It was the fish dealer's bill. It seemed to Alayne exorbitant, as it always did. She asked — "Is he waiting?"

"Noaw, madam. I told him there weren't noaw use." For the thousandth time the mingled deference and impudence of his manner infuriated Alayne. With her cheeks burning she turned her back on him and lifted Adeline from the saddle.

Either something in her mother's face or the thought of her dinner prompted the child to acquiesce, but she objected to leaving the saddle behind.

"I must take it upstairs to my room."

"Wragge," said Alayne, "take that saddle away. I don't know where it came from."

"From the cupboard under the stairs 'm. That's where the old mistress kep' it. Liked it near 'er, she did. Many a time she 'ad me carry it into 'er room and she'd stroke it and sniff the smell of the leather. She was a grand rider in 'er day and no mistike." Wragge spoke as though he had known old Mrs. Whiteoak in her years of strength though he had never seen her till she was past ninety, when Renny had brought him home after the War. Rags had been his batman. But this, thought Alayne, was his way of showing his intimacy with the affairs of the Whiteoaks, of making her feel an outsider whenever possible, she who had been married to two Whiteoaks, who had experienced heaven and hell in that fusty old house. She said tersely:

"Well put it away."

With a sliding provocative glance at Adeline, he picked up the saddle. She raised her crop threateningly and glared up into his face. He backed away in exaggerated fear of a blow. Alayne could barely restrain an access of anger at them both.

She tore the riding crop from Adeline's hands and put it into Wragge's. She would have liked to strike him with it. "Put it and the saddle away," she said sternly.

But the child now threw herself face down on the saddle, clutching it with arms and legs and indeed the whole of her strong little body and filling the air with her yells of rage. They sounded as though she were being strangled. For a moment Alayne and Wragge looked down on her with equal consternation.

Then a quick step crunched the gravel and Renny hurried toward them. He looked frightened.

"What's the matter?" he demanded.

"Just 'er 'igh temper, sir," answered Wragge, speaking before Alayne could. She made a peremptory sign and he reluctantly withdrew though she was sure he lingered just inside the hall.

The blind spaniel threw up his muzzle and howled but the Cairn puppy, darting to Adeline's side, began to snuffle ecstatically against her face and in her thick tumbled hair. Her crying was stopped as if by magic and she rolled off the saddle and looked up into her father's face.

She blinked her streaming eyes, her mouth changed miraculously from a square exit for howls to a very throne of laughter. Her dress was up to her armpits. The puppy took hold of her drawer leg and began to pull at it. She kicked delightedly and gurgled with laughter.

"I simply can't do anything with her," said Alayne. "Her behaviour is enough to ruin my nerves. I can't enjoy flowers or have any peace for her. Look at her dress — fresh an hour ago. My head aches. Here is the fish dealer's bill. Do take her up, if I touch her she screams."

Renny took Adeline into his arms. His face was stern but he could not keep the tenderness out of his eyes when he looked at her, and nothing escaped her. She put both arms about his neck and planted her mouth on his. She gave him a long, fragrant kiss. Alayne shot a look of positive resentment at her plump back and picked up the saddle. With sweet placidity Adeline watched her carry it into the house, then gave a sidelong glance at her father. He said:

"Poor little Mother. You do upset her. Why are you so naughty?"

Adeline stroked his arched nose with her forefinger. "Am I good with you?" she asked.

"That has nothing to do with it. The question is, why are you naughty with her?"

"You are naughty with her too."

He gave one of his sudden bursts of laughter and was still laughing when Alayne returned.

"I can't help it," he said apologetically. "She says such extraordinary things."

"What sort of things?" asked Alayne coolly.

"Well, she says I am naughty with you too."

"She has an instinct for hurting me."

"What absolute nonsense!"

"It's true."

"Why, she's only a baby — not four yet!"

"I can't help that. She knows how to hurt. And she knows how to draw you always to her side."

"I'm not on her side!"

"You are — or you would not show such evident glee at her precocity."

"Glee — what a beastly word!"

"It seems to express the tone of your laughter."

He stared at her baffled, then took a quick turn across the gravel drive, the child in his arms. He did not know what to say.

She thought — "I am being detestable. But I can't help it. He doesn't know how Adeline worries me. He wouldn't understand. If only she would love me as she loves him. But she is antagonistic towards me."

Alma Patch, the anemic village girl who came daily to look after Adeline, now appeared.

"Baby's dinner is ready," she announced in her accustomed timid whisper. Renny's presence always frightened her. Now she stood blinking her pale eyelashes and staring at his shoes.

He set down the child, who ran and thrust her white fist into Alma's freckled hand. Then she broke from her and threw both arms about her mother's knees and hugged them.

When Alayne was alone with Renny she leant against his shoulder and her hand slid inside his coat. She felt the muscular roundness of his chest and his strong heartbeats. Her lips trembled.

"I'm such an unsatisfactory mother. I haven't the animal magnetism or whatever it is that makes one's offspring love one."

"Adeline adores you. Look at the way she ran to you."

"Yes … I know." But the image of her child faded from her mind. It was obliterated by Renny's nearness, the smell of his tweeds, of his flesh, the feel of his heartbeats.

He laid his face against the smooth pale gold bands of her hair. But he drew suddenly away.

"What is it?" she asked.

"Your hair!" he exclaimed. "I see a white one — right on the top."

"I know. I saw it days ago."

He looked aghast. "But you're not going white, are you? At thirty-eight?"

She laughed. "What a catastrophe! But I don't think so. My mother found grey hairs at twenty."

He looked relieved. "Let me pull it out."

It was characteristic of a strain of stubborn New England Puritanism in Alayne that she would not pull out this grey hair. She backed from his predatory hand. "No, no, let it be! Why should you want to pull it out?"

"Because I don't like it."

"Well, I do." She really hated the white hair but she resented his flurry over it.

"You like it because your mother had one at twenty. I can imagine your father saying — 'Really, my dear, this is a most interesting hirsute phenomenon. I must immediately write an obscure thesis on it!'"

She returned tartly — "You ought to understand ancestor worship. You are eternally quoting your grandmother and your aunt."

Showing his teeth he pounced on her, held her tightly while he tweaked the hair from her head. She gave a little cry and he held up his trophy triumphant.

"I think you are horrid," she exclaimed but in her heart she was glad the hair was out. It was as though with it some of her irritation had been uprooted. She winced but she smiled.

"Do throw it away," she said.

He looked at her, scandalized. "For birds to weave in their nest! You know that's bad luck, don't you?"

"Don't tell me that you believe in such a ridiculous superstition!"

"Gran always said —"

"There you go — 'Gran'!"

"She said it meant death."

Alayne laughed. "Well, I can think of people whose hairs I should like to cast to the birds."

"I shan't risk it." He struck a match and touched the blanched hair with its flame. She looked on amused yet with a ridiculous feeling of sadness as this minute part of her shrivelled and turned to a puff of ash. She said suddenly:

"You do love me, don't you?"

"What a question!"

"But you do? " Her eyes filled with tears. "I want you to say you do."

"Otherwise I might have given your hair to the birds." He put his arm about her, then gave an exclamation of pain. "I believe I shall have to see the doctor," he said. "I've hurt myself."

Instantly her brows puckered in anxiety. "But when? Where? Why haven't you told me?"

"It's my shoulder. I was lifting something."

She gave an exhalation of relief. A wrenched shoulder was not likely to be serious. She said, with more irritation than sympathy — "I have never known anyone who so often gets hurt. You are too impetuous really. You throw yourself into things so. What were you lifting?"

He returned, frowning — "I don't throw myself into things. It's nothing serious. I'll get Piers to drive me over to the doctor's."

"But not before dinner." They had dinner at one.

He agreed to wait till after dinner because Alayne disliked the hours of meals upset, but he had little appetite. He returned from the doctor's with his arm in a sling. He had broken his collarbone.

III

THUNDERCLAP

THAT EVENING CLARA Lebraux divested of her daffodil-strewn apron, sat on a rather uncomfortable rustic seat before the door of her own house and inhaled with deep enjoyment the smoke from a Russian cigarette. Her enjoyment of the cigarette had an edge all the more keen because of her deep unhappiness. She stared into the twilight of the trees beyond her small garden and reviewed her life. It was divided into three parts — her girlhood in Newfoundland, her married life in Quebec, and the years since coming to the vicinity of Jalna. Her father had made money in the fisheries. He and his family had lived extravagantly. Clara had married young and enjoyed a kind of bickering happiness for twelve years, clinging more and more to her child as she cared less for her husband. She had lived the open air life that suited her, tobogganing, snowshoeing, in the winter; sailing her yacht on the St. Lawrence in the summer. Then, when Pauline had been a long-legged child of fourteen, Clara's father had lost his money and, in the same year, Antoine Lebraux had developed the disease which had proved fatal. From that time Clara had never known what it was to be free from anxiety and care. Her brother had moved to Ontario. She and Lebraux with their child had followed him and bought a small farm with the object of rearing silver foxes. In the long illness and death of her husband Clara had found a friend in Renny Whiteoak. He had been friend and protector to Pauline and her. Clara remembered how in her husband's terrible illness she had depended more and more on Renny, how, after Antoine's death, love had come to her. But not in place of friendship. They were good friends always, he never suspecting her love — not till that night last September when, in the twilit wood that now opened before her, they had found each other as lovers. They had come together in friendship and in passion. The harvest moon had burned in the dusky sky above them. She wanted him, had been wanting him for years and hiding her desire. She had exulted in giving herself to him. They had seemed small under the great harvest moon, but not insignificant. Their love had had an exultant meaning under the night sky. All through the autumn they had met, but not since then. She understood that she was no longer necessary to him in that way and she acquiesced. She was more primitive than passionate. Nothing could take from her what she had had. Now that the warm weather had come she sat smoking every evening staring into the wood, wondering if he might come to her.

Pauline, dressed in white, came out of the house and leaned against the back of the bench. She looked pale.

"I find these first warm days depressing," she said, in her low voice that had a hint of her father's French intonation.

Clara's hand reached back to hers. "Do you, darling? But they are nice, after such a terrible winter, aren't they?"

"I like the winter. I never mind the cold."

"I know. But the cold is awful to me, even though I was brought up in Newfoundland.... Look here, Pauline."

"Yes, Mummie." She answered as a child, but her eyes dwelt, with a woman's appraisal, on her mother's blunt, healthy face, her hair cut without elegance, her chest on which there was a red triangle of sunburn. Pauline suspected the relations between Renny and her mother, and the suspicion poisoned her life. She loved Renny with her passionate girl's soul, with a piercing, hopeless love. And soon she was to marry Wakefield. Sometimes she felt that she was wrong in marrying Wakefield, but she had a deep affection for him, and she could not waste her life in love for a man who cared nothing for her as a woman, only loved her as a little friend. She had told of her indecision in the confessional and the priest had advised her to turn her heart confidently to Wakefield. He was sure they would be happy together. She must put Renny out of her mind. Her love for him was a sin.

"I've been thinking," said Clara.

"Yes?" Pauline was scarcely interested. Her mother would certainly be thinking about the tea shop, and they had talked and thought so much of it.

"I've been thinking," went on Clara, "that I ought to go away."

"Go away? But where? And why?" Pauline's words were almost a cry. She could scarcely believe her ears. Her mother go away!

Clara went on quietly — "Well, since your uncle's wife has died, he needs a housekeeper."

"He doesn't need you!" said Pauline passionately. "He's never been kind to you. I don't like Uncle Fred. Why, Mummie" — her voice broke — "you couldn't go away? You couldn't!"

"You and Wake would be better alone. Any young married pair are better alone."

"We don't want you to go. We don't want to be alone." But even as her lips framed the words, her voice faltered. She was not convincing. Clara experienced a cruel pang. Yet how natural that the boy and girl should want to be in the house alone!

But Pauline was not thinking of Wakefield. A glimmering brightness had risen in her mind. If her mother went away there would no longer be the torture of seeing her and Renny together, of seeing them go off together talking intimately about some trivial matter.

"I have quite made up my mind." Clara was saying. "Of course, I shall often come to see you. And I'll write two or three times a week." She spoke in a stolid matter-of-fact tone.

Pauline looked down at her curiously. What was behind that blonde impassive face? Why had she come to this decision? Pauline suddenly wanted to throw herself on Clara's breast and cry. The twilight of the spring evening, the strangeness of her approaching marriage, the thought of parting from her mother, gave her a lost, frightened feeling. But she spoke calmly.

"Of course, if you want to go, Mummie. But you know how I feel about it. Why, I've never been away from you a night in my life. It will be horrible."

Clara laughed teasingly. "Horrible! With Wake! It's a good thing he can't hear that."

"He would understand."

"Is he coming tonight?"

"No. He has gone to town to a mission for men. It is the Paulist Father's mission. Wakefield is becoming more Catholic than I am. He really knows much more about the ritual. He's wonderful, and he appreciates the beauty of it so."

"Yes," agreed Clara thoughtfully. "But I wish he had come to see you. It's a night for young lovers. Do you smell something sweet on the air?"

"I've noticed it. I don't know what it is. I'm perfectly happy with you. Shall we go for a stroll?"

Clara's feet ached from being on them all day, but she was never too tired to walk with Pauline. She so habitually thought of Pauline before herself that a wish expressed by the girl became her own also. She rose and put her arm about Pauline's waist.

"Which way shall we go?" she asked.

"Through the wood and down into the ravine."

"Don't you think it will be damp there?"

"I don't mind." Pauline's childishly egotistical answer overrode any further objection Clara might have had. Clasped together they crossed their plot of shaven grass and from it found the narrow path that led across an open field into a copse of oaks. Here the path wound steeply into the ravine, from where the hurried murmur of the stream could be heard.

As they entered the wood a blackbird, hidden among the dense branches, let fall his last low whistle before, startled by their steps, he sought a still more remote shelter for the night. After that came the whirring cry of the nightjar who seemed not to fear them. He spun his velvet flight about them as they moved, now singly, toward the little bridge that crossed the stream.

All this belonged to Jalna, and from the other side of the water another path led upward to the house. Along this path they now heard a third person moving. The young bracken, crushed by his footsteps, added its scent to the already sweet-scented air. A bright spark, making a downward curving arc, showed that he smoked.

In the minds of both mother and daughter was the certainty that the descending figure was Renny Whiteoak's and both felt an almost equal pang of regret that she was not to meet him alone. No regret dulled the eagerness with which he greeted them. They had not yet spent a summer in the place where they now lived, and it came as a pleasant surprise to him to find them standing together on the bridge on this first warm evening.

Clara noticed before Pauline that his arm was in a sling. She gave an exclamation of dismay, then asked curtly:

"What did you do to it?"

"Nothing!" he laughed. "Honestly, nothing."

"Well … if you are going to answer me as though I were a fool …" she said sulkily.

"What is it really?" asked Pauline. She drew close to him, trying to see his features, but she could only make out the brightness of his eyes, and the line of his lips against the cigarette.

He answered — "I was wrestling with the Daffodil tea shop and put it in its place too."

"It's a damned shame!" exclaimed Clara. "I'm absolutely sick about it. Is anything broken?"

"The collarbone."

"And you're due to ride in the Show in a few weeks. How awful!"

"It's only a crack really. I shall be all right."

Clara put out her hand and laid it gently on his shoulder. "I had rather the old tea shop had fallen down," she said.

She kept her hand on his shoulder because she could not take it away. It was as though the maimed shoulder were a magnet that held her hand irresistibly. If he had backed from her across the bridge, she would have followed him as unconsciously as the iron the magnet. In the semi-darkness Pauline was aware of this irresistible drawing of her mother and she felt a wild rage against her. "When she goes," Pauline thought, "I shall never be tortured like this any more. I shall be far happier." She said — "I think I shall go back to the house. Wakefield may come."

Without turning her head, Clara answered:

"I thought you said he had gone to the mission."

"He may not stay. He said he might come rather late."

"Oh, very well."

Clara spoke, almost without knowing that words left her lips. But, after a few moments, she made a great effort and said to Renny:

"I am going to keep house for my brother. It is better for Pauline and Wakefield to be alone together."

"Going away!" he repeated incredulously. "You can't. It's perfect nonsense. They don't need to be alone together. I've never heard of such a thing. Why should they want to be alone together?"

"It's better for married people. They get on better."

He returned hotly — "None of us have been alone when we were first married. Not Eden and Alayne. Not Piers and Pheasant. Not Alayne and me."

She gave a little laugh. "Well, have the lot of you always got on?"

"My Uncle Nicholas and his wife were alone together and they got to hate each other."

"I have another reason."

Something in her voice made him try to see her face. "What is it, Clara?" he asked.

"I feel that it is not safe for me to be near you."

"You need not be afraid of me."

"You have shown me that. But I can't trust myself. I must take my hateful self away."

His voice broke out harshly. "Clara, I need you! I can't let you go away! I want you near me!" He put his uninjured arm about her and drew her to him so that their breasts were together. She did not answer but, with supreme effort, tried to draw every particle of bliss possible from his embrace for her solace later. Yet she did not falter in her resolve.

Pauline had retreated to the top of the path but had not yet returned to the house when she heard Renny's voice raised in what, in the extreme stillness of that place, amounted almost to an outcry. She stood transfixed in an ecstasy of jealousy. She was not the only person who had overheard his excited words. He stood in the singular position at that moment of a man who holds in his arms a woman who loves him, while two other women who love him, stand as listeners unseen and unable to see the principal actors in the drama.

Having seen Renny go toward the ravine, Alayne had a sudden desire to follow him there. She had last seen the stream frozen and the bridge arched in snow. She would stand on it with him·and listen to the talking of the stream. A passionate tenderness toward life stirred her emotionally. She felt the largeness and strength of the springtime renewal. A heaviness, as though her own body partook in it, caused her to move slowly. She made no sound as she opened the wicket gate and stood at the top of the descent into the ravine.

When she heard his outburst of "Clara, I need you! I want you near me! I can't let you go away!" — she did not stop in her slow descent but moved forward, as though by a power other than her own. The path seemed to flow under her feet and yet she was able to move steadily. It was her brain that felt as though it were falling, in a dizzy flight down into the darkness. All the while she had a hard pride in the thought that she could walk so steadily after hearing words like these. She planted one foot after the other among the curled green heads of the bracken fronds. She carried her electric torch in her hand, unlighted, but, when she reached the bridge, she turned on its beam and pointed it, as though it were a weapon, at the two who had drawn apart in consternation.

She flashed the light across Renny's rigid features then turned it full into Clara's face that showed, not so much shame and mortification, as sullen resentment. Her light-lashed eyes blinked, but she stared at Alayne's black figure and said curtly:

"This is just a goodbye you've interrupted, Mrs. Whiteoak. There's nothing to be melodramatic about."

Alayne answered in a voice she scarcely recognized as her own — "Let it be a goodbye! Let it be a goodbye!"

"Renny will explain."

"I ask for no explanation," answered Alayne bitterly, as though she threw their secret unopened in their teeth.

Clara turned from the bridge and began quickly to mount the path toward the wood where Pauline listened. She felt no surprise when she found her still there. She gave her shadowy figure one glance, then passed doggedly on. Pauline remained where she was.

The dusk in the ravine deepened to darkness across which the first firefly outlined the pattern his followers would elaborate in their season. A tree toad set up its liquid warble. The torch fell from Alayne's hand and went out. She clasped the railing of the bridge and bent over it, as though she were going to be sick. She felt in her face the chilled breath of the stream.

Renny came and put his hand on her back, but she pressed her breast against the railing, writhing away from his touch.

"How long has that woman been your mistress?" she asked.

"Alayne — don't!"

"I asked you how long."

He returned fiercely — "She is not my mistress."

With the insistence and hollowness of a bell she repeated her question. The firefly sketched his design more intricately on the darkness.

Renny said — "Now, Alayne, pull yourself together. Don't be hysterical. This isn't the first time that a man who loves his wife —"

"Don't use that word to me," she interrupted harshly. "*Love!* Yes — I suppose you do love me — as a man loves his fireside chair — his old coat — all I want to know is — how long?"

"Come up to the house. There's a horrible chill rising from the water."

"*Chill* —" she repeated scornfully, "I feel no chill, I feel a fever of heat!"

He took her forcibly in his hands. He said quietly:

"You must come to the house."

She straightened her body and allowed herself to be led, as though blind, along the path. He picked up the torch and dropped it into his pocket.

He led her into the dining room and turned on the lights. He closed the doors and said, in a tone almost matter-of-fact — "Now, I'm going to give you something to drink."

He was shocked by her grey-white pallor, her expression of outrage and hate.

"Yes," she said harshly. "I need to be drugged, doped. Give me something that will make me forget all this — if you can!"

He poured a little brandy into a glass and offered it to her. She struck it violently away with her hand and the glass lay shattered on the floor.

She looked at him as though she saw him for the first time, and every hard-bitten line of his face was hateful to her. He scowled ruefully at the spilt brandy, and said:

"I wish you wouldn't carry on like this."

"I dare say you do," she returned bitterly. "It's very troublesome of me. I'm not at all the sort of wife you should have." She looked steadily at him for a space, then she began to cry loudly and brokenly. He remembered with swift relief that the servants were out for the evening. They were alone except for the sleeping child. His highly coloured face was now almost as white as Alayne's. He stood transfixed till the noise of her crying subsided, then he repeated:

"Clara is not my mistress."

"Oh, why do you lie to me?" she exclaimed brokenly.

He was silent a moment, then said, in a low voice:

"I don't deny that she and I were once intimate."

"When?"

"Last fall. But I do deny that there has been anything between us since."

She said, in a shaking voice — "Perhaps you can explain that passionate outburst of yours on the bridge."

"I value her friendship."

"Her friendship! That woman's friendship! I tell you she is sex personified."

"And I tell you that she is a colder woman sexually than you."

The implication of these words transfixed her for a moment, then she said violently:

"I don't want to hear anything about her! I refuse to hear her name spoken!"

"You never will hear it spoken by me."

She spread her left hand in front of him.

"Look at that hand! It has worn the wedding ring of two Whiteoaks and both of you have been as false, as faithless — as I suppose all your precious ancestors were before you."

Renny looked up at the portrait of his grandfather in Hussar's uniform. "He and Gran quarrelled a good deal but he was faithful to her. At any rate, she thought so."

He had spoken in pride of his grandfather's fidelity. Of what was he made? She looked at him standing there, with his narrow red head, his arched beak of a nose, his horseman's back and shoulders, and she hated him, every bit of him, from the point of red hair on his forehead, to his worn brown shoes.

She said, with an icy close-lipped sneer — "What a pity you did not model yourself on him rather than on old Renny Court who from what I hear was the rake of the countryside!"

He was stung and burst out — "Is love a matter of conscience?"

"Not with you!" Her mouth looked positively ugly with its sneer, he thought. "Nor with Eden. Neither of you had any conscience."

From white a deeper red than usual flamed into his face. He said, in a hard voice:

"You had better leave Eden out of this. He is dead and — if he was unfaithful to you — he knew damned well that you didn't love him any more — that you'd turned to me."

"How could he know that?"

"How could he help? Uncle Nicholas told me since that everyone in the house knew it. They were just waiting to see what would happen."

"So — you talk me over with your family!"

He disdained to reply to this but went on — "And let me tell you, Alayne, that you were far more provocative in your behaviour toward me at that time than Clara Lebraux has ever been!"

It was as though he had struck her. But she controlled herself and said bitterly — "But you were able to resist me!"

He answered with dignity — "You were married to my brother!"

"You make my head reel!" she cried. "The fact that I was married to your brother had a restraining influence — but the fact that I am married to you has none."

"I have used more self-restraint than you know," he returned sternly. "Besides, things were different with me then. I was a happy man. I had not the same need. Last fall I was — well, you know how things were with us."

"I know that last summer you mortgaged this place and took money needed for other things to move that hideous house on to your land for Clara Lebraux to live in! Now I know why!"

"Alayne!" he cried. "I had no such thought when I brought Clara and Pauline to live on the estate. They were in terrible difficulties. I had been Lebraux's best friend."

"Well," she answered, with a gesture of finality, "I don't want to hear any more about it. I can't bear any more."

He began to pick the broken pieces of glass from the floor, bending awkwardly because of the sling he wore. She looked at his dense red hair and thought — "I shall go white before he does." She looked at the lines that indented his forehead and felt a bitter satisfaction.

He took out his handkerchief and mopped up the little puddle of brandy. Then he stood up and pressed the wet handkerchief to his forehead. He stood almost impassively while she left the room. But when he heard her crying in her room he bounded up the stairs and throwing open the door appeared before her, his face contorted like a child's.

"Don't!" he exclaimed brokenly and would have taken her in his arms.

She put out her hands to keep him off.

"Darling — you know I have never loved anyone but you!"

"*Will* you go away!" she answered. "I couldn't bear to have you touch me." She went and threw herself on the bed. She felt like one shipwrecked, as though her legs were weighted by seaweed that dragged her down.

Little Adeline stirred in her cot and made a sighing sound. Renny went to her and she stared out of her bright eyes, remote and impersonal, like a little animal in its burrow. Her hair stood like tawny fur.

Alayne sat up on the side of her bed.

"Ask your child — our child — to forgive you," she said. "That is our child. I bore it and I wish I'd died then."

He put his face down to Adeline's but she was only half awake. She stared with her bright impersonal look as though she did not see him. He drew the covers close under her chin and went out.

IV

THE LONG NIGHT

NOT A SNATCH of sleep came to help her through the long hours. Mounting, mounting, up to midnight, declining, sinking, to the dawn, the hours carried their load of misery to her. In her fancy she saw them deposit their separate loads in the passage, between her door and Renny's, till a great black mound was formed, barring them away from each other forever.

During the first hours she could think of nothing but the fact that Clara Lebraux had lain in his arms, as she herself had lain. Over and over again she pictured licentious details of their meetings. Had he lied when he said that they had not been together since the autumn? It did not matter — it did not matter — they had been together! She heard their very whispers in the woods, whispers that came to her like shouts. Clara's face was riveted against the darkness, mouthing her passion.

Alayne hated herself for these thoughts. With all the strength in her she stripped them from her mind and left it naked, cold. She thought coldly of her position in this house. Ten years ago she had come to Jalna as Eden's wife, a sedate, carefully guarded young woman, conventional, inexperienced, feeling herself unconventional, experienced beside these Whiteoaks, with their hidebound traditions of family, of churchgoing, of male superiority, even while they were dominated by the old grandmother.

She had, coming from a great Metropolis, felt tolerant of them in their unworldliness and, in this backwater, under their Victorian guidance, what emotions, fears, hates, and anguishes — she had plumbed! Two marriages to Whiteoaks, and both of them unfaithful to her!

Then Renny's words came like a whip. "If Eden was unfaithful to you, he knew damned well that you didn't love him any more — that you had turned to me!" Had Eden known that? No, he could not have known! He could not! She had kept her secret. Eden's love for her had been a shallow volatile stream, only too eager to turn aside to a fresh outlet. And those other cruel words that Renny had said — "Let me tell you that you were far more provocative toward me at that time than Clara Lebraux has ever been!" What had she done, said? She could not remember. But she remembered the fever of her love for him that gave her no peace. If Eden's love for her had been a shallow stream, hers for him had been no more. To Renny she had thrown open the passionate recesses of her spiritual being. She had created for him a new Alayne, a woman reckless, desirous, abandoned to his love. "You are a more passionate woman sexually than Clara Lebraux." She rolled her head on the pillows and tears poured down her cheeks.

Oh, the birth of this new hate for him! It was far more agonizing than childbirth. It tore at her every organ. It nauseated her very soul. A dreadful metallic taste came into her mouth. Her hair was dripping with sweat. She felt as though she would go mad.

She rose and went to the window. It was a black night and had turned extraordinarily cold for the time of year. There was no breeze, no sound, no feeling of life, no promise. The air touched her face like a cold hand. There were no stars, no moon, the sun might well forget to return to such a world.

Out of the darkness Adeline spoke — "Mummie!"

"Yes, dear."

"I want a drink."

"Very well. I'll get you one."

"No. I want Daddy to get it."

"He is in his own room."

"Call him."

Alayne went to the side of the cot and spoke sternly.

"Baby, you are not to ask for Daddy. You will take the drink from me or do without. Will you take it from me?"

"Yes." The little voice was self-possessed. Adeline sat up and drank deeply. She emptied the glass and asked for more, her eyes looking challengingly into Alayne's.

"You cannot have any more water."

"Why?"

"Because you have had enough."

"Why?"

"If you drink too much you will wet the bed?"

"Why?"

Alayne put her hand on Adeline's chest and pressed her down on to her back. With a touch she could rouse all the antagonism in Adeline's fiery nature. Now she made her body rigid and, putting her hands above her head, clenched them into fists. She began violently to kick the bedclothes from her.

Like a sulphurous hot spring the hate that Alayne felt for Renny boiled up to engulf his child. She had to turn away and look out of the window. Adeline began to scream, giving herself up to the abandon of a tantrum as though it were noonday instead of midnight. Alayne let her scream.

Renny appeared in the doorway. He asked:

"Are you having trouble with her? Shall I take her?"

"I suppose you had better. I can do nothing with her." She spoke without looking round.

He came into the room on tiptoe in his thick-soled shoes. Why is he walking like that?" thought Alayne. "One would think there was somebody dead."

Adeline clutched him round the neck. She showed every tooth in her head in a joyful smile. When she was on his arm with her little pale blue silk quilt about her, she rolled her eyes triumphantly toward her mother.

"I'll keep her the rest of the night."

"Thanks."

"Would you tell me what she was crying for? Was she hungry perhaps?"

"She was crying for more water. She has had enough."

She could scarcely endure it till the two of them were out of the room. At once she locked the door and began to undress. She felt chilled through and drew the bedclothes over her head.

In the black seclusion beneath them she saw a series of pictures of Renny. She saw him with uprolled sleeves felling a tree on that day when she first discovered her love for him. She saw him, with her happy self by his side, galloping along the lakeshore in the autumn wind. She saw him, in the glare of electric lights, leaping barriers at the Horse Show amid a storm of applause. She saw him as he knelt by her bed on the day their child was born, his eyes wet with tears of tenderness for her.

Oh, how she had loved him! How she had loved him! Her love for him had made her into a different woman — yet not different enough to accept him as he was! Always she had wanted to change him — to force him into congeniality with herself, even while it was the bitter sweetness of their antagonism that enhanced their passion.

Hours passed while she went over and over the scale of their relations, always ending in the shock of the discovery. At last her brain refused to work coherently. Like a worn-out mechanism it moved erratically, feebly. Still she could not sleep.

Toward dawn an irritating tickling set up in her throat. At regular intervals she gave a dry hacking cough which she tried in vain to smother. When she found she could not smother it she gave in to it letting it tear at her throat without hindrance.

The handle of the door was turned, then Renny's voice said — "Alayne, I have brought some of my licorice tablets. Open the door."

"No," she answered, in a muffled tone. "I don't want anything!" And she allowed the cough to tear at her throat. She knew that, since Eden's death, the sound of coughing was horrible to him.

"I'll put them on the floor here," he said. She heard the sound of the little box being placed on the floor. A faint light showed Adeline's empty cot.

Her mind went back to her married life with Eden, that first flawless, happy love. She recalled her joy in the poems he had written then, a joy as over children they had created together. What a short while it had lasted! Yet this imperfect, troubled, tortured love for Renny — how it had persisted! Like a vivid, tough-fibred thread, it had dominated the pattern of her life for ten long years. It had so dominated her life that all that had gone before seemed to belong to a different person, to be almost meaningless to her. But she would unravel that thread! She would unravel the fabric of her life to the drab and pallid warp, so that nothing of that love might remain.

Her cough was less troublesome and might have ceased altogether but she began to cry again. She made choking, coughing sounds.

He was at the door again. "Alayne, I'm going down to get you a hot drink. You must take it. Do you hear?" He did not wait for an answer. He padded along the passage in his felt bedroom slippers. But he was fully dressed.

"She's got to take it," he kept muttering to himself as he went down the stairs. "She can't help herself. She's got to take it."

He descended the basement stairs and was in the brick-floored kitchen where the big coal stove was throwing off a steady warmth. His spaniels were lying on a mat beside it. They rose, yawning their surprise at his early arrival. Merlin uttered the deep-toned bark which, since his blindness, expressed his easily stirred emotions. Renny quieted them and went to the stove. Luckily there was hot water in the kettle. He poked the fire and opened the draught. The reflection from the living coals made a rosy glow over his haggard face.

She must be hungry, he thought. He would take her some bread and butter and a pot of coffee. She loved coffee. Nothing else so refreshed her, she often said. He went to the cupboard where he knew it was kept and took out the red enamelled container with the picture of Windsor Castle on the lid. The heavy sound of Mrs. Wragge's snoring came from the bedroom beyond the narrow dark passage.

He was a little puzzled about the making of the coffee. He supposed that the process must be very much the same as for tea but the steeping rather longer. While he waited for the kettle to boil he went to the larder. A gliding step approached and Rags, in cast-off pyjamas of his own, stood at his side.

His sharp little face showed his surprise at finding the master of Jalna, fully dressed, in search of anything so innocuous as bread and butter at that hour. He said:

"Can I 'elp you, sir? Shouldn't you like something a little more substantial?"

"It's not for myself."

"Ow, it's for the mistress! Just let me get it, sir. I know 'ow thin she likes it. Nothing more than a wifer."

He did indeed cut the bread delicately, while Renny looked on and Mrs. Wragge's snores echoed through the basement room. Watching Rags preparing food took Renny's thoughts back to France. He saw him making an appetizing dish out of some odds and ends from dilapidated tins. Rags remembered it too. Cocking an eyebrow, he said:

"Well, they weren't such bad toimes, sir. I think they were the best toimes of my life. I shouldn't tike it amiss if there was another war. Not if I could be your batman again, sir."

"There are worse things than war, eh, Rags?"

"I'll s'y there are, sir! There's comradeship in war. Folk are kind to each other. There's only one enemy. We all knoaw 'oo 'e is. But in peace, my word, there's enemies all about us and, 'arf the toime, they're posin' as friends! Noaw, I 'aven't much use for peace, sir." He arranged the bread and butter on a plate, with little finger crooked. "There, that looks temptin', doan't it?"

The boiling water was poured on the coffee. Renny carried the tray to Alayne's door. He knocked and her voice said — "Come in." She had unlocked the door while he was downstairs. She was sitting on the side of her bed with a blanket about her shoulders. As the door opened she turned her head and fixed her eyes on him with a look of almost impersonal wonder. She thought — "Let me look in his face again and see if there is no sign there of what he has done. Surely there is some change in his face." But when she looked in it she saw nothing different. He wore the same look of concern, she thought, which he wore when he was worried about a sick mare. No added sensuality to mouth or cunning to eyes marked the months of deception he had passed through. He was made of iron, she thought.

He had a feeling of poignant compassion seeing her sitting there, dishevelled, in the grey dawn. He had a feeling of anger too, at some unseen force of fate that had made this so unnecessary discovery possible.

All was over between him and Clara — excepting their friendship. Why could not their few amorous encounters have passed unrevealed!

He set the tray on the table by the bedside.

"If you would only," he said, "try to look on this sensibly. If you would just keep in your mind that you are the only woman —"

"The only woman!" she interrupted hoarsely. "The only woman! Please don't ask me to keep anything quite so grotesque in my mind. My mind is put to it now to keep its balance."

He said loudly, "You are the only woman in the world I could want as my wife. Clara —"

"Yes — I know — a wife and a mistress!"

"Not a mistress! Not a mistress! You can't call her that. Those special feelings came and went. They left no mark. On my word of honour, Alayne, I have been true to you all our married life except for this one lapse and you know that at that time we — you and I — were not on good terms."

She stood up facing him. "Will you leave me alone! I can't bear anything more." She put her hand to her head. Again her legs felt heavy, as though they were dragged down by wet seaweed.

He made a grimace of despair. "Please taste your coffee then — before I go." He filled a cup for her with the clouded liquid. She took a mouthful then set down the cup with an expression of disgust.

"I couldn't possibly take it."

"Is it made so badly?"

"It is horrible." She lay down on the bed and turned her face away.

"Will you have some of the bread and butter?"

"I couldn't eat. Please leave me."

With a look of deep chagrin he carried the tray to his own room.

Its window faced the east. In the first tremulous sunrays Adeline lay curled on his bed fast asleep, her expression one of beatific calm. On the foot of the bed slept the Cairn puppy, its plump body giving little hysterical jerks in a dream.

Renny drank the coffee Alayne had left and poured himself another cup. He folded two pieces of the bread together and took it in a single bite. He was terribly hungry.

V

THE LONG DAY

He had remembered that it was Sunday when he was shaving, and he had suspended the action of the blade while he considered whether or not the day would be better for his situation than a weekday. He decided that on the whole it would make things more difficult, both for himself and Alayne. He would, in the ordinary course of living, spend more time in the house. He could not so easily absent himself from meals. On the other hand Piers and Pheasant always came to Sunday dinner and, of course, there was church.

He had a sudden desire to take little Adeline to church. She was surely old enough. He remembered sitting through a sermon on his grandmother's knee, when he was even smaller. He thought it would take his mind off the misery of last night, if he could see her in the family pew. It would be amusing, considering her likeness to dear old Gran. It would take Adeline out of Alayne's way. The nursemaid always had Sunday off. Alayne would certainly not feel like being troubled by a stirring child, after the night she had spent.

Would she appear at breakfast, he wondered. He shaved himself with difficulty because of his injured shoulder. Adeline and the puppy were tumbling together on the bed. Suddenly she sat up and stared.

"Why did you make that funny face?"

"My shoulder hurt me."

"Why?"

"I've broken a bone."

"Let me kiss it."

He came to the bed, one half his face covered with lather, and bent over her. She planted her mouth on his arm. "Is it better now?"

"Much better."

He returned to his shaving. "A good thing I am almost ambidextrous," he thought.

The puppy yelped and he turned sharply to see Adeline kissing it extravagantly. He asked:

"What were you doing to him?"

"Kissing his sore bone."

"Humph. Well, I must take you to Mummie to be dressed." He washed his hands and took the child to Alayne's door.

"You call her," he said.

She called — "Mummie, Adeline wants to be dressed!"

He went back to his room and heard Alayne's door open and close. She would have stayed in her bed but there was the child to be cared for.

Adeline strutted about the room on her bare, beautifully shaped feet. Alayne was dressed. She wore a blue dress that accentuated the violet shadows under her eyes. She sprinkled a little cologne on her fingers and held them to her temples.

"Me. Me, too!" cried Adeline, holding up her flower-pink face.

Alayne, with a sad smile, put a few drops tenderly on the russet locks.

In glee Adeline showed every tooth.

"More! More!"

"No. You have had enough. You must be dressed."

But it was like handling a young wild thing. She turned this way and that, wriggling, shrieking with laughter. The putting on of every little garment was an ordeal. The room swam about Alayne.

When Adeline was dressed she went to where the bottle of cologne stood and emptied it down the front of her fresh yellow frock. She strutted up and down, looking at Alayne over her shoulder.

"I laugh at you," she said.

Then Alayne saw what she had done. With an icy look that cowed the child, she took her by the hand and led her downstairs. Renny and Wakefield were in the dining room waiting for her. Wakefield looked heavy-eyed and morose as if he too had not slept. He seemed to flourish his depression, as though in defiance of the bright sunshine that poured between the yellow velour curtains.

Renny achieved a conciliatory grin and said, addressing the air midway between Alayne and Adeline — "What a nice smell! Sunday morning scent, eh?"

Alayne was beginning to eat the half grapefruit which was served to her alone. She said:

"She has emptied my bottle of cologne on herself."

Adeline made her mouth into a rosebud and rolled her eyes at her father. She bent her head so that Rags might tie the bib on her white nape. His pale glance travelled from one face to the other and, as was his habit when he felt stress in family relations, he was assiduous in his solicitude for Renny, drawing the principal dishes a little nearer to his side and whispering a message he had had from Wright, the head stableman.

It seemed possible to talk a little when he was in the room but, when he had gone, the two men and the woman could find no word to say and the child greedily applied herself to her porridge.

Delightful spring sounds came in at the open window, the bleating of young lambs, the rival notes of two songbirds, the soft rush of a caressing wind. Renny cast a swift look at Alayne and noticed the smooth brightness of her hair, the fastidious order of her person. He was filled with admiration that she could look so after such a night. Yet, at the same time, he had a feeling of baffled anger that she could be meticulous under stress of such emotion. Still, he had dressed with more care than usual and, if she had come dishevelled to the table, he would have deprecated it. "What can I do to make her forgive me?" he thought. He felt powerless before the walls of her desolation. A hard bright rage crept over him. He turned and stared into Wakefield's face, then broke out:

"What the hell is the matter with you that you haven't a word for yourself?"

The sombre lines of Wakefield's face broke into astonishment and hurt as though he had been struck, then he gathered himself together and answered:

"I did not know I was expected to make conversation."

"Well — you are not expected to look as though you were at a funeral."

"Neither of you looks very cheerful." He scanned their faces shrewdly and divined the cause of Renny's irritation. He turned to him almost pleadingly. "If you knew the sort of night I had you would not expect me to be cheerful. I am at my wits' end to know what to do."

"Why — what is wrong, Wake?" Renny's tone changed to one of anxiety.

Wakefield crumbled a bit of toast on his plate and answered, almost in a whisper — "I have decided that I should not marry. I want to go into a monastery."

Renny looked at him dumbfounded; Alayne with a bitter smile. She said:

"I think you are very sensible. It is better to shut yourself away from life—not give yourself to anybody."

Renny exclaimed harshly — "How can you say that? What about Pauline? It would break her heart. As for me — why, Wake, you don't know what you are talking about! It's a ghastly life — unthinkable for a Whiteoak."

"I've been thinking of nothing else for a month."

"But — only yesterday — you were perfectly natural — you and Pauline — at The Daffodil."

Alayne's eyes, icy, accusing, pierced him. So — he was there, with Clara, yesterday morning! She said, "I suppose it was there that you hurt your shoulder."

He coloured but with a sudden defiant grin answered — "Yes. I was raising the porch of the tea shop."

Wakefield ignored the interruption. He said — "The time to speak had not come. Now it has come."

Renny sprang from his chair and began to walk up and down the room.

"You can't do it!" he cried. "You can't! It's appalling. I forbid it! You're not of age. I'll see these damned priests."

Wakefield answered calmly. "I wish you would. You'd find that I had no encouragement from them."

Renny thrust out his lips in scorn.

"Ha! They'd never let you know! They're too sly for you. Well, I'll put a stop to it! God, if Gran were here, she'd raise the roof with her shame for you!"

Wakefield returned — "You forget that one of the reasons why Grandfather left Quebec was that Gran showed Catholic sympathies."

"Rot! She was young. She was in a strange country. She got bravely over it. And so must you. Lord — when I think that you'd turn religious — when other young fellows are turning pagan!" He took out his handkerchief, wiped his forehead, sat down resolutely at the table and drank his tea in a few gulps. Then he said:

"We'll not talk about it now. We'll have it out later, Wake, when we're quite cool and composed."

"I am cool and composed now," returned Wakefield with gravity. "I have had it out with my soul. That is the important part. And Pauline will understand. I think she will be very happy for my sake."

The mention of Wakefield's soul took the pith out of Renny. He leant back in his chair helpless, staring disconsolately at his untouched breakfast. Alayne looked at him with cruel amusement. She could not help herself. He had made her suffer. Now let him suffer — in his love for Wake, in his pride, in his tenderness for those Lebraux women!

Adeline finished her breakfast. She was sweet and good, taking no notice of her elders. A heavy scent of cologne came from her. She liked it and drew up the front of her dress to sniff.

Renny turned to Wakefield. "I suppose you have been to early Mass," he said.

"Yes — I am going now to see Pauline."

Renny turned to him almost tragically. "Wakefield, I want you to promise me one thing. I want you to promise me that you will not speak of this to Pauline till I have seen your priest. You must promise me that."

Wakefield answered irritably — "Oh, I suppose I can promise you that! Though it makes it difficult for me. And I can promise you something else and that is that nothing anyone can say will prevent me doing what I have made up my mind to do."

"But you promise — mind, you promise!"

Wakefield gave a muffled assent then rolled his table napkin meticulously and put it into his napkin ring drawn by a small silver goat. He had always loved the little goat, now he gave it an unconscious caress.

Adeline looked at it enviously. She said — "I wish I had a little goat like that."

Wakefield gave her his charming smile. "You shall have it, Adeline! I am going away soon and must give away all my belongings. You shall have the little goat."

She laughed delightedly. "Go today, please!"

"I wish I could."

At these words, at the thought that Wakefield wished he might leave his home today, Renny's mouth went down at the corners as though in physical pain. He gave a short nervous laugh, then said to Alayne:

"I don't suppose you'll be coming to church this morning?"

She shook her head, looking down at her clasped hands.

"I have a mind," he went on, "to take Adeline with me. It is time she began to go to church and she will be off your hands for the morning. She can sit with Pheasant."

"Very well, though I think she is much too young."

She could not deny her relief at the thought of being free of the child's activities for an hour or two.

But she kept Adeline with her until it was time to go. For the first time that spring they heard the church bell across the fields. She put a fresh dress on Adeline, her little fawn-coloured coat and new straw hat and led her to the front porch. She sat her on the seat there and said — "Wait here till Daddy comes." She bent and kissed her, but coldly. She wondered suddenly how Renny would manage his surplice with his arm in a sling.

He thought he would like to take the path across the fields with the child. He could not drive the car and he wanted no one with him. He remembered the family party that used to set out on a Sunday morning — the old phaeton, driven by Hodge now dead, Grandmother, the uncles and young Wakefield established in it, the car following with himself, one or two of the whelps and perhaps Aunt Augusta and, of course, Pheasant.... Finch walking across the fields as he was now — what a tribe! But that was the way to live — one's flesh and blood under one's own strong roof!

Adeline was serenely happy. In her almost four years she had never felt quite so good and so happy as this. She tried to express this in her very walk, in the way she clutched her father's fingers. Every time he looked down at her or pointed things out to her she smiled up at him in utter goodness. She would not ask to pick the tiny wild orchids that showed in the grass. Alayne had not known that she was to walk and had put on her thin patent leather shoes. The path became wet and Renny was forced to heave her up on his one efficient arm. It was more effort than he could have imagined and he was glad when they reached the road to the church. The last bell was ringing.

He felt proud of his daughter as he led her along the aisle. He saw people looking at her, surprised and pleased. Meg stared out from the Vaughan pew, round-eyed with amazement. Renny put Adeline in the Whiteoak pew beside Piers, Pheasant, and their boys. Piers gave Renny an amused look. Pheasant and the boys were in a flutter. It took them a moment to decide on the best place for Adeline to sit. Miss Pink began to play the organ.

A live bee was clinging to the rector's surplice as he was about to put it on. He carried it, resting with spread wings on the snowy surplice, to an open window and flicked it with his finger out into the sunshine. He found Renny with compressed lips, struggling to get into his surplice. Ever since the building of the church a Whiteoak had acted as lay reader.

"Why, my dear fellow, what has happened? Your arm — nothing serious, I hope." But though his tone expressed solicitude he felt no real concern. He could scarcely have recalled the various occasions when his lay readers had appeared before him, in slings, in bandages, or limping. They spent their days among horses. They were headlong. They were always getting hurt. And they were a tough-fibred lot. He had seen old Mrs. Whiteoak, rather than miss the christening of one of her grand-children (Piers, he thought it was), carried to the family pew by a sweat-ing coachman and groom, when a fall from a horse had done something to her kneecap. She had never ridden again. She must have been nearly eighty-three.

"Collarbone," returned Renny laconically, "broken."

"Tch — is it very painful?"

"Only when I aggravate it."

Mr. Fennell noticed then that his usually high-coloured face was pale, that his eyes had not their customary brightness. "I'm afraid you had a bad night with it."

"Rather. It's time we went in."

One arm only projected from his surplice. His other side looked oddly bulky. Against the dark wood of the chancel his sculptured head stood out incisively. In the hymn, "The strife is o'er," his voice dominated the rather feeble choir of four men and seven women who, always defeated in their contests with the vigorous Whiteoak voices, felt themselves defeated before they had opened their mouths.

In the general confession Renny looked from the shelter of his hand at Adeline. She was being good. He felt his heart strengthen in pride. She was a fine child and the spit of old Gran. He had begot her. Alayne had borne her. Together they had produced that rosy flower of a child. Then the thought of all that had transpired the night before came to taunt his spirit. It was characteristic of him that he scarcely gave a thought to Clara. His mind was concentrated on Alayne's alienation from him. His mind dwelt on it darkly. There was projected into it a scene of passion in which he would forcibly overcome her antagonism, but he thrust this from him. His lips mechanically repeated the words of the confession. "We have erred and strayed from Thy ways like lost sheep.... We have left undone those things which we ought to have done; and we have done those things which we ought not to have done...." Alayne's face was blurred. In its place came a picture of Wakefield in a monk's robe, with shaven crown. Wake, whose engagement to Pauline had seemed so promising of happiness — Wake, his boy! He remembered his delicacy — the nights he had sat up with him, the fear that he would not rear him. The fear that he would be a poet like Eden. Then his pride in the boy's growing strength, in his eagerness to work, to make a place for himself. It had been a sting to his pride to see Wake's name over a filling station but — now how desirable that seemed when Wake wanted to give up his name and become Brother Something or Other! Well — he would see the priest and do everything in his power to prevent it! He felt a sudden hot anger at the boy. The young shuffler — to jilt Pauline for a whim! He had always been full of whims — a spoilt boy. What was it Gran had said? "The ingratitude of the spoilt child is sharper than the stallion's tooth." He was so absorbed in his thoughts that he remained kneeling after the others had risen, his face shaded by his hand. He realized what had happened and stood up imperturbably. His vigorous voice was heard — "Glory be to the Father and to the Son and to the Holy Ghost." Adeline dropped her penny and it rolled beneath the seat.

When the time of the First Lesson came, Renny mounted the steps behind the brass eagle. Meg watched him with sisterly pride. She thought — "How nice and white his surplice looks! Of course, they were all laundered at Eastertide. It makes such a difference. And the Easter flowers are lovely. I do like things bright and cheerful about a church because it's naturally rather a depressing place. What was he reading?"

"Speak, ye that ride on white asses, ye that sit in judgment and walk by the way…. Awake, awake, Deborah: awake, awake, utter a song: arise, Barak, and lead thy captivity captive, thou son of Abinoam."

She thought — "I always did like this Lesson, though how people went through the things they did then, I can't imagine … strange how Alayne let him come to church alone, when it is a wife's duty to encourage her husband in any religion he may have…. To think that Maurice would come with those old tight trousers on! His legs look ridiculous."

Maurice thought — "He looks seedy this morning. I suppose it's his arm. But he wouldn't stay away — no, not if he'd cracked both collarbones! Churchgoing is more and more of a bore to me. I wish Meggie cared no more for church than Alayne does. I'd be satisfied to stay at home with the Sunday papers. Darling little Patience — drinking in every word! Wonder what she makes of it."

"They fought from heaven; the stars in their courses, fought against Sisera. The river of Kishon swept them away, that ancient river, the river Kishon. O my soul, thou hast trodden down strength."

Maurice thought — "Why is Meggie staring at my trousers? Oh yes, they're the tight ones! But I must have another turn out of them." He tried to make his legs look smaller.

Patience thought — "I like to watch Uncle Renny's face when he's talking. He does nice things with it that make me want to hug him. I don't care a bit what he's reading. I just like watching his face. I wonder what it feels like to have a broken collarbone. Very disagreeable, I expect. I hope I don't fall off my pony and get anything broken. What lots and lots of flowers there are! What funny ears that old gentleman in front has! I think they might have put Adeline in the pew with me. Why is Mummie looking at Daddy's trousers?" She too peered at them.

The voice, in a level tone, proceeded — "Then were the horse hoofs broken by the means of the prancings, the prancings of their mighty ones."

Piers thought — "I don't see how that could be. I've seen a good many horses plunge about in my time but I've never known them break their hoofs doing it. I wish Pheasant would stop fussing over the children. It only makes them fidget more. I guess the best thing to do is to put Adeline at the end of the pew. Lord, I hope she goes to sleep during the sermon!" He moved Adeline to the place next the aisle. She was delighted and gave him a look of beaming gratitude before she began to loll over the end of the pew and try to see what was going on along the aisle.

"Blessed above women shall Jael the wife of Heber the Kenite be, blessed shall she be above women in the tent. He asked water, and she gave him milk; she brought forth butter in a lordly dish. She put her hand to the nail, and her right hand to the workmen's hammer; and with the hammer she smote Sisera, she smote off his head, when she had pierced and stricken through his temples."

Pheasant thought — "Those were the days! If a woman didn't like the way a man behaved she hit him on the head with a hammer. They talk a lot about the new freedom of women, but I don't see it.... Renny is almost handsome this morning. It suits him to look pale and tired. He has such good bones in his face. Adeline is surprised to see him up there in a surplice but she's awfully good. I rather wish I had a little girl. Perhaps the next.... No, no, I don't want to go through that again! Please, God, don't let there be a next! Not that I don't love all my little children

— but I did mind having them — especially young Philip who was so robust.... Mooey has a funny expression. I wonder what he's thinking."

Mooey was thinking — "That was a hard tumble the grey pony gave me yesterday. I feel more and more sore, the longer I sit. I'm afraid of the grey pony and he knows it; Daddy says that's why he acts so skittish with me. Next time I ride him, I'll set my teeth and show him I'm not afraid. But it would only be pretending. He'd know. I wish I didn't have to ride at the Show...." The voice of his uncle was borne into his consciousness.

"At her feet he bowed, he fell, he lay down; at her feet he bowed, he fell; where he bowed, there he fell down dead."

Mooey thought — "Funny how just bowing down killed him dead. If he'd had the fall I did he'd have had something to die for.... I do like Uncle Renny. Those were delicious candies he gave me.... I wonder if his shoulder hurts as badly as my sore spot."

Adeline, lolling on the end of the pew thought — "What a big big house! God's house. This is His party. We must be good. I am good. I am as good as — oh, I see Daddy's legs under his white dress! Daddy, Daddy, Mummie, Mummie, I can say prayers as well as anybody — Gentle Jesus — I know more words every day. I look like dear old Gran. Soon I'll be four. I know all the words Daddy reads. Uncle Piers holds me too tight."

Daddy was reading — "So let all thine enemies perish, O Lord: but let them that love him be as the sun when he goeth forth in his might. And the land had rest forty years." He paused, then — "Here endeth the First Lesson."

Adeline yawned, showing without reserve the charming interior of her mouth. She too had had a poor night. Piers took her on his knee and she rested her head against his shoulder.

She was good all through the service, even when he left her and joined Maurice in taking up the offertory. But she was a little troubled till Mooey whispered to her — "Have your penny ready." She held it tightly while she watched the progress of her uncles up and down the aisles. At last Piers held the alms dish in front of her. She was amazed by all the silver and copper she saw on it. She placed her penny in the middle and would have taken a piece of silver in return had not Piers passed on with the dish.

He and Maurice stood shoulder to shoulder at the chancel steps while Mr. Fennell advanced to meet them and Miss Pink sounded triumphant notes on the organ. As churchwarden, Renny cast a speculative glance at the offertory.

The service seemed long that morning. The air coming in at the windows was so inviting, so filled with the promise of fine days to come that Whiteoak flesh and blood longed passionately to be out in it. Those living ones gathered about the green plot for an exchange of greetings as they always did while the rest of the congregation was departing. The Easter flowers on the graves were still comparatively fresh. It was Meg who had laid them there and, while no grave was flowerless, the offerings were ranged in importance from the wreaths on her grandparents', parents', and Eden's graves to the few daffodils that marked the graves of her stepmother and infant half-brothers and -sisters.

Renny was the last to join the group. She turned to him with an affectionate — "Well, dear, I'm glad to see that you are able to be out this morning. But you look quite pale for you. How sweet Adeline was!"

"Next Sunday," said Piers, "you may have her in your pew."

"Oh, Piers," exclaimed Pheasant, "she was no trouble at all! We liked having her, didn't we, Nook?"

Nook smiled doubtfully. He was rather afraid of Adeline. The children began to run about the low iron fence that enclosed the plot, enjoying the new springiness of the grass, the escape from restraint.

Renny looked from Meg's face to Maurice's, from him to Piers and then to Pheasant. There was a frown on his brow that drew them visibly closer together. They looked enquiringly at him. He said:

"Well, I've a pretty piece of news for you. I haven't heard anything in many a long day that has made me as sick as this."

Maurice took off his hat and passed his hand over his greying hair. Meg's mouth became an "O" of apprehension, Piers stared and blew out his cheeks and Pheasant exclaimed:

"I'm not surprised! I have felt something hanging over us. I walked under a ladder at the stables yesterday. The last three times I've been to the pictures I've had seat number thirteen. Last night I dreamed of wild animals and at breakfast Piers upset the salt."

Meg said disapprovingly — "I think those are queer sayings for a Christian just come out of church."

Renny glared at them. "Have you finished? Now, what I want to tell you is this — Wakefield says he is going into a monastery — going to be a monk — going to throw Pauline over and be a monk! What do you think of that?"

The news was so different from anything she had expected that Meg scarcely knew how to take it. If it had been fresh money losses she would have groaned. If it had been bad news of absent loved ones she would have wept. But for this she was quite unprepared. She closed her eyes and said — "I think I'm going to faint."

Maurice, with conjugal skepticism, said — "I don't think you are — just keep calm."

But Renny clasped her in his sound arm and said excitedly:

"Run to the pump quick, Piers, and fetch water; she *is* fainting! She'll be unconscious in a moment."

Piers ran, leaping across the graves toward the old pump in the rear of the church. The children, not knowing what was wrong, ran joyously after him. Pheasant began to fan Meg with her prayer book. They supported her on the iron railing till Piers returned with the water in a tin mug. She kept her eyes closed till he approached her, then, fearing he might dash it in her face, she opened them and sat upright.

"Just give me a drink of the water," she said. "It will revive me."

The children gathered about, staring into her face.

"I knew she'd take it hard," observed Renny.

Piers said — "There's no use in our getting upset, we'll simply not allow it. He's not of age. He can't do it."

"Do you think he is in earnest?" asked Maurice.

"Absolutely. He's been wrestling with the idea for a month, he says. Had it out with his soul, he says."

They turned the words over in their minds. Meg took a draught of water from the rusted mug. Piers gave it to Mooey to return to the pump and the other children trailed after him.

"This comes," said Piers, "of allowing his engagement to Pauline. I always thought it was a mistake. I never thought that he really knew his mind. Now this is just something new that attracts him. But he must be stopped before it's too late."

Meg exclaimed — "I will go to him — on my bended knees! I will tell him what it will mean to the family if he deserts us. Oh, to think of it! To think he'd not confide in me! I've been a mother to him. I wore myself out nursing him — a puny little baby, with such eyes and such a mass of dark hair! Do you suppose they'll shave his head? I couldn't bear *that*! I'll go to him at once!"

Maurice put it — "You can't, Meggie. Remember the P.G.s' Sunday dinner. You like to oversee that."

Meg rose. "Yes. I must be home for that. But, this afternoon — we will come to tea. My child shall implore him not to do anything so dreadful." She looked almost serene as she saw this scene in mind's eye, saw the deferential faces of her men folk.

Piers said — "Among us we'll put a stop to it. He's a queer kid. And look at Finch. He's certainly got a queer streak in him."

They remembered Finch's queer streak. They remembered Eden. Meg looked down almost accusingly at her stepmother's grave. She pointed a suede-gloved finger at it.

"There," she said, "is the source."

Piers looked uncomfortable. "Oh, I don't know about that. Some of the Courts had queer streaks."

"But not this sort!" cried Meg. "Did you ever hear of a Court entering a monastery? Did you ever hear of a Court doing the sort of thing Finch has done? No, Piers, you cannot deny that your mother was different. You might well kneel here by the graves of our loved ones and thank God that you are a Whiteoak — even while you respect her memory."

Piers looked mollified. He did indeed thank God for it.

The four children trooped back. Adeline crept beneath the iron railing from which chains and spiked iron balls depended, as though to restrain the dead within their cramped divisions, and seated herself astride her grandmother's grave. She jogged up and down, as if on horseback, clucking her tongue and slapping the grave in encouragement.

"Young ruffian!"

"Oh, Adeline!"

"Look at her!"

"Take her from the grave!"

"Oh, naughty — naughty!"

"Ha, ha, ha!"

The laughter from Renny. Piers said sternly:

"I don't see how you can laugh at her. It's beastly disrespectful toward Gran."

"Gran would laugh too, if she were here. She'd say — 'A pickaback, eh? I like the youngsters about me.'"

"Renny," said Meg, "I command you to take your child away from there. If you are willing to let her behave so, Piers and I, at least, don't want to see such an example set our children."

"I should think not," agreed Piers.

"Adeline," said Renny, "come to Daddy."

Adeline jumped from her imaginary mount, her round, bare thighs flashing. She now stood astride a small mound marked by a headstone bearing the words — 'Gwynneth, Died April 13th, 1898, aged five months.' Piers exclaimed angrily:

"Now she is on my little sister's grave! I won't have it!" He grasped Adeline by the arm and lifted her roughly over the railing. She smiled up at him daringly.

"You talk," said Renny, with equal heat, "as though Gwynneth were your sister only. What do you mean by it?"

"Well, she was only your half-sister."

Renny was cut. "Do I cast it into your teeth that you are only my half-brother? I care as much for Gwynneth's memory as you do. As a matter of fact, you never even saw her."

"Yes," agreed Meg, with one of her inexplicable veerings in fraternal discussion. "Gwynneth might never have a flower laid on her grave if she had to depend on you, Piers. It is I, her half-sister, who bring them." And she looked down complacently at three narcissi and a spray of pussy willow.

Piers did not know what to say. He stared sulkily at his boots.

Maurice examined his wristwatch.

"Our P.G.s will be starving, Meg."

She gave an exclamation of consternation.

The very mention of the paying guests was distasteful to Renny. He said sarcastically:

"I suppose you dish up for them and Maurice ambles round with the trays."

"You seem to think it is all right," declared Meg, "for Mrs. Lebraux to run a tea shop."

"Yes," said Piers, "he goes to the length of breaking his bones to help her in the work."

"Oh, to think of it! And you allow Wakefield to keep a filling station!"

Renny retorted in exasperation — "Don't worry! Mrs. Lebraux is going to live with her brother and Wake is entering a monastery."

Before Meg could answer this she was led away by Maurice who took the welfare of his guests deeply to heart. Patience ran after them. Renny and his child crowded into the car with Piers, Pheasant, and their boys.

A tremor might well be supposed to have quivered through the dense earth that lay on old Adeline's coffin as the group departed, and her spirit have exclaimed — "What's the to-do? I will not be kept out of things!"

Alayne was waiting for them in the sitting room. She had often felt it rather an ordeal that these relatives should always take Sunday dinner at Jalna. Today she welcomed them.

She had a flat, strange, unreal feeling. The thought of making conversation took from her what strength she had. She would let the others do the talking. The Whiteoaks had one never-failing subject of absorbing interest — horses and the breeding and training of horses. For all his keenness in farming, Piers could not make it pay. He and Renny were breeding more horses, polo ponies and children's saddle ponies. Curiously little Maurice had not inherited his parents' love of horses. He loved the sounds and scents of the fields and woods, but he desired no stirrups between him and the earth. An erratic swift-moving creature beneath him filled him with nervous apprehension. Even Pheasant did not realize the depth of this emotion though she shielded him from rough experiences as much as was in her power. Mooey lived a double life, feigning a keenness unnatural to him in the activities of the stables, disappearing when he had the chance into the great depths of the woods or hiding in his attic room to pore over the old books which the Miss Laceys had left stored there.

Alayne liked Mooey and she felt a compassionate understanding of him, but it was little Nook who was her favourite. He was the sort of child she would have liked for her own. He was sensitive, shy, aloof, slow to give his affection but staunch in the giving of it. Between him and Alayne there was a curious understanding. He ran to her now and clasped one of her hands in both of his. She sat down and took him on her lap. She and Pheasant were in the sitting room while their two husbands, Adeline between them, had gone to the stables before dinner. Mooey hesitated in the hall, uncertain whether or not he should follow his father.

Pheasant glanced shrewdly at Alayne. She saw the heaviness of her eyes, the lines about her mouth. Something was wrong, she thought, something beyond an ordinary quarrel. Alayne looked ill. Her skin had a sallow tinge. "Men *can* make you suffer," she said out loud before she could stop herself, and then added, breathlessly — "Oh, Alayne, I should not have said that!"

Alayne sifted Nook's fine hair between her fingers. "It doesn't matter. I expect I do look awful. I couldn't sleep last night."

Pheasant burst out — "As long as you love each other, I don't believe in lying awake suffering in your mind! I say it's better to make friends at any cost — dignity or high ideals or — anything! And I know you have lots of both."

Alayne's lips twisted in a little smile. She answered composedly, not being able to enter into intimate depths of marital discussion.

"We are naturally worried about Wakefield."

Pheasant was unconvinced. She could not believe that Wake's decision to enter a monastery could make Alayne look like that. She said:

"Nothing that young man could do would surprise me. I pity him when Renny and Piers get after him. But I didn't expect you to mind so much."

Alayne answered irritably — "I don't mind. It is the sort of thing one must settle in oneself. But it is upsetting to Renny and very hard on Pauline."

"Not half so hard, *I* think, as marriage with him would be! But Mrs. Lebraux will be terribly disappointed. It must be hard, when you think you have your daughter settled in life, to find that it's all off. Not having a daughter, I shall never have to go through that."

The mention of Clara Lebraux's name quivered through Alayne's nerves like the striking of a gong. She got up abruptly and carried Nook to the open window. "Let us see," she said, "if we can find any buds on the lilac."

Alayne retreating as usual! thought Pheasant. And she began resignedly to talk about the children: baby Philip's new tooth and how good Adeline had been in church. Alayne remained at the window till she saw Renny and Piers coming toward the house.

She remembered how the first time she had seen Renny it had been from a window, drooping in his saddle with that accustomed air, unconscious of being watched. At that first moment the shape of him had been imprinted in the most sensitive recess of her mind and never again could be effaced. Now he was walking toward her after ten years and how little changed outwardly! Yet she felt as though she saw him for the first time, unaccountable, mysterious, threatening. Yet there was nothing to fear. She had experienced the worst — he could not hurt her now. A feeling of repulsion toward him, amounting to nausea, rose in her. She turned from the window.

He did not enter the room with Piers but said from the doorway:

"Could you come here a moment, Alayne? There is something you must attend to."

She set Nook on his feet and went into the hall. Renny stood in the doorway of his grandmother's room. He said in a low voice — "Come in here — I have something I want to say to you."

"No," she said, out of the constriction in her chest.

He took her by the arm and drew her into the room. She did not resist because of Piers and Pheasant across the hall. He closed the door behind him.

Although the window was open the air of the room was close, impregnated by the odours of the Eastern rugs and fabrics, the formidable dresses, dolmans, and mantles that still hung in the wardrobe. It seemed to Alayne that she must stifle if she remained there for more than a moment. She faced him, her antagonism quivering like a flame in her eyes. She put her hands behind her on the handle of the door.

He said, with a perceptible tremor in his voice — "Alayne, I brought you into this room purposely, into this room that belonged to a woman who understood more about life than anyone I've ever known. She knew men and she knew women, and she knew human weakness —"

"What is all that to me?" she exclaimed passionately. What help is that to me today?"

"But only listen —"

"I will not listen —" She turned the handle of the door vehemently in her hands.

His face softened to tenderness, his eyes were suffused by tears. "You know I love no one but you — that I never have and never shall love any woman but you!"

She pointed to the bed with its rich-coloured covering. "You might have told that to her — she might have believed you. Perhaps she condoned such things in her husband. But you can't make a Whiteoak out of me — you can't make a Court out of me — not after ten years! I'm the child of my parents. Do you suppose that if my mother had found that my father had been meeting another woman in the wood — been intimate with her there — oh, I have no right even to mention their names in such a connection! It's horrible! I wish I had not even mentioned my father's name with such thoughts in my mind. But I have mentioned it and I tell you, Renny Whiteoak, she would never have forgiven him! She would never have allowed him to touch her again! And I am her daughter."

"Does that mean" — an odd embarrassed expression flitted across his face — "does that mean that you will never sleep with me again?"

"It does." She opened the door and stood in it. She saw him place his hands on the footboard of the bed and stand staring at it as though he actually saw his grandmother lying there. His lips moved but she did not hear what he said. She turned with a quick strong step into the hall just as Rags sounded the gong for the Sunday dinner.

Rags stood by the gong with bent head. He looked up at her slyly from under his light brows. She had an uncanny feeling that he knew all that went on in the house, understood all, with no more than a word caught here and there to inform him. He was like some strange god, she thought, standing there by the gong, beating their entrances and exits in the futile drama of their lives. In the sitting room they stood waiting for Renny, Piers talking with an added heartiness because he was conscious of some crisis other than that brought about by Wakefield.

Adeline was in a gale of spirits. She tossed back her head and laughed up in their faces, showing her teeth which were extraordinarily white even for a child. She would not let Nook be and he made no effort to hide his fear of her. Piers's chagrin at his son's timidity deepened the colour in his fresh-skinned face. Mooey felt embarrassed for Nook's sake, but he also felt a certain satisfaction in the thought that he was not the only one who did not come up to Piers's standard of what a boy should be.

As Renny entered, Piers said to him — "I guess this one will have to go into a monastery too. I think it's the only place he'll be fitted for. Adeline can frighten him with a look."

Renny stared at the children, not seeming to see them. He said — "Did I hear the gong?"

"Yes," answered Pheasant. "And I don't think it's fair to say such things about poor little Nook, because Adeline certainly has an intimidating way with her, don't you think so, Alayne?"

"She intimidates me," answered Alayne. She took Nook by the hand and moved toward the dining room.

"She grows more like Gran every day," said Piers approvingly. Adeline hung on his coat, dancing beside him.

Following them, Pheasant asked of Renny — "When do you expect the uncles? They're coming to visit, aren't they?"

"I'm expecting to hear any day that they are on their way. This will be a pretty mess for them to return to." He looked so sombre, indeed so black, that Pheasant felt a sudden pity for Wakefield. She said:

"Perhaps everything will be happily straightened out before they come."

He drew a profound sigh. "Indeed I hope so." His eyes rested on Alayne standing facing him across the table.

Wakefield was late, not so much because he shrank from the concerted attack of the family as with a sense of the dramatic significance of his entrance. He was disappointed to find that Meg and Maurice were not present. With a little smile at Pheasant and a non-committal nod to Piers he dropped into his chair.

Contrary to his usual air of protest against Wakefield's tardiness, Rags placed his plate as though making him a formal presentation of it, but it was near Renny that he hovered with an air of solicitude.

It was customary on Sunday to have red wine or ale on the table, but to Piers's disappointment there was neither today. He showed his discontent by pushing the glass of water away from him and throwing a glance of sulky enquiry at Rags. Rags received it with almost smirking pleasure because he felt in his master's perverse refusal to have anything stronger than water on the table a gesture expressing depression of a peculiarly searching nature.

There was roast duckling and Renny presented a drumstick to each of the children. It was almost unendurable to Alayne to sit during the exhibition of eager gnawing that followed. Adeline was conscious of this and threw her mother daring looks out of eyes humid with greed.

When this course was removed and large glistening table napkins were being used to wipe small sticky hands and mouths, and Renny had loudly cautioned Rags not to let the dogs have the duck bones, the gathering heaviness of the atmosphere was broken by Piers saying to Wakefield:

"Are you in earnest about this affair or are you just showing off?"

A quiver passed over Wakefield's face. He gathered some crumbs of bread by his plate into a little mound. Then he turned to Renny and said:

"Do you think it is fair that I should be asked such a question?"

"I don't doubt your sincerity."

"Thank you. Then if you don't doubt my sincerity, and if I tell all of you that I have fought this out in the very sweat of my spirit and that I've come to a fixed decision, I don't see what more there is to be said about it."

"But, Wakefield," cried Pheasant, "you don't realize what you are doing! You're just throwing away all the lovely things in life for a dreary existence in some dreadful cell!"

Wakefield smiled at her almost compassionately. "That speech shows how little you know of life in monasteries. I expect to work as hard as

I ever have only in a different way. And don't imagine, Pheasant, that I haven't considered the lovely things of life that I must give up. I have considered every single one of them and I don't mind telling you that it was a bitter thing giving them up, but it would have been still more bitter to have given up the lovely things of the spirit."

"But can't you have both?"

He answered gravely — "Not in the way necessary to me."

Piers said — "What about Pauline? You don't mind depriving her of all she has looked forward to? Not that I consider a life yoked up to you a very desirable one!"

"I don't think that this will come as a very great surprise to Pauline. I think she must have seen it coming. No one who loves me could have failed to see that I was passing through a great crisis in my life."

Piers returned — "No one who knows you could fail to see that you're a confirmed play-actor and have been all your life. I make my guess that this monastery stuff will last just about a month — just long enough for you to break your engagement to a girl who is a damned sight too good for you!"

Wakefield gave a crucified smile. "I must learn," he said, in a steady voice, "to bear such remarks as that — even to welcome them. I must be ready to pass through fire to attain —"

"Shut up!" shouted Piers. "I won't listen to such tripe! What I'd like to do to you is —"

Renny interrupted — "That's not the way to take him, Piers. We must try to show him calmly that he's not fitted for a monastic life, that no Whiteoak is. Just think, Wake," he turned his penetrating gaze on his youngest brother, "you will be cut off forever from all the things our family have delighted in! From a free outdoor life, from liberty of speech —"

"Ho!" exclaimed Wakefield, "I like that!"

"I repeat liberty of speech. As a family we say what we think even though we get hell for saying it."

"I call the oath of silence liberty as compared to that!"

"My God!" ejaculated Piers, and overturned his glass of water.

"Naughty, naughty," cried Adeline.

Pheasant began to mop up the water with her table napkin. Renny proceeded — "You're young. You're very young even for your years —"

"He's a whining puppy," interjected Piers.

Renny turned on him fiercely. "*Will* you let me go on! Now, Wake, what do you think your uncles will feel about this? Your father, your grandmother, if they were living? They would feel that you are contemplating an impossible thing. Because they all would know that a Whiteoak cannot live without women." The disastrous import of his last words as relating to the crisis in his own life struck him into silence the moment they had passed his lips. Wakefield, Piers, Pheasant, and the children faded from his sight. He was left alone with Alayne, the bitter accusation in her eyes, the sneer on her lips piercing him. He stared at her fascinated, the muscles in his cheeks and about his mouth alternatively flexing and relaxing, his forehead corrugated in consternation.

She held him with her gaze, caring for once nothing for what the others thought. The tension was only cut by the entry of Rags who placed a deep rhubarb tart in front of Renny and a bowl of whipped cream.

"Rhubarb tastes so nice this time of year," observed Pheasant, while she pressed Piers's foot under the table.

"Yes," he added, "and the cream whips so well."

"Me!" cried Adeline. "I want tart! I want tarts with cream! Lots of cream!"

Her father turned on her sharply and gave her a rap on the hand with the spoon with which he was about to serve the tart. "Mind your manners," he said sternly, "and behave yourself!"

She drew back her hand and hid it under the edge of the table. She thrust out her lower jaw and glared at him half abashed, half defiant.

He served the tart, raising his eyes to the pulse throbbing in Alayne's throat and asked — "You, Alayne?"

"No, thank you."

There was silence for a space whilst Mrs. Wragge's flaky pastry was consumed and the warm sunlight coming between the heavy yellow curtains brought out not only the richness of the mahogany and silver but the shabbiness of the rug, the wallpaper and Rags's coat. The mind of each one at the table drew back on itself, ignoring for the moment the pressure of the egos surrounding it. Alayne felt a kind of exhausted triumph after her silent encounter with Renny. She had reduced him as she had not seen him reduced before, and she had a mordant comfort in the thought that he could know shame. The only one who seemed near to her at this moment was little Nook who sat on her left. She took his hand in hers and helped him with the eating of his tart.

Pheasant had seen the look exchanged between Alayne and Renny and her mind was in a whirl of curiosity. Her sympathy lay with Alayne but, for some reason, she had hated to see that expression on the hard weather-bitten features of the master of Jalna.

Piers was experiencing a feeling of irritation at himself in that he was unable to enjoy the good food according to his wont. He could not remember a time when a family disturbance had dulled his taste, that is when he was not the centre of it himself. But it was certain that neither duckling nor peas nor rhubarb had their accustomed flavour. Then observing the damp spot by his plate he realized that it was being given only water to drink that had taken the zest from his palate. He pushed out his lips and toyed with the pastry on his plate. Renny shot him a sideways look.

"What's the matter with it?" he demanded.

"Oh, I expect it's all right."

"Why don't you eat it then?"

"I don't seem to want it."

"I shall be sorry," said Wakefield, "if the spiritual crisis I am passing through takes away anyone's appetite, most of all yours, Piers. Home wouldn't seem like home if you —" He smiled ironically.

Piers's blue eyes turned on him truculently. "My loss of appetite has nothing whatever to do with you or your plans," he said hotly.

"The truth is," said Pheasant, "that Piers is simply sulky because he has had no spirituous liquors to quaff at this repast."

"We are economizing," returned Renny curtly. "But, if you find it impossible to eat without drink, if you find that you must overturn your glass of water and sit sulking throughout the meal, I can have Rags fetch something. What would you like?"

Piers returned stolidly — "Nothing will help me now but a whiskey and soda."

"Whiskey and soda, Rags."

Rags opened a door of the sideboard and peered into it defensively. He produced a decanter half-full of Scotch and a syphon of soda water.

Renny asked — "Wine, Pheasant? Alayne?" He kept his eyes on his plate.

Both declined. Alayne said — "Wragge is taking coffee to the drawing room. Shall we go on, Pheasant?"

They rose and collected the children. As they passed out, Renny, at the door, gave Alayne a fleeting look. Her face revealed nothing but a weary endurance of the situation. He returned to the table and poured himself a drink.

Wakefield sat between his brothers lighting a cigarette. He got to his feet then and said:

"I think I'll follow the girls. There's no object in my staying here. My mind is irrevocably made up."

"Remember," said Renny, "that you have promised me to say nothing of this to Pauline till I have talked to your priest."

"I'm not likely to forget it. And I'm anxious for you to see Father Connelly and discover for yourself how little encouragement I have had from him."

"Sit down," urged Renny almost tenderly, "and let us talk it over quietly together, now that the women are gone. Have a drink with Piers and me."

"No, thank you, Renny. I'm not taking anything of that sort. I forgot myself when I lighted this cigarette." He stubbed it out on the plate before him and left the room.

He met Alayne at the foot of the stairs. She was bringing down a large cretonne bag in which Adeline kept a jumble of small toys. All three children had followed her to the attic for this. Now their faces were as expectant as if they had never seen its contents before. Wakefield went with them to the porch and saw the bag turned out on the floor. Nook timidly picked up a dishevelled mechanical bird.

"Mine!" exclaimed Adeline and snatched it from him. "His name is Boney. He used to talk but he can't talk now. He used to say — '*Haramzada — haramzada — chore — chore!*'" She was triumphant over her delivery of the Hindoo words.

"Now," said Alayne, in a flat tone, "you must amuse yourselves with these while we have coffee. Adeline, you must share your things with Nook. Mooey, will you please play with them?"

Adeline, her hair a bright red in the sunlight, went down on her knees among her treasures pushing toys arrogantly into Nook's hands while he still gazed longingly at the bird. Mooey dropped to his knees beside them and began languidly fitting a puzzle together.

As Alayne poured the coffee Pheasant asked Wakefield — "Have you heard from Finch and Sarah lately? Is there any talk of their coming home this summer?"

"Yes. But I don't know just when. Finch is giving recitals here in the autumn. He's been doing awfully well in Paris."

"I know, I saw the press cuttings he sent. They seemed to be good though Piers and I couldn't make out all the technical terms. Our French is as rusty as our everyday conversation is bright." She was nervous before Wakefield. She did not know what to say to him. He had a queer sort of halo round his head, she thought, as though he were already half-sainted. She believed in him as Piers could not.

"I wonder," he said, putting four lumps of sugar in his coffee, then taking three of them out again and laying them on his saucer, "whether he and Sarah are happy. Tranquilly happy, I mean."

"I don't see how they can be. They seemed to me oddly matched. Finch is so open, so anxious to please, and Sarah is so closed in and doesn't give a damn what anyone thinks of her."

"That seems to me a good combination." He spoke rather cynically, his bright eyes resting on Alayne's face. She said:

"Sarah and Finch have their love of music in common. And not only that — they love all beauty. I think they are perfectly suited to each other."

"You may think so," returned Pheasant sententiously, "but, if I were a man, I'd sooner do what Wake is doing than be linked up with Sarah."

"I do expect understanding from Finch in the new life I'm undertaking," observed Wakefield. "He was very interested and nice about my conversion. There is something religious in him too that the others haven't got."

Pheasant looked at him enviously. "I wish I had! But I've no more real religion in me than a gypsy. I'm full of pagan superstitions!"

Wakefield answered gravely — "They show that you are not dead spiritually, Pheasant. All may come right with you yet."

Again a wave of nausea was passing over Alayne. The two in front of her were no more real than figures in a dream. She could not clearly follow what they were saying though she made the effort. She sipped her coffee clear and held all the nerves in her body tense.

Mooey drifted into the room. "They're playing very happily," he said. "Adeline has given Nook the bird now as well as most of her other toys. I wish I had something to amuse me."

Wakefield went to the cabinet of Indian curios. He took out a small ivory elephant. "My grandmother gave me this when I was a kid like you. I've liked it better than anything I've ever owned, almost. It's so nice to hold and the carving is so delicate. I'm going to give it to you, Mooey, to remember me by." He put it into Mooey's hands.

Mooey had always been rather afraid of Wakefield who had liked to tease him and bewilder him with long words. He was almost overcome by pleasure in the gift. His face flushed. Wakefield bent and kissed him on the forehead. "Bless you, young Maurice," he said.

Pheasant burst into tears. "Oh, Wake," she sobbed, "you make it all seem so sad!"

Alayne clenched her hands between her knees and closed her eyes.

Renny and Piers, left together, sat in silence for a space, then Renny said:

"Our mistake was in tackling him simultaneously. But I'll take him myself to the stables this afternoon and have it out in my office. I may be able to do something with him."

"Silly young blighter!"

"Well, I shouldn't say that. Wake has always been thoughtful for his age. His delicacy when he was a kid made him different from the rest of us. He's in dead earnest about this so we mustn't be too hard on him."

Piers pushed out his lips. "No, we mustn't be hard on *him* even if he breaks Pauline's heart! She's mad about him."

Renny rested his head on his hand, shielding his eyes. With an almost physical effort he put from his mind the thought that Pauline loved and always had loved him more than Wakefield. He said indistinctly:

"She'll get over it."

Piers mixed himself another drink. He eyed his brother speculatively. The bent head that had something stark and aloof about it, the lean shapely hand shading the eyes, the mouth with its downward curve of miserable gloom. There was a misery, there was a gloom about him like a palpable essence. Piers felt almost startled by it. Good Lord, no need to take Wake's defection so hard as that. He put his hand on Renny's arm.

"It will probably turn out all right. And it's not final yet — he hasn't gone into the monastery and when they've had a month or two of him they'll probably reject him."

Renny muttered — "I'm in deeper trouble than that, Piers. I'm in the hell of a mess and — the doors have shut on me — it's irrevocable —"

Piers's fingers pressed his arm. Piers's mind flew to the mortgage on Jalna. Surely nothing less than the thought of losing Jalna would make Renny look like this. He asked, rather unsteadily:

"What is it, old man?"

Renny raised his head and looked at him sombrely. "You know about Clara Lebraux and me?"

"I've guessed."

"Alayne has found out."

A weight rolled from Piers's chest. So it was not Jalna! But it was bad enough to make old Renny look like a mask of tragedy. He asked:

"She's not going to leave you, is she?"

"Leave me? God, no! It's not as bad as that. But it's bad enough. And the hard part is that it is all over between Clara and me — has been for months — and Clara is going away. She was telling me that she was going away, down in the ravine, and Alayne overheard."

Piers gave him a shrewd look. "Was there something then — in the way you took the news —?"

Renny broke out harshly — "I still care for Clara, as a friend! It was hard to think of losing her. I have talked to her ... as I couldn't to anyone else ... well, she's been a complete pal — if you know what I mean."

"It's a beastly mess," said Piers. After a little he added — "I am glad Mrs. Lebraux is going away. Things may come right between you and Alayne when she is gone."

"Never! You have no idea what Alayne is like. It's been horrible to her. She sets before me the standards of her father — not of my father or my uncles."

"What of that old Dutch sea captain ancestor of hers? Was he a paragon?"

"She only knew her father. And she knows what her mother would have done in her place. Or so she says."

Piers asked abruptly — "Was all this going on last night? Between you and her, I mean?"

"Yes. Piers, you must not let fall a word of this to Pheasant. It's in absolute confidence."

"Not a word, old man!"

There was no need for Renny to have warned him. The subject of infidelity between a man and woman was one which Piers and Pheasant avoided with a determination almost fearful. Piers muttered:

"But it's not half so bad for her as it would be for you if she ..."

Renny gave a harsh laugh. "My dear fellow — I could forgive her! I could forgive her twice over!"

Piers saw that his lip trembled, that his eyes were full of tears. Poor devil, he was taking it hard! As for Alayne — Piers's mind moved slowly back over the past. He recalled the atmosphere of Jalna when Alayne lived here as Eden's wife and had not been able to hide her love for Renny. He took another drink and muttered:

"Uncle Nick could see it — I could see it — I'll bet Eden knew it.... If you had ... I wonder if she would ..."

"I hope you're not getting drunk," observed Renny.

"Not a bit of it. But it's a difficult thing to put into words. What I mean is I believe Alayne had it in her to be unfaithful to Eden with you."

Renny's mind also turned to the past but it turned with a passionate swiftness. He saw himself standing by an old apple tree he had felled, Alayne in his arms, their first unforgettable, unpremeditated kisses, for she had kissed him back ... she had kissed him back ... he would never forget the feel of her lips on his. He saw himself with her again, in the porch at night, a rainy wind scurrying about them, dead leaves blown to their feet. She standing rigid, rain drops on her cheeks like tears. He saw the longing in her eyes. Through all his nerves he felt her wild reckless desire for him, the desire to be held close to his breast, to be kissed again by him. But he had restrained himself with a grim effort, remembering that she was another man's wife. He had kept from her his understanding of her, though, if young Finch had not just then come on the scene his resolve might have melted before the burning desire in her eyes. He saw a third picture. Night again and again rain. This time they were in a motorcar in a secluded spot. He had been driving her home from town where they had left Eden. Yes, they had left Eden, they had left him behind them as they had moved into the dark depths of a world of deeper desire. All during the drive they had not had a thought but for the nearness of each other, the wish to make that nearness complete. Yet Eden had come between them when he would have stretched out his hands to take her for his own. He remembered how the reluctant words had been dragged from him — "If you were not Eden's wife I should ask you to be my mistress. A man might cut in on another man that way, but not one's brother...." Again he had reminded her that Eden was his brother, that time in the bright sunshine on the lakeshore and she had reminded him, in a strange harsh voice, that Eden was only his half-brother. That had somehow chilled him. He had answered — "I never think of that." The smell of wood smoke from a fire his brothers had lighted on the beach came back to him now with the remembrance of the leap his heart had given when she had whispered — "I will do whatever you tell me to." And when they had said goodbye — it was the night of Gran's hundredth birthday, he remembered — she had clung to him and, half fainting under his kisses, had whispered — "Again — again!"

He sat so motionless, the lines of his face so set, that Piers dared not speak to him for a space, but sat sipping his whiskey and soda, studying with unabashed eyes the profile turned to him. But suddenly he could restrain himself no longer. He leaned forward and struck the table in front of Renny sharply with his fingertips. He exclaimed:

"Let her deny it! She'd have given in to you if you had pressed her! I saw you kiss that night of Gran's birthday."

"Well — I don't know — it may be one way or the other. But I do know that I never could throw that up to Alayne. Ours was a great love. She was perhaps willing to put aside everything for it. I couldn't put aside Eden. This affair — Clara and me — is quite different. I went to her for comfort when everything was wrong at home, when Alayne seemed to have turned away from me. And indeed she has now. I'm afraid I've messed things up horribly and I'm damned if I know how I've done it. When I was eighteen a woman old enough to be my mother told me that I could have women's love for the asking. I guess what she meant was that I would attract them physically. If she had known me longer she might have added that I could not satisfy their spiritual or intellectual side."

"You're muddled up in your mind, that's certain," said Piers. "You're no more to blame than she was. You've done nothing that she wouldn't have done. But you're ready to take all the blame while she is self-righteous. She has always put herself on a pedestal, by God!"

Renny gave a wry smile. "Let that be your last drink," he said. "I'm going to find Wake."

He hesitated outside the drawing-room door unseen by Alayne but seen by Pheasant. He and she exchanged a curious, intimate glance. It was an intimate look of understanding. He passed on into the porch, watching for a moment the children at their play. The sudden sight of him always filled Adeline with rapture. She dropped her toys and scrambled to her feet. As he bent over her she clasped his wrist in her hands and depended her weight from it. He uttered a shout of pain in response to the fiery stab in his shoulder. He pushed her from him and stood leaning against a pillar of the porch nursing his arm. Pheasant and Alayne appeared in the doorway.

"Whatever has happened?" demanded Pheasant, her small face showing the anxious lines that were only too ready to shadow its youthful smoothness.

Alayne looked frowningly from husband to child, a fresh wave of nausea dimming their figures. She did not speak.

Renny gave an apologetic grin, his eyes fixed beyond them in the empty hall. He muttered:

"This young woman had a sudden fancy for swinging from my arm."

"Oh, how awful!" cried Pheasant. "No wonder you howled! It gave me a fright, didn't it you, Alayne?"

Alayne gave a wintry smile and turned back to the drawing room. Renny strolled across the gravel sweep. Adeline ran after the women demanding — "Why did Daddy cry? Why did he push me? I don't like to be pushed. I'll push him back next time!"

Mooey was troubled by what had happened. There was something strange, something unnatural about all the grown-ups today. Even in the sweet warm breeze that blew in at the door there was a sense of sadness. A little round bunch of hepaticas, the first spring flowers, stood on a table in the hall. He and Nook had gathered them in the wood that morning and brought them to Alayne. He stood by them now admiring them and he held the small ivory elephant warm in his hand, yet his heart felt heavy. He thought he would go into the dining room and peep into a recess of the sideboard where sometimes candied fruit was kept.

He was surprised to find his father there and would have retreated but Piers, with a jerk of the head, indicated Renny's chair and said:

"Sit down and keep me company. I'm in a bad mood."

He had never spoken to Mooey in this intimate way before, as though he were another grown-up, and the little boy, sliding on to the chair, felt proud and rather anxious. He did not know what was expected of him.

Piers studied his son's face with a contemplative, not altogether approving gaze. He wanted Mooey to grow up to be a pal of his and doubted very much if he should. And certainly not little Nook. But there was young Philip — a chip of the old block. He looked up at the uniformed portrait of his grandfather relishing, as often before, his own resemblance to it and now, added to that, the resemblance of his third son. And he himself was a third son! And his own father, through whom he had got his looks, had been a third son! He had never thought of that till this minute. It was a most remarkable thing. Something special in third sons, no doubt about that! And, in the fairy tales of his childhood, it had always been the third son who had come out on top. Very remarkable. He pondered over this with a solemnity that Mooey found almost overpowering. He stared at him fascinated across the table.

Piers asked suddenly — "What was the matter out there?"

In one of the strange reticences of childhood, Mooey could not find words for a reply. He just looked at Piers with an odd veiled smile.

"Why the devil don't you answer me?" demanded Piers.

Mooey still smiled but did not speak. Piers leant forward and stared into his face, a sudden surging fear shaking him to his depths. That smile — that detached veiled smile — why — why, there was no doubt about it — he caught Mooey's chin in his hand, his staring eyes making the colour retreat from the little boy's face. But still the smile remained! It was Eden's smile — and Pheasant had — oh, God — it couldn't be! It was too horrible!

Then relief swept over him like a cooling wind. Eden was in Europe when Mooey was conceived! He was a fool — he was half drunk — or such an idea would never have entered his head. He threw himself back in his chair with a laugh of deep relief. He said:

"You're going to make a fine man, aren't you? Horses and farming and outdoor life — all that sort of thing, eh?"

"Yes," breathed Mooey, out of strained lips. He twisted his fingers together under the table.

Another thought assailed Piers. He remembered how mares and bitches sometimes reproduced characteristics of former sires in their off-spring. Was it possible then that this smile of Eden's which had almost a look of pain in it had come to Mooey because of Pheasant's past intimacy with Eden? Piers felt a leaping antagonism toward both Pheasant and Mooey and the old bitter hate of Eden pained in his breast. Then again came relief. Eden had been like their mother. And she, of course, was Mooey's grandmother. Easy for a boy to look like his grandmother. There was Renny — the spit of old Gran! Piers put out his hand and rumpled Mooey's hair. He said:

"I want you to do well with the ponies this summer. If you do I'll give you something nice on your birthday, see?"

Mooey put back his shoulders and forced courage into his eyes. He said:

"Yes, Daddy, I will"

Now Piers's mind moved away from his son to Alayne. As always with him when he had drunk too much he could not remain seated. He rose and stood on his strong legs, his glass in his hand and a lowering shadow on his flushed forehead.

"I want you to go to the drawing room," he said, "and tell Auntie Alayne that I must see her alone. Not your mother, mind. Just Auntie Alayne."

By the time Alayne was inside the dining room the shadow had become an ugly blackness. His eyes were hot with resentment. She looked at him first enquiringly, then defensively, but she could not imagine what he had to say to her.

"Yes?" she asked tentatively.

"I've always hated the thought of Eden," he said. "The very thought of him makes me feel as black as hell."

He had been drinking too much, she thought, and said "Why think of him, then?"

He looked into his empty glass. "Because I'm forced to think of him. And the queer thing is that I begin to sympathize with him where you were concerned. What's a man to do but turn to another woman when he sees his own wife throwing herself at another man's head? The fact that that other woman happened to be my wife has obscured every feeling but rage in me." He felt that he was becoming eloquent. He repeated — "Yes, it has obscured every feeling but rage. But he's dead and I see now you have driven your second husband ..."

Alayne put up her hand to her throat. Her face was stony but her voice broke harshly as she exclaimed:

"He has talked me over with you!"

Piers raised his own resonant voice.

"And why not? He knows he'll get sympathy from me. And sympathy is something he's lacked all his married days. You poured that out on him before you were married, when he didn't need it. He needed no man's sympathy till he was hitched up to you, and no *woman's* either!"

Alayne backed from him toward the door. She said — "You are utterly contemptible. Will you please go! As for the pair of you — you and he — I can only repeat — you will please never speak to me again!"

"The thing for you to do is to think over what I've said and try to see yourself as the family see you."

"The family! It might have been different with him and me if there hadn't been always the family!"

She went out and shut the door behind her. She did not go back to Pheasant but upstairs to her own room and threw herself across the bed. She clutched handfuls of the soft pillows and pressed her face into the darkness between them. There was a bluish shining spot before one of her closed eyes. She rubbed the eye, opened it and shut it sharply, but when she closed it the bright spot was still there. Even tears did not wash it away.

She had thought that the bitterness of her anger toward Renny could strike no deeper, but the discovery that he had confided in Piers gave an unexpected blow to her pride and Piers's words had filled her with a rankling shame. She had always felt that neither Eden nor the family had been conscious of her infatuation for Renny. All their faces rose before her, strongly marked, individualistic, big-nosed and fierce-eyed. She saw them as vultures rejoicing over the pale corpse of her pride.

In that moment she wished that she had never met one of them, that she had never planted her foot within the domineering gates of Jalna, that she had never spent a night under that roof, in the arms of one brother or the other — Eden who had come in his bright youth and swept her, in the music of his poems, from the drabness of her office life in New York — Renny who had roused to its height the passion only half woken by Eden. She remembered the professor, the friend of her father, who had asked her to marry him and whom she had refused. There would have been her proper place! With him she could have lived the life for which nature had calculated her. She could have had a child who would have been the fruit of her bosom as well as her womb. Not one who would have stared at her laughing out of alien eyes, tormenting her when she dared. Above all, she would have never had to face the desolation of this hour.

She dreaded the return of Renny. She dreaded the uneasy darkness of his eyes, the inward purposefulness of him that was a mystery to her.

She thought with complete detachment of the child left to work her will in the rooms below. Piers and his family had gone some time ago. There was silence for a time she heard Adeline's laughter coming from the distant basement where the Wragges had taken her in charge. Unconsciously she was relieved by the laughter and, face downward as she lay, fell into a deep sleep.

He did not return to the house till the hour of their evening meal. They were to eat it for the first time that spring by daylight. Rags had got a few sprays of wild cherry blossom and had placed them in a vase that did not suit them, on the supper table. Alayne noticed the clash before she drank in the beauty of the blossoms. She kept her eyes fixed on them, praising them to Rags who could not proceed with the serving of the meal till this was accorded.

Renny asked — "Is Adeline asleep?"

"Yes. Mrs. Wragge gave her her bath and put her to bed for me."

Rags oozed devotion as he offered Alayne the salad. Renny stood by the sideboard, fork in hand. "That was kind of her. Some cold beef, Alayne?"

"No, thank you. Just salad."

He dropped a scrap to the spaniels who sat on either side of him, then returned to the table and spread mustard on his beef. He was afraid that Rags was going to leave them, yet perhaps it would be better if he did. Silence or even a scene might be easier than the effort to make conversation.

"Those flowers are pretty," he said, staring fixedly at them. "What are they?"

Rags had left the room and Alayne answered:

"You know the names of fruit blossoms better than I do."

He felt baffled. He tried talking to his dogs but they lay, muzzles on paws, with an air of resignation.

He made a more determined effort. "Well, I had a long talk with Wakefield in my office. We came through it very well. Both kept our tempers. And I'm going to see his priest tomorrow."

"That is good," she returned.

"Wake is having supper with him tonight and, of course, preparing him for my visit. But I do believe that no pressure has been put on him. He's always had a religious bent and turning Catholic has been rather too much for him. But I have hopes that I hadn't this morning."

"That is comforting," she observed, biting into a radish.

He raised his eyes to her face. "Comforting —" he repeated, "comfort — that's what we need, isn't it, Alayne? Comfort to make us forget the things that go wrong…. Oh, my darling, if you knew how I hate to see you look like you do now. Why, you're ill!" He got up and went to her side.

She said vehemently — "It is no wonder if I am ill! If you have hopes that you hadn't this morning I have despair that I hadn't this morning."

"What is it now?" he asked.

"You have talked me over with Piers."

A storm of reproach could scarcely have exceeded the bitterness of the few words. A tremor passed through her limbs and her heart beat heavily.

He exclaimed — "I did not talk you over with Piers! I told him what I had done and that you took it very hard. That is the truth. I don't even know what you mean."

She gave an exclamation of contempt. "Please don't expect me to believe that! Like your grandmother you are clever when you are cornered. But you should choose someone less terribly candid than Piers for your confidences. He told me just how I had driven Eden to Pheasant's arms and you to Clara Lebraux's. He told me how I had thrown myself at your head. Oh, it must be splendid to have a brother like Piers to share your little troubles with!"

They heard Wragge's step on the basement stairs. Renny dropped quickly into his chair. Alayne took another bite of the radish and sat rigid, its tiny green stalk in her fingers.

Renny exclaimed — "I have just heard of a most promising two-year-old I can buy for a surprisingly low figure, considering that her sire is a champion. She's going to be a grand one. What would you say if I were to win a big event with her? There's still money to be made in show horses, you know, if you only have the luck."

"Yes, I should imagine so."

She could see his hands across the table and she was fascinated by the amount of mustard he put on his beef.

Wragge asked — "Shall I close the window, ma'am? This evening h'air strikes coald."

Alayne assented. From above came the sound of screams from Adeline. "One of her bad dreams," observed Alayne, rising.

But Renny was on his feet ahead of her.

Wragge asked — "Shall I ask my wife to go to the young lidy, ma'am?"

"No, no, I'll go!" Renny was already halfway up the stairs.

Alayne again sat down, her eyes fixed on his untouched meal. Although she had seen him leave the room she still saw him, with the utmost clarity, seated at the table. She saw the evening sunlight on his red hair and thought — "Not a grey hair there! He looks young, young!"

Adeline was in a state of wild distress. She sat upright, her face contorted, her nightclothes wet with sweat. In an ecstasy of relief she strained toward her father.

He bent over her. "Daddy's pet — Daddy's pet girl! There, there, now ... what was it all about?"

She looked at him with tranced eyes, scarcely seeing him but drawing comfort through every pore from his presence; the scent of him associated in her mind with comfort and protection. She began to laugh through her tears, not knowing what to say to him, for her dream had faded from her mind.

She asked, fingering a button of his coat:

"Why did you cry when I pulled your arm?"

"You hurt me."

"Sorry."

She took his hand projecting from the sling and pressed her lips to it. She began to mumble it, like a puppy, and even nipped it with her sharp teeth. But when he put her down and covered her she snuggled docilely into her nest.

He stood looking about the room, at Alayne's intimate, delicate belongings, her thin silk dressing gown, her tortoise-shell toilet articles ranged on the glass with which she had lately had her dressing table covered. He saw her cloistered there, for the rest of their married life, separated from him by the hate he had seen in her eyes. He had been shocked by the cold hate he had seen in her eyes. He could not believe it possible that their marriage had come to that. If only she cared more for Adeline, that might hold them together! But she didn't, there was no use in mincing matters, she was cold toward their child. If Adeline had been like herself, Alayne would have understood her. Yet he could not bring himself to wish that the child of his loins were different.

She still clasped his fingers and he bent and kissed her hand before he withdrew. Then — "Good night," he whispered, "and no more bad dreams!"

Her lips curved, her lashes lay on her cheek.

Alayne was alone when he returned to the dining room. She did not speak. After the dewy freshness of the child's face, hers looked more haggard, more unhappy, than before. She saw that he had difficulty in cutting his beef. He scowled at it with lips compressed but she could not bring herself to go to his assistance. When, at last, the meat shot into the air and was caught by Floss, she clenched her hands and bit her lip painfully.

Renny broke into loud laughter. "This is too funny," he said. "It's too ridiculous." He gathered his table napkin into a ball with his good hand.

Alayne rose from the table. "I could not sleep last night," she said. "I believe I'll have to go to bed now."

"Yes, yes, I think you'd better," he said. "You need rest — but," his eyes scanned her plate, "you've eaten only a radish!"

"It is enough." Her tragic tone, the thought of the radish, almost sent him off again. He sat, grinning up at her. He could no more have gone to the door with her than she could have helped him cut his beef.

Floss stood drooling, stung by the mustard, yet wagging her tail for more. She looked idiotically good-natured. Wragge returned from the basement and Renny said curtly:

"More beef, Rags. Cut it up."

"Ah yes, sir. That h'injured shoulder is a great 'andicap for you." He glanced inquisitively at Renny's plate.

"Floss got that, Rags."

Almost tenderly Wragge prepared his food for him but neither salad nor cold beef had any flavour. Bit by bit he fed the meat to blind Merlin.

He could not endure the house and though the darkness was abruptly closing in he went to the stables. It was turning cold too and the wind blew strongly from the lake. It pressed on his forehead like a steadying hand. Outside the stables he stood facing it a moment, his eyes resting on the dark bulk of the house. Only two lights glimmered there.

He remembered the days when its bright rows of windows repelled the darkness which now seemed powerful to engulf it. And soon Wake would be gone from it who had scarcely spent a night from under its roof! And gone forever! In his mood of depression he saw that calamity coming inevitably toward him. He could do nothing to prevent it. He was going to lose Wake whom he had thought to have always beside him! He had lost Alayne!

He remembered his free days and how he had carried love lightly, as a rider wears his colours in a race. But Alayne would have him wear love as a chain, and his restive spirit winced at its galling.

He went into the stable and, in the dim light, passed from stall to stall. They all knew him and bent their heads to touch him, to be caressed by his hands, cunning in knowledge of their responsive nerves. When he came to his favourite, Cora, he put his arms about her and kissed her. Her velvet nostrils snuffled against his cheek and her primitive quiescent peace was absorbed through all his being.

VI

THE CELIBATES

THE NEXT EVENING Wakefield went through the ravine to break the news to Pauline. His mood was one of pensive joy. His spirit was exalted, yet a strain of tender sadness increased the beauty all about him, made him pause to observe the charm of the tiniest flowers, to notice the whitish green of the fern fronds. Before long he would be saying goodbye to the scene which had been the background of all his life! He had often longed to travel, to see the places which had seemed so magical when he read of them in books, but now he wanted to make only one journey and that was to the cloistered seclusion of the monastery where magic lay in the ceaseless service of Christ and His Mother. The monastery was opening its walls to him. As he walked he could feel in anticipation the soft flapping of the robe against his legs.

He was eager to tell Pauline of his decision, yet he shrank from hurting her in her pride and possessive love of him. But she herself was devout and, even though her suffering might be almost intolerable at first, she would come to see that in giving him up she would reach heights of spiritual joy she might never have attained in the possession of him as a husband. She would marry; she was designed for marriage and happy motherhood; she would think of her engagement to him as a period exquisite and untouched by the crudity of sex. Perhaps she would name her youngest son for him…. He pictured himself going to see her and her husband (a robust, fine-looking man not unlike Piers) and taking the infant Wakefield on his knee while her other children stood about in awe of his thin ascetic person and monk's robes. He was not sure that such a visit could be permitted but hoped that because of some special circumstance it might.

Pauline was waiting for him, looking pale, he thought. She was heavy-eyed, as though she had not slept, withdrawn into herself as though in contemplation. Was it possible that she guessed his intention? His voice shook a little when, after kissing her gently, he said:

"You look tired, darling. Have you been doing too much?"

She shook her head, her fingers gripped his closely. They dropped into their accustomed seat on the verandah. He put his arm about her, then withdrew it and thrust his hand in his pocket. It was going to be harder than he had thought. He longed to have it all over and to be free. The world about him, the dim sea of purple twilight, seemed meaningless to him apart from his great desire.

"I have something to tell you," he said. "I'm almost sure that you have guessed it and that it is hurting you even more than I was afraid it would."

She turned to him, her face pale and startled. "What is it? Has anything happened at Jalna?"

"Pauline — don't you guess?"

"What do you mean? I don't guess anything. Is it about Renny … Alayne?"

"No, no — about me…. Haven't you noticed anything different about me lately?" He looked steadily into her eyes. The moment was upon them now. He steadied himself to tell her. There was a wounded look in her eyes, as though she already felt the blow. She answered, gravely:

"I have noticed that you seem very happy, and very — religious."

"Then you do guess!"

She looked at him blankly. "No, I can't possibly guess."

"Then I must tell you." He had a sudden aversion from putting his resolution into words, sounding, everyday words. He muttered, almost inaudibly:

"I must go away. Can't you guess where?"

"No, I can't guess." She sat waiting, her dark impenetrable gaze fixed on his, her long brown hands folded on her lap.

He took his hand from his pocket. It felt almost powerless, as though it did not belong to him. He laid it on her folded hands, his fingers pressing their engagement ring.

"Pauline — I am going to ask you to take off this ring that I gave you.... No — not really to take it off — I want you to keep it always in remembrance of the lovely time we've had together. But — I can't marry you! I find that I'm simply not meant for marriage. I am meant for something very different. I want to go into a monastery, Pauline!"

She looked at him unbelievingly. "Oh no, Wake — you can't mean that!"

"Darling — you can't feel the cruelty of it any more than I do! But it's better for me to discover my vocation now than after marriage, isn't it?"

She seemed incapable of taking in his words. She said incredulously — "You! Vocation! Why — you can't really mean it! What are you saying, Wake?"

I'm telling you, darling, that I want to enter a monastery. I broke the news to Renny yesterday. I promised him that I wouldn't speak to you about it till he had had a talk with Father Connelly. He went to see him today. You can't imagine how splendid the Father was — how clearly he made him see that I had the right to direct my spiritual life. Renny came home quite different. More controlled and apparently quite willing to let me have a try at it, but, of course, he's terribly anxious about you and so am I. I realize what a blow it is."

She said in a low voice — "He is anxious about me!"

"Yes, terribly anxious. But he doesn't know you as well as I do. He doesn't realize how full of character you are."

She gave a little laugh. "No — I suppose not."

Her laugh jarred on him. He took his hand from hers. His eyes were luminous in the dark. He said, almost assertively:

"Of course, it is awful for you. I know it, and I've suffered accordingly. But what must be must be, and it is as inevitable for me to enter a monastery as for that stream down there to enter the lake. No matter what obstacles are put in its way it goes on to its ordained destination."

"Oh yes, I understand. And I sympathize — more than you know ... now that I have taken it in. At first I was absolutely astounded. You seem the last one on earth for such a life."

He returned, almost huffily — "I don't see why you say that. I've always had a desire for solitude. When I was a small boy they used to talk about my thoughtfulness. Of course, I was generally up to mischief then. Still — I think I've always had a contemplative nature."

She said hesitatingly — "I have often thought that I should like to enter a convent."

"Not take the veil!" he ejaculated.

"Yes, take the veil."

"I have never heard of anything so ridiculous! Why, you're absolutely cut out for marriage and motherhood. Don't let such thoughts enter your head, Pauline. They're positively wrong — for you. Some other chap will come along, someone far worthier of you than I am. And you'll love him and you'll have children and perhaps" — he smiled tenderly — "you'll name a little boy for me. That would please me if — the news reached me in my cell."

"It sounds very pretty," she answered. "But I'll never marry. If you are going to enter a monastery I'll go into a convent. As I said, I've often thought I should like to, and now it seems the natural thing."

Wakefield did not like the idea at all. He had anticipated comforting a heartbroken Pauline, but to find her calm, taking his announcement with no more than astonishment, ready herself to throw aside the world at a moment's notice, seemed somehow to belittle his act of renunciation, to steal his thunder, as it were. He experienced an almost childish resentment and was searching for words to translate this into dignified disapproval when the door opened and Clara Lebraux came on to the verandah. She carried a tray with glasses of lemonade and a plate of cake.

"I thought you children would like this," she said, setting the tray on a low table before them. She turned away then to fasten a verandah blind that hung loose and Pauline took the opportunity to whisper — "Don't speak of this to Mother. I had rather tell her when we are alone."

Wakefield nodded glumly. He would have preferred a dramatic disclosure to this too easy acceptance of their changed relations.

Pauline turned the little pearl ring on her finger and said, with a flitting smile:

"I wonder what I shall do with this! Nuns can't have possessions, you know — any more than monks!"

Wakefield thought that he had never known Pauline to be guilty of bad taste before. He sipped his lemonade which was too sour, in silence. Clara suspected a quarrel between them and talked cheerfully of plans for their future. She had already told Wakefield of her intention to live with her brother and relinquish the tea shop after her short essay in running it. Wakefield had a sudden pity for her as she talked of visiting him and Pauline after they were married. For the first time in his life he was wretchedly uncomfortable because of feeling for someone else. What would Clara's life be, with himself in a monastery and Pauline in a convent? Instead of gaining an affectionate and brilliant son, she was to lose her daughter. He could not endure the situation for long and, after muttering an excuse and kissing the two on their foreheads, he left. Everything had turned out different to what he had expected. Pauline had accepted his withdrawal with no faintest outcry of pain. She had seemed even more willing to retreat from him than he from her. Now Clara's staunch tenderness for them both oppressed him to the point of tears. In truth his eyes were wet when he kissed Clara, and he experienced a filial uprooting in his breast that was more painful than his farewell to Pauline.

The two women watched his slender figure, so quickly absorbed into the twilight. A shadowy moon appeared above the trees and a smell of wet earth rose from the fields.

Clara, sitting on the step, lighted a cigarette, its flare discovering her blunt blonde features set in an expression of affectionate concern. Pauline swayed softly in a hammock in the shelter of the verandah. She curled herself up and put an arm across her eyes. She waited for Clara to speak.

Clara did so in her usual matter-of-fact tone. "What's up, darling? Anything you can tell me?"

Pauline's answer startled her. "Yes, Mummie. So much that I don't know where to begin."

"Nothing worrying, I hope?"

"I'm afraid you will not be very happy about it."

So many vicissitudes had come to Clara Lebraux that her spirit was alert with its answer of defence. Now, in a veiled tone, she said:

"Don't keep me in suspense, Pauline. I'm ready to face most things, you know."

Pauline lay curled up, as though she would make herself physically remote from Clara's anxious maternity. She answered, almost coldly:

"Wakefield and I — he came to tell me that he doesn't want to be engaged any more. He is going to enter a monastery."

"Oh, my darling!" The exclamation was sharp with anger against Wakefield and fierce with pity for Pauline. "How could he? How dare he? That church … all my married life…. He can't do such a cruel thing to you! Why didn't you tell me while he was here?"

"I wanted to be alone with you."

Clara threw away her cigarette and her hand groped toward Pauline in the dusk. Pauline took it in both of hers.

Clara said — "You know that I wouldn't have made a scene. But I should have talked sound sense to him. He's a romantic boy and he is simply carried away by the vision of a mediaeval life. But to have him treat you like this! I won't bear it!"

Pauline interrupted — "It doesn't matter nearly so much as you think."

"Not matter! Why, darling — what are you saying?"

Pauline's body swayed with the deep breath she drew.

"Mummie, I have never really loved Wakefield. I've tried to and often thought I had succeeded — and I do love him but — not in the way you want to love the man you're going to marry. There is only one way for that, isn't there?"

Clara came to the side of the hammock and took Pauline in her arms.

"No, no, there are different ways. Many different ways. That's the wonderful and strange thing about it. There are different ways."

Pauline said stubbornly — "There is only one way for me, and I've never loved Wakefield like that. Perhaps it was wrong for me to be willing to marry him but I was willing."

She gave a strange little laugh. "I took a lot of pleasure in preparing for it but it was a kind of game of pretence. It was as though I was pretending it was someone else I was marrying."

Clara shrank from something in her voice. She was afraid that Pauline was going to say something that would be even more painful than what had gone before.

Pauline was helpless against a desire for further self-disclosure. What she had so assiduously guarded she longed to bring into the light, even though she knew what it would cost them both. She said almost defiantly:

"I don't suppose you've even guessed the real truth. You've had no idea, have you, that I've really loved another man?"

Even in that dim light she saw the whiteness of Clara's face, how all its wholesome sunburnt colour fled from it, leaving it white and drawn. They had been isolated too much together, the understanding between them was too deep to make the speaking of his name necessary. Clara turned and went to the edge of the verandah. She said, in a heavy, choking voice:

"You have felt this way about him for a long time, I suppose."

"For years."

The words were dragged from Clara against her will. "Does he know?"

The jealousy which Pauline had felt for Clara now rose from its smouldering to a cruel flame.

"Yes," she breathed, and kept her face turned from her mother.

Clara asked — "What does he feel?" A cold sweat broke out on her lips. She was so afraid of what Pauline's answer would he. She felt herself unable to bear it. She sat down again on the steps and buried her head in her arms.

She is afraid, thought Pauline, she is terribly afraid that he has made love to me too. It would be unbearable to her to think he had kissed me. But if only I had something worth confessing, I should be glad! I don't think I could stop myself from telling her.

She said, almost humbly — "He loves me as a child, nothing more."

It seemed to Clara that her heart was eager for suffering that night. Every remark that Pauline made, even one like the last which should have been a relief, cut her cruelly. She said:

"You have been unlucky in your love, Pauline. It's very hard for you, my darling. I don't know what to say to help you. I simply don't know what to say. It's so unbearable to me to see you suffer."

Pauline's disclosure had given her relief. She felt a new compassion for her mother and a sense, already cloistered, of watching the world from a different plane. She scarcely realized what significance her next words would have for Clara. She spoke them almost indifferently.

"There is no need to worry any more about me, Mummie. I'm going into a convent. I've made up my mind to do that. So there's no use in saying things against it."

Clara put up her hand, as though against a blow. Her jaw dropped and she stared fixedly at Pauline out of her round boyish eyes.

"You're not in earnest, really," she gasped. "You don't know what you're saying — all this has upset you so. But you mustn't say it, darling — it frightens me too much."

"But I am in earnest. I'm not upset.... I tell you I shall be a thousand times happier in a convent than married to Wake —"

Clara interrupted fiercely — "If you don't want to marry — I shall be the last one to urge you. But why the convent? You have no vocation, I'm sure of that. There's so much in the world for us to do together. Think of me, Pauline! Don't leave me! Why — if I lose you —"

She began to cry frantically, with hoarse, tearing sobs. She clutched Pauline to her, hurting her in the vehement embrace by which she seemed to feel that she could restrain her.

But it was of no use. The child who had been so malleable in her hands was as resolute as though her decision was the outcome of long months of thought, instead of the outcome of a swift recoil. They crept to bed in the grey drawn, like two boats seeking harbour after a night of buffeting.

Pauline slept dreamlessly as an exhausted child, but Clara lay awake thinking of how Pauline's love for Renny had flourished, side by side with her own, and been undiscovered by her. She brooded passionately on the brief fructifying of her own desire. All was gone from her forever, she thought, her child, her lover, her very life.

VII

RENNY AND CLARA AND PAULINE

SEVERAL DAYS PASSED before Renny was seen by either Clara or Pauline. Wakefield wrote to them both long letters full of poignant feeling and touched by a tender regret for the happiness they had known together. After reading hers Pauline burned it, but Clara laid hers away in a little box to keep. Her feeling of bitterness against Wakefield was gone. With her usual resignation to the inevitable she now accepted the new design of her life with outward composure. She spent most of her time in the tea shop, and at night she felt tired out and went to bed early.

One morning, when the newly budded boughs were being tossed by a fresh wind on which floated downy particles from birds' nests in process of building, Clara did not go to the tea shop but remained at home for necessary household tasks. She and Pauline were talking with an attempt at unconcerned cheerfulness when they saw Renny dismounting from a roan mare at the gate. They both became motionless as though they had been moved by some secret spring that now ceased to act. They looked out of the window at horse and man as though to imprint the image on their minds. Clara noted with sensuous pleasure the harmonizing colour of the mare's sleek hide, Renny's mellowed riding boots, the heather-toned tweed of his clothes, the russet of his hair and his weather-beaten face. Pauline was conscious only of the approach of the exciting and powerful personality that had dominated her adolescence.

He fastened his horse to the fence and knocked formally at the door as he always did. They looked at each other but neither moved. Pauline glanced mechanically toward a mirror above the sideboard and raised her hand to smooth her hair. It was unruly, vigorous hair that had always framed her face in a dark halo. She had a startling vision of her head close-cropped and shrouded in a black veil.

She stood, a strange smile lighting her face, as Clara admitted Renny. She knew at once, by his expression of profound melancholy, that Wakefield had told him what she was about to do. She said, almost lightly:

"You know about me, don't you?"

He took her hand and held it tightly, looking down at its slender length, its pale deep-set nails. Already it looked to him like a nun's hand.

"I'm baffled," he said huskily. "I'm simply baffled by it all. I've read of suicide pacts but this beats any suicide pact."

Pauline answered, still wearing the smile — "It may be suicide socially but that is all. I think we shall be much happier — at any rate I shall — where we are going. Please don't say anything against it, Renny! Mother and I have had it all out and I can't bear any more."

Renny dropped her hand and looked at Clara who returned his look stoically.

"It's quite true," she said; "there's no use in trying to dissuade her."

"When are you going?" he asked Pauline. "Wherever it is, let me tell you that I consider this temporary in both your cases. You've gone neurotic and I'm convinced that inside six months you will both be back with your people."

She moved her head from side to side in grave negation. Her eyes were full of tears.

Seeing her, as he thought, weakening, he exclaimed:

"Have you no pity for your mother? She will be left alone."

Pauline could not speak. She swiftly left the room and they heard her sobbing as she ran up the stairs. Renny turned an incredulous face to Clara.

"I can't bring myself to believe it," he said. "Wake and Pauline! It was a good match.... I was very glad of it."

He was aware of something different in her attitude toward him. She was looking at him curiously, speculatively, as the male whom Pauline loved. He had become two men to her — this man and the lover from whom she was parting. The knowledge that he thought of Pauline only as a child was a relief so poignant that it gave her courage to face all other evils. If she had felt that those hands had touched Pauline, those lips had met hers, in ever so tentative an amatory caress, she could never forgive him — not from jealousy but for the hurt he had given her child. In Clara sexual love was overshadowed by maternal. In Alayne passion dominated maternity, while in Pheasant the two were equally balanced.

"Where will she go?" he asked.

"To a convent in Quebec where an aunt of her father's is Mother Superior. She will be very kind to Pauline."

He made a grimace of distaste, then said abruptly — "That priest of Wake's is a nice man and a very sensible one. He was so thoroughly understanding. He came the next day to see my horses and you should have seen Wake's face when he discovered us in a loose box holding a confab — not about him but about a brood mare."

"That was good," answered Clara, and she looked at him compassionately.

Then, with an effort of lightness, she offered him a cigarette and his accustomed chair. She said:

"All this has to be gone through. I expect that in a year we shall look back on these scenes with equanimity. It's when you brood on things that they are so awful."

He looked into her round face of which the bony structure was becoming visible and the blackness beneath the eyes looked as though it had been hammered there. He laid a hand on her knee. "I should never have consented to your going away. I need you too badly as a friend.... But now I believe it's the best thing for all of us." A quiver passed over his face.

Clara broke out bitterly — "I bring unhappiness to everyone! Let us hope that I'll be a ray of sunshine in my brother's house."

"It's foolish to talk like that. No one can ever know what you've been to me — and coming to this house as I have — and watching Pauline grow up."

Her self-control failed her. "Pauline has told me." Her face reddened.

He looked at her blankly. "Told you what?"

She would have given much to take back her words. Now she did not answer him but sat staring at the polished leather of his riding boots.

In acute embarrassment he muttered — "She is a child."

He remembered the scene in this very room when during a heavy storm, Pauline had thrown herself into his arms and formed with her lips the words — "Kiss me." His heart was wrung for her as he answered:

"She is too sensitive for life. Perhaps where she is going will be best for her."

Clara said — "I suppose Alayne — your wife — was upset. Still, I was only saying goodbye to you."

He answered stiffly — "It was terrible for her. I have never known her so — well, she's ill. You only have to look at her to see that."

"Do you think you should have come here this morning?"

"She couldn't possibly know. Besides she must understand that I have business arrangements to make with you and this affair of the youngsters' to talk over."

"I will have a sale."

He looked about the room, at the blinds he had helped to put up, the pictures he had hung. He said:

"It was fun, settling you here."

"Yes," she agreed, "lots of fun."

"The time has gone quickly."

"I can scarcely believe in it all. So much has happened!"

"Yes. It seems only yesterday that my uncles went to England. Now we are expecting them home in a fortnight. They'll stop the summer, I hope."

"And Finch and his wife, are they coming?"

"Yes. Finch has to have a rest. He's been working too hard, it seems. He's feeling seedy. Nerves, I expect."

"Will you be glad to have the house full again?"

He looked at her almost pathetically. "I can't tell you how glad I shall be. Jalna is like a tomb these days. I'm sure having other people about will help — Alayne and me."

His tone, in coupling their names, brought home to Clara her position as an outsider. She said:

"I don't think anything will do her so much good as knowing that I am a hundred miles away."

She set her face determinedly toward the future and began to talk of plans for the subletting of the tea shop and the sale of her furniture.

As always her calm acceptance of events tranquillized him. He became animated on the subject of making the most for her out of the transactions.

Upstairs Pauline lay listening to the steady flow of their voices, filled with an aching curiosity to know what they talked about. When she heard him leaving the house she went to a window and looked down on her mother and him. In an agony of jealousy she saw Clara accompany him to the gate and stroke the bright flank of his mare and then, almost caressingly, touch his stirrup.

She met Clara at the door. They were startled to see each other, like friends long separated by a rift. Clara said then, rather breathlessly:

"He is coming back again to see you. He wants to say goodbye. He couldn't bear to do it today."

"I don't want to see him!" cried Pauline passionately. "I don't ever want to see him again! I know about you and him — I understand it all." She fled back up the stairs.

VIII

RETURN OF THE UNCLES

RENNY DISCOVERED A business trip to Montreal that coincided with the arrival of Nicholas and Ernest. For the first time in his life he found the atmosphere of Jalna unbearable. The separation of a few days, he thought, might lighten the weight of depression. Relieved of his presence, the tension of Alayne's mind might be eased. With him out of her sight the weakness of his flesh might appear less heinous.

An expression of relief did indeed cross her face when he told her of his intention. Adeline alleviated the situation for them both by her demands for a fine new toy. She seemed to care nothing for the fact of his going away. It was just what would he bring her? What would the now almost forgotten uncles bring her? For the hundredth time Alayne was impressed by her egotism, her greed.

Alayne had never been able to bring herself to perform those wifely duties of preparation for Renny's journeyings from home. He was so capable, so Spartan in his belongings that she would have felt self-conscious in so doing. Yet she had seen Pheasant fussing distractedly over Piers's packing for the absence of two days, and he had seemed to like it.

There was nothing unusual then in his making his preparations alone, but when it came to the moment of departure under Wragge's penetrating eye she had to draw on her resources of dignity and calm.

She followed him to the door. Wright was waiting in the car and Wragge had installed the one suitcase with officious care. She asked casually:

"When will you be back?"

"Inside the week, I expect."

"I hope the uncles will have had a good voyage."

"Yes, I hope so too."

Adeline shouted — "What do you think they will bring me?"

He snatched her up and kissed her. "Little rogue Why should they bring you anything?"

She gave him a strangling hug, wrapping her bare legs about him, clinging like a leech.

"Because I'm *so* good!"

"Who told you that?"

"God. He said in my ear — 'You're the best child of all!' And so are you — aren't you, Daddy?"

He smiled grimly at Alayne and set the child on her two feet.

"Kiss him! Kiss him, Mummie!" cried Adeline.

He bent, touched Alayne's hair with his lips, and was gone. She and the child watched the car disappear, Adeline holding tightly to her fingers, her small face suddenly grave. A quivering sigh rose from Alayne's chest. Nearly a week! she thought. Now that I have this week alone, I shall be able to bear it!

In the days that followed, Adeline seemed keenly aware of her isolation with her mother and also of something unusual in Alayne. The child had never before been so demonstratively affectionate toward her. She was continually running to her, clasping her about the knees and laughing up into her face. But to Alayne there was more of blandishment than affection in these embraces and she saw in the child's eyes a searching, appraising look. And why did Adeline speak so little of Renny? What instinct told her that there was something amiss between her parents? But she was determined to earn her presents by goodness; she had never been so little trouble, so obedient.

Wakefield was seldom at home except to sleep. Chalk, the blacksmith's son, was taking over the filling station and there was business to be done with him. He spent part of each day at Vaughanlands or with Piers and Pheasant. Though his family gave him no peace he seemed to welcome these long conversations of heart-probings and determined essays to shake him from his purpose. The more Meggie implored, Piers derided or Pheasant gave him sagacious counsel from her store of experience, the more inflexible he became, the more austerely happy. He was glad that he would still be at Jalna when his uncles arrived because he expected from them a dignified onslaught such as he had not yet experienced. He wanted to be tried in every respect, to feel supremely sure of himself before he entered the monastery.

It was a balmy day at the end of May when Nicholas and Ernest found themselves again under the roof of Jalna. It was a playful, caressing, wild May day. Ernest declared:

"I had forgotten there were such days, Nick! One gets them nowhere but here."

Nicholas took a deep breath of the clover-scented air and ejaculated:

"How good it feels to be home again! After all, there's no place like Jalna! Alayne, my dear, you're looking very peakish. I wish you could have made the sea voyage with us. It was really delightful."

Ernest too thought that Alayne looked badly in need of a change. The long Canadian winters were very trying. But, now that he and Nicholas were here, they would liven her up. Perhaps she would go away for a visit. They stood on either side of her exuberant and affectionate, Nicholas a little heavier, a little more stooped, wearing his grey hair a little longer; Ernest, looking younger and stronger than when they had last seen him.

Renny stood a little apart from the rest giving swift looks from one face to the other, noticing, with a deep sense of relief, that Alayne looked less worn, less ill than when he had left. Her eyes refused to meet his.

Now Adeline rushed in, newly washed, newly dressed, her hair in a flutter of waves. Her uncles could not make enough of her either to satisfy themselves or satiate her. She ran from one knee to the other, ignoring her father, till at last she threw herself tired against his side and whispered:

"Have they brought me anything, do you think?"

They had indeed brought presents to everybody. Pheasant and Piers and their three boys arrived just as they were being unpacked. Piers was examining his cigarette case, Pheasant twirling her bracelet, the children on the floor with their toys when the Vaughans' car arrived and Meggie came panting in, overflowing with embraces, followed by Maurice and Patience, hand in hand.

Nicholas and Ernest had never had a heartier welcome, not even when their dear Mamma was living. Each member of the family looked with warm approval on their return, even though, and, in some cases because, it was for only a visit. To Renny it renewed the background of his life, without which he felt insecure, the design of his days fragile. To him and to Alayne also their full deep voices, which seemed not to age with their bodies, made endurable the hollow space between. Both Pheasant and Piers felt that the combined wills of the uncles would reduce Wakefield to submission, while for the Vaughans, their presence made Jalna a much pleasanter, more genial house to visit.

In the two old men Adeline found new heights to climb, new pockets to explore, new hair to rumple, and new necks to squeeze. Already she showed a positive preference for men. She was tolerably amiable to Meg and Pheasant but on Piers, Maurice, and the male portion of the tribe she lavished her fervour. To Nook alone she was a terror.

Ernest and Nicholas succumbed to her absolutely.

"She is the very incarnation of Mamma!" exclaimed Ernest.

"And will be a beauty later on," said Nicholas. "Just now her nose is too big and her eyebrows too definite for such a small child."

Ernest agreed and added regretfully:

"I wish we might see her grow up, Nick."

"Not much chance of that," returned his brother gruffly.

"But look at Mamma! She lived to be a hundred and two."

"Yes, and look at us! We'll never do it."

It was amusing and rather touching to see Adeline take them by the hands and lead them where she willed. Alayne seeing them pass slowly along the hall to the drawing room, the light from the stained glass window falling over them, had a moment's feeling that here was a macabre re-embodiment of the trio that had so impressed her when she first came to Jalna.

Toward Wakefield's resolution they were unexpectedly tolerant. Real consternation was felt by the family at this lack of support in its opposition.

"Well, well," Nicholas growled, "there are worse places than monasteries. For my part I had rather see the lad in a monastery than running a filling station. That has been a thorn in my flesh, I can tell you."

"I agree," said Ernest. "A movement toward monastic life is taking place in England. Religious houses are springing up all over the country with their triple vows of celibacy, poverty, and obedience. The cosmos of the Victorian age no longer exists. Young people find themselves with nothing to hold on to. They are bewildered. I confess that, if I were a young man today, I should have a decided leaning that way."

He and the boy had long sympathetic talks on the subject. Nicholas was tolerant but believed that he would never stick it out. Both brothers felt a renewed vigour and an exhilaration in the family contacts. The long autumn, winter, and spring spent in their sister's house, with her accustomed presence removed, had been a period of pensiveness, even though the fact that they had inherited her income had kept them from melancholy. Now they took pleasure, not only in the vigorous life about them, but in the fact that they were financially independent and could come and go as they chose. They had in fact let their house furnished to a tenant who would be willing to extend his short lease indefinitely.

Their rooms had been spring-cleaned for their reception and all the familiar time-worn objects shone back their welcome. Renny's Cairn puppy took a fancy to Nicholas and established himself in the armchair that had been Nip's stronghold. Ernest carried the parrot cage to his room and endeavoured to cajole Boney into renewed speech, but he remained silent and aloof.

A good deal of amusement was created in the family when Ernest disclosed to them his new hobby. The amusement was changed to respect when they saw the beauty of what he created and were made the recipients of such charming gifts. In going over Augusta's belongings he had discovered a half-finished piece of *gros point* in a delightfully coloured Italian design. She had always been a skillful needlewoman and evidences of her needlework were displayed in every drawing room among the connection. Still, this was something new, a bold and strikingly handsome effort, and Ernest had felt keen regret that it had not been finished. His regret had merged into determination. He had taken up Augusta's needle and delicately, carefully proceeded with her work. A neighbour had kindly given him help. He had been an unusually intelligent pupil. And, when that piece of work was completed, he had gone to London with the express purpose of selecting new patterns.

Meggie, Pheasant, and Alayne each owned an example of his work and now he planned new coverings for the seats of the Chippendale chairs in the drawing room.

His eyesight was excellent while that of his brother had failed considerably. Nicholas liked to lounge in his easy chair, the puppy on his knees, and watch Ernest's long figure bent above the embroidery frame while they discussed in turn the affairs of each member of the family which for them had a never-failing fascination.

IX

THE RETURN OF SARAH AND FINCH

AS THEY PASSED through the railway station followed by porters with Sarah's profusion of luggage and her maid carrying a bundle, Finch wondered which of his brothers would meet them. Scarcely Piers, for it was his busiest time of the year. Scarcely Wakefield, who had a filling station on his hands. He decided that it would be Renny — who was always able to get away. His eyes swept the line of faces behind the barrier. He had a longing that it should be Renny's face that he would see first. The nine months he had been away seemed unconscionably long. He strode forward on his long legs till Sarah's voice, petulant from heat and weariness, restrained him.

"You will have to go on alone, if you go at that speed. I simply cannot walk any faster."

She advanced in her peculiar short gliding step, at which Finch had once scoffed, saying that she moved as though she were on wheels. Now he slackened his step resignedly and put his hand under her elbow.

He did not wonder at her petulance. He himself felt ready to drop. The sleepless night in the stifling heat of the train had been an experience never to be forgotten. The throbbing of the wheels, the crashing and jolting of the trucks as the train stopped and started, still beat in his temples.

She exclaimed suddenly — "There he is! It's Piers."

Finch felt a moment's disappointment but it vanished at sight of Piers's welcoming grin, his sunburnt face in which his eyes looked surprisingly blue.

They grasped hands and Piers said:

"Hullo! Is that mountain of stuff yours? Sarah, you look as cool as a cucumber!"

He took the arm on her other side and together they guided her to the car. It was the one Finch had given him. Piers said facetiously:

"It's still in pretty good shape but I'm ready to exchange it for the latest model whenever you are." Then he noticed that Finch was wearing glasses, and added — "By George, you look highbrow! Is it affectation or do you really need them?"

Finch answered nervously — "I've been having the devil of a time with my eyes."

His nervousness came, not from the trouble with his eyes, but from his agitation over the bundle which Sarah's maid was carrying. Piers recognized the woman and smiled at her amiably. Then he saw that what she carried was a sleeping child of between two and three years.

His expression changed to one of bewildered astonishment. He stared stupidly at Finch and Sarah. He opened and shut his mouth without uttering a sound. Sarah had a malicious pleasure in his bewilderment. Finch searched in vain for words to explain the child to Piers. Why had he come? Of all the family been the one to whom the first explanation was necessary! He cursed himself for having given in to Sarah's desire for melodrama. Melodrama in a railway station, at nine in the morning and at a temperature of ninety degrees, was unthinkable and yet it had to be faced. Well, let Sarah break the news to Piers in her own way! With a lift of his eyebrows he shifted the responsibility to her.

Piers exclaimed — "I say, you've been rather beforehand, haven't you?"

Sarah answered, in her low, sweet voice — "This is your brother Eden's child. His and Minny Ware's. She brought it to us in Paris. She was ill and couldn't keep it any longer. So we have brought it here."

Piers did not start or change colour. He stood stock-still, his eyes fixed on Sarah's face, absorbing in its full significance what she had said.

If she had hoped for an outburst of anger from him, she was disappointed. He turned to Finch and said simply:

"As affairs are at home you could scarcely have done a worse thing. Renny and Alayne are at the outs. Alayne and I aren't speaking and, though Eden's dead, he was dragged into our quarrel and the sight of his child won't help matters. You must be mad to think of bringing it here."

Finch answered loudly, in a shaking voice — "What else could I do? There was nothing else to do, I tell you Minny came to us — a sick woman. She's in Switzerland now!"

Piers interrupted with a note almost of despair in his voice:

"Is there no end to the harm that fellow has done?"

"Well, this is his child," said Finch, "and there was nothing else for me to do but to protect it."

"Are you sure it's his child?"

"Look at it and you'll not ask that."

Piers strode to the side of the maid who did not understand English but who now spoke cooingly to the child which sat up with a startled expression and looked about it. It was a girl with delicate features and rather sallow. She looked composedly into Piers's face while leaning against the maid's shoulder in an attitude of languor. Piers saw in her a curious blending of Eden and Minny. She had Minny's slanting, strange-coloured eyes and high cheekbones but Eden's bright golden hair and the lower part of her face was shaped like his.

Piers turned abruptly from his survey of her and got into the car. He placed his hands on the wheel and looked straight ahead of him. The porters had installed the smaller luggage and Finch had to busy himself in arranging for a lorry to carry the trunks. When he returned to the car, Sarah, with the maid and child, were already in the back seat. He got in beside Piers. He dreaded the long drive to Jalna. He wondered what he could find to say to Piers that would calm his resentment. Again he cursed himself for not having prepared the family for such an advent. He blamed himself for being too much under Sarah's influence. He was too much under the influence of all those closely connected with him yet he did not seem able to help himself. He took off his glasses and began to polish the lenses while he slid an enquiring, propitiatory look at Piers.

"I repeat," said Piers, "that it is the most insane thing I ever heard of two people doing. Have you taken the child yourselves? Or are you bringing her home to Renny? I wish you'd tell me that!"

"I want to pay for her education but we can't adopt her. Sarah doesn't like children. Renny is so fond of them that I thought he'd be willing to give her a home. Or perhaps Meggie will."

"Well, you may leave me out of it. I certainly will not have her in my house."

"No one would expect that. You have three of your own already. But Patience is an only child. I thought perhaps Meggie —"

"Meg has her hands full with her P.G.s."

"Then there's little Adeline. The child would be a companion for her."

Piers gave a bark of sardonic laughter. "God help the child! What's her name?"

"Roma. Poor Minny told Sarah that she called her that because she was conceived in Rome where they had the happiest time they ever knew."

"Tch! What a name! And what a way to come by it! Poor young devil! Is Minny going to recover?"

"I'm afraid not. She was hopeful but she looked terribly ill. A friend, a rich Jew I think, has been awfully kind to her. She's to have the best care. I'm afraid the disease was deep-seated before she knew of it."

"A pity she had the child! I don't believe Eden ever told Renny of it."

"He never knew. For some reason Minny didn't want him to know. Do you think Renny will be very angry with me for bringing her home?"

The tone in which he asked this was so like the tone in which, as a boy, he had asked — "Do you think Renny will give me a licking, Piers?" — that Piers turned a curious glance on him. What sort of fellow had this queer younger brother grown up to be? Piers realized that he knew very little about him. He had been married, and that to a strange creature like Sarah, for more than half a year. He had lived in Paris, he had played to foreign audiences and been written about in the press, yet none of these experiences seemed to have left much mark on him. He had the same half-starved look, the same too-sensitive mouth, the same nervous way of putting his hands between his knees as though to restrain their excited movements. Piers felt rather sorry for him.

"How does it feel to be married?" he asked.

"Oh … fine!" But, to Piers, his tone was strangely detached. He remembered now that Finch had asked him a question, and he felt a sudden desire to reassure him. So he answered:

"I dare say old redhead will be delighted. If there is one thing above another that pleases him it is an addition to the clan."

"And Alayne — how do you think she'll take it?"

"I don't think for a moment that she'll tolerate it."

Finch raised his voice excitedly — "Well, she needn't! She needn't! I'll look after Roma! I'll find a home for her. Perhaps Mrs. Lebraux would look after her."

"She's leaving to keep house for that brother of hers. Pauline has gone into a convent."

Piers felt a distinct relish in delivering this counter-shock to Finch's introduction of the child. He relished still more the announcing of Wakefield's entering a monastery.

But he had not counted on the effect of the first piece of news on Finch. He caught Piers by the arm and exclaimed:

"That's not so, Piers! You're joking! You aren't in earnest!"

Piers narrowly avoided a collision with a motor lorry. The French maid screamed and Finch sank into a corner, crimson with shame, his heart pounding violently.

"I'm sorry," he gasped. "I'm a blasted fool!"

He grunted under the prod Piers gave him with his elbow. Piers growled — "You'd better get into the back seat with the women and let the baby sit with me. It would have more sense than you." He looked reassuringly over his shoulder at Sarah. "It's all right, Sarah! I've not been drinking. But your young husband is rather too emotional."

Piers lighted a cigarette. Sarah asked, inquisitively introducing her pale face with its pointed chin, between them:

"What did you tell him that upset him so?"

Piers thought — "I'll bet she's a devil of jealousy. I must protect this young fool." He said, out of the side of his mouth:

"I was just telling him that young Wake has gone into a monastery. I had no idea it would be such a shock to him."

Finch sat up in his seat as though galvanized, then sank back speechless.

"There he goes again," said Piers jocularly. "We'd better get him home." He started the car and did not look in Finch's direction again till he saw, from a swift glance, that he had recovered himself. Then he imparted to him, in desultory snatches, such news of the farm, the horses, and the new ponies as he thought would interest him. While he talked, his own mind was heavy with the thought that Eden's child was in the seat behind. He had hoped that they were done with Eden, except in the dark recesses of memory, but now his child had come as an ever-growing reminder of him. But Finch must take her away again! Alayne would be on his side in this and he would stand by her. That child must not live in their midst!

Any doubt as to the truth of Piers's first piece of news was dispelled for Finch by his manner of imparting the second. It was a cruel truth and it cast him down into a depth of melancholy that was unaccountable to him. He was not sure that he loved, or ever had loved, Pauline but he had felt her presence in his life as something beautiful. There were always in his thoughts of her a regret and a sense of promise. She had inherited something from her mother that made her presence restful and magnanimous toward men. Neither of them was capable of any antagonism of sex. He had envied Wakefield his long acquaintance with Pauline. He wished he might have been Wakefield's age and grown up beside her in his stead. He had resented Wake's engagement to Pauline. Now he felt an impassioned curiosity to know what the two had experienced that had driven them to such a recoil from marriage. He·pictured them in nun's and monk's habit and strangely the pictures he conjured up looked natural and even inevitable.

Sarah disliked being in the seat with the maid and child. It would have been much nicer if she could have had Finch beside her on the first drive to Jalna since their marriage. She was irritated by the maid's slavish adoration of the child. When Sarah, who cared little for the services of the maid beyond the mere packing and care of her clothes, had suggested that she might look after the child on the journey, the rather hard-faced French woman had indifferently agreed. No sooner was the little one in her care than it became the object of lavish caresses and a continuous babbling of infantile endearments. The maid was a changed woman, shown in her true colours which were most unattractive to Sarah. She turned her shoulder on the pair. She fixed her eyes on Finch's profile. Its fascination for her never lessened. Nor the intense study of his face when his eyes looked deep into hers. The contrast between him and Arthur Leigh, her first husband, in every aspect of their life with her provided her with material for profound brooding. The contrast was always in Finch's favour. Arthur had given her wealth, social position, and travel. He had been charming to look at and charming to live with but he had never really pleased her. He had been too vulnerable, too easily elated or cast down by her moods. What was perhaps only a slight perversity he had taken too seriously. He had translated a little gaiety into an ecstasy of happiness. She had owned so few belongings that she had been bewildered by the presents he had lavished on her; and it was not till after his death that she had developed an acquisitive sense and had guarded her possessions.

Finch's timidity combined with his harsher vein increased her infatuation for him day by day. She marvelled at what he said. She sought to penetrate his mind, to know the thoughts he kept secret. He was so often wrapped in his thoughts. He sometimes ignored her and he seldom gave her presents because, with Whiteoak hard-headedness, he saw that she already had too much.

They left the town and passed foamy stretches of orchards in bloom. The lake slid to the side of the road and although it was scarcely ruffled they felt its coolness. Finch took off his hat and closed his eyes. He wished that Piers would stop talking. It was hard to keep his mind on what he said. Harder still to find words for a reply. Over and over he was saying to himself — "Pauline in a convent.... Pauline a nun.... I shall never see her again! Everything is changing for me.... I am alone...."

Nicholas, Ernest, and Alayne were at the door to meet them. Piers stood, with an air of resolute detachment, waiting to see what welcome would be given the newcomer. Sarah went to Finch's side as soon as they had alighted from the car, and they advanced with strained smiles. The child sat rigidly on the maid's arm, her bright hair, which had never been cut, hanging in uneven locks about her face.

When greetings had been exchanged Ernest asked of Finch — "Who are the woman and child? Is Piers giving them a lift?"

Finch, in his present state of mind, longed to declare — "Yes, yes, they are going on. I don't know who they are." He saw Piers staring fixedly at his uncles. He saw Sarah's smile fade and her lips move without making a sound. He gathered himself together and said, in a shaking voice:

"Uncle Ernest, this child is Eden's. Minny brought her to me in Paris. Minny is terribly ill. She couldn't keep the child. Eden never knew about it — the baby, I mean. I'm going to look after her."

Ernest, Nicholas, and Alayne stood rooted. Nicholas could not take it in. He turned to his brother and demanded testily:

"What's he say? Who is the child?"

"Eden's," returned Ernest, with surprising composure. "Eden's and Minny's."

Nicholas stared, stupefied. "But — but — Eden is dead! What's all this talk? I can't understand!"

"It's Eden's child," repeated Ernest and his clear blue eyes searched Alayne's face to see how she would take the news.

She looked almost as mystified as Nicholas. She went slowly to the child and scanned its face. Then she turned almost pleadingly to Piers, to whom she had not spoken for weeks.

"Do you think this is true?" she asked.

Nothing she could have done could have drawn Piers's sympathy to her as this appeal to his judgment. He gave her a look of almost tender solicitude.

"It's rough on you," he said, "having it brought to Jalna."

Nicholas repeated — "I don't understand."

Sarah smiled almost maliciously. "It's easy to understand. Minny was that sort of girl, you know. And Finch is the sort of man who would come to her rescue."

"It's rough on Alayne," repeated Piers.

Finch exclaimed loudly — "It has nothing to do with Alayne! I should think Alayne would feel sorry for the poor little thing."

At this moment Adeline, freshly dressed for the occasion, rushed out of the house. Instantly her eyes discovered the other child and she had no interest in anyone else. She reached up to her, trying to drag her from the arms of the maid.

"Set her down," commanded Ernest. "Let us see her."

The child stood motionless, dazed but not afraid, its dress, of a foreign cut, crumpled against its thin body. The maid encouraged her in staccato French.

Adeline was enraptured by the sudden appearance of the girl child smaller than herself. She inspected her with beaming assurance then grasped her wrist and led her toward the house. The child hung back timidly.

Nicholas's voice came, as though shaken out of him. "Finch, do you tell me that this is Eden's and Minny's child?"

"Yes, Uncle Nick."

"Well, well, I don't know what Renny'll say to this. I can't think what he'll say to it." Suddenly he picked up the little creature and held her in front of him. "Minny's eyes and cheekbones!" he growled. "No doubt about that…. I must tell Renny of this! I am the one to tell him! Where is he now? Why isn't he here?" He stood irresolute holding the child in his hands, the thin legs with soiled knees, dangling.

Alayne said — "Where would he be but in the stables? A new arrival there is more important than one at the house."

Finch exclaimed eagerly — "I do wish you would tell him, Uncle Nick! It's just as you say. You are the one to do it." He thought — "I'm scarcely home…. I'm not inside the door before I feel the pressure of all their spirits on mine and I get bewildered…. I can't remember whether or not I've spoken to Alayne…. How ill she looks!" He said — "What a crowd of us to descend on you, Alayne! It's a beastly nuisance for you, I know."

"It is nothing," she said, and she returned his kiss affectionately.

Sarah came and stood close beside them. She looked at Alayne as though she would snatch Finch's kiss from her. Alayne said to her:

"I suppose you have had a wonderful time in Europe."

"For itself I hate Europe," answered Sarah. "I was dragged about it too much by my aunt. But wherever Finch is, is wonderful to me!"

"That's the way to feel!" exclaimed Ernest. Then he added — "I do wish Nick wouldn't be so impulsive! Why can't he wait till Renny comes instead of rushing off like that!"

Nicholas was indeed clambering into the car, very stiffly because of his gouty knee, and still carrying the child. Piers had returned to his place at the wheel.

"Do let him go, Uncle Ernie!" said Finch. "He's taking a load of responsibility off me."

"But I wish we could see how Renny receives Roma," said Sarah.

"Yes," said Ernest. "It's scarcely fair to the rest of us to present her so secretly."

"Secretly!" Alayne gave a harsh laugh. Finch turned to her quickly.

"Are you angry with me, Alayne?" he asked timidly.

"Angry? No. You couldn't help yourself. You had to be yourself. Just as Eden couldn't really die."

He answered — "Do you feel that way about him too, Alayne? I'm just the same. I never can believe that Eden is really gone from us — especially since I've had Roma."

Adeline had insisted on getting into the car with Nicholas and the child. Piers drove them straight to that part of the stables where he knew Renny was. He sent a message to him by a stable boy who was passing with a bucket of water. The boy hurried off, slopping the water a little as he went.

Piers lighted a cigarette and said over his shoulder — "If you want my opinion of this affair, Uncle Nick, I think Finch has acted like a damned fool."

"But what could he do? Minny was desperately ill, he says."

"That's possible. It's possible too that she was deceiving him. In any case she had rich friends who could have provided for the kid. It's an imposition on Alayne, bringing it here, I say."

"Well, well, we'll see what Renny says."

"It doesn't require much imagination to guess that. He'll receive it with open arms."

The stable door was opened by the boy and Renny appeared carrying a few-hours-old foal in his arms. He exclaimed:

"The boy told me you were here, Uncle Nick, and I wanted you to see this. Isn't it a beauty?"

He was in trousers and shirt with uprolled sleeves. His hair was on end and his face wore a look of exultation. The foal hung limply in his arms, its disproportionate legs dangling, its neck arched with the stark strangeness of some prehistoric beast.

Adeline shouted — "Let me see it! Let me see it!"

When Nicholas opened the door of the car she scrambled out and ran to Renny's side. She was in ecstasy over the foal, pressing her hands into its soft coat, caressing its little hoofs.

Renny stared surprised at the child Nicholas was holding on his knee. Nicholas exclaimed:

"Yes, yes, I've never seen a better! Splendid little fellow!"

"Whose child is that?" asked Renny.

"Why — Finch and Sarah brought it."

"Coltie! Coltie!" cried Adeline. "Bring the little girl to see it, Uncle Nick! She wants to see it. Daddy, let me hold it!"

Renny advanced to the side of the car carrying the foal. There had been something fateful, something deliberately impressive, in Uncle Nick's voice. What the devil has happened now? he thought. There's something up! He said:

"So they've arrived! I hope you apologized for me. I must go to the house." He stared at the child that stared fearfully at the foal.

"Stroke it! Stroke it!" cried Adeline.

Nicholas put out his hand and filled it with the foal's delicate hide. It lay weakly in Renny's arms, giving itself to their handling. Renny dismissed the stableboy with a nod.

"Whose is she?" he asked, as his mind revolved around strange possibilities. Uncle Nick would not look like that if it were an ordinary child. Something in its face held him fascinated. The pupils of its slanting eyes were dilated with fear as it stared at the foal.

Before Nicholas could answer Piers said roughly — "It's Eden's. His and Minny Ware's."

Nicholas scowled at him for thus forestalling his news. Piers jumped out of the car and said, half apologetically:

"Well, tell him all about it. God knows, I don't want to! I'll take the foal to its dam."

For a moment, Renny, while he scrutinized the child's features, retained his statuesque pose with the foal. Then he surrendered it to Piers who bore it away, weak and resigned, its head now drooping over Piers's arm. Adeline, forgetting her absorption in the other child, danced at his side. She carried one of the foal's hoofs in her hand with careless familiarity.

"You say she is Eden's?" To Renny the child was, at first glance, feminine and a personality. It would have been impossible for him to use the impersonal pronoun of it.

"Yes. Minny brought it to Finch in Paris. She is ill. T.B. I'm afraid. Not going to get better."

"But Eden never spoke of a child!"

"He didn't know. But look at it."

He put the child out of the car into Renny's hands. Its legs dangled and it gave itself, helpless and unprotestmg, as the foal. Renny's eyes pierced it and its face quivered. An odd veiled smile passed across its pale face.

"By Judas! It's true!" exclaimed Renny. "She is Eden's daughter! Eden's little girl! Why — it's wonderful! It's staggering! But it's true! Uncle Nick.... Uncle Nick.... I can't tell you how.... Why — it's like getting word from him! God — I can't tell you how glad I am to have his child! The way Eden had to suffer ... and die ... well — it was all so unnecessary ... and there was always the thought that he had gone and left nothing behind him but hard feeling ... but now ... this little girl...." He pressed the child against his shoulder and bent his head to touch hers. She curved her arm about his neck and snuggled against him with an air of submissive satisfaction.

Nicholas said — "Finch is going to bear the expense, and I'm quite willing to help. I'm glad, on the whole, that he has brought her home. I feel as you do about Eden.... But who will look after her? Will Meg, I wonder?"

"Meg has enough on her hands. She couldn't possibly manage a young child. Even if it had a nurse. No, no, her place is at Jalna. I like kids about. She will be a companion for Adeline."

Nicholas pulled the end of his grey moustache. "What about Alayne?" he asked.

Alayne's unhappiness rose before Renny like a black curtain that he could touch. He said:

"I must talk it over with her."

X

Changing Winds

HE COULD STILL feel the tangibility of her unhappiness when he found her alone in the dining room counting the table silver. She was laying the various sizes of forks and spoons in neat piles. When he came in and closed the door behind him she paused in what she was doing and looked at him. But she waited for him to speak. He felt his heart beating heavily. When he was away from her he forgot her power to make him feel uncontrolled. To steady himself he said:

"Counting the silver, eh? Anything missing?"

She picked up a thin, worn teaspoon with the crest almost obliterated. "One of these," she said. "But it must be somewhere about. That girl Bessie is so careless. These spoons are favourites of yours, I know." She spoke in a low polite voice.

"Yes, I've always liked those little spoons." He took one up and laid it against his cheek. "They're so smooth and fine. I hope that missing one will be found."

"Yes, I hope so." She proceeded with her counting and he stood watching her intently, conscious of the delicate scent of her hair and her flesh, and of her antagonistic remoteness.

When she had meticulously laid the last fish fork in its place, she said:

"I know exactly what you are going to say, so please don't worry yourself about the manner of saying it. Subtleties are quite unnecessary with me."

He thought: It's all this unhappiness that has made her so baffling. I can't say anything in the way I intend. I can't get near her. He said:

"Well, if you know just what I'm wanting to say, what have you to say about it yourself?"

"Nothing." Her eyes, looking into his now, had become frozen, shallow. "You must do just as you please.... There will be nothing new in that."

He said, bitterly — "What a brute you make me out!"

"No. But you have always done as you've pleased. You can't deny that."

"I do deny it!" he said hotly. "When I look back over my life it seems to me I've had a lot of hampering and thwarting."

"I dare say it does.... But I shall certainly not hamper or thwart you in anything anymore."

"You will not object to the child's living with us?"

"Haven't I said that I won't hamper you?"

He answered gravely — "I wish I could thank you. But how can I? You make it impossible." Then, in spite of himself, warmth and eagerness came into his voice. "Alayne, I do think we shall never regret taking her. After all, you loved Eden once and he loved you.... I expect that the worst thing he ever did to you was to make way for me."

Her mouth began to shake.

"Don't!" he cried. "I can't bear it!"

"Bring the child here!" she gasped. "Bring her here!"

"Not if it's going to make you feel like this!"

She steadied herself, her hands clutching the spoons. "Her coming means nothing to me — one way or the other ... now."

He gave his shoulders a despairing fling. She again began to count the spoons, her lips moving inaudibly.

He went out and stood in the hall. He thought: "What sort of life have I now? Everything hopelessly muddled.... I can't see how it's all come about ... Clara going ... Pauline and Wake gone ... Alayne hating me ... Eden's child here.... If only I knew some way out of the mess.... That white-faced Sarah and the mortgage.... Funny name — Roma! Poor little thing.... Must go and see her.... God! That was a nasty twinge in my shoulder!"

He went up the stairs and found the child in the nursery where Adeline had laid out all her treasures before her. The child looked doubtfully at them and at her, but, when Renny came in, she went to him and raised her slanting eyes to his and a smile flickered across her face. He took her by the arm and lifted her from the floor. There was nothing to her!

"Why, you're a mosquito!" he said. "Have they fed you enough, I wonder?"

"Lift me! Lift me!" cried Adeline, pushing her plump shoulder against his hand.

But she showed no tendency to be jealous of Roma. There was something unchildlike in her arrogance of security. She gave her favours or she denied them. She was honey-sweet or she flew into tantrums. But she always felt herself in the very centre of her world. She ate, drank, slept, was petted or punished, firm in this assurance. Beside her Roma was fragile as an eggshell, her dry, fair hair like moonlight compared to the exuberant sun of Adeline's auburn curls. For the first weeks Roma scarcely spoke at all. Then she began to talk a little in an odd mixture of French and English that delighted Adeline who picked up the French words eagerly, declaring that she had made them up herself. The two children were inseparable. Adeline was more amenable than ever before. Roma did just what she told her.

Renny never saw the two playing together without a fresh surprise, a deeper satisfaction that Eden had sent back this token of himself to be reared, to be cherished at Jalna. The broken link was re-forged, the circle complete.

He gave up trying for Alayne's forgiveness and spent most of his day in the stables. He had bought the mare, of which he had spoken to Alayne. He had bought her against Maurice's advice, against Piers's advice, even against his own better judgment. For, though she had been offered at a low price, she had already got the reputation of a hysterical nature and a half-mad habit of walking on her hind legs when being shown. She was a bright chestnut with a blonde mane and tail and so long-legged, long-necked, and small headed that she seemed to have stepped from an old print, rather than from an Ontario stable. She had full, proud eyes, with a kind of noble fear in them, as though she had not yet grown accustomed to the strange world in which she found herself. Her eyes slid from stall to stall, warily observing her new companions. Her wide nostrils snuffed the flesh of her new master. In the possession of the mare, in the problem of schooling and showing her, Renny found solace from the unsolvable problem of his own life.

Finch felt a relief that was almost painful, in being once more at Jalna. His other absences had seemed as nothing to this last. It had cut him off, thrown him into a new and mystifying life. He had been struggling for months against the torture of his nerves.

Now he would relax, he would learn to sleep again, the pains in his neck and temples would subside. He would plunge his spirit in the cool deep of the woods, try to put out of his mind all he had been through.

His relief was so great, he was so tired in that first week, that he did indeed sleep better. There was a temporary dulling of all his overwrought senses. He talked, scarcely knowing what he said, but it passed for sense. There did not seem to be much wrong with him. Over and over again he traced the paths through wood and field. He stood watching the farm labourers at work. He stood watching Renny, Piers, and Mooey schooling the horses. He walked when all the house was dark and the stable dogs barked at the sound of his steps but he would not set his foot outside the gates of Jalna.

At the end of the week he longed to see his old friend, George Fennel, the Rector's son. George was so tranquil, so receptive, so easy to talk to. Finch could not understand the change that had come over Alayne. He had strained toward the hour when they would be alone together. He felt sure that she would understand. But now she was changed. She was withdrawn into herself. She was almost silent and, though she appeared to listen attentively to what he said, her answers came at random. Her face had a closed-in look and she gave Finch no encouragement to open his heart to her.

He could not talk to George Fennel as he might have talked to Alayne, still he craved the comfort of George's sturdy presence, and one night, after a hot sunset, he walked to the Rectory across the fields and along the paved road that he liked to remember as the dusty country one he had known as a boy.

He saw Mr. Fennel in the vegetable garden digging potatoes. He was in his shirt and, his beard now grey, was crisp and lively from heat. His face had grown rosy with years and he beamed affectionately at Finch.

"Glad to see you back," he said, holding out an earth-stained hand. "We're all proud of you, Finch. You're becoming famous, they say. Well, well, it's nice. Yes, very nice."

Finch's hand sank in his. He felt the dry film of loam between their palms. He wanted to hang onto the Rector's hand. He wanted to lead him somewhere, far away from himself, but Mr. Fennel returned to his spade and, in answer to Finch's stammered greeting, said:

"I suppose you want to see George. I think you'll find him in his room. Lucky you came before he went out." There was a humorous twinkle in the Rector's eyes as he heaved up a spadeful of small, sallow potatoes.

George was in his room, which was next the roof and blazing hot. He was changing into snowy duck trousers and a mauve, silk, tunic shirt. His stocky figure exuded heat and purposefulness. He beamed at Finch as his father had done, but there was something mysterious in his bearing.

"It was hot as blazes in town," he said. "You simply don't know anything about it here. The pavements were melting. The motors stank. I have got a lot of mosquito bites from sitting by the lakeshore last night and they all itched at once." He plastered hair cream on his tousled hair and brushed it into repose.

"Look here," said Finch, "if you're going out, don't let me keep you."

"Oh, I have time for a chin before I go."

George was different. He who had always been comfortably untidy was now slick as a ribbon. And look at his nails! Clean, polished, and being polished again! For the first time in his life Finch felt suspicious of his friend.

He said rather stiffly — "I'll not keep you, Jarge!"

He thought, by using the old familiar "Jarge," to draw him closer. "I just dropped in as I was passing."

"Right," said George, and put his face closer to the looking glass.

Finch sank into the depression in the sofa and took off his glasses and rubbed his eyes. George had not even noticed that he was wearing glasses.

He now asked Finch how Sarah was, if he had liked living in Europe, and whether he had broadcast in England. Then after a silence, during which George hung his town clothes on stretchers, he said, reddening:

"I want you to meet Sylvia. I've talked a lot about you to her. She's dying to meet you."

So that was it! Sylvia! And this was what was left of their confidence and friendship! Finch listened to all George had to tell of Sylvia, he examined three photographs and half a dozen snapshots of her. He even walked as far as Sylvia's gate with George but he declined to go in. He had a glimpse of her waiting on the verandah. George and she were engaged.

XI

THE NOVICE

To FINCH THE house seemed very strange without Wakefield. The boy had always been at home, had always been in evidence. His voice had been heard raised in the airing of his opinions, in complaint or in the mere delight of hearing himself talk: his slender body had been gliding along the passages, sliding into rooms or darting from restriction. He had grown manlike in his love for Pauline and less interesting. In his natural buoyancy, unscrupulousness, and patronizing airs he had maddened and fascinated Finch. Finch had secretly envied him his assurance. He remembered him as a baby, sitting on Gran's arm, not at all afraid of her, playing with her earrings and chains, tugging at her cap. Finch remembered how he had lain pensive in bed after his heart attacks. Now he was gone!

What had happened to him and Pauline? Why had they thrown aside their love like an unbecoming garment and put on the robes of monastery and convent? Curiously the news of Wake's entering the monastery had been the greater shock. In imagination he tried to follow the steps in Wake's life that had led to this. Surely something terrible had happened to him spiritually or he could never have given up the world so young, so untried. Finch discovered in himself a feeling of relief in the knowledge that Wake and Pauline were cut off from each other. By degrees he thought with resignation of Pauline kneeling before a crucifix in nun's apparel.

He could think of this calmly, but the thought of Wakefield was black with mystery, almost unbearable. He began to think of him as dead. He woke once in the night convinced that Wakefield was dead and that the family had decided that his nerves were not in a fit state to bear the news and had concocted this tale of the monastery.

He got out of bed without waking Sarah and went to Renny's room. Inside he could hear the crude ticking of the alarm clock and the soft snuffling of the Cairn puppy. Renny's breathing came strong and deep. "What breathing!" thought Finch. "To breathe like that a man's mind must be at peace." He went close to the bed and put out his hand in the blackness. He touched the puppy and, giving itself up to the unexpected nocturnal caress, it turned up its warm round belly and wriggled. Finch pressed his fingers on the puppy and felt the soft flutter of its heart.

"Renny," he said. "Renny!"

"Yes — who's that?"

"Finch. I want to ask you something. May I turn on the light?"

He could feel Renny heave his body with the effort of answering. He muttered "Yes," and flung his arm across his eyes as the unshaded light struck them. For an instant Finch saw his mouth unguarded by his eyes. He had a sudden desire to bend and kiss it.

But now the brown eyes stared up at him and Renny asked sharply — "Anything wrong?" Again he was on his pedestal and Finch a schoolboy. He answered, trying to keep his voice calm:

"It's about Wake. I think you're deceiving me."

"*Deceiving* you?" Renny raised himself to stare.

Finch's voice came loud and hollow.

"I believe Wake's dead! I'm sure of it! You've made up this story of the monastery to deceive me. You think I'm not well enough to hear the truth. But I tell you I must know."

Renny beat down the stammered words with a laugh. But he looked anxiously at Finch as he answered:

"I think you're well enough for a good hiding. And you'd get it if you were ten years younger. You talk like an idiot! Wake dead! Well, I'm damned! What will you imagine next!"

He turned out of bed in striped pyjamas and went to his chest of drawers and began to search in one. "You must think we take it coolly."

"You all seem different. There's something wrong in the house. I feel it."

"Hm, well, we're depressed about his shutting himself off like this. But *dead*! Here's one of his letters. Read that." He put the letter, with its small, erratic handwriting, into Finch's hand.

Finch's body curved over the letter, the hollows in his cheeks accentuated by the ceiling light. It was the simple out pouring of a boy happy in a new life. A schoolboy's letter, though it ended with the tentative urge toward conversion.

Finch laid it down and muttered shamefacedly — "It's all right. I can see that. I don't know what put such an idea into my head. I'm not well, Renny. My nerves are hellish." He dared not look into Renny's eyes.

The puppy was sitting smiling at them. Gaps showed where his milk teeth had come out. One ear was cocked, the other drooping. His forelegs looked as though they were about to give under the weight of his round body.

Renny pushed the puppy out of his way and got back into bed. He said:

"Now you go back to Sarah and forget this nonsense. You'll be all right in a little while. A month at Jalna will make a new man of you."

Finch put his hand on the switch and looked enviously at the pair on the bed. "I'm awfully sorry, Renny," he said, "to have got you up like this. I'm a damned fool. You see," he put his hand to his head, "it's the pain here. It makes everything seem different to me."

"Neuralgia. That's what the doctor said, isn't it? Nervous strain. Just try to keep your mind off it. You'll soon be all right."

Finch looked at him out of the cage of his pain, and said huskily:

"I hope so. I can't go on like this. It's been getting steadily worse."

"Ever try liniment?"

"I've rubbed on Baum Analgesique. But this pain is all over my head."

"Look on the top shelf of that small cabinet. There's a largish bottle. The label is stained. That mixture is put up for me by a vet. An old Scotch remedy. I've used gallons of it on horse and man. Always put it on the grooms when they get kicked. It smells like the devil and acts like a charm."

Finch went to the little cabinet which he had seen planted against the faded wallpaper all his life. He remembered its mystery to him as a small boy, how he had been caught investigating the contents of a bottle of laudanum and had his seat warmed. The tenseness in his head was temporarily relieved. His nostrils drank in the smell of the liniment.

"Rub it in well," said Renny. "It won't hurt your hair."

Finch acquiesced, feeling tired and peaceful. He stood under Renny's eye, in the comfort of his jocular directions and rubbed on the liniment. It stung and it smarted his eyeballs. He gave himself up to its stinging and smarting and the pain was eased. His strong bony fingers rubbed and rubbed.

"My God!" exclaimed Renny. "You'll have the skin off! Go to bed now. But you can't go to Sarah smelling like a sick stallion. You'll have to sleep in your old room. The bed may not be made up. Take that quilt from under the puppy. Take the liniment too. You may keep it. I'll get another bottle. You'll soon be all right." He grinned up at Finch, showing all his strong teeth.

Oh, the wonderful, harsh comfort of him! Finch could have wept with the ease of it. He pressed the sticky black bottle against his chest and stole up the attic stairs. He was a boy again, creeping up the narrow dark stairway. The window of his room showed grey against the blackness. It stood open. A cold mist was blown across his bed.

He did not mind. He did not mind. Nothing mattered. The pain was still. It lay curled up sleeping like a snake in its nest somewhere in the middle of his head. He touched with his fingertips the sore places in the back of his neck. They quivered like jelly beneath his touch, horribly sensitive. When he touched them he felt as though he would scream, like some horrible instrument whose too sensitive keys had been drummed.

He curled his palm under his cheek and lay very still, absorbing the quiet cool night. It spread over him like a wing and all his pain was gone. Only the sore spots remained. He lay still and peaceful, as when he was a young boy, safe in the darkness after a day of bewilderment or unhappiness. He had shared this room with Piers till Piers had married. He could almost feel Piers's sturdy body in the bed with him, feel that sense of both fear and security in his nearness.

Now the vine that always tapped on his window when there was a breeze began to talk to him. Shadow answered shadow as the early dawn disturbed the darkness. Oh, that peace of his own dear room! He rested on it. He drew it about him. It folded itself over him.

Purposely he kept Sarah out of his mind. She stood just outside it waiting the first chance to enter, ready to make herself thin as a knife, if she could but enter. But he turned his thoughts peacefully away from her. His mind was a blank; he was sinking into sleep when, not the thought of her but she in the flesh, stole into the room and bent over the bed.

"Why did you leave me?" she whispered.

He kept his eyes shut, pretending to be asleep, but she saw that he was awake.

"Why did you come up here?" she asked, and her black plaits fell across his body.

"It was the pain," he answered, keeping his eyes tight shut. "I smell of liniment."

She sniffed him, the cold point of her nose touching his face. "I don't mind. It's rather a nice stinging smell."

"It's beastly! Do go back to bed, Sarah."

"No. I don't mind the smell. I'll get in here. I like this room because you were a boy in it."

He scowled up at her. "There are no sheets. Just the mattress."

She laughed so that he saw all her small teeth. "I don't mind. It will be fun lying on just the mattress. I'd love to sleep on the ground with you. You know that." She crept under the quilt and pressed close to him.

"You'll be sick," muttered Finch. "I smell like a horse."

"I don't mind." She snuggled closer.

Peace was gone from him but a restless sleep came. In the morning he felt better and he made up his mind that he would go to see Wakefield that very day. Ernest had already been and was eager to go again. Sarah was determined to accompany them. It was Nicholas who ordered them to let Finch go alone. The boy might have a nervous breakdown, he said, if he were harried by constant companionship. Solitude was what he needed. Nicholas's leonine head, his deep voice, the sombre lines cut on his face lent might to what he said. Finch took a train after breakfast and arrived at the monastery soon after the midday meal.

He felt very nervous as he waited at the broad low door, the ugly brown paint of which was blistered by the sun. But before it was answered, Wakefield ran across the parched grass to his side and threw both arms about him.

"Hullo, Finch! Hullo — hullo! How splendid to see you! I was reading over there under that tree and I looked up and could scarcely believe my eyes. I've been hoping every day you'd come."

Finch grasped his hand and searched his face to see what change was there. Wake looked stronger than he had ever seen him. His eyes did not appear so luminously large with his cheeks fuller and his skin as brown as a berry. There was a certain severity about his mouth, a look of reflection, and his nose was developing a fine Court arch. He returned Finch's gaze smiling and asked:

"What do you think of me in this?" He gathered the skirts of his gown in one hand and strode, with what seemed to Finch some of his old vanity, along the walk and back.

"It looks rather funny," said Finch, "but I suppose I'll get used to it.... You look happy, Wake."

"I am. Happier than I dreamed was possible."

"But then you've always been a happy fellow. I mean you were always sure of yourself, rather —" Finch hesitated for a word.

"Cocky," supplied Wake. "I know just how you must have felt about me. I think I was full of conceit. But I wasn't really happy. I was too self-conscious for that. But now I've given up all self. Come along to my tree and we'll talk about me." He caught Finch by the arm and drew him toward a bench beneath a chestnut tree that was turning prematurely brown. Other black-gowned figures were about, some slender like Wakefield, some thick-set or rotund.

It was evidently a time of recreation. They strolled together in groups or sat reading. On the bench where Wakefield had sat lay a volume of St. Thomas Aquinas. He picked it up and his fingers closed caressingly over its worn leather covers.

Finch thought — "If only I could know what is in his mind! And how he came to do this strange thing and how much of his happiness is real and how much play-acting! But I'm a beast to suspect him for a moment. He is absolutely sincere. The look in his eyes ... the very movement of his hands...." He said gently:

"Will you tell me something about it, Wake? I thought that you were terribly keen on Pauline. What changed your feelings? Would you mind telling me?"

"Well, you know, Finch, I was always rather religious. Do you remember how I used to pray for my grandmother when I was a kid? Of course, that was presumption and very irritating to my uncles, but it showed that I had a feeling for prayer. Then I stopped praying and began to write poetry. But I wasn't really a poet, like Eden was. With me it was just a phase and it passed. Then I fell in love with Pauline and everything was different. What I wanted above all things was to have her for my own. I wanted to work to make enough money to marry. And I did work, didn't I?"

"Yes, you did," agreed Finch. "You worked damned hard."

Wakefield looked pleased. "You're the first one who has said that, Finch. No matter how hard I worked I was looked on as a sort of playboy who couldn't do a man's job. I worked hard in the garage too. Later on I expect to work hard at teaching. There's a tremendous lot to be done." He looked capable of doing his share.

Finch thought — "Is this novice really Wakefield? Is this Wake in the long black gown? Am I Finch? Are we two sitting together under this chestnut tree with those black crows of men flitting about? If only the pain keeps off ... I can believe in anything ... I can believe in God ... if only the pain and confusion leave my head...."

He picked up the book of Thomas Aquinas and opened it. The print was blurred before his eyes. He took off his glasses and pressed his eyeballs. Then he looked again. Now he saw the letters. But there were two of each. He turned his eyes to Wake's face and saw his features grotesquely duplicated. He closed his eyes.

"You aren't well, are you, Finch?"

Wakefield's voice was warm with sympathy.

"I'm all right." Finch spoke gruffly. "I'm just tired. Those concerts were a strain."

Wakefield laid a brown hand on Finch's knee. "If you weren't married, I'd be after you! I'd never rest till I had you, Finch! You could be so happy in this life. You were not made for the stupidities and futile excitements of the world. You could make such wonderful use of your music. And, if I could have you beside me here, well — I'd ask for nothing more."

Finch thought — "How deep does it go with him? Is he just exhilarated by this new life or has he really found something that will last always?"

He asked — "How did you come to do it? Which of you — I mean, surely you didn't give up Pauline of your own free will."

"No — not of my own will. But God's."

Finch moved restlessly on the seat.

"You see, I had to be a Catholic to marry Pauline. At first I didn't think much about it. She was the important object. But I was willing. It seemed rather a picturesque thing to do. I began after a little to get interested in my talks with the priest. Then I went to a mission for men. And I began to be unhappy. Every day I got more miserable and I lay awake half the night. But I kept it all to myself." His lips set in a firm line.

Finch thought — "Who *is* he like? I see Gran's face in his, and Renny's, and Eden's, and even Piers's. He's like all of them but me! I'll never get nearer to him than I am now."

Wakefield went on — "Then suddenly I found out that I wanted the religious life. Nothing but that. Nothing else would do. I consulted my priest. He was doubtful. But I knew I had a vocation. You can imagine what the family said."

"Yes…. What I can't imagine is what Pauline said. It must have been a shock to her."

"That was the remarkable thing. That is what makes it all seem so divinely ordered. Almost the first thing she said to me was — 'I sympathize more than you know. I have often thought I should like to enter a convent.'"

"She said that, did she?"

"Yes. And her look told me even more than her words. She wasn't playing up to me. My belief is that we turned off the path we had taken at the very same moment. The same thought had been working in us both, though we were unconscious of it."

Finch looked down at his glasses dangling between his fingers. "And you don't regret her? I mean, you can bear the thought of never seeing her again?"

"Oh, I am sure I shall see her again. I look forward to that. But it will be different — naturally."

"I don't suppose there is a chance of my ever seeing her again."

"Uncle Ernest told me that she is going to be at her mother's sale, to help her. You might see her there. If you do, Finch, please give her my love and tell her I hope she is as happy as I am. Give my love to her mother too."

Finch remembered the blonde, stocky woman and felt a sudden compassion for her. He felt a pang in his heart at the thought that Pauline was going from them all forever. A thin old priest came to them across the burnt grass. Wakefield introduced Finch to him and the three proceeded to join a group of other novices.

They were all natural and friendly with Finch. Wakefield must have talked a good deal of his family. They asked Finch questions about his concerts and his experience in the world of music. To Finch it seemed that Wakefield already occupied in the monastery something of the position he had had at Jalna. He seemed a favourite with the older priests.

He took Finch over the grounds. To the vegetable garden where lay brothers were working with an industry Finch had never before witnessed. He wished Piers might have seen them. He was shown over the monastery and saw Wakefield's room. He looked at him curiously, out of his long, large-pupiled eyes.

Finch had a good tea and was extraordinarily hungry.

He stood beside Wakefield in the chapel at Benediction. The light from the stained glass windows fell across the heads and shoulders of these men withdrawn from the world. They seemed suddenly cold and aloof from him. The air was rich with incense. As he fixed his eyes on the glittering monstrance the pain in his head began again. He wanted to get away.

At the gate the brothers shook hands. Wakefield said:

"Remember, Finch, you will never be out of my thoughts. I shall always be praying for you. I have hopes that you may become a Catholic. And Renny too. I even have hope for him."

"What about Piers?" asked Finch grimly.

Wake gave one of his old mischievous grins. "Well," he said, "I haven't much hope of Piers."

XII

Sale at the Fox Farm

The atmosphere of an auction sale was not a novelty at Jalna. Once a year Renny and Piers held a sale of surplus stock. The bustle in preparation for it, the actual event, the rearrangement of stables afterward, and the gratification or disappointment in the result, were a solid part of each year.

But the sale at the fox farm was different. It was still called the fox farm though the foxes had disappeared. Their wire-netted runs stood forsaken or sagged to the ground. But the little house was charming inside. Clara and Pauline had delighted in keeping it so. Now it would stand bereft, its associations torn from it like a clinging creeper. To Renny it was a black day. He would be glad when it was over and the door locked on that chamber of his life. He had done all he could to arrange for a successful sale. Now he had only to stand by and watch the familiar objects disappear one by one.

There was nothing of much value in the house. The furniture and rugs had been bought at haphazard, with regard to cheapness rather than any scheme, but Clara had, with effective walls and curtains, some pieces of family china and the pictures Lebraux had bought, when he could not afford them, given the house that air of well-being which she contrived in her material surroundings.

She and Renny stood together at one end of a table of ornaments she had arranged, while at the other Finch fingered a little china box with the figure of a shepherdess on the lid. Clara looked reflectively at his face, at his hands.

"The boy looks tired," she said.

"He is. He has worked too hard. He's not strong."

Clara gave a little grunt. "I wish he had cared for Pauline, instead of Wake. He's more stable."

"I wish he had. Things might have been different." Then Renny remembered Sarah. "But still — he's got a wife who is absolutely devoted to him. Lots of money too."

"Hm, yes. It was God's mercy to you."

"She's a strange girl. I'm glad I'm not married to her. She makes me uncomfortable."

Clara's eyes turned from Finch to him. Her short strong features softened to tenderness. Her eyes embraced him.

Finch asked — "Was this Pauline's?"

"Yes. Her French grandma gave it to her."

People began to trickle into the room. The air was hot, sticky. There seemed nothing to breathe. The auctioneer's voice could be heard from a bedroom. A woman wearing black cotton gloves with a hole in the thumb picked up the china box and peered into it. The auctioneer's clerk came and took Clara away.

Finch muttered to himself — "If she drops that box...."

The woman said to a friend — "Cute, isn't it? I believe I'll buy it for Betty's birthday."

The room was filling up. It was insufferably close. Finch moved to Renny's side.

"Do you think," he asked, "that Pauline is here? Do you think she will be in — nun's things?"

"Lord no! She's in brown. There she is. Just by the door. She's looking for Clara."

Pauline stood in the doorway, childishly indecisive. She was bareheaded and her thick, dark hair, more closely cut than Finch had before seen it, hung unevenly about her ears. She looked mildly at the collection of people. Her lips parted as though she strove for a deep breath.

She saw Renny and Finch and came to them and spoke in a low, even voice.

"I'm glad you have come. Mummie and I have felt awfully confused by it all. It's ages since I've seen you, Finch." She held out her hand.

Finch took it. He said — "I saw Wakefield last week." Then he coloured deeply, wishing he could withdraw the words. She did not seem to mind. She looked just the same only there was something a little cold, a little detached about her that was new to him. Her lips had less colour. She kept looking at Finch as though he was a shield between her and Renny.

"Has the sale begun?" asked Renny.

"Yes. In Mother's bedroom. It's packed with people."

"Two-thirty — two-thirty — going at two-thirty!" came the auctioneer's voice from above.

The people in the dining room were not interested. They settled themselves to remain where they were till the things they wanted were put up.

"Let's get out into the air," said Renny.

The three went out and stood by the empty fox run. Pauline said:

"Do you remember my pet fox?"

"Yes" answered Finch. "What became of him?"

"He died. I was terribly sorry. I cried and I cried didn't I, Renny?"

He took her arm in his hand. "It's all over, Pauline," he said.

Finch moved away from the others and made as though to look for gooseberries on some neglected bushes.

Pauline raised her eyes to Renny's face. "How I have loved you," she said.

He looked back at her without speaking, cut to the heart. She went on breathlessly — "That is the last time a word of love shall ever pass my lips. But I had to say it. You understand, don't you?"

"Yes, I understand."

They followed Finch who held out a few prickly berries. They each took one as though it were some sort of rite. The fruit was sour on their lips and the prickles stung them.

After a little they returned to the house and Pauline and Clara shut themselves up in a small, empty room, sitting on two boxes to wait the end of the sale.

When the auctioneer reached the dining room the bidding slackened. The bedroom furniture had gone well, but the furniture of the dining room was almost given away. Finch bought the china box and Renny the brass coffee table across which Clara and he had so often discussed their plans.

He became more and more depressed. The things were going for nothing. He towered above the group straggling about the dining room. He had a picture in his mind of himself and Clara, Wakefield and Pauline, dancing through these rooms. The gramophone to which they had danced was almost given away. Now a walnut cabinet was being offered.

He nudged Finch in the ribs. "Buy it," he urged, "buy it for yourself! You'll be needing some furniture."

Finch flew into a panic.

"B-b-but what should I do with it?"

"I'll keep it for you. As long as you like. Hurry up! Don't let it get away from you!"

Finch, scarlet, nodded to the auctioneer. New life was put into the bidding. He got the cabinet, two chairs, and a chesterfield.

"You'll be needing just such things one day," urged Renny. "You'll never have another chance like this."

"But Sarah will hate these things."

"No she won't. She can't. They'd look well if they were re-upholstered. You'll never have another chance like this."

Renny bought a large watercolour of the rocky shore of the Saguenay, a bookcase full of books, and a little cabinet with a fragile tea set in it. By the time this was done he was in a state of exhilarated good humour and Finch in one of resigned depression.

What had he done? What would he do with these things he had acquired? The close atmosphere of the house made him sick. The hands of the village women pawing the curtains and clutching feather pillows made him sick. He had a mad desire to run after Pauline, to hammer on the door of the room and shout to her that she must come away with him and find peace somewhere. Renny stood beside him, leading that charmed secure life of his. Finch thought — "He is as tough as steel. If only I had a face like his I could look into other faces without flinching. It's strange to think how all these people packed in here have no pain in the head."

Renny said — "Let's go and speak to Clara before we go."

Finch followed him to the door of the unfurnished room and Clara answered their knock. She had a piece of bread and butter in her hand and there was a smudge on her cheek. Pauline sat on an upturned box, her back to the door.

"It's nearly over," said Renny. "It's gone very well. This young man bought quite a lot."

"Oh, that's nice," answered Clara.

Finch could see Pauline's hands clasped on her lap.

XIII

THE END OF ENDURANCE

ONE OF PIERS'S farm wagons drawn by two bay geldings brought to Jalna the things Renny and Finch had bought at the sale. Not to the house itself but to an empty cottage on the estate known as Fiddler's Hut. Piers lounged by the door as the furniture was carried in, smiling sardonically. Renny stood filling his pipe and trying to look unembarrassed.

Piers remarked — "You say young Finch bought all this stuff of his own accord?"

"Why not? He will be needing furniture."

"Not this sort."

"How the hell do you know what he'll need!"

"No use in being irritable. I just marvel at him."

"Don't speak of it to Sarah — not yet."

"So, it's to be a surprise for her? Birthday, or something?"

"Well — he should be allowed to tell her of it himself."

"Didn't you buy anything?"

"That black cabinet. And the bookcase and picture."

Piers bent his knees in front of the bookcase and ran his eyes over the titles of the books. His silence expressed tolerant amusement.

The couch refused to go in at the door.

"Could you keep it for Finch?" asked Renny, almost pleadingly.

"Not possibly. Our rooms are full." Still squatting he raised his eyes to Renny's face and said — "Finch doesn't imagine surely that he can hide this junk —"

"It isn't junk!"

"It's junk as far as Finch is concerned. Maurice was at the sale. I saw him look in just as the chairs were knocked down to Finch. I saw him afterward talking to Uncle Ernest in the yard. You and Finch are pretty sanguine."

"I'm not concealing anything. The things I bought are going to my room."

Piers said thoughtfully — "You're taking a good deal of trouble, aren't you, to make things worse between you and Alayne?"

Renny returned sombrely — "Nothing I can do matters one way or the other."

Piers took a book from the case, rose, and opened it. Then he muttered — "Everything matters — when two people are trying to live together."

"We're not," Renny answered harshly.

He had the furniture reloaded on the wagon and taken to the house. What Finch had bought was carried to an already overcrowded box-room in the attic and the cabinet, tea set, and bookcase set up in his own room. By the time this was accomplished, every member of the family knew what was going on. Ernest and Nicholas added their bulk to the room. Sarah and Alayne stood in the passage looking in. Renny affected not to notice their presence. He placed the anemic-looking tea set in the cabinet with hands more accustomed to the handling of horses.

After a little Alayne turned away and went into her own room. Sarah followed her and asked, in her sweet impersonal voice:

"Why did they do it?"

Alayne answered abruptly, out of set lips:

"Don't ask me! Just be thankful, Sarah, that those two women are out of the way before your marriage is wrecked."

"Was the daughter after Finch?" asked Sarah.

"They're utterly unscrupulous!"

"Was it the mother, perhaps?"

"I say only this — be thankful they're going."

Alayne was losing control of herself. Her outrage would not be kept in durance. It raged and sickened her. To see him handling those cheap, fragile cups … those books, now to be kept by his bedside!

She went to her desk and bent over an unfinished letter to her aunt. She said:

"I'm sorry, Sarah. I must finish this letter for the post." She bent close to the writing as though she were short-sighted.

Sarah thought — "If only I could get out of her what all this is about! How fascinating Finch is with his strange moods! How wonderful life is!" She glanced at herself in the mirror, patting the convolutions of her sleek braids.

As she went out, Adeline passed her coming in. She was carrying a box of small lead toys and when she reached the middle of the room she emptied them to the floor with a clatter. Alayne had not seen her come in. She sprang from her desk, terrified.

"Oh," she gasped, "what are you doing? You can't have those in here."

"I can," said Adeline. "I've just bought them at a sale. I want them in my room."

"Adeline, pick them up at once and take them out!"

"I won't!"

"You shall!"

Adeline began to kick the toys in all directions. Alayne caught her by both arms and held her rigid. Adeline began to dance with rage. Alayne pressed her fingers into the child's flesh. Adeline struck at her face and kicked her. Her screams were piercing.

Nicholas stood in the doorway.

"My, my, my," he said, "this is awful. What has angered her so, Alayne?"

"Take her," said Alayne. "Take her away. I can't stand any more."

Nicholas took the child in his large calm hands and laid her against his shoulder. Her screams became sobs and she clasped her arms about his neck.

He carried her to his room and Renny now appeared in the doorway. Alayne thought — "It is like a play…. They come one after another to the door…. All bringing more suffering to me…. I can't bear any more."

Renny said — "It seems strange that you can't get on with your own child for five minutes at a time. Why should you make her suffer for your anger against me?"

"Her suffer! Her suffer!" repeated Alayne. "And I was just thinking — no one cares about my suffering — please go away and leave me."

He said, trying to calm her — "Now look here, Alayne, there's no sense in your getting upset about my buying those few things at the sale. As a matter of fact, they're things I always liked and I didn't want to see them just given away."

She turned her tortured face on him.

"No — you didn't want anyone else to have them! You wanted them near you. You wanted them in your own room by your bed. When have you bought anything new for the house? Tell me that. When have I bought anything new that you didn't object? Tell me that. You've always said that the house was overcrowded already. Yes — it is overcrowded! And I am the one too many!"

He had come inside and closed the door behind him to shut in the rising of her voice. They faced each other above the scattered toys.

"Alayne, you don't know what you are saying!"

"I do! And I tell you I refuse to stay in this house with those things you have bought from your mistress. I won't stay in the house with them — or with you!"

He stared at her, turning pale.

"What shall you do?" he asked.

"I will go to my aunt. I am writing to say that I will go to her." She made a tragic gesture toward the letter on the desk.

"Very well," he returned coldly. "I think it's probably the best thing that you can do. We certainly can't go on like this. It's too — too awful." He added quickly — "Don't imagine that I will let you take the child."

"You may keep the child." She sat down by the desk and when the door had shut behind him buried her face in her arms. She looked wonderingly at her tears absorbed by the blotting paper. "I could write a letter in tears," she thought, and wondered at herself for crying so much because she was not by nature that sort of woman.

Absolute silence fell on the house. From the farm came at intervals the persistent lowing of a cow for her calf. The land was heavy with thick midsummer sunshine. The old house was warmed through and through. The mellow sunshine was kind to it. The faded curtains and threadbare spots in rugs were enriched and glossed over by its radiance. The house looked its best but no one noticed it. It sat like a drowsy old cat absorbing warmth in its every fibre. Only Alayne gave it a thought and that was — "I shall soon leave it forever and I have made no impression on it, even though I have given it another Whiteoak to shelter."

She took her pen and wrote at the end of the letter, in which she had not mentioned the possibility of visiting her aunt: "Expect me some day this week. I find that I cannot endure life here any longer. I have tried and failed. It just can't be borne. Please don't feel upset. I think I am doing what is best for us all. I am sure you will want me. You will hear from me again before I leave." As she signed her name she thought:

"I will give up his name and become Alayne Archer again."

XIV

ESCAPE

SHE HAD A fugitive feeling as though she were being pursued, even though her departure from Jalna had been so arranged as to give the semblance of a visit to an aunt who was pining to see her, also a journey for the benefit of her own health. Both she and Renny were anxious to keep up the appearance of naturalness. Neither had felt that they could bear curious glances, sympathy, blame, family discussion of their affairs, attempts to draw them together again. They had in truth been drawn nearer together than for a long while in their desire for secrecy, their nervous determination to hide their wounds.

They had made their arrangements with dignity, looking calmly into each other's eyes, noticing calmly the ravages the past weeks had made on the faces of each. Adeline was to remain at Jalna but she was to visit her mother when Alayne wished. Later Renny was to tell the family that Alayne was not coming back. Then he would take down the pictures from her room and send them to her. When Adeline was older she would have this room for her own.

Renny had taken Alayne to the train. He had gone into the railway carriage with her, arranged her smaller pieces of luggage in a neat pile on the seat opposite. He had sat down on the arm of the seat and made jerky attempts at conversation. He had gone out and returned with magazines and newspapers for her. The worst moment had been when it was necessary to say goodbye. He had stood up rigid, his nose looking prominent and bleak. She had stood up, her legs trembling. A grating jar had passed through the train.

"Hurry!" she had gasped. "It is starting."

His body had swayed, as though he were tearing himself physically from her.

"Goodbye," she had gasped, and their hands, hers in fresh white gloves, had touched.

He had had a jerk from the train as he sprang to the platform. She had seen him recovering his balance, people staring at him. Then the relief — the blessed relief — it was all over between them. The train was whirling her into another life.

Still she had that feeling of being pursued. She lay hunched in her berth, her hands clenched under her chin, and she seemed to hear the beat of feet running in pursuit. In the blackness she saw the Whiteoaks pursuing her, tireless and unyielding. She saw Ernest first, with long, limber legs, stitching at his needle point embroidery as he ran. She saw Nicholas leaping strongly, unhampered by his gouty leg. She saw their mother, with closed eyes and folded arms, as she had seen her in her coffin, but running too. She saw Eden clinging to old Adeline's skirt, his yellow hair streaming a yard long. She saw Piers and his family — little Nook weeping. She saw Meg and hers.... Wake in his monk's robe flitted in the shadow.... Finch took off one pair of glasses and put on another so that he might see her clearly.... Last she saw Renny, carrying her child.... Then her clenched hands moved upward and pressed her lips against her teeth.

It was while she was filling in the form for the immigration officer that her nerves had begun to get the better of her and the nausea that had been troubling her returned. She had scarcely been able to make out the questions or to control her pen between the narrow lines. The officer had been considerate. He had sat down on the seat opposite and given her help. But he looked a little suspicious when she had trouble in remembering the name and address of the aunt whom she was going to visit. When he had left her she had gone to the ladies' toilet room and been sick. After that she went to her berth.

The heat in Canada seemed as nothing compared with the heat in New York. The great marble station seemed a sepulchre for a demon of heat. But her little aunt, who met her, looked as fastidiously cool as ever and had aged little since Alayne had last seen her. She took Alayne and her luggage in hand, and they were transferred to an electric train that carried them to the pretty house on the Hudson where Miss Archer lived. It was five years since Alayne had been there. She had been estranged from Renny then, but that estrangement had been only as a cloud in the sky of their love compared to the chasm that now separated them.

Miss Archer had been troubled by the abrupt addition to Alayne's letter — even the handwriting had looked unnatural. She was still more troubled by Alayne's appearance and, when she had her settled comfortably in the cool living room with a cup of coffee and some cookies before her, she said:

"Now, my dear, you must tell me all about it."

Alayne tried to look unconcerned.

"About what?"

"Well" — Miss Archer gave a nervous little laugh — "this is all very sudden, isn't it?"

Alayne fortified herself with a drink of coffee. She must get it over at once. She had had enough of leading a double life. She could endure no more. She raised her heavy eyes to Miss Archer's face and answered

"It just means, Aunt Harriet, that I have left Renny. I'm not going back to him — ever."

Miss Archer's delicate face was suffused by colour and her mild eyes by tears. She half rose as though to take Alayne in her arms but Alayne held up her hand. "Don't, Aunt Harriet! I'm not in any mood for sympathy. I just want to speak of this matter coldly. I want to say what must be said and then try to put all that behind me. I want to make a new life with you — if I can — if you'll have me."

Miss Archer half rose once more, and again, at Alayne's look, sank back.

"Very well, dear. Tell me just what you want to and then we'll speak of it no more. As for welcoming you to my house — you know there's nothing on earth I want so much as to have you with me." She kept her voice steady but her handkerchief was twisted in her smooth ringless hands.

"I have left him," repeated Alayne. "I can't stand it any longer. He's — been unfaithful to me — with a woman named Clara Lebraux. She lives next door to us — that is, she did."

"Another woman," said Miss Archer. "A neighbour! The brute!"

"I tried to stay in the house with him after I found out. I did stay for a while. But — things happened and I just couldn't."

"I should think not! Oh, my poor dear, what you have been through! The second one of that family. What a pity you ever met them! If only you had married that nice man — that friend of your father's. How different your life might have been!"

"Yes." Alayne tried to picture what her life might have been but she could not. "I can't picture it," she said. "I'm too worn out by what my life *has* been. It has been hell, I tell you, Aunt Harriet. I wasn't made for such a life — such a wife."

The harshness of Alayne's words, the vital life thrust suddenly before Miss Archer repelled her. She felt shaken. She said — "Let us be thankful that your dear parents have not lived to see this day." She said after a moment:

"It seems so strange that I have never seen him." There was a note of reproach in her tone, for Alayne had never urged her to visit Jalna. Alayne had felt that there were too many things at Jalna, too much seething life there. She had felt that it would have frightened her aunt. She said:

"You would not have admired him. Still — you might. I don't know. I can't tell. He isn't at all like Eden. But you've seen snaps of him."

"He has a good figure," said Miss Archer.

Alayne began to count the stripes in a casement cloth window curtain. Her lips moved silently. One — two — three — four — five —

"What are you saying, dear?"

"I was saying he has."

"His face is unusual. Not at all like Eden's. Eden was so attractive."

Six — seven — eight — nine — Her lips moved.

"I didn't hear you, Alayne dear."

"I was saying he was."

"It seemed such a perfect marriage. But I mustn't talk of that. Alayne — what of your child?"

"I am to have her a part of the time."

"Poor little mite! She will be missing you terribly. Are you assured that she will be properly cared for? The bringing up of children is so scientific now."

"She will flourish. She won't miss me."

"Not *miss* you! Alayne!"

"She adores her father."

How hard Alayne was! Marriage with this man had certainly changed her. Miss Archer had a moment's doubt as to her congeniality as a companion in her house, but it was swept away by sympathy.

That sympathy was never failing. Alayne relaxed, lapped in it, relaxed as she had not for months. She burrowed into the downy quiet of the new life. She drew long breaths of the air that was never tainted by smell of dog or horse. Her ears gratefully drank in the tones of Miss Archer's soft thin voice. She looked out on the tidy street where each little lawn had its ornamental shrubs kept moist by water from a hose and where boys and girls flitted by on roller skates.

But, though she rested and a new peace came to her, her health did not improve. One day unknown to her aunt she went to see a doctor. He confirmed what she suspected. She was going to have a child.

She made up her mind to keep this a secret as long as possible.

XV

THE ADORING WIFE

THE UNCLES, FINCH and Sarah, Renny and the two tiny girls, now constituted the household at Jalna. Nicholas and Ernest had never been more content to be in their old home. England was no longer for them as a permanent home. They had got on each other's nerves in the damp days of the Devon winter. They had felt isolated. The fact that London was near and they were too old to take part in the life they had once loved, even if it had existed, saddened them. Nicholas's gout and Ernest's indigestion had got steadily worse. Now, back in Jalna, they felt like new men.

The long hot summer agreed with them. They had the food they were used to, cooked just as they liked it. They took care to give periodical presents to Mrs. Wragge which kept up her interest in their favourite dishes. Their Devon house was let to satisfactory tenants.

They set about the congenial task of embellishing their own rooms. Nicholas had his repapered in a rich design with a good deal of gilt. He had his couch and chairs upholstered in mulberry and the woodwork of the room painted ivory. Ernest selected a mauve monotone as his scheme of colour and he had brought a rug with him from Augusta's house. It was one which he had not wanted to leave to the mercy of even a well-recommended tenant. He had brought it to Jalna with the

intention of presenting it to Alayne but he found himself less drawn
to her than ever before. For one thing, she had gone off terribly in her
looks and, as he said to his brother, she was appallingly self-centred.
He was disappointed in her and he simply could not make up his mind
to give her the rug. He kept it in the attic rolled in canvas as it had
crossed the ocean, till she went away. Then, when he had his room
redecorated, he had it brought down and laid on his floor. When he
saw the effect he could not be thankful enough that he had had the
good sense to keep it for himself. Now he was working on *gros point*
covers for the seats of his chairs.

The effect of these two rooms side by side was rich. Renny was
elated by the sight of the house so beautified. The fact that his own
room, which had always been ugly, was now made hideous by the crowding into it of the bookcase and black china cabinet from the fox farm,
did not impress him. Inside and out the house was in order. Though
there was a mortgage on it, the mortgage was held by Finch's wife. It
was Finch himself who held the mortgage on Vaughanlands. So behind
the depressing word mortgage was the solid security of kinship. Though
Maurice could not dig up his interest, Finch would certainly never make
a move against him. Though Renny was equally vulnerable, Sarah would
never foreclose. Yet consciousness of the power held by the young couple
secured them certain immunity from criticism. When Maurice would
have scoffed at Finch's nerves, Meg would have laughed at the idea of
his not being able to fill his autumn engagements, they remembered the
mortgage on Vaughanlands. When Renny would have ridiculed what,
to him, were Sarah's affectations, he remembered the mortgage on Jalna.

He came to dislike Sarah. He resented her enigmatic smile, her look
of sly pleasure in her own thoughts, her small-mouthed, curved-nosed,
pointed-chinned profile always turned toward him at table. She disliked
him more every day. She was jealous of Finch's love and loyalty for him.
She resented his air of masculine hardihood even while she wished that
Finch had some of it. In Sarah he met a woman for whom he had no
physical attraction. Nor did he wish to have any. He forced his grandmother's own grin to his lips when he encountered Sarah, and longed
for her visit to be over.

Nicholas and Ernest admired her. They enjoyed her talk of European capitals, when she brought herself to talk, for she was a silent creature except with Finch. They liked the dresses she had brought from Paris and the scent of her Russian cigarettes and exotic perfumes. She was lavish with herself in expensive trifles to make up for the years of penury, and the fact that her income was greatly decreased by the falling of stocks did not impress her at all. In spite of her strangeness she was more readily absorbed by the family than Alayne, for she was a Court, and the life of the house was congenial to her. She longed for no life outside it except for the life of concert hall and travel connected with Finch's work. She practised on the violin for an hour every morning but never opened a book. Her only reading was love stories in magazines which she devoured but never discussed. She did not throw them away when she had finished but kept them in a corner of her room where the pile grew from week to week. She went to church every Sunday, delighting in showing off her Paris clothes before the little congregation. Once she played the violin at a church tea party. The Rector liked her better than he had ever liked Alayne. On her part she was glad of Alayne's absence. Little by little she gathered in what authority she could in the house. Rags and his wife both approved of her and flew to do what she asked.

Little Adeline held herself aloof. She was conscious, with a child's instinct, of the dislike between Renny and Sarah. In a subtle way she felt that Sarah was trying to usurp her mother's place in the house. She frowned when she saw Sarah pouring tea from the silver pot. On her birthday came a beautifully made frock from Alayne. Adeline was enraptured and strutted about, saying:

"This is from my Mummie. She's coming back soon. I want to see her."

Roma, the other new member of the household, expressed no opinion either by behaviour or words of the strange environment in which she found herself. She was so shy, so speechless, that she might have been dumb. She was an inactive child who preferred to sit rather than run about with Adeline. She did not care much for toys, liking better to play with coloured pebbles from the lakeshore or a handful of acorns or some petals of flowers. Yet she accepted what Adeline offered, only to discard it when Adeline's back was turned. She cared even less for food than toys, sometimes refusing to touch her meals. At these times Renny alone could persuade her to eat. He would sit with her on his knee, the spoon in his hand, cajoling, petting her into emptying the dish. He scowled at her thinness. She was a feather compared to Adeline's white-fleshed weight. "Eat this!" he would exclaim. "Your legs are a sight." And he would add, in horrible French — "*Menge cela! Tes jambes sont trop maigres.*" And she, opening wide her mouth, would murmur — "*Merci, beaucoup.*"

He was really delighted to have her, partly because she was a companion for Adeline and brought out the best in her, even more because she was Eden's child. His love for Eden's memory increased as he resented more deeply Alayne's attitude toward him. He often talked of him, now jocularly of his difficulties with him as a boy, now gloomily of his last illness. There were several copies of Eden's two books of poems in the house. He arranged one of each on a table in the drawing room. The others he stood in the bookcase in his bedroom. Sometimes, at night, he would take one up and sombrely read a poem through, his pipe drooping from a corner of his mouth. Finch, passing his door one night, discovered him and stood unseen watching. Why was Renny doing that? What did he find in Eden's poems? Pity for Renny who never pitied himself, pity for Eden, filled Finch with sadness. He remembered how Eden had given the money he had made from a series of talks on poetry to Wakefield to buy an engagement ring for Pauline. Where was that ring now? Discarded — hidden away, as the symbol of a futile love. And for that Eden had driven himself to the last ditch!

Finch saw his own reflection in the mirror behind Renny's chair, his hollow cheeks, his questioning, troubled eyes. His reflection seemed to brood over Renny, to cast a spell over him. Finch stared, not able to move away, till he was not sure whether the figure in the chair were Renny's own or a reflection of him, whether the reflection in the mirror were not his own true self and the figure in the doorway a mere shadow.

The lithographs of horses on the walls rolled their eyes at him, their bodies seemed to palpitate in fear. Renny moved uneasily in his chair. His head slanted, as though he listened. The puppy on the foot of the bed sat up and yawned. The yawn strengthened into a whine.

Finch moved away. He thought — "I can't sleep with Sarah. It would be too unreal being in the bed with her. Those creeping pains in the back of my neck will drive me insane unless I can be alone. But I'm afraid to tell her for fear she will object...."

He thought he would write her a note, and went up to his old room where he knew there were paper and pencil. He tore a leaf from an old exercise-book and wrote: "Darling — I am feeling so —"

But the pencil would not move. He put all the force of his body into his arm, his hand, but he could not move the pencil. It reared itself, clamped to the paper, inexorable.

For a time he could not even loosen his fingers from their iron grip on it. Then it fell to the floor and he tore up the paper. The noise of the tearing shot through his head in a dreadful pain.

He went unsteadily down the stairs to Sarah. She was propped up in bed reading a magazine. A glossy braid lay over each shoulder, black as night. The lacy jacket of her pyjamas glimmered over the firm whiteness of her body.

He stood leaning against the door, his heart beating heavily. But he spoke in a low steady voice:

"Look here, Sarah, the beastly pain is after me again. There's only one thing for it and that is to be alone. I'm going up to my old room. You don't mind, do you, darling?"

Her eyes looked into his over the edge of the book.

"You know," she said, slowly, "what it means to me to be away from you."

"Yes, yes, I know. It's wonderful your feeling like that — about me ... but I've got to get over this rotten thing ... and the only way ... I can't bear anyone near me...."

He pulled off his glasses. His long, large-pupilled eyes became very bright.

"It can't be your eyes. They look so lovely."

"No, no. I don't know what it is.... Just nerves...." He came to her and gently touched her. "You understand, darling — just till I get over this.... You won't mind."

Her arms reached up to him. They seemed to him like naked feelers reaching up to drag him into an abyss. He started back.

"Good night. Tell me good night."

"No," he said loudly. "I can't even do that! Can't you see ..." The harshness of his own voice surprised him.

He left the room quickly and returned to the attic.

Oh, the peace and darkness of it! In the darkness he pulled off his clothes and got into bed. He burrowed his head into the pillow and lay waiting for the pain to ease.

It crept up from between his shoulders, circling his neck, its shrewd fingers pressed even to his throat. The roots of his tongue felt it. His head seemed to swell, as though his brain would burst from an iron band. There was an orchestra playing in the room with him, accompanying the exquisite solo of the pain.... He drew himself into a knot and lay listening.

The next morning he woke in peace. He went downstairs, ate his breakfast in the sweet peace. He was almost afraid to speak for fear he would break its sweet fragility.

But, at ten o'clock, the pain began again and stayed with him till he slept at late night. And so on, day after day, week after week. He grew gaunt and dishevelled and had to force himself to speak gently to Sarah.

He had a sudden longing to see Wakefield. He went to Renny and said — "Do you think Wake could come home for a few days? I've scarcely seen him, you know. After he takes the final vows it won't be so easy for him to leave."

Renny looked pleased at the mere thought of a visit from Wakefield. He said — "I'm sure they will let him come, knowing you've been away and aren't feeling yourself. Just write a nice letter — you know how to put it — I'm sure there won't be any difficulty."

"You write, Renny. I — I'm afraid I can't do it." As he made this admission the pain in his head increased.

"Can't do it!" Renny stared at him, then looked embarrassed. He answered, with forced heartiness — "Yes, of course, I'll do it. I'll write today.... Have you tried aspirin? Alayne found that it helped her headaches."

It doesn't help this. Nor the stuff the French doctor gave me. Nothing seems to help it. I — don't know when I shall be able to play again."

Renny put a reassuring arm about his shoulders. "It will pass away — just keep your mind off it and stay outdoors all you can." He looked anxiously into Finch's haggard young face. "I'm glad you thought of having Wake come to see you, only mind you don't let him convert you. He'll be after you if he thinks there's a chance."

In a few days Wakefield came to spend a week at Jalna. In his black robe his figure looked fuller, his face browner. He looked serene and secure in his happiness. The family regarded him with wonder. It seemed such a short while ago that he was a bare-kneed little boy, imitating his elders, busy in the expression of the intricate life he had made for himself in the family circle. Now he was aloof from them all but so affectionate and understanding. He hung with Ernest over his embroidery frame. He had long talks with Nicholas and read the London *Times* aloud to him. He visited every corner of the stables with Renny. Took sugar to his old pony and groomed it down. He even hitched up his robe and mounted Renny's new horse to try its gait, savouring with serene pleasure the wonder and admiration of the stablemen and farm labourers who had gathered to see him.

He went to tea every day at Vaughanlands or with Pheasant and her boys. Meg showed him off to her paying guests. Pheasant poured out to him her problems in the rearing of her small sons as though he were already an experienced minister of souls. Even Piers began to take him seriously. He visited Mr. Fennel who had taught him almost all he knew, and stirred him up to controversy in the matter of religion. It was delightful to him to go to the Rectory as a monastic emissary. In truth Wakefield was in the seventh heaven.

Eden's little girl forgot her shyness with him. When they were alone together she would even talk to him in her odd mixture of baby English and French. She followed him wherever she could, clutching a fold of his robe in her thin little hand. His name fascinated her. She kept repeating it as they went. "Wake ... Wake ... Wake ..." in a strange little singsong. Her straight hair was so fine that whatever touched it left it standing in a pale wisp ... it always stuck out so, on the side nearest Wakefield.

The idea came to him of re-colouring the walls of the nursery. With one of Mrs. Wragge's aprons tied over his robe he applied a wash of sunny yellow to walls and ceiling. He went to town and bought pictures of the legends of saints for a border. Between the windows was St. Francis surrounded by birds and animals. Alma Patch, the nursemaid, was breathless in her delight. Ernest had brought her from England a nurse's outfit which raised her to a new pinnacle of prominence in the village. She found Roma easy to care for except in the matter of persuading her to eat her meals. The difficulty with Adeline was to persuade her to stop.

But the greater part of Wakefield's day was spent with Finch. They had long walks together or lay talking on the glossy brown needles in the pine wood. Endlessly, with calculated soothing monotony, Wakefield talked of his life in the monastery, of his joy in his religion. He read aloud to Finch who lay, only half listening to what his mind refused to accept, but drinking in the reassuring peace of Wakefield's presence.

At night they slept together in Finch's old room, their long limbs in peaceful relaxation, Wakefield's arm thrown protectively across Finch. He felt the elder of the two now. He felt immensely strong and proud in his protection of Finch. Finch was the young brother, the weak, the fearful, the clinging. Wakefield realized, as did no one else in the family, that Finch shrank from Sarah's demonstrative love, that her feverish interest, which was never apart from sex, in everything he said and did, was irritating and exhausting to Finch. To Sarah, Wakefield's attitude was conciliatory and confidential. He listened gravely to her accounts of Finch's playing in Europe. He promised that Finch would be able to undertake the series of recitals in America which his agent had arranged for him. Just now, he said, relaxation and solitude were what Finch needed most. She must go to see Meggie and Pheasant, keep out of Finch's way, so that his love for her might not distract his nerves. Artists were temperamental beings and had to be humoured. Wakefield clasped his hands on his stomach and felt fifty.

It was an amazing thing to Finch that the boy who had always irritated him by his cocksure ways and assumption of superiority over him should now be his comfort and his strength. But he surrendered himself to Wakefield. As he lay in bed watching Wake at his prayers in the candlelight, listening to the steady murmur of prayer from his lips that sometimes showed a curious resemblance to his grandmother's in their flexible line, Finch felt that there was something present stronger than either of them, a mystery and a symbol in the room. Day by day the pain in his head lessened.

Still he was not regretful when Wakefield's week was up and he returned to the monastery. He wanted to be alone with his growing peace. He felt that only by himself could he find the way back to normal life, the work that lay before him ... the years that stretched before him, the years with Sarah.

She followed Wakefield's advice and left Finch to himself, but he was never out of her thoughts. With Wakefield gone Finch became conscious of Sarah's thoughts always reaching out to him. He shrank from them because their feminine vitality was more than he could bear. They were hot sparks from a furnace. They were electric waves. She conceived the idea that by playing her violin she could draw him back to his music. She began by playing it softly in the drawing room when she knew that he was nearby. Then she played more loudly, choosing the pieces he liked best, in their own room when she knew he was in his old room above. She even came to the foot of the attic stairs. She came slowly up the stairs, the violin held fast under her white, pointed chin, playing as she came.

When he had heard her violin in the drawing room he had slipped out by the side door. When he had heard it in her bedroom he had crept down the stairs and escaped. But when she mounted the stairway, playing as she came, there was no escape and he flung up his window and leant far out, calculating the distance to the ground.

She was as insistent and ruthless as a child. She had a child's egotism. The door of Finch's room was thrown open and he stood on the landing looking down at her.

"Don't!" he said hoarsely.

She raised her pale glittering eyes to his and went on playing.

"Stop!" he repeated fiercely. "You mustn't play to me, Sarah! I can't bear it!"

The hand that held the bow dropped to her side. She smiled up at him.

"Why?" she asked. "I think some music will do you good."

"No, no, it hurts my head! Can't you understand, Sarah! The notes hurt those nerves in my head that keep paining all the time. They beat like little hammers. They tear like little claws. You must put your violin away, darling. Just for a while, till I'm better."

Sarah drew her bow caressingly across his hand that lay on the banister. She came nearer to him, smiling. "I'll not play anymore," she said.

The violin bow burnt his hand. He drew it back and for something to do with it took off his glasses and rubbed them on his sleeve.

"Darling eyes," she said, and came close and kissed them.

He stood motionless, scarcely breathing, surveying himself as an outsider, a body — a skull surrounding a horrible pain.

She put both arms about his neck and held him tightly. A cold wind blew on them through the open window.

"I am so cold," she breathed, and she put her lips on his and wound one of her supple legs about his calf.

He tore himself away from her, backing into the doorway of his room. She stood her violin on the floor, leaning it against the wall, and came toward him showing her small white teeth.

"No, don't come!" he said loudly. "Can't you see that I don't want you?"

"Darling, you don't mean that! Not want your Sarah?"

He controlled himself and spoke more quietly. "It's just that I'm tired, Sarah. You know how it is with me, darling. You don't want me to go quite to pieces, do you? You've got to let me alone — till I'm better. Wake told you that, didn't he? He told you that what I needed was to be let alone."

"Wakefield spoiled you," she said.

She slipped past him into the room and laid herself down on the dishevelled bed. She held out both arms to him and put all her seductiveness into her smile.

"Come," she said. "Love will make you well."

He stood swaying in the doorway. Should he run down the stairs and escape? But no, if he did that she would have his room, his blessed retreat, the place where he had been happy with Wakefield.

He came to the bed and, taking her by the arms, dragged her wildly from it and thrust her out into the passage. She struggled with him. They struggled on the stairway. She screamed and, as though the scream had loosed something in her, followed it with others loud and piercing.

Renny had just come into the hall below followed by his spaniels. At the sound of the screams Floss dropped her tail between her legs and backed to the door but Merlin lifted his blind face and barked as though in anger. Renny came to the foot of the stairs, his jaw dropped in consternation. "My God, what's the matter?"

Finch loosed Sarah and hung against the banister.

"She won't let me alone!" he shouted. "I tell you she won't give me any peace! She's driving me mad!"

Renny turned to Sarah who was leaning against the wall. He asked — "What's the matter with him?"

"Wakefield has been turning him against me," she moaned. "He won't let me touch him."

"It's maddening!" shouted Finch. "I tell you, she gives me no peace. She's been fiddling on the stairway — right to my door — and she knows how it hurts my head! I tell you — I can't bear any more!" He broke into hysterical crying, clinging desperately to the banister.

At the sound of his crying Sarah began to cry too, with a wailing sound like keening at a wake. Ernest who had been busy at his needlework in the drawing room, came into the hall carrying it. Anxious, in the midst of his excitement, not to lose a stitch, he tried to set his needle in the canvas but instead thrust it into his thumb. He doubled over with pain. Merlin continued his angry barking. Nicholas, confined to his bed with gout — the first attack since his return to Jalna — beat on the floor with his stick and shouted:

"What's going on out there? I say, what's going on?"

Renny bounded up the stairs and put his arms about Finch. He led him into his own room and set him on the bed. Then he returned to the passage and shut the door behind him. Merlin was grinning at his side, snuffling at the door, but Floss stayed below with Ernest. Renny called down:

"Uncle Ernest, take Sarah down with you. Give her a glass of something. Make her shut up!"

"I'm all right," said Sarah. She went slowly down the stairs to Ernest who led her into the drawing room.

All was quiet now but for the thumping from Nicholas's room. Renny opened his door and looked in. Nicholas was sitting on the side of his bed, his face contorted as he tried to put his bandaged foot to the floor.

"Get back to bed, Uncle Nick," said Renny. "It's all over."

"But what was it?" asked Nicholas almost piteously. Gladly he heaved up his leg and got under the covers again. Merlin went to him, nosed for his face, found and licked it.

"Down, you old fool," said Nicholas, cuffing him.

"It was a row," said Renny, "between Sarah and Finch. They've got on each other's nerves, I guess, and no wonder, with the way he carries on with his head and all. It's enough to drive the girl crazy. Still — she's no right to go fiddling at him when she knows how it hurts."

"Fiddling at him!" groaned Nicholas. "Fiddling at him!"

"Yes. Who does she think she is? Nero? I tell you, she'll find her Rome burning one of these days if she doesn't look out. Finch is in no condition to cope with a high-strung wife."

"I call her a harlot," said Nicholas.

"Well," Renny's forehead was knit. "I'm going back to the poor young devil to see what I can do with him. If he keeps on like this he'll be in a sanatorium. This house is enough to drive a man to drink. Come, Merlin —" He went out, followed by the spaniel.

XVI

His Own Room

NICHOLAS WAS PROPPED up in bed reading when Renny returned. He laid down his paper and looked expectantly into his nephew's face. Renny said:

"He's quiet now. But he's in a bad way. I wonder if I ought to send for the doctor."

"What is it all about?" asked Nicholas irritably.

Renny sat down on a chair by the side of the bed, folded his arms and drew down his mouth at the corners.

"Are you going to tell me, or aren't you?" demanded Nicholas.

"He's turned against Sarah, Uncle Nick. He can't bear to have her near him. Do you think he may be going out of his mind? They say it's a sign, when you turn against those you love."

Nicholas returned his look with one still more sombre. Then he said, emphatically:

"No, no, I don't believe any such thing. She's just got on his nerves. He's been under a strain ... all those recitals ... he's tired out. Then — she's a queer girl — I never could make her out."

"She's damned passionate — behind that cold face of hers."

Nicholas growled — "Hmph, well, my wife was damned cold, under an alluring exterior."

"You turned against her, didn't you?"

"Absolutely. But in a normal way — no hysterics on either side."

"He says he can't stay in the house with her. He looks awful. I believe he'll go nutty if she starts her fiddling again."

"Send him away for a change."

"When I suggested that, he said he wouldn't leave his old room. He said he never wanted to leave it again."

Nicholas ran his hand distractedly through his tumbled grey hair. He said:

"Bring me a whiskey and soda. I want to think."

"Remember your gout."

Nicholas groaned back to his pillow.

"Lord, yes! Give me a little plain soda, then. I'm thirsty. Just put a spot in the soda, enough to flavour it. I'll cut out meat today."

While he was sipping Ernest came into the room his thumb bound in a handkerchief.

"It was a strange coincidence," he complained, "that I should have had my needle in my hand when Sarah screamed. The result is that I gave myself a disagreeable wound. I'm wondering if there might be a possibility of lockjaw."

"Not a chance," growled his brother.

"Well, I am relieved to hear you say that, but really it is very painful," He turned to Renny. "How is that young man behaving now?"

In brief sentences Renny told him.

"They must be separated for a time," said Ernest. "My idea is this — let Sarah go to the fox farm. She can make it quite nice with the things Finch and you bought and some of the furniture from our attic. She won't have much to buy. I've suggested it to her and she falls in with the idea. She does not want to be far from Finch yet she realizes that he must be humoured."

Nicholas looked admiringly at his brother, then deprecatingly at Renny.

"Trust old Ernie," he said, "to find the solution. I think it's the best plan possible. That house is standing empty. Let Sarah live in it. Let her pay a good rent for it."

"No, no," said Renny. "I couldn't ask her to pay rent."

"It would be in very bad taste," agreed Ernest. "Especially as she holds the mortgage on Jalna."

"All the more reason," said Nicholas. "Get out of her all you can."

Renny shook his head. "Impossible. But Uncle Ernest's idea is a good one! We'll shoot Sarah over there as soon as possible. I shan't be sorry to have her out of Jalna. I don't wonder that she gets on young Finch's nerves."

"It will be nice to have another house in the family to visit," said Ernest.

That very day two scrubbing women were sent to prepare the house for Sarah. Noah Binns was sent to cut the grass and tidy the flower borders. The next morning a farm wagon conveyed two loads of furniture and Meg went to town with Sarah to buy curtains and kitchen utensils. A cousin of Alma Patch was discovered who could both cook and wait at table. At evening Sarah and her French maid glided through the ravine to the fox farm. Sarah was excited as a child.

Before she left she wrote a note to Finch and slipped it under his door, running down the attic stairs afterward with a tapping of high heels. She did not resent that he refused to see her. She would not have had things other than as they were. It was all a part of the wonderful game of marriage with Finch whose every mood, every gesture, fascinated her. She pictured him behind the door watching her note appear, going fearfully to fetch it, reading its passionate fearless phrases with a quickening heart, struggling feverishly against the physical longing for her. Soon, soon, he would cry out that longing!

Finch listened to the tapping of her retreat, saw the note appear under the door. He saw it appear, and disappear under the edge of the worn carpet. He left it so hidden. He turned his head on his pillow, looking peacefully at the dim flowers of the wallpaper. He wanted nothing but to remain where he was. In this room he could come breast to breast with the soul of his boyhood. The walls spoke to him. The leaning roof bent like a wing above him. The faded patchwork was a shield between him and the world. Sometimes the pain was with him; sometimes he lay weak and calm, free from it.

He refused to let the servant come in to make his bed but got up when it became too tumbled and put it in order himself. He went to the linen cupboard along the passage and got clean sheets when there was no one about. He loved his room so, he wanted no one but himself to enter it.

He lay listening to the noises of the house. Adeline's laughter and rages, the boom of Nicholas's voice, the barking or growls of dogs, the shuffle of Bessie's carpet sweeper. Sometimes he heard the thud of horses' hoofs beneath his window and once a stableboy's shrill whistle sounded like the notes of a violin. He sprang up in bed, starting with sweat, and was only reassured when the whistle ended in a guffaw. When Renny or his uncles came in to see him he pretended to be asleep or that the pain made talk impossible. He was ravenous for his breakfast but the other meals were carried away almost untouched.

At the end of ten days Piers, without warning, appeared at his bed-side. In all this time Finch had scarcely given him a thought except to remember him as the grand and tormenting companion of his boyhood. Now he looked up at him in wonder, at his fine shoulders, at his face enriched by a long summer of outdoor work, his hands strong and firm from the handling of horses.

Piers said, with his derisive grin, but not feeling as sure of himself as he looked — "Taking a rest cure, eh? How do you feel?"

"A bit better, I think," mumbled Finch, the old sheepish look flickering into his face. "I was pretty tired."

"Well, you've had time to rest and, if you stay here much longer, you're going to make yourself into an invalid. What you need now is some exercise."

Finch turned his face away. "I'm not up to it yet." he muttered.

"And never will be — if you don't make the effort. I've come to take you out — anywhere you like. I'll leave that to you — but you've got to get out of this bed and out of this house."

"Look here — I simply can't — when I move, the pain — you don't understand, Piers."

"I think I understand you — about as well as anyone can. And I know that, if you're let alone, you'll never get up."

"Rot!"

"It isn't rot. You know it's the truth. You have a long stretch of life ahead of you and a lot of work to do. Come now" — Piers's tone changed to one of almost entreaty — "let me help you on with your clothes. I have the car at the door. I'll take you for a nice run along the lakeshore. There is a glorious breeze. The leaves are beginning to turn."

For answer Finch rolled over and drew the bedclothes over his head.

In an instant Piers was on him. Grasping the coverings he stripped them from the bed and gave Finch a sounding smack on the buttocks.

"Come now, up with you!" he said.

Finch suddenly discovered that he wanted to surrender himself to Piers. He wanted his strong hands to master him. He let Piers help him on with his clothes, half laughing, feeling very shaky in the legs.

Piers held his arm as they went down the stairs. "Does he know," thought Finch, "that I am dizzy, or is he just bullying me?"

Not a soul was about. Had Piers warned them out of the way? The car, bright after a hosing, stood on the drive. Piers put Finch into the seat beside him.

Softly the car rolled beneath the arching trees. A change had taken place since Finch had last looked about him. The leaves of the birch trees were turning to gold, the oak to russet, the maple to blazing red. The stubble fields lay swarthy in the sun and goldenrod and Michaelmas daisies rose, bright-headed and tough-stemmed, by the fences. Fragile flowers were gone and red mountain ash berries told of frosts to come. Finch leant back in the seat, absorbing the scene, not speaking.

They passed along the shore of the lake that lay ruffled under the harebell-blue arch of the sky. A fringe of foam crept up the sandy shore, subsided and again frothed up. I must forget, thought Finch, how I once tried to drown myself in it. It was too beautiful, the way I sank into its brightness. I was stronger when I was drowning than I am now. Why did Eden save me?

Piers let the car slow down and lighted a cigarette. Everything he did with his hands was right, Finch thought. Not a hair's-breadth of indecision, just strong, easy, capable movements.

Piers slid his blue eyes to Finch's face and away again. There was something benevolent in the glance. He said carelessly:

"You've always taken things too seriously."

"I know," muttered Finch.

"Even as a young boy, you were the same."

"No need to tell me that."

"I was a callous cub."

"Don't let's talk, Piers."

"I'm not going to. But I do want to get you out of the rut you're in. I know that I'm not artistic — no imagination, or that sort of thing. But I know when horse or man is headed for a fall. I knew that Eden was. But he was never any good. You are. I knew that spoiling Wake was bad for him but no one else could see that. I always felt that Renny's marriage to Alayne would turn out badly for them both. But nothing could stop them. I'd like to see you make a good job of your life. You started out so well. You got all Gran's money. You have a talent that ought to make you famous — according to what the critics say. You've married a rich wife. But — you took your legacy too seriously. I know that we made it hard for you but shouldn't have let a little criticism drive you to —"

"Don't," interrupted Finch twisting his fingers together.

"I'm not going to…. Then you took your music too seriously. You let it be your master, instead of mastering it…. Now you are taking your marriage too seriously."

"My God!" broke out Finch, "you took your own marriage seriously enough — when you found out —"

Piers's face darkened. "I did take it seriously. But not too seriously. I kept my head. No one can deny that. I wasn't going to have my marriage wrecked."

"You *loved* Pheasant!"

Piers stared. "And don't you —"

"I hate her! No … not hate … It's more like fear —"

"There you go — Fear!"

"I tell you, she stifles me…. She takes the life out of me…. I can't live with her, Piers!" His voice rose. He looked so wild that Piers let out the speed and growled:

"No one is going to ask you to. Not till you want. But — will you just put yourself into my hands — do what I say for a few days? Perhaps a week?"

"What do you want me to do?"

"Come for a drive with me every day. I'll not trouble you by talking like this again. You'll just get the air and a change of scene. Then, at night, I want you to take a good horn of Scotch — enough to make you forget your troubles. You have no idea how much good it will do you. It's the best medicine you can have. Will you do it?"

Finch gave a little laugh. "It sounds easy," he said. "I don't mind taking the whiskey if you think it will do me good. I'm not sure about the motoring. I like my own room, you know."

"You will never get well while you stick in it. I know what I'm talking about. What you need is movement in the open air. Why, you look better already!"

Finch gave in. That night Piers came to Jalna and administered the dose of Scotch with a steady hand and a benign eye. A rich glow enveloped Finch. His nerves tingled, then relaxed. He fell into a heavy sleep. But next day the pain in his head was worse and he refused to leave his room.

XVII

Early Autumn

RENNY WALKED BESIDE the wagon that conveyed Clara Lebraux's furniture, together with some pieces from the attic at Jalna, to the fox farm. The load did not include the things he himself had bought at the sale. He liked having the bookcase and cabinet in his bedroom and he had taken the coffee table to his office in the stables and had arranged his smoking things on it. He could not bring himself to return these pieces to the fox farm.

As he helped Sarah to arrange the rooms — Meg was also there, her presence adding comfort to the scene — he reflected on the vicissitudes of this house. He could scarcely believe that Clara and Pauline were gone from it forever and he would have given much to have seen Clara's sturdy figure capably putting the place in order, Pauline, by turns serious and gay, in place of Sarah gliding helplessly about and her French maid making a mountain out of every molehill. They were unreal to him and he liked reality. That was what he had liked best about Clara, her warm vibrant reality. Still Sarah was taking this affair with admirable calm. She was in a difficult position but was uncomplaining. Indeed she seemed to feel more pleasure than unhappiness in making this separate home to which she expected to bring Finch as soon as he was fit.

Meg was affectionate toward Sarah. She praised her openly for unselfish devotion to Finch, comparing it with the cold selfishness of some wives, and if her lips did not frame Alayne's name, her tone breathed it.

All the family began to find Alayne's continued absence suspicious. As they watched the mails and no letters came from her to Renny they were certain that she had left him for good. Before long she acknowledged this in a letter to Pheasant, who kept her posted on the welfare of her child and who indeed never failed to send the most minute gossip connected with the family. Pheasant felt an isolated pride in being the only one to whom Alayne wrote but she wished that Alayne would write more frankly to her. There was something detached and impersonal about her letters. Pheasant felt sure that she had more to tell than of the trivial doings of herself and her aunt.

Ernest and Nicholas were hurt by Alayne's not writing to them. A coldness had sprung up between them and they felt that the fault was on Alayne's side. She was changed, she was cold and her old graceful charm seemed to have left her. At the same time they were not ill-pleased that Sarah had removed her presence, for it was an emphatic one and now they felt freer to live their own lives in their own way. They laughingly called Adeline the little mistress of Jalna. She liked this and put on an air of authority in the house. She was four years old and she was a woman of authority. So she felt, and Alma Patch could no longer control her. She got up, went to bed when she pleased, and ate what her keen taste demanded. Food that would cause pain to Pheasant's boys affected her not at all. She ate hard russet apples, juicy peaches skin and all, slices of current cake between meals. She drank strong tea, lemonade, cider, or buttermilk. She threw off all authority and marched fresh-skinned and firm-fleshed to meet life.

Renny had bought her her first riding suit, had it made to order by his own tailors, who marvelled at her proportions, so fine for her age. In truth she looked noble with her auburn curls shortened a bit and her legs as straight as God could make them.

Soon she vied with Mooey in schooling the ponies. He was envious of her daring and strained every nerve to hold his superiority as a nine-year-old. Renny gave his time to preparing his horses for the shows.

His hope lay in the newly acquired mare, tempered by the doubt that he would ever break her of her strange habit of walking on her hind legs. These legs were so thin and she held them so stiffly that the stableman nicknamed her "Mrs. Spindles," and the name stuck. In her lay Renny's hope of paying Sarah the interest on the mortgage, of which two install-ments were now due.

The Vaughans' position was not so straightened as it had been. Meg's paying guests had been profitable, but to produce the interest for Finch was out of the question. This caused Meg and Maurice little anxiety because Finch apparently did not notice that the time for payment had arrived. He spent his days in his room, only getting up to tidy his bed and not again repeating either of Piers's prescriptions.

With Piers and Pheasant things had improved. Crops had been munificent, fruit and stock had both sold comparatively well. The Miss Laceys had decided to spend the rest of their lives in California and agreed that Piers should buy their house on easy terms. Piers made his first payment and came home to tea hilarious. He kissed Pheasant and the baby and gave each of the boys twenty-five cents to spend. He walked round the garden saying "My garden" — Pheasant knocked loudly on the door crying "My door." The boys, taking it up, ran all over the place shouting "Mine — mine" to everything they touched.

Heavy autumn rains came and Sarah's longing for Finch grew beyond all bounds. She came to Jalna at dusk on a day of gales and rain, wrapped in a white waterproof cape. She looked like one of the silver birch trees given motion and sight for its longing. The rain dripped from her as she stood waiting for Wragge to open the door. A black tendril of hair lay flat against her cheek. Once more the leaves of the Virginia creeper were beginning to fall into the porch, as every autumn they closed the chapter of the past summer. Merlin, dripping wet after a prowl, came snuffling at Sarah's heels. He raised his blind face and gave her a deprecating grin as he recognized her, then pushed ahead to be first to enter the house.

Wragge was long in answering the door. She could hear his steps coming, then he waited to put on the light. Merlin could scarcely endure his anxiety. He pushed his stern against Sarah, scratched the door and whined. There were so many scratches on the door that these new ones made no impression — no more than another fallen leaf on the porch.

When the door opened Merlin shot into the hall and, placing the side of his head on the carpet, propelled himself in an effort to dry his long ears. Wragge looked surprised.

"Oah," he said, and hesitated, as though he were a jailer.

"I came to see Mr. Whiteoak — Mr. Renny," Sarah said, softly.

"Oah, you can see 'im," said Wragge. "Will you come in, please?"

Sarah smiled and asked — "How is my husband?"

Wragge's defences melted before that strange sweet smile which lighted only the lower part of the face, leaving the eyes cold and grey beneath their fine black brows. He glanced toward the door of the sitting room and spoke almost in a whisper.

"Pretty bad, I should s'y, ma'am. 'E takes very little nourishment — 'im as always was the 'eartiest heater in the family. And 'is nerves! Well — if nerves ever was unstrung, 'is are."

"Wragge, I must go up to him," said Sarah.

Wragge's face puckered in worry. "I doan't knaow if I ought to let you, ma'am — without permission. It might set 'im off. 'E won't see no one."

"But I must," said Sarah. "I promise you I won't set him off. It will do him good to see me."

"Well, 'm, if you do, I 'ope you won't mention music to 'im, for 'e's turned clean against it. Only the other day Miss Adeline began to strum on the pianner and 'e came tearing down the stairs enough to frighten you and shouted to 'er to stop. 'E looked 'alf mad."

"I'll not talk of music, Wragge." She slid past him into the hall and was halfway up the stairs when the door of the sitting room opened and Renny came out. In two strides he was at the banister. He thrust his hand between the spindles and caught hold of her cape.

"You dare!" she said. "You dare try to prevent me seeing Finch!"

"I can't let you go up! It would upset him."

"It is you and your brothers who are coming between us…. Let me go up!" She tore open her cape at the throat and let it fall in his hand. She ran like a hare up the two flights of steps to Finch's door.

He was after her, two steps at a time.

Merlin raised his muzzle and gave his deep, bewildered bark. Wragge picked up Sarah's cape and hung it carefully on the rack from the top of which the carved fox's head grinned down at him.

Renny caught her just as she laid her hand on the doorknob. He held her tight, their two hearts pounding. He said, in a fierce whisper:

"No — no — you're not going in!"

"I am! Let me go! Finch!"

Renny stifled her mouth against his shoulder. He pressed her body against his and carried her struggling down the stairs to the hall. He took her inside the sitting room and shut the door behind them.

"Don't be a fool," he said. "You'll spoil all your chances with him — if you force yourself on him now."

"You are determined to keep us apart."

"Sarah, you are a stupid woman Can't you *feel* that sometimes a husband may want to be left alone?"

Her eyes shone with hate. "I feel why your wife has left *you* alone! You are absolutely ruthless!"

"Now you're talking nonsense. But I have a sick boy on my hands. Can't you be patient for a little? You were brought up to be patient. You weren't allowed to put yourself first."

"I am in love."

She stood before him, sleek, black-haired, not disarranged after the struggle. Everything about him was repellent to her. She hated the look of authority in his eyes, as though his word were law in that house, hated his hard, shapely hands with their close-cut nails that looked as though they were scrubbed with a stiff brush. The hate was all the more poignant because she envied him, for Finch's sake, his formidable strength.

"I am in love," she repeated. "And the one I love is ill and you are keeping us apart. Your own sister thinks we should be together."

He made a contemptuous grimace. "What does Meg know of his condition? I tell you, no one knows but Wakefield and me."

"And both of you hate women," she cried, "or you couldn't treat them so! He drove Pauline to a convent and you drove Alayne back to her old life. You are trying to turn Finch —"

He interrupted — "I am trying to save Finch from an absolute breakdown."

"I demand one thing," she said. "He must be seen by a specialist. I will bring one here myself. Finch must see him."

"Very well — do."

"If the specialist says he can be moved I will take him to my house."

"Very well — do."

"Oh, you think you're safe! You think you have his spirit broken! You think you've got him fast. You want to rule the house — as your old grandmother did! She stood up like granite while other people stumbled and fell. If you were put out of this house your strength would go. It's the awful pride of this house that makes you so arrogant. Jalna reeks of pride and tyranny."

He grinned at her, not ill-pleased.

"The house is all right," he said. "Gran was all right. We are all all right. But you are letting your feelings run away with you. No one wants to see Finch on his feet — back at his work — more than I do. Bring the specialist along. Perhaps Finch will see him. Perhaps he won't. We can only try."

"I will see one tomorrow," she said. She passed him, hating the smell of tobacco and horses that came from him, and went into the hall. With great deference Wragge took the white cape from the rack and put it about her shoulders. Only the moment before he had deftly stepped back from his position with his ear at the panel of the sitting-room door. There was a humorous melancholy in his eyes.

A gust of wind, with a splutter of rain on it, came in when the front door was opened. Floss came too, wet and draggled. Merlin met and kissed her. They both looked expectantly at Sarah, wanting her to go so that the door might be shut on the night. Renny asked:

"Shall I go with you through the ravine? It's getting dark."

"No — thank you. I'd rather go alone."

The door was shut on her. Renny and Rags exchanged a look. Rags said:

"I think I'll fetch you a little gin and water, sir. There's nothing like it to steady the nerves."

"Thanks, Rags. Where are my uncles?"

"Just in the drawing room, sir. It's a blessing the wind's 'owling like all possessed. They've 'eard nothink."

Renny joined them, pausing by Ernest's chair to admire the progress he had made with his needlework that day. Nicholas was reading aloud from *Henry Esmond*, in his sonorous voice. The wind strove against the French windows and cried out in the chimney. But Boney sat silent on his perch, muffled, somnolent, one half-open eye sufficing to show him all he wanted of the world.

"Sarah's been here," observed Renny tersely.

Nicholas laid down his book. "Well, well, why didn't she come in to see us?"

"She was rather upset. She wants to bring a specialist to see Finch. I think it may be a good idea. But I dare say Finch won't see him. Sarah's a bit of a fool."

"Why?" asked Ernest putting his needle into the calyx of a flower.

"Well — she seems to think I'm trying to keep Finch and her apart."

"I'll tell her that's not so," said Ernest.

"If you ask me," said Nicholas, taking out his pipe, I think her case is hopeless."

The shadow on Renny's face deepened. He had a feeling almost of dread toward Sarah.

He talked for a while with his uncles then went to the room where the two children slept. The wind had disturbed them and they looked up at him from their cots like two small, alert animals. Which one would he go to first? Roma invited him with her slanting eyes while she kept her lips folded together. Adeline wriggled her toes against the sheet, inviting him. He went and caught the toes in his fingers and tweaked them. She was galvanized into activity. She leaped from under the bedclothes and sprang up and down on the mattress. She threw him daring looks from under her lashes.

"And you were tucked in so neatly!" he exclaimed.

"I don't mind! You'll tuck me in again, won't you? You get up too, Roma! You jump too! Up and down — up and down — *très jolie* — *très jolie* — I talk French, Daddy!" Roma scrambled to her feet also. The two tiny girls jumped and chanted in unison. Then Renny gathered them both into his arms and they smothered him with hugs.

He hated what he had to do when they were tucked into their cots and he drew a deep breath before he went to Finch's room.

Finch started up from the corner where he was sitting in the darkness, when the door opened. In the light from the passage Renny saw him standing, tall and gaunt, a dressing gown over his pyjamas.

Renny asked casually — "Don't you want a light?"

"No — perhaps — I don't care," muttered Finch.

Renny closed the door and put on the light. The room was unspeakably forlorn. Finch, with that look of suffering on his face, the dressing gown slack on his thin body, brought Eden poignantly to Renny's mind. He said anxiously:

"You have no cough, have you?"

"No — I don't think so.... Renny, I know who was out there."

"She came to see you but I wouldn't let her in. She's gone."

"Don't let her in — ever! I — I — don't want to see her ... she tires me with her talk and her ... You see, Renny, this pain makes me different. I'm not like I was when we married. I loved her then — I think — and I loved music but ... I can't bear to think of either now ... love and music are torture to me...." He began to bite at his thumbnail almost violently, as though to steady the shaking of his hand.

"Don't bite your nails! You may be sure I'll never let her in. You shall not be forced to see anyone you don't want to see."

"But — supposing you weren't here?"

"I don't think she'll come again. But she wants you to see a specialist and I think you ought to do it. We are — none of us — satisfied with the way you're getting on. He would probably fix you up in no time."

"I have seen a specialist!" said Finch excitedly. "I saw that French specialist. He was a nice man. He understood. He understood that all those recitals and the travelling were a strain and he understood about Sarah too — without my ever telling him. And he said the only thing for it was rest and to keep to myself. Sarah never understood that I needed privacy. She was always there. She loved going from place to place — meeting people — showing me off. She would sleep half the day but

— she wouldn't let me sleep at night! I forgot how to sleep. And my eyes hurt and then the pain began."

"I know," said Renny. "Still I think you ought to see a doctor whom she will choose. You can tell him just how you feel — about everything. She will believe it if she hears it from him."

An idea came to Finch. He would see the specialist and through him make Sarah understand that he could never live with her again.

The next day she brought the doctor to see him, waiting in the drawing room with Nicholas and Ernest while the interview took place. She sat rigid and almost silent except when Renny came and stood in the doorway for a moment, then she pointed to him and said:

"There's the man, Uncle Nick and Uncle Ernest, who is trying to separate me from the one I love."

"The uncles know that is not true," said Renny.

"They can't deny it!"

"It was Uncle Ernie who suggested your going to the fox farm and Uncle Nick agreed."

"It is you who stand between me and Finch," she repeated sullenly.

"It will all come right, my dear," said Ernest.

Nicholas puffed silently at his pipe.

In his room Finch was being diagnosed by the specialist. He was a spare, grey-faced man who looked rather ill himself. He had neither heart, humour, nor understanding, and did well in the diagnosis of sensitive patients. He had even written a book on diseases of the nerves, a copy of which always stood upright on the desk in his office. He dressed in and copied the manner of Harley Street. His handsome car and chauffeur in livery waited outside. The antagonism Finch instinctively felt towards him made the interview easier. He answered the doctor's questions in a cold, hostile voice. When the doctor said that a special ultraviolet ray treatment was called for, Finch agreed apathetically to go to a hospital three times a week. He would agree to any treatment he said, looking with cold hostility into the specialist's eyes, but he could never agree to live with his wife again. Would the doctor make her understand that? It would be well if he could.

Renny took Finch in the car to the hospital in town for the prescribed treatments, calling for him promptly at the specified time. Finch envied him the interval which he knew would be spent with his horsey friends, while he lay stretched on a cot, all his nerves tingling under the electric rays, the experienced fingers of a nurse massaging his neck and spine. He lay there supine under the hands, listening to the strange cries of a dumb child who was being treated in the next cubicle and the voluble groans of a stout Italian on the other side. He rather liked the treatment. He liked his nurse and she liked him. She seemed dubious as to its efficacy but the specialist dropped in for a few moments each time and pompously encouraged her.

At first Finch felt that here, after all, was something that was going to help him. He liked the drives to town, slouched in the car beside Renny who drove so differently to Piers. One never knew what Renny or the car would do next — the car seeming to try to behave like a horse, while Renny viewed its efforts with suspicion. The weather was wild and rainy. The lake tossed foam from its greyness. The ugly suburbs of the town were hidden in a sweeping mist. The windshield steamed. There was ease in Finch's pain and he looked forward to the firm manipulation of the nurse's hands. How often she would pause and ask — "Do you think this is really helping you?" And Finch would answer — "Yes, I am sure it is. I slept better last night." When he had got home he had fallen into an exhausted stupor. The grey-faced specialist now looked at him with approval. He almost beamed when he entered the cubicle and found Finch prostrate under the powerful ray, the nurse skillfully kneading his spinal nerves. But, driving home, Renny slid anxious looks at him.

Then, one black afternoon of blowing leaves and gusty clouds, Finch began to cry on the way home. Renny, with set face, looked straight ahead of him for a space. Tears rolled down Finch's face. He felt too weak to wipe them away.

Renny said — "You're all right. We shall be home soon. Come now — there's a good fellow." He spoke soothingly, as to a frightened horse.

Finch tried to speak but he could not. He felt the tears running down his cheeks, warm and salty. He felt the car leap forward. Renny was speeding to get him home ... back to Jalna — back to the safety of his own dear room....

When they were there, behind the closed door, Finch said — "I can't go on with it…. I can't go on…. The pain is worse … it's like claws tearing." He turned his long grey-blue eyes, full of suffering, on Renny.

Renny answered curtly — "No need to go on. You shall do just as you like."

"What I want is," said Finch, "what I want …"

"Yes, what is it that you want?"

"I want to go back there" — he made a tragic gesture toward the bed — "and stay till I am well."

"All right. I think it is the best thing you can do."

Finch's gratitude hurt him. He helped Finch to undress, laying his glasses on the chest of drawers, hanging his coat in the cupboard.

"I'll be better soon," said Finch. "Only I can't go to the hospital again and I can't see Sarah. You'll make her understand that, won't you, Renny? I can't see her!"

"You'll get over this."

"I'll play again — I think. But I'll never live with Sarah. She — she — oh, I can't explain! But — I tell you — look here — I tell you —" He looked wild; he became incoherent.

"See her and tell her so."

"No!"

"Write to her."

"I can't write. I can't hold the pen. It — isn't legible."

"My God, you have got yourself into a mess! Is your head paining now?"

"Horribly."

Renny drew a sharp breath. "Well — get to bed! We'll see what that will do for you. I'll tell Sarah."

"I wish you'd get her to go away from the fox farm. She seems — so near."

"I can't drive the woman out of her house. She is barely settled."

"But you'll see her today? And tell her about me? You'll tell her I can't…."

"Yes, I'll see her today. Keep your hair on."

As Renny walked through the ravine to the fox farm he considered with acute discomfort the position into which he was now forced. He had to tell Sarah that the husband she apparently doted on could not and would not see her, that he refused to contemplate a life anywhere near to her. This at a time when she held a heavy mortgage on Jalna and had already accused himself of coming between her and Finch! How many distasteful things he had had to do of late! He could scarcely reckon them up. Indeed to reckon them up was the last thing he wanted to do. He wanted to put them out of his mind during the respite of this walk through the ravine.

He felt rudderless without his spaniels at his heels. He had left them at home because of Sarah's pug who would go into spasms of barking at sight of them, persist in barking throughout the visit. He was a spoilt little devil.

The rain beat down on him, the wind beat the wet branches of the trees that seemed all too ready to sacrifice their leaves on the icy altar of winter. The trees this season seemed to have no pride in rich foliage, changing to despondent yellow and brown instead of their brighter tones. Their wet limbs discovered the forsaken birds' nests and a faint twitter of birdsong came from the naked branches of a wild cherry tree.

The boards of the little bridge were plastered with wet leaves and edged with vivid green moss. The stream, welling full, hurried between the rank borders of long grass, harsh iris leaves, and a few pale forget-me-nots. It gave back no reflection but detached, sullen, occupied solely by its own swift progression, slid under the bridge, its voice lost in the wind and rain.

Renny laid his hands on the slippery smoothness of the railing and looked down into the stream. His eyes followed its turnings almost unseeing so familiar was the scene, yet an essence rich and comforting entered into him from it. It held so many memories for him — memories from his very infancy — that he knew its changes as the changes on the faces of his own family. But, unlike them, it was yearly rejuvenated.

An inner chamber of his mind opened and out of it came the remembrance of that scene between him and Alayne, after she had discovered him with Clara. Again he saw Alayne, shadowy behind the electric torch as she turned it full on him. He saw her bending over the stream, clinging to the rail, in an agony of jealousy, in this very spot. Where he now stood. Her body had hung over the rail here ... her dear body....

He was startled by that sudden feeling of her dearness. That, combined with the great distance between them.... She had gone out of his life ... gone away.... She was not going to live with him ever again.... Not until this minute had he taken it completely in, the fact that she was lost to him. And it seemed a strange moment for this realization to come, when he had his mind so filled with the affairs of someone else.

Now the stream, as though it reversed its mood, gave him back the reflection of Alayne — not tortured by hate but happy, relaxed, her blue eyes beaming up at him, her white arms round his neck. He saw her body — her dear body — strong and sweet in love for him. Yet he had not been able to shield her from what had come between them. And it was false, a traitorous disruption of their love, because no woman could ever put her out of her place in his heart and no man rivalled him in hers.... He had loved Clara. He still loved Clara. It had been a wrench to give her up — as a friend who understood him without explaining, who accepted him as he was, without yearning to make him over. Their interval of passion had, to him, been only as a red poppy blossoming in the rich grain of their friendship. It had been garnered with the grain. It had, now that all was over, taken on the sober hue of comradeship.

It seemed almost unbelievable to him when Sarah herself opened the door. It was unnatural to see her in that house. For an instant he saw in her stead Pauline, as a long-legged child, holding her pet fox in her arms, her dark hair framing her face. His heart contracted as he remembered how that face was now framed. And the little fox was dead....

Sarah looked at him startled, then said:

"You look like a brigand!"

"Do I?" He grinned, trying to look amicable.

"Yes — with that battered-looking hat pulled over your eyes and your collar turned up."

"I need to — it's raining like the devil." He took off his hat and the rain ran from its brim.

She looked at his head disclosed in the electric light. It was to her the head of an enemy, stark and invulnerable. His bright eyes roused a fierce antagonism in her.

After an embarrassed pat to the pug he followed Sarah into the living room. She sat down, arranging her skirts about her and touching the twists of her sleek hair, as though for his inspection. He waited for her to speak, which she did in a sweet, rather pleading tone.

"I hope you have brought me good news of Finch."

He looked at her speculatively. "No I'm afraid not. He won't go on with the treatments."

"Not go on! But he has just nicely begun."

He could not resist answering sarcastically:

"It may seem *nice* to you. He doesn't find it so. It drives him crazy."

"It is often like that at the first. It will help him later. It is helping him. The doctor says it is."

"Well, he ought to know. But Finch doesn't agree. He refuses to go to the hospital again or see the doctor again."

"You're glad!" she said hotly.

"I can't pretend I'm sorry. I've seen him going downhill for weeks."

"What is going to draw him up again? Tell me that?"

"Rest."

"Rest!" She spat out the word scornfully. "He's had nothing but rest for months! I must see him. I must see him at once. Nothing shall stop me!"

"Sarah, you cannot see him!"

"You shan't stop me!"

"I don't want to stop you."

"You do! You do!" she interrupted, not raising her voice but charging it with hate. "You are trying to take him from me. You want to see me cast out — alone!"

"What rot you talk! Why should I want to separate you?"

"Because you're jealous of his love for me. You know it has changed him."

He looked at her in wonder. "The things women get into their head!"

Sarah put her elbows on her knees and her chin in her palms, bending toward him. He had never seen her sit in this attitude before. She looked familiar yet unfamiliar and, like a highly strung horse, he mentally shied from her.

She said — "You really hate women. That is why you are so fascinating to the weak ones. But I see you just as you are." And she bent nearer as though for that fuller view.

"Your idea of me is as false as hell," he answered morosely. "I don't hate you or any other woman but I have to think of my brother. He's a sick boy —"

"Boy!" she interrupted. "There you go! Keeping him tied to you — calling him boy! I say he is a man — and my husband!"

"He acts like it, doesn't he?" He shewed his teeth at her and she had a desire to strike him. He added — "And like a husband!"

"He would be both — if he were away from you!"

"Sarah, in God's name, what do you want me to do?"

"I want you to let me go to see Finch."

He answered emphatically — "Finch will not see you. There is no use in persisting. Give him time. Go away somewhere. The change would do you good."

"Join Alayne, eh? Yes — tell me to join Alayne!"

"Now you're being just silly."

She twisted her fingers together. "Oh, I could be so happy here, in this little house — if only he would be his old self! I'd ask nothing better of life."

"Not Finch's music?"

"Our life would be a song."

She embarrassed him. He said:

"You talk like a crooner, Sarah. You only need to add — 'And nothing could go wrong!'"

Her pale face became paler. She rose and went to a window and looked into the dusk.

"You think none of my emotions are deep," she said, with her back to him, "but they are. I am in earnest when I say that I love this place. I love it because it is a part of Jalna. It was that way from the day I first saw it."

He went to her, smiling his gratification.

"Do you really, Sarah? It is nice, isn't it? You know, I don't want to hurt your feelings but I do think you're being pretty difficult about Finch.

I don't understand your attitude toward him but I do understand your feeling for Jalna."

She returned his smile with her small mischievous one, that had something wicked in it, like the lifting of a feline animal's lip.

"I like it so well," she returned, "that I wish I owned it."

His eyebrows shot up. "Do you really?"

"Yes…. I wish I owned it."

"Not much chance of that, Sarah!"

"I suppose not…. Will you stay and have dinner?"

The thought of a meal with Sarah in that house was repellent to him. And he did not like dinner at night. He was used to his evening meal of cold meat, some hot made dish, biscuits, and cheese.

The pug was so pleased at his going that it was genial, rubbing the wrinkled velvet of its nose against Renny's hand, seeming to screw its tail tighter. He gathered a handful of its fawn-coloured hide and gently rolled it. Sarah looked at them, enigmatic and smiling.

Under cover of the pug's good humour Renny said — "About the interest, Sarah…. It's overdue, I know…. It's been mounting up…. But I'll have it for you after I've been to the New York Horse Show. I expect to do something there with this new mare of mine."

Her laugh was almost inaudible. "You had better," she said, "or I may own Jalna yet."

He straightened himself to rigidity and said, incredulously:

"Surely such an idea has never entered your head!"

"Many a time," she answered coolly. "You would be surprised if you knew how often."

His incredulity was tinged with pride. He said, with a certain grimness:

"There isn't money enough in the world to buy Jalna. Why, I can't believe you have entertained such a thought! But I'm glad you appreciate it, Sarah. It's a fine old place. Gran put a good deal of herself into the building of it."

Sarah folded her arms, not aggressively but rather with resignation. "If I cannot have Finch," she said, "I shall try to get Jalna."

All the way home those words sounded in his ears. He ran, crushing the wet grass and ferns, repeating aloud — "Try to get Jalna! Yes — try it — do try it! By God — the cheek of the woman! Get Jalna — from me — she's out of her wits — if she ever had any!"

He crossed the bridge in two strides and mounted the steep path without slackening his speed. He threw open the little gate, stood on the lawn, his breath coming sharp and strong, and stared at the house as though to make sure of its invincibility. To think that Sarah, that queer cousin, that snaky wife of young Finch's, had cast acquisitive glances at the old house! It was enough to raise its roof — to shatter its windows in outrage.

But the house stood there, serene and even stolid under his inspection. It looked massive surrounded by the blackness of its evergreens. Light showed in the hall, the drawing room, and the nursery. The one in the drawing room came from a leaping fire. The uncles were there. Upstairs the babes were being put to bed. What of Finch?

Renny went to the side of the house and looked up at his window. There was no light. Lying there — the poor young devil — in the darkness — alone with his thoughts and his pain!

XVIII

A Day of Adeline

ADELINE WOKE ON this clear frosty morning even earlier than usual. There was a fanciful mystery in the first pink rays of sunlight that penetrated between the reddening leaves of the Virginia creeper which during the summer had begun to festoon across the window. The rays fell on to the quilt embroidered in blue forget-me-nots that her mother had made her and she lay still a moment remembering how she had used to sleep in her mother's room. She could remember her mother bending over her and the way her hair looked bright. Alayne! That was her name. Some day she would come back and bring presents. But Adeline liked sleeping upstairs in the nursery. She did what she liked. There was no one to say — "You shall not have another drink," or to stand quelling her with steady blue eyes till she stopped laughing and shouting. Adeline could do what she liked up in the nursery with Alma and little Roma. She was past four and no one in the house could make her mind except her father and she knew how to manage him.

She closed her eyes and lay looking at the pretty colour behind her lids. She knew that in another moment she was going to do something that would dispel the immobility of her body as a swift breeze would dispel the stillness of a little pool. Even now she felt the first ripples of motion running upward from her toes, flowing through her tender yet elastic muscles.

She broke into a ripple of laughter and scrambled to her feet. She stood in the middle of her crib and looked across the room at Roma, lying curled like a shell, fast asleep. Adeline laughed again, this time loudly and consciously, trying to wake Roma but she curled herself closer and slept on.

Adeline jumped up and down, enjoying the bouncing of the mattress beneath her, her red hair flying, her brown eyes shining, a being so thoroughly refreshed by sleep that it seemed she could never be tired again.

She jumped so high that she all but lost her balance. This sobered her a little. She put her hands on the railing of the crib and looked over. She noticed a worn spot on the carpet that she had not seen before. She thought she would spit on it.

She gathered a supply of saliva in her mouth and let it dribble over her pouting red lip on to the carpet. It did not hit the worn spot. She tried to gather saliva for a fresh venture but apparently she had used all there was.

Masterfully she threw a leg over the side of the crib, then turned on her stomach and slid toward the floor. Her nightdress was caught and her deliciously dimpled body glowed pink in the frosty air. So she hung for a space, then found her feet and trotted to the window.

She saw on the ledge a small, blue butterfly, late beyond reason, opening and closing his wings like two gently waving diminutive fans. A roguish smile dented her cheek. She put out a hand, with fingers curled, just over the butterfly. It folded its wings, watching her. Her hand swooped, closed. She had it safely. She squeezed it in glee. Then she cautiously opened her hand and again shut it, after one glance. An expression of ferocity darkened her brow. She put her shut hand between her knees and pressed knees and fist together, jumping up and down to gain force. Then suddenly her face became a blank, she straightened, spread her palm and gazed long at it.

She wiped her hand against her nightdress. She felt lonely and pouted out her lips.

Then she saw Roma and galloped to her. She pressed her face between the bars of the cot and put it close to Roma's. How funny the face looked with the eyelashes pressed close together and the two round holes in the nose, the mouth open a little! She looked closely into Roma's mouth. She laughed into it, their breaths mingling.

"*Ah, non, non, non!*" said Roma, pushing at her. But Adeline would not go. She began to roar like a lion and in a moment they were romping together.

Alma came to dress them, looking apprehensively at Adeline. She carried a jug of warm water which she emptied into the basin.

"I won't be washed!" said Adeline.

"Just your face," pleaded Alma.

Adeline snatched up a washcloth and wet it in the cold water in the ewer and scrubbed her creamy cheeks to flame. She dried them on a corner of a bath towel. Alma stripped Roma of her nightdress and she stood, a white sliver of humanity, shivering by the washing stand.

Adeline went to the cupboard where her riding breeches and coat were hung and threw open the door. Alma rushed at her. They scuffled.

"I will wear them!" stormed Adeline.

"You mustn't! 'Tisn't allowed, first thing in the morning!" hissed Alma.

Roma began to rub herself with a jelly-like cake of soap.

Adeline lay down on the floor preparing to roll and scream, then she changed her mind, got up and went to a chair where the clothes she had worn yesterday lay. These were a pair of outgrown breeches and jersey that had belonged to young Maurice. Alma watched her with relief and disapproval. She said:

"I should think you'd want to put on one of your pretty dresses and look like a lady."

"I must ride," returned Adeline briefly. "Help me with these. I'll keep my best ones clean."

Alma helped her into the breeches whose seat reached Adeline's knees, and turned back the sleeves of the jersey from her round white wrists.

"Look at Roma," said Adeline. "She's had a scare."

Roma, covered by a sticky lather, shook like a leaf. Alma ran and began to rub her with a towel. "*Froid — froid!*" chattered Roma. "Cold!"

"She comes from a warm country," explained Adeline. Hands in pockets she swaggered to the door.

"Hair!" begged Alma. "Your hair! It's like a brush heap!"

Adeline slammed the door after her and swaggered along the passage. At Finch's door she stopped and put her eye to the keyhole. She could see the bed and a hump in it.

"Hullo, Unca Finch!" she called.

"Hullo, darling!"

"Can I come in?"

"Not today, Adeline."

"Are you better? Will you soon be well?"

"Quite soon."

She tried the handle. She would have liked to romp with him on the bed, but the door was bolted.

"Listen! I'm giving you a kiss."

She placed her mouth on the keyhole and kissed through it repeatedly. Finch made kissing sounds in the bed.

"Does that make your pain better?"

"Yes."

"I'm going to ride my pony."

"Good."

"Bye-bye."

"Bye-bye."

She went down the stairs and looked into her father's room. Its emptiness made her thrust out her under lip in disappointment. She went to Ernest's door and heard him steadily snoring. She stood there for several minutes imitating him. Then she went to the door of Nicholas's room and thumped on it.

"Come in! Come in!" rumbled the deep voice.

He was sitting up in bed drinking a cup of tea. A small tray with the teapot on it lay on his knees. She skipped to the side of the bed.

"Unca Nick! Unca Nick!"

His grey moustache swept her face. He put an arm about her and hugged her close.

"Little woman!"

"I want to whisper something."

His eyebrows went up in pretended surprise. "Whisper? But why? We're alone."

"I must whisper. Shall I get up on the bed?" Already she was climbing.

"No, no!" he pushed her down but he bent his head toward her.

She pushed back his thick grey hair and fully exposed his ear. She put her mouth to it and whispered loudly:

"May I have some tea?"

"Tea? Tea? You? You would take my poor mouthful of tea?"

"Yes." She smiled ingratiatingly.

He tasted it, added more milk and held the cup to her lips. She drank deeply, her face flushing at the unusual heat, her eyes rolling up at him.

She would have stayed on for a while but he got rid of her by admiring her riding togs and the day's work ahead of her. Fortified by the drink she descended to the dining room.

She gave the bell-rope a tug and Rags came up from the basement. He grinned admiringly at her. "Good-morning, Miss."

"G'morning. I want my breakfast."

"Better come along down to the kitchen. Cook'll give it to you."

"I want it here." She climbed to the seat of a chair and held out her bib to him. "Put it on me," she ordered.

He tied it on her nape while she held up her curls.

"Wot d'you fancy?" he asked.

"Sausage."

"There ain't none."

"He had some." She pointed to her father's plate.

"'Ow do you knoaw?"

"There was a crumb left. I ate it."

Rags looked shocked. "You! The mistress of the 'ouse, peckin' abaht on other folk's plates like a sparrer!"

"Sausage! Sausage! I want sausage!"

She sank in her chair and put a stubby shoe on the table and kicked it.

"If your mother could see you!" But he was really amused. He clattered down the stairs to the kitchen and returned with two sausages and some fried potatoes on a large plate. She was sitting upright now, eating cold toast spread with bitter orange marmalade. Rags took this from her hand and placed the plate in front of her. His wife had already cut the sausages into pieces suitable for the child.

"And wot do you plan to do today?" he asked, leaning on the back of a chair and watching her genially as she ate with gusto.

"Work," she answered, with her cheek bulging.

"Wot at, may I ask?"

"Schooling the ponies."

"You're getting them ready for the show, eh?"

"Yes."

"That grey one is a 'andful for you."

"Ha, ha!" She laughed joyously. "I'm not afraid."

"You're wot I calls a well-plucked 'un."

"Oh!"

"*And*, w'en you're older, an overdose of sex appeal, or I miss my guess."

"Ha! ha! ha!"

"And you've beauty, you knaow — of a kind. Though not the film type — which, I may say, appeals most to me."

"Ha! ha! ha! ha!"

"Come now, you mustn't laugh so. You'll choke. Besides, there's nothing to laugh at. I'm tryin' to 'ave a serious conversation with you."

"No you're not. You're funny. I like fun."

"You've never said a truer word than that. I never saw anyone that likes it better. 'Ave some more marmalade?"

"No. Lift me down."

"Please!" he admonished.

"Please."

"Wot abaht your grice?"

Docilely she bent her head, folded her hands, and murmured:

"For what we have received may the Lord make us truly thankful, For Christ's sake, Amen."

He lifted her down, wiped her mouth, and took off her bib.

"A 'appy day to you!" he said. "And mind you doan't fall and break your neck."

She stood in the doorway in her baggy breeches and baize green jersey and waved her hand to him.

When she was gone he looked up at the portrait of her great-grandmother that hung over the sideboard. "A chip," he said, "off the old block, if ever there was one."

Outdoors the air was so crisp, so brilliant, that Adeline scarcely knew what to do with herself. She could not remember a morning that looked like this, so frosty in the shadow, so bright in the sun, so strange, so wild. Under the old pear tree on the lawn a few brown pears lay on the cold grass. Glossy cones lay under the evergreens. Adeline began to run in circles.

Faster and faster she ran, her eyes bright like a wild thing's, her heart going like a little engine. She ran till she fell and lay with the world going round and round with her. She was the very heart and centre of the world. She could make it whirl round and round. When she took a tumble the sky bent over her in surprise. All the frosty little marigolds in the border were staring. She snuffed their pungent scent. The smell of the ponies came from her jersey. She screamed for joy.

She rolled over and over on the grass, screaming. She flung her arms and legs about.

Old Merlin who sometimes now allowed Renny and Floss to go off without him, was disturbed from his dream in the sunny porch. He came across the lawn and licked the back of her neck as she lay face downward. She rolled over and looked up into his blind eyes. He beamed down at her, his tongue dangling, ready to give her another lick. How she loved him!

To show it she clutched handfuls of the wavy hair on his neck and pulled down his head. She laughed up at him, thrusting out her under jaw and making little savage endearing noises. She kicked him on the underside while she pulled his coat with all her might.

Suddenly he gave a yelp of pain and jerked himself away from her. He went and sat down on the steps looking offended. Then he lifted up a front leg and licked himself underneath.

She lay on her stomach, her dimpled elbows in the grass, staring at him, an amused smile flashing over her face. She began to pluck handfuls of grass and put them on top of her head. The tiny spears fell over her face in a shower and tickled her neck. She got up and began to trudge toward the stables, putting a pear in her pocket on the way.

She stuck out her lips and exclaimed — "You would, would you?" — to nothing in particular, and slapped her own thigh. Doing this she discovered that she was on a pony and began to gallop at top speed.

She discovered that her breeches were slipping down and she hitched them up and held them. Standing so she moved aside to let the new stableboy Wilf pass through the door leading a horse. Seeing her the horse swerved and knocked his hip on the doorpost. He reared.

Adeline glared at the boy. "Why don't you walk backwards, silly?" she said.

Wilf looked confused and Wright, appearing at the door, grinned. "Right you are, miss," he said. "I never knew a clumsier boy."

Adeline looked critically at the horse and then went toward her father's office.

"Are you coming to help with the ponies?" called Wright, grinning at the back view he had of her.

"You bet!" returned Adeline.

At the door of the office she gave her breeches another hitch and knocked with the side of her fist.

"Hello!" said Renny. "Who's there?"

She made her face into the very emblem of sweetness and showed it inside the door. He said:

"I'm doing accounts. You'll have to keep still."

"I don't mind," she returned, and sidled into the room. She liked it better than any of the rooms in the house.

Its yellow oak desk, littered with ofttimes not too clean papers, with the swivel chair where Renny sat, the shiny lithographs of racing horses on the walls, the ugly stove with which it was heated in winter, were to Adeline admirable objects, unchangeably connected with the being she loved best.

Floss came to meet her and she stroked her carefully.

"That's right," said Renny, with an approving glance.

"I always stroke them this way," she said demurely.

He looked at her from under his lashes. "Come and pet me."

She rushed to him and caught his hand in hers.

"I will kiss your hand," she said.

She began to kiss it with great tenderness, as though it were something fragile. Then her kisses became more fervent and she pressed her lips hard, first on the back, then on the palm of his hand. She closed his fingers on the last kiss and looked gravely into his face. "I love you, Daddy," she said.

He hugged her close. "Do you? Now you must be quiet and good while I finish these accounts. Then we'll get to work."

She slid on to a chair and took the winter pear from her pocket. It was so hard that she could take only small bites but it had a nice taste and it gave her something to do. She crunched it on her back teeth, staring hard at the spot where she would next bite.

Renny shot her a look. "Don't chew so loudly. It's bad manners."

She returned his look blankly, then swallowed whole what she had in her mouth. She swung her legs against the chair and gazed at the pictures of the horses, saying over their names in her mind.

"Stop kicking the chair leg. I'm adding up figures."

She desisted and became limp, the nibbled pear cupped wetly in her hand. She gazed at Renny, wondering at the corrugations on his forehead. She scowled, trying to make some on her own, and felt the velvet results with her fingers.

For all her high spirits she was able to keep still longer than most young children. She finished the pear as quietly as she could, wiped her palm on the corduroy velvet of her breeches, then waited patiently, getting colder and colder.

There was a mauve tinge to her cheeks when Renny at last shut the drawer of the desk with a bang and got to his feet. In this low room he looked immensely tall and strong to her. He snatched her up and kissed her.

"Why, look at your breeches! They're falling off!"

He set her down and did what he could to put her clothes in order. In the stable they met Wright. Renny said — "You should shake hands with Wright, Adeline. He and his wife have a nice little baby."

Adeline gave Wright her hand. "Many happy returns," she said.

The men exchanged amused glances.

"I want to see the baby. Is it in the stables?"

"Not yet," answered Wright. "But you may see it. Could I take her, sir? My missus would be proud to show it."

"Good. But don't be long."

Wright took her hand and they crossed the stable yard and climbed the stairs to Wright's rooms over the garage. Adeline was filled with excitement and delight when she saw the infant. She had no more than a glance for Mrs. Wright's chalk-white face on the pillow. She snuggled the baby, hugged it, kissed it, tried to take it from its mother and carry it about.

"No, no," said Wright. "It's too young."

"Is it a boy or a girl?"

"A boy."

"What is its name?"

"It has no name yet."

"No name!" She was astonished.

"Should you like to name it, Miss?"

"Yes. Call it Jim."

"Are you willing, Missus?" asked Wright.

"Jim's a nice name."

"All right. We'll call it Jim."

"I want one like it for my own."

"You're too young."

"Can only grown-up people have them?"

"Yes."

"Babies are nice but I like colts better?"

"Ah, you're a character."

"My mummie has gone away. She's gone away to get a baby, just like yours. Only smaller, even. About this size." She held her hands six inches apart.

Wright and his wife exchanged looks, then he led Adeline full of importance to the paddock where Piers was, and Mooey mounted on the grey pony. Piers had just been dunning Renny for the last year's supply of fodder he had had from the farm. A stableman was setting up low white gates for the schooling.

The grey pony looked beautiful, his coat sleek and a white star on his forehead. He was being schooled for a hunter. Mooey trotted him around a few times on the flat, looking anxiously at his father and uncle.

"Now then!" called out Piers. "Go to it!"

He was dissatisfied with the jumps though they were quite good ones. "The pony did it all by himself. You might as well not have been on him. Buck up, and ride as though you had some guts! Sit farther back!"

Around and over the gates the pony circled, again and again, his bold roving eyes alight for mischief. Mooey was keyed up to master the pony, to take the jumps better, not to be tossed off, as he knew the pony had it in his mind to do. He was thrown but scrambled quickly to his feet, caught the pony and mounted again, turning his face, set in a strained smile, toward Piers.

Adeline appeared from the stable riding Wakefield's old pony. It was a dark bay with a small neat head and kind eyes. She pressed her knees against it, her lips pouted in pride.

"Look at her!" exclaimed Piers. "Look at her feet and her legs! Just right, by gosh! Look at her hands and her wrists! Adeline, round your wrists just a *bit* more! *She's* going to make a good one." He grinned triumphantly at Renny. "*She* won't be tossed off like a feather pillow!"

"I want to jump!" cried Adeline. She headed her pony straight at one of the gates.

"Look out!" shouted Renny to Wilf, who sprang forward and laid the gate flat.

"Pig!" said Adeline to the boy, as her pony jumped like a grasshopper over nothing. "Dirty pig! I want to jump!" She rolled her eyes accusingly at her father.

"Lay down the pole for her, Wilf," said Renny.

The boy ran and fetched the white pole over which Adeline was accustomed to practise. She looked on with disfavour and, as it was being put in position, turned her pony's head toward another of the gates.

Jumping was in the cold autumn air. The old pony did not mind showing what he could do. Adeline made movements with her arms as she had seen Wright do, who believed in lifting his mount over the jumps. She jogged the pony's mouth and Renny and Piers looked around just in time to see Adeline dive forward toward the pony's ears as he cleared the gate. He slowed up and she regained her place in the saddle. She gave a shout of triumph as she cantered past the men and straight into Mooey.

The grey pony was startled but not ill-pleased. Here was more mischief! He reared, ducked, bowed, and sent Mooey over his head.

"Good God!" groaned Piers. "The boy is fit only for a rocking horse!"

Renny darted forward and caught the bay pony's bridle as the grey wheeled, kicked at it, and galloped the length of the paddock.

Mooey gathered himself up, his face muddy, one hand clamping his knee.

"Are you hurt?" asked Renny.

"No," lied Mooey and threw a furious glance at Adeline.

Patience Vaughan appeared on the pony she was to ride at the Show and the schooling proceeded. The sun pushed back the mist and shone out almost as hot as in summer. The grass of the paddock looked green again and the muddy spots by the jumps glistened. Pony after pony was put through its training.

Adeline, petted and arrogant, was always getting in the way, having to be rescued from danger. She was gloriously happy, with an animal instinctive happiness. She saw nothing beyond this morning.

But it came to an end and Piers asked her if she would like to go home with him for dinner. Renny had lifted her from her pony and he smoothed the red hair back from her hot forehead.

"Want to go?" he asked.

"No. I'll stay with you."

"But I'm going out to lunch in Stead."

"I'll go with Uncle Piers, then."

It was lovely at the Harbour, she thought — small and sunny, with zinnias and marigolds close to the door, and Baby Philip running and falling down and picking himself up again. She liked the looks of Pheasant in her yellow dress and necklace of beads like scarlet berries.

Pheasant washed her and tidied her hair.

"Did you ever see such hair!" she exclaimed to Piers, as it flew after the comb. "And such skin! Oh, I wish I had a little girl!"

"It's a pity Mooey isn't one," answered Piers.

"Didn't he do well this morning?"

"I did well!" put in Adeline.

"I'll say you did!" said Piers. "But he had two tumbles and both unnecessary."

Pheasant looked reproachfully and pityingly at her eldest when he came to the table. He sat very straight, avoiding her eyes. She bent over him, whispering in his ear:

"Corn for lunch."

He brightened and looked up at her with gratitude, not for the dish he liked best but for the sweet comfort in her tone.

After the roast pork, potatoes, and apple sauce, the corn came in a large dish. The full, smooth-pearled ears were wrapped in a snowy napkin. Adeline's eyes glowed as Pheasant selected an ear for her.

"Golden Bantam!" she said, smacking her lips.

"It's not. It's Country Gentleman," said Mooey, glad to contradict her. The schooling had made him nervous. He slid a piece of butter along the rows of his ear of corn and, when it had melted, buried his teeth in the kernels.

"Me! Me!" cried Baby Philip.

"No, no, darling," said Pheasant, "you're not big enough."

Philip hurled himself back in his high chair, rage and misery in his blue eyes.

Piers already showed a tendency to humour this son. He put a small ear of corn into his hands and grinned approvingly as the baby attacked it.

"Well," said Pheasant, "if he has colic all night, you may sit up with him."

Philip rolled his eyes truculently at her over his buttery prize.

Nook knew that he could not digest corn and ate his baked potato pensively. He was thinking of how he had hidden his latest treasure — a wild canary's nest in two tiers, with an unhatched cowbird's egg in the lower one — at the first sound of Adeline's voice. Now he could enjoy playing with her. Here he was on his own ground and was less intimidated by her than at Jalna.

Pheasant put them to rest together on a big bed, out of hearing of the baby. They rolled and laughed and shouted till Nook's cheeks were a wild-rose pink and Adeline's eyes glittered like a young animal's. Mooey had gone off by himself to the woods.

After tea Renny called for Adeline. He tied his horse and had a cup with Pheasant, who had the baby on her knee.

"Philip is quiet, for him," he said.

"Yes. He's just been getting up the corn Piers gave him at dinner. Piers is so reckless with the children."

"You should control him." He spoke severely.

"Control him! Could Alayne control you?" Alayne's name was out before she could stop herself. Well, surely there was no harm in speaking that name, when Renny had never acknowledged a break between them! She felt that she would rather like to force him to some admission.

He was startled but he stared at her as though he would stare down any intrusion on her part into his affairs. Then abruptly he answered her question with another, so shrewdly put that it forced a direct answer.

"You hear from her regularly, don't you?"

"Yes."

"Has she said when she is coming back?"

Well, two can play at hedging, thought Pheasant, and asked:

"Are you expecting her?"

"No." Again he stared, and the blood surged to his hard, high-coloured face.

"It is a great pity."

He rose instantly and looked at his wrist watch. "Where is Adeline?" he asked.

It was an unnecessary question, for the children were making a hub-bub overhead.

Pheasant went into the hall and called:

"Nook, bring Adeline down. Her daddy is here."

They could not hear her. She went halfway up the stairs, calling to him. The noise ceased and the children appeared smiling and flushed. Nook was so happy that he ran and fetched his bird's nest to show Adeline. Proudly he displayed the chamber with the cowbird's egg unhatched in it.

"You mustn't touch," he warned, but Adeline had already snatched it.

Pheasant wiped the sticky yolk from her little hand, Renny carried her off. Nook, in despair, was rolling on the floor. Philip found a piece of the eggshell and ate it.

Going home Adeline was in a state of bliss. Beneath her was the great powerful horse, at her back the muscular wall of her father's body. When the horse turned his head she saw the glint of his teeth against the bit. Her father's arm was the strongest in the world. The frosty air almost drove her mad with joy. Never before had she seen a new moon glitter out in a frosty sky — and she on horseback. She shouted at the top of her lungs. She rocked from side to side, testing the power of that never-failing arm. She would have liked to go on riding so forever.

But he would not even take her to the stables. He put her down at the door of the house and Rags called down the basement stairs to Alma that she was back. There was nothing to do but go to bed. She felt resentful toward the whole world.

She mounted the stairs reluctantly, dragging on Alma's hand. She was a sight, Alma declared, with her jersey torn and her breeches sagging to her heels. She must be very quiet for Roma was fast asleep.

She realized that she was very tired. She could hardly drag one foot after the other. Outside her mother's door she stopped and pointed a grimy finger.

"I want her," she said.

"Well, you can't have her," said Alma. "She's hundreds of miles away."

"I know. She's gone to get a baby. Like Wright's. Only just so big." She held up her hands two inches apart.

Alma smothered a laugh. "Oh, the things you say," she giggled.

"'Cause I know," said Adeline sturdily.

She was good and very quiet while she was undressed and washed. She ran naked to peep between the bars of the crib at Roma curled up, with a wisp of hair that looked white, starting from her white forehead. Adeline pushed out her lips to kiss her but Roma was too far away.

She felt very small and alone when the light was out. She comforted herself by remembering a little blue butterfly that, long ago, in the morning time, she had seen opening and shutting its wings like a fan. She wondered what had become of it.

XIX

ALAYNE AND THE NEW LIFE

LIFE IN THE charming little house up the Hudson was not so easy as Alayne had expected. Not that she had looked forward to happiness, but she had expected the serenity, the simplicity of living which she had known there in the old days. She found that living alone had made a difference in Aunt Harriet. After spending her days in thought for her sister's comfort, she had turned to spending them in thought for her own. It took little to upset her — a window opened that she had left shut — a disarranged couch — a newspaper thrown down carelessly. There was no doubt Alayne was less tidy than of old. Yet at Jalna she had been held up, sometimes as a paragon, sometimes as a tyrant of orderliness. Now she found herself intensely irritated by her aunt's fussiness, her exacting care over things that were not, after all, of great value. It irritated her that Miss Archer should refuse to let the maid dust china that, at Jalna, would have been handled by the Wragges without restraint. Sometimes the very smallness of the table at which they ate their meals irked her. She was too conscious of her aunts fastidious preparation of each mouthful.

Yet, at times — nearly always, she was warmly grateful for the refuge of this house. To no other place could she turn for love and kinship.

She and Aunt Harriet talked for hours of days gone by. They recalled every incident of the visit which she, as a child, had made to the Miss

Archers'. All Alayne's childish sayings were recounted, not once but again and again, in the long autumn evenings. Hearing them she could not help thinking how much cleverer and more spiritual she had been than her own child. At other times she felt that she had been a little prig.

When the tale of Alayne's childhood was exhausted Miss Archer turned to her own early life with her sister and brother, Alayne's father. She brought out old photographs and daguerreotypes and recalled the very price and pattern of the dresses in them. She retold the lives of her own parents and grandparents. She even shed tears over the pathetic death of a young son of her great-grandmother's. Living intimately in the memory of these forebears of hers Alayne could not wonder that she had found the Whiteoaks alien. She recalled the faces in the old photograph albums at Jalna and the anecdotes she had heard of their owners; how Nicholas would growl — "That old blackguard! Well — he was the scandal of County Meath, and that's saying a good deal." Or Ernest would exclaim — "That was Fanny Whiteoak — a beauty, but what a temper! Her husband used to beat her, and small wonder!"

Alayne wondered when her aunt would become conscious of her condition. It seemed extraordinary that her state of health aroused no suspicion. But then, Miss Archer had never had anything to do with maternity. Still she often seemed to be worrying privately over something. It was possible, Alayne thought, that Aunt Harriet was getting tired of having her with her, and one day she bluntly put the question.

Miss Archer burst into tears. "No, no, dearest Alayne," she sobbed, "it could never be anything but joy to have you with me. It is my investments that worry me. They are getting worse and worse."

Alayne was aghast. "Have you seen your lawyer?"

"Oh yes. He has done all he can. But how could he know that my stocks would go down so? He is terribly disturbed." Her pretty, old face quivered and was wet with tears.

"Now let us keep calm and go into this," said Alayne.

They went into it and it was even worse than she had feared. The room began to go round with her, as it always did now, if things were upsetting. But she kept on patting Aunt Harriet's plump back. "You must not worry so. It will be all right. I have enough for both of us and your stocks will recover. I am sure they will." In her heart she did not believe they would. She found herself prone to look on the dark side of everything. She saw the money which she had so relentlessly guarded from Renny's predatory hand, being spent to keep up this house — leaving nothing to bequeath to her child — her children! With terror she put from her the thought that her own income might shrink so that there would not be enough of it for them to live on. Still, she could always get a job with her old friend, Mr. Cory the publisher. She was sure of that. But who would care for her baby while she was away? Certainly not Aunt Harriet. She knew nothing of infants and was too old in any case. No, she would have to engage a nurse — and she pictured her aunt and herself in an apartment in New York being kept awake by the crying of a child.

Oh, if only this had not happened to her! She writhed spiritually as she considered all that it implied ... if only she had found Renny out before this had happened to her! For a second it flashed into her mind that perhaps it would be better if she had never found him out — considering that then all was over between him and Clara.... Fiercely she put this weakness from her. She was glad she had found him out, glad she had escaped from the degradation of such a situation — glad that she had taken from him the power to say, "I have deceived her and got away with it. A man has to have a fling once in his married life. Mine was successful." And how could she know that he would not have repeated the infidelity?

She was morbidly determined to hide the fact of her pregnancy from the family at Jalna. In a curious manner the knowledge that Minny had concealed the birth of her child from Eden worked on her mind. She conceived a strange connection between herself and Minny. The thought even came to her that her own child would be a girl and of the same pale colouring as Minny's child. She pictured herself as dying at its birth and Aunt Harriet taking the child to Jalna — a companion to Roma.

In the dark fall days she took an unhappy solace in such thoughts as these. Her health was better and she forced herself to take long walks for the sake of the unborn child. She took them in the afternoon and it was at this hour that the postman made his rounds. As she turned homewards she could scarcely restrain her impatience to see if he had brought a letter to her from Canada. She said to herself that it was Pheasant's letter she strained toward, with its news of Adeline. But in truth she was always expecting a letter from Renny — a letter demanding or imploring her return. The sight of the Canadian stamp set her heart pounding.

But the letter was always from Pheasant. She was a good correspondent. Alayne was the only person to whom she wrote and she had a deep sense of secret importance when she sat down to detail the doings at Jalna for her benefit. Alayne always carried the letter to her own room and first read it there, later on reading such parts as she wished to her aunt.

If Miss Archer thought that she kept anything back she gave no hint of her suspicion. Indeed suspicion could not describe any feeling of hers toward Alayne. Alayne had a right to her own privacy and the thought of infringing on that was obnoxious to Miss Archer. They were a family who always respected each other. Some of the extracts from Pheasant's letters made it easy to realize what Alayne must have gone through in such an environment. And it had had its effect on her! One could tell by the way she read aloud, without turning a hair, things which she would once have found distasteful.

Miss Archer could not understand Alayne's attitude toward little Adeline. To her it seemed lacking in tenderness and natural solicitude. Once she said to her:

"Aren't you afraid, Alayne dear, that she will grow quite away from you? Don't you think we should manage for her to visit us soon?"

Alayne had disconcertingly exclaimed:

"Adeline here! You little know what you are suggesting. She would drive you mad in this little house. As for her growing away from me — she's never been near me, since her first year. I can do nothing with her." As her lips formed the last words the figure of Miss Archer faded from her sight and in its place she saw Renny's tall, spare form, his lips bent in an expression of embarrassment. She had so often flung these words at him.

The room seemed suddenly suffocating. She rose and went to the window a crack of which was open and beneath which a steam radiator sizzled forth its heat. She added:

"You must think me an unnatural mother. But — I'm simply not able to have her with me now. Later on it will be different." She drew herself up, facing the cool inlet of fresh air. Her body looked strange and misshapen. Miss Archer gasped as the revelation struck her like a blow.

"Alayne! You — why, you — oh, my dear!" Her face became crimson. Life was suddenly horrible, indecent to her.

"Yes," answered Alayne coldly, "I'm going to have a baby. It can't be helped. There's no use in making a fuss over it." She had never spoken so to her aunt before. Miss Archer was hurt and showed it.

Alayne went and put her arms about her.

"Don't mind me, Aunt Harriet. I'm not myself these days. I've been so worried that I haven't known what to do."

Miss Archer clasped her close. "My poor child! It's all too terrible. To think that — when you knew he was unfaithful!" She could not keep a note of accusation out of her voice.

"But I *didn't* know! Not when this happened! You don't imagine I ever lived with him after I found them out, do you?"

"Did you know that you were — like this — when you left Jalna?"

"No. I went to a doctor here."

"But you should have confided in me! Not borne all this alone! Oh, my poor little girl — what you have been through!" Miss Archer began to cry but kept on talking. "When I think of all that your parents hoped and planned for you! They both thought you would do something very much worthwhile.... If only you had never met Eden! Then you would never have met this man. I just can't say his unspeakable name! I hope I am a Christian but it seems to me that nothing is too bad to punish him. He deserves to *suffer*."

"He's no worse than lots of others, I suppose," said Alayne sullenly. She was heavy and tired and felt that she could bear no more talk.

Miss Archer, on the contrary, could not stop talking. Her mind was fastened on Renny, rather than on Alayne's state which she could not yet bring herself to face, and on his head she poured out her bitterness of spirit. Alayne was glad when she heard the postman. She hoped there would be a long letter from some old friend of Aunt Harriet's to take her mind off their difficulties. For once she did not look for the Canadian stamp. Yet there it was, on an envelope addressed by Pheasant.

Contrary to her use she did not take the letter to her room but opened it at once and began to read it aloud:

DEAR ALAYNE —

I've been intending to write to you for weeks but there always seems so much to do at this time of year, getting ready for winter and having colds and helping with the Harvest Festival. And then there is always the Horse Show. We did pretty well at the Show. That new mare of Renny's is certainly a bad actor. She walked on her hind legs through all the events and won nothing. But he has great faith in her. Piers tries to talk reason into him but you know what he is like when he gets infatuated. We got a first in the Corinthian Class — two firsts and a third in Middleweight Hunters. The polo ponies did very well and we made several good sales after the Show. I was especially bucked by Mooey's performance, as Piers has rather a low opinion of his powers. Of course Patience is a born rider and was a favourite with the crowd. But you just wait till your little Adeline gallops on the scene! She'll carry all before her. Even now she will get on any sort of pony and stick there too. She's a picture of health and loveliness. I only wish that Nook had her digestion. But he's a darling, really, and often asks when Auntie Alayne is coming back. Philip is growing to be a grand lad and a chip from the old Whiteoak block.

To go back to the Horse Show. Do you remember the carriage that the grandparents had built in England in the old days? It stood in the carriage house, rusty and covered with cobwebs. Piers cleaned and polished and enamelled it till it simply glittered and I, wearing a bustle and a sailor hat over one eye, perched on the

driver's seat, while the bays glittering and rattling their
harness high-stepped round the ring. Renny agreed
that I handled them well and I certainly got masses of
applause. That young bay mare is a great disappointment. She has been ...

Alayne stopped reading, coughed, searched for a handkerchief.
"You are not catching a cold, I hope, dear," said Miss Archer.
"No. Just a tickling. Let's see, oh yes —"
"The mare. What a lot Mrs. Piers knows about horses."
"I'd finished with that. Here we are:

The Harvest Festival was a great success. I did the font in
masses of purple grapes and their leaves. It looked lovely
but Meg thought that grapes were not suitable, being
suggestive of Bacchanalian revels rather than innocent
babes. She and Miss Pink did the chancel in dahlias and
gladioli. Piers did marvellous things with pumpkins and
ears of corn and Renny came in with some gorgeous
branches of scarlet maple leaves. They were the last
touch in beauty.

"I should think," interrupted Miss Archer, "that he would have the
decency to keep out of the church."
"Why?" asked Alayne brusquely.
"Well — I shouldn't think you'd ask that."
"I suppose he never misses a Sunday — reading the Lessons."
"Doesn't it seem horribly hypocritical to you?"
"No. I think that the Whiteoaks look on that little church as their
own — whether they are being good or bad."
"You speak of them as though they were children."
"They are, in a way. That is — they are natural."
"But no family has a right to look on any particular church as its own.
Religion is universal."
"I haven't any."

"Well, of course, I mean in theory."

"The Whiteoaks don't theorize. That church is as much a part of their life as Jalna." She returned to the letter, feeling herself surrounded for the moment by the old life, scarcely conscious of her aunt's presence. She read in silence.

"Aren't you going to finish the letter to me? I am always so interested in that family."

"Oh, there's not much more. She speaks of how they miss Wakefield and of Finch's illness. The poor boy doesn't seem to be improving very fast." She spoke in an unnatural voice. A strange brightness had come into her eyes.

Miss Archer looked at her steadily.

"I'll tell you what it is," said Alayne, her voice trembling. "He is coming to New York! Renny!"

"I've been expecting it: Alayne, you must stand firm."

"Oh, not to see me! To the Horse Show — in Madison Square Garden. You know! He's coming to ride that awful horse Pheasant speaks of!"

"Yes, dear," said Miss Archer soothingly. "I wish that good luck may attend him, I'm sure."

"Aunt Harriet, I must see him! Not to talk to him! I don't want him to know I am there. But I must see him ride. There is something in me that simply demands this final glimpse. I can't tell what it is but it's there. I've got to see him! You'd like to come too, wouldn't you, Aunt Harriet? It is the sort of thing you have never been to. It would be an experience for you — even if you didn't particularly enjoy it."

Miss Archer was quite eager to go. She delighted in new experiences and anything was better than sitting at home mourning the loss of her income. She trembled to think what would have become of her if Alayne had not been at hand with her support. And Alayne must be humoured. If she wanted to see this dreadful husband of hers do high jumps on an impossible horse, why — she must see him! If only Alayne were not going to have his child! That was the complication that rose dark and almost overpowering. When Harriet Archer thought of that she was frightened by the hate that flamed in her. Once, in the privacy of her own bathroom she heard herself exclaim — "Serve him right if he fell and cracked his ugly red head!"

She heard herself say this in a harsh voice quite unlike her own. She looked in the looking glass and saw her face puffy with hate, her mouth in a new shape. She stared at her reflection fascinated. For the first time she was conscious of a second self, whose existence she had never even suspected, a vindictive self who could wish suffering to another.

But she was not ashamed. She wished him ill, only because he had caused suffering, and would be the cause of how much more, to the one she loved best in all the world. She let herself go and repeated:

"It would serve him right if he cracked his skull at this very Show!"

She was struck with horror by the thought of what such a sight might mean to Alayne, in her present state. It might be the end of her and of her unborn child! Indeed it was not safe for her to risk witnessing an accident of any sort. She must give up the thought of attending the Show.

But Alayne was stubborn. Her heart was set on going.

"But in your delicate condition it is dangerous. Just think if there was an accident — not to Mr. Whiteoak, of course, but to some rider — what a shock for you!"

"Aunt Harriet, if I can survive what I have been through, nothing can hurt me. The change will do me good."

In truth the thought of it seemed to do her good. Either that or because in the natural course of her pregnancy she developed balance and endurance. Her appetite was good, her skin clear, she felt a desire for movement. This was well because the strictest economy was now necessary. They parted with the one maid and did the work of the house themselves. Alayne found that she enjoyed this. The house was small, in perfect order, there were all the conveniences of electric appliances, perfect plumbing and hearing. She and Miss Archer did things in their own way, to their great satisfaction, without waste and without irritation. Again and again Alayne recounted the maddening perversities of the Wragges: how on a mild autumn morning an enormous fire would blaze on the hearth, and how on a cold wet one only a handful of coals would struggle against the chill: how when the uncles had tea by themselves an enormous potful of the best tea — enough for six — was carried up to them: how there was never anything made of leftovers, which were fed to the dogs: how Rags spent hours in cleaning silver but never swept underneath the furniture: how they both were enough to drive anyone, descended from New England housewives, stark, staring mad. Miss Archer never tired of hearing of their evil deeds. They exhilarated her almost to the point of forgetting her own adversities.

She and Alayne rivalled each other in making dainty dishes. Almost every day they telephoned to the drug store for a pint of delicious ice cream. Alayne felt that she could never have too much of it.

They decided to spend the night of the show in New York at the apartment of a friend of long standing — Rosamond Trent. Alayne made up her mind, with the suddenness to which Miss Archer was becoming accustomed nowadays, to take an early train to New York and buy herself a new hat and coat on the afternoon before the Show. She was tired of looking dowdy, she said.

Rosamond Trent was delighted to have Alayne with her again — they had once shared an apartment — but she was dismayed by the change in her, which she absorbed in one swift glance. She turned to Miss Archer and said:

"After our shopping I must carry Alayne off to my pet beauty parlours. I have never seen her hair look so dull. Her skin is lovely still but there are those shadows under her eyes — and, I hate to say it, lines about her mouth! But Madame Sonia will do wonders for her."

When she had Alayne alone she clasped her to her well-corseted bosom. "Oh, my poor darling! How appalling it all is! And how my heart aches for you!"

Alayne rather enjoyed being fussed over, wept over. She had become a stranger to that sort of thing in her life at Jalna. The air was crisp, the sun gleamed brilliantly between the quick moving purple clouds as they set out on their shopping and beautifying expedition.

Rosamond Trent's ideas were large — especially where the money of other people was concerned. Nothing would do but that Alayne should buy a smart, military-looking, fur-trimmed coat and a little French hat to go with it. The shape of the coat was concealing and both were black, a colour which had always suited her.

As Alayne lay supine in a cubicle in the midst of the whirring, buzzing activity of the beauty parlour and gave herself up to the manipulation of practised hands, she wondered what desire had driven her to spend her money and her time in this fashion and on such an occasion. She could not tell. It was as though her nature had cried out for some respite from gloom and a denying of beauty. She had been heavy, she had been slack, she had been dragged down by the weight of her own thoughts for so long! Now, on this wild, boisterous afternoon, in the urge and press of the life about her she would behave as though all were well, as though she were enfolded in happiness and well-being instead of — she moved her head uneasily beneath the patting fingers of the masseuse and a quivering sigh escaped her.

She had forgotten that her hair could look like this, all sleek waves and glistening little curls. The beauty treatment had refreshed her and the slight makeup, so skillfully applied, had made her eyes look bright, made her look ten years younger.

Oceans of tissue paper billowed about the little room in Rosamond Trent's apartment. Rosamond and Miss Archer stood at delighted gaze as Alayne appeared dressed for the show. She looked lovely, they declared, and the silent thought of both was that her position was tragic and they wondered what she was going to do with her life.

She seemed almost girlishly inconsequent. At the table next theirs, in a restaurant where they dined, a young man sat alone. He could not keep his eyes off Alayne. Every now and again one of the three women caught him in an admiring glance. To feel that she could attract the eyes of a man, of a young man used to the company of girls who thought of little else but their appearance, made Alayne feel almost recklessly exhilarated. She ordered wine and wondered a dozen times what Renny would think if he discovered her there. But this was the last sort of place he was likely to come. He had his own peculiar haunts among men of his own sort. What was he doing now? Was he nervous before the Show? At the thought of him a contraction, as of fear or hate, she did not know which, caused her heart to miss its beat. She lifted the glass of wine in a trembling hand, but forced her lips to smile back at Rosamond Trent. She resolutely put the thought of him, as a man, out of her mind and bent it toward the thought of him as a rider. She experienced a feeling of pride in the thought that Aunt Harriet and Rosamond would see tonight what sort of horseman he was.

She stood silent between the other women as they waited in front of the restaurant for a taxi. A cold, blustering wind raced between the tall buildings. In the taxi she was still silent. Everything about seemed suddenly unreal. She wondered where she was going and why. She could not take in what Rosamond Trent was saying. Her mind became concentrated on the vital stirring of the child within her. Marvellous, inexorable being, that unseen fourth in the taxi…. It's imagined face flashed before her, smooth, white as an egg, with fine white hair like Roma's. Why should she always think of Roma in connection with it? But she thought of it with aloofness, with coldness. There was no tenderness in her heart toward it.

Miss Archer looked at her anxiously as Rosamond was buying the tickets. Alayne had slipped the money into Rosamond's hand.

"Aren't you feeling well, dear? You are so quiet."

Alayne forced herself to smile. "I'm all right. It is just the crowd. I have got out of the way of mixing with such hordes of people."

Miss Archer squeezed her arm excitedly. "Isn't it amazing? I never imagined … and such an interesting crowd … all sorts of people!"

They had good seats. Rosamond had seen to that. All about them there rose the vast tiers of faces. Below spread the course with its white gates and oxers. An event was already in progress. As they took their seats a storm of clapping broke forth. The band began to play. There was an animal vitality in the air that was almost frightening to Miss Archer. But the people about looked respectable.

Alayne held the bulky catalogue. She had herself in hand now. She looked competently through the pages for what she wanted. "Isn't it amusing to see her, Miss Archer? She knows all about Horse Shows now," said Rosamond.

She saw his name again and again on various days. She knew the horses he was riding. The knowledge of all she had absorbed about horses, without being conscious of it, made a gulf between her and Rosamond and her aunt. This was the fifth night. She found his name.

Champion Sweepstake — Value one thousand dollars guaranteed. No. 56 … Mrs. Spindles … ch. M. 15, 8, 5 years…. R.C. Whiteoak …

It was so strange to see his name there. So strange … so strange … and the thought that she would soon see him in the flesh…. It seemed to her an unthinkably long time since she had seen him…. She felt that everyone in the Garden must know that she had come to see him.

They watched foreign Army teams competing … French, Italian, South American officers. They watched an exhibition by Troopers of the Royal Canadian Mounted Police, in their red tunics, broad-brimmed hats and black breeches. There was a glamour about them, a precision, a fineness. Miss Archer joined almost wildly in the applause.

Alayne sat rigid, her hands tightly clasped. All that passed was a dream to her, a fantasy, a nothingness till he came on. She picked him out at once among the other riders, sitting the tall, lean chestnut easily, with that accustomed droop of the shoulders. She saw the dark coat — she knew just where it hung in his wardrobe — the riding boots — she could see the row of them on their wooden trees. She was filled with wonder that he could sit there so easily, the mare sidling into her place, and be unconscious of the look that pierced him from where she sat.

The mare had been shown in other classes during the week. It was evident that she was known by some, looked on with amusement. But she had a lovely shoulder, a smooth sweep to her flanks, an iron neck and a little, clever head. Her eyes beamed, as though with a candid return of the crowd's amusement. There were performances ahead of her that were difficult to beat. She swung in an easy canter over the tan-bark and cleared the first gate with a space to spare. But, almost as soon as she had landed, as though in an access of perversity, she reared and walked on her hind legs toward the next obstacle. A gasp of surprise followed by laughter came from the tiers of seats. Surely she could not clear the next gate But they had heard strange things of her and they held their breath to see what would happen. Her rider had evidently been prepared for this performance for, though the colour flamed into his face, he appeared calm and headed her toward the next gate.

Almost at the take off the mare lowered herself, looked closely at the gate, dropped her head, reared and again jumped clear with many inches to spare.

There was a thunder of applause which the mare accepted with an air between the mischievous and the vixenish and the man with an embarrassed yet triumphant grin.

Again she was on her hind legs! Again she minced coyly along the course. Again she lowered herself and cleared the gate like a thunderbolt. The applause thundered to the roof. The crowd loved the mare because she was strange, perverse, and triumphant.

Alayne's hands separated, each seeking a hand of those on either side. She gripped their fingers. Hers seemed made of iron they held so fiercely. She laughed outright as the mare, on hind legs, stalked from the course and out of sight. She could imagine the hilarious stream of curses fired off above her head when those two were alone.

"Will they give him the prize?"

"Oh, but they should!"

"But how can they, when the horse behaved so?"

"She's a devil!"

"How that man can ride!"

"There'll have to be a tryout with the best of the others."

Alayne's ears drank in these ejaculations. She looked eagerly into the faces about her. She talked eagerly to Miss Archer and Rosamond Trent. They were mystified by her. She seemed beside herself with excitement. A brilliant spot burned in either cheek. She wanted the people about to know that that man was, or had been, hers.

Suddenly, at a distance, standing with some other men, she saw Piers looking unbelievably natural, laughing and talking.

In the tryout all the others had faults but the mare never ticked a bar though again and again she approached the obstacle in her own peculiar fashion. The crowd was jocular and joyful when she was awarded the prize. Now she stood immobile, beautiful, aloof, her rider scanning the faces of the audience as though for one he knew.

But that face, white and tense, was lost as a drop in the sea.

The journey home seemed very long. Snow began to fall. There had already been a few flurries but this was the first time it had come down in earnest. The flakes stuck to the windows of the taxi, which was not a very good one, and an icy draught moved the dead air in it. Miss Archer kept talking rather nervously about the show. She was very much afraid that she would take a chill and her mind was in a state of confusion after the strange evening. She was glad when they had boarded the electric train and she could snuggle into a corner of the seat and close her eyes. She thought — "There is no use in making conversation. Alayne is tired out, poor girl. How lovely she looked at dinner! And at the show! I like that narrow fur collar on her! What strange pictures come before my eyes ... all sorts of coloured lights ... horses bounding and caracoling — *is* there such a word? *And* that *man*! My first thought was he hardly seems human!... Later on I had a feeling of something very human in him ... that was when he was sitting motionless on his horse ... but not the sort of humanity I am used to, and the last man I should choose as a husband — if I were choosing one ... I *do* admire his back ... there's something about it ... and the way he rode that impossible horse.... I never cared for the word mare.... It is strange how in some cases the male name of animals is best and in others the female.... I rather wish Alayne had been willing to go back to Rosamond's apartment to supper. It would have been nice ... but Alayne has always liked her own way.... I do wonder if perhaps ..."

The very inmost chamber of Alayne's mind was drained of thought. She sat sunk in her seat staring straight ahead of her, seeing nothing, feeling nothing but the weight of her body, her spiritual exhaustion. She planted her feet on the floor of the train, and through them its vibrations hummed to the very core of her.

The snow flickered past the steamy pane. The platform of the little station was white with it. The taxi they had ordered was waiting for them and, at last, they found themselves in their own living room.

"Are you glad you went?" asked Miss Archer over their hot coffee.

"Yes. I'm very glad."

"Are you pleased that he won the prize?"

"Very.... What do you think of him, Aunt Harriet?"

"My dear, I think he is a violent-looking man. I could understand your loving Eden but ... *this* man ..."

"This man," repeated Alayne. "No, I suppose you couldn't understand that."

In her own room she carefully put away the new hat and coat. Then, as though her body were of much less importance, she threw it passionately on the bed and cried far into the night.

XX

THE COMING OF WINTER

MEG AND MAURICE were effacing as well as they could the ravages that a summer of paying guests had made in their living room. Though they hoped to get other guests as agreeable next summer it was very pleasant to be alone again, to let oneself go, without regard to the opinion of outsiders.

Patience was at this moment practising on the piano with the loud pedal down: Meg was cleaning the spot on the wallpaper above the couch where a gentleman with oiled hair had been accustomed to rest his head; while Maurice, in an old shooting jacket, was putting a fresh covering on the seat of an old-fashioned, much-carved walnut chair. The noise of his hammering did not at all perturb Patience, only causing her to press the loud pedal more firmly. A canary, struck by the last pale shaft of sunlight, was singing himself hoarse in his cage.

Meg beamed.

"Well, that looks better, doesn't it? Really, I was almost hopeless of getting it clean. Look, Maurice ... Maurice, look! Are you deaf?"

Maurice, sitting on his heels, obligingly admired her work. "You've certainly made a good job of it. I hope the old blighter won't want to come back next year. He made that spot on the wall and burnt the seat of this chair with his cigarette. He seemed only half awake."

"But he was very nice and so well-informed."

"If only he had been satisfied to keep his information to himself!"

"Maurice, you mustn't be ungrateful! Think of the money we got out of him. And his digestion being so bad he brought most of his food in packages."

"Look what he did to the wallpaper and the chair."

"That's childish. Remember that we got over a hundred dollars from him."

"I don't see how you make that out," He hammered noisily.

"Why, six weeks at —"

"He wasn't here six weeks."

"Of course, he was! Don't you remember how the very day he arrived —?"

"I can't hear a word you say."

"Why do you go on hammering when I'm talking?"

"Must get this chair covered sometime. He's weakened the springs, too."

"What?"

"He's weakened the springs, too. My father sat in this chair for seventy years —"

"What utter nonsense! You don't suppose he sat in it as a baby."

"Why not?" Maurice stared at her truculently.

"What would be his weight then? In any case your father was never a heavy man. As compared with my father and my grandfather —"

"Good Lord! I don't suppose they ever sat in this chair."

"What has that to do with it, I'd like to know."

"Then why did you bring them into the discussion?"

"I didn't. I was just comparing."

"Why compare?"

"What did you say? Why are you muttering?"

"Muttering! If you'd choke off that canary you might hear me!"

"You said only yesterday that he'd scarcely uttered a peep for weeks!"

"What?"

"Patience, darling, could you put down the soft pedal?"

Patience wheeled on the antiquated stool. The door bell rang. She ran and looked out of the window.

"It is Uncle Piers!"

"Whew!" said Piers. "It's turned cold, I can tell you. We're in for a real snowstorm."

"Yes," said Meg. "I was just noticing that great purple cloud above the sunset. I was just comparing it in my mind to the way the sun shines out in one's life, in spite of clouds."

Maurice looked at her stupidly.

"I see that your morale is good," said Piers. He sat down and took Patience on his knee. She rubbed her cheek against his firm cold one.

"Oh," she said, "how nice and frosty you feel!"

"He always has a good colour," said Meg. "I was like that as a young girl. But I had a terrible shock and an illness and I was always pale after that."

Maurice stared stupidly at her.

Piers asked of Patience — "How are you getting on with your lessons?"

She smiled without answering. Meg did it for her. "Oh, she's practising very well now that the P.G.s are gone. I couldn't insist on it when they were here. Now Maurice begins to realize that it was worth going to the expense of a good teacher for her. He begins to appreciate her talent."

Maurice stared at Meg. "It's a pity," he said, "that with a musician like Finch in the family we should have to pay for music lessons."

"Yes, isn't it?" agreed Meg. "When I think of the months and months he has been home and all he might have taught Patience in that time! Well — it's depressing, to say the least of it."

Piers answered gloomily — "It is Finch's condition that depresses me. I don't know what is to become of him. The weeks and the months go by and he lives the same appalling life. I'll tell you plainly what I think. I think he is headed for a sanatorium or his grave — I don't know which."

"Oh, don't say that!" cried Meg. "Not before the child. Don't even think such things. Thought does affect a sick person. I'm sure that all Finch needs is complete rest. That's what Renny says."

"Renny baffles me," said Piers. "He lets that boy lie there getting weaker and weaker. He does nothing. Whether he's fatalistic or merely slothful, I don't know. For my part, I feel absolutely discouraged. I went in to see him yesterday. He was lying on the bed looking perfectly peaceful. He hadn't a book, a newspaper, a cigarette — anything by him for amusement. I said to him — 'How's that pain in your head?' — and he answered 'It's a lot better. It only comes now and then.' Then I asked him if he didn't think he ought to get up and he said that if he got up the pain would come back again, that he wanted to stay where he was till he was quite well. He said he wanted to be left alone and not worried and — when I told him what I thought about it the tears began to run out of his eyes, easily — without any effort, you might say. It was awful."

"Patience," said her mother. "Go and tell Katie to bring the tea."

"I don't like her to hear disturbing things," she said when the child was gone.

Maurice asked — "What do the uncles think of his condition?"

Piers gave a short laugh. "They don't take anything very seriously, except their own comfort. 'Finch has had a breakdown. Time will mend him. We must do all we can to bring him and Sarah together again. She's a nice girl though rather eccentric, and devoted to Finch.' I tell you that the whole family — yourselves included — are either blind or willfully unobservant — I was going to say callous."

"Oh no," interrupted Meg. "Don't say callous! After all, the uncles have had ten times the experience that you have had, Piers. *I* have had the experience of a breakdown and time healed *me*."

Piers pushed out his lips and looked unconvinced.

Maurice asked — "Do you like this new covering I've put on the chair?"

Piers grunted approval.

Meg sat down beside Piers and took his firm hand in hers. "Piers, if anything should happen — oh, I can't put such a thought into words I should never have let it enter my mind!"

Maurice looked at her uncomfortably, Piers blankly. "What thought?" he said.

She almost whispered — "If anything should happen that Finch ..."

"Well — I'm prepared for it, as I've just said."

"Piers, what about our mortgage? Who would hold that?"

"Sarah, if he has made a will in her favour. But I don't think he has made a will. In that case she would get a third and the rest be divided equally among us."

Meg pondered.

"I hope it won't come to that," said Maurice. He sat nursing his hand which had been crippled in the War and now had rheumatism in it.

"What a thing to say!" cried Meg. "Just as though the thought of such a thing was not horrible to all of us!" She began to cry, her plump breast rising and falling with her gasping breaths.

"Don't work yourself up," said Piers. "There's lots of life in Finch yet. Here comes the tea."

"For heaven's sake," added Maurice, "don't let Patience see you crying!"

With an effort Meg controlled herself. A neat maid placed a silver tray on the table beside her. From a covered dish came the smell of hot, buttered muffins. A jar of blackberry jelly caught the light like a jewel. A round sultana cake and a pierced silver basket of thin cookies spoke well for the fare enjoyed by the summer's paying guests.

Patience handed about the muffins with a troubled glance at her mother's face. Meg at once spoke brightly of the wins at the New York Horse Show. Piers agreed complacently, putting half a muffin in his mouth, that they had done well.

"I should think," said Meg, "that Alayne would feel humiliated. She hadn't a good word for that new mare. She never appreciated Renny's flair for picking up unusual horses. She doesn't know the first thing about them herself but she's eternally setting up her opinion."

"I think we've seen the last of her," said Piers. "She's been away for months and hasn't even asked to have Adeline sent to her on a visit. She's an unnatural mother."

"There is nothing natural about her!" exclaimed Meg. "Have you ever seen her give one yearning, brooding mother-look at poor little Adeline?"

"I've seen her look daggers at her."

"And Renny! Does she ever give him that understanding, maternal look that a natural wife gives her husband?"

Meg demonstrated this look in a way that caused Maurice to hang his head and grin sheepishly.

Piers said — "She writes to Pheasant, you know."

"Surely Pheasant shows you the letters."

"Sometimes. I don't ask to see them. Pheasant doesn't think she'll come back. She thinks her mind is in a sort of morbid condition."

Patience was feeding the canary.

Meg leant close to Piers and whispered — "Whatever was it all about? Mrs. Lebraux?"

"I dare say. They haven't confided in me."

"Well, I certainly think Renny should in me. I am his only sister and he well knows that nothing he could tell me would ever pass my lips." She took a fresh helping of jelly and poured herself another cup of tea. "This is almost the first food I have eaten today."

"That's true," confirmed Maurice.

In silence Piers spread jelly on a cookie and covered it with another. Patience called from the window — "Sarah is coming in at the gate!"

When Piers had come he had remarked that it was going to snow. Now Sarah's small fur hat was white with it. Flakes clung to her smooth, black hair. While Piers had brought with him a sense of boisterous but not unkindly weather Sarah brought the feeling of white relentless winter — the snow on her hat, her pale chiselled features, her penetrating, light grey eyes.

Meg welcomed her with effusion, and ordered a fresh pot of tea. Maurice gave her his chair by the fire and Patience seated herself on a stool close by, admiring Sarah's beautiful clothes.

"Really, Sarah," said Meg, "you are wasted in this place. There are so few to appreciate the way you look."

"I like clothes for their own sake," said Sarah. "But if you like the way I look I am glad. I hope you don't mind my coming. This time in the day is very lonely, it's neither light nor dark and the sky is heavy with snow."

"I don't see how you stand it!" exclaimed Meg. "I simply must have people about me! To live in a house alone — with the trees crowding so close — I'd go mad!"

Sarah gave a small smile. "I've been used to a quiet life but — sometimes I feel — as though I couldn't go on — as though something must happen to me."

Maurice put in — "Why don't you go South for the winter? I certainly should if I were in your place. By spring you would know — well, things would have settled themselves in some way."

"No. I must stay here. I must be near Finch. And I love this place. I can't tell you how much I love it. It's just that at this hour of the day —"

Meg said warmly — "My dear, we're delighted to have you. Come every day at this time if it cheers you. We have just been talking about poor Finch ourselves and feeling simply terrible about him."

Sarah turned to Piers. "Have you seen him lately?"

"Yesterday."

"And how is he?"

"The same."

"Did he — speak of me?"

"No. He wasn't very talkative."

"But I asked you — last week, wasn't it? — to try to find out what he feels about me the very next time you saw him!"

Piers lighted a cigarette. "It's no use, Sarah. You would have known that if you'd been there. It seems a strange thing to me but I do earnestly believe that two marriages are broken up in this family. And, if one is more finally broken up than the other, I believe it's yours."

"I have not given up hope."

"Nor I!" said Meg. "I'm positive that it will be all right with you and Finch in just a little while."

Sarah looked as though she could have embraced Meg for her words.

Piers regarded her pessimistically. He said — "What do you know about it, Meg? You haven't been near him for weeks. It would be more to the point if you went to him — tried to rouse him, instead of being so sure that everything will come right."

"What is the use of my going?" cried Meg, angrily. "The last time I went he wouldn't see me and Renny was gruff and irritable. He said he wouldn't have Finch bothered by anyone whom he didn't want to see. I tell you, Sarah, you're not the only one who suffers!"

"What is it to you as compared to me?"

"It is a very great deal to me. Finch was a little boy of seven when his mother died. I brought him up. I was a mother to him. Family ties may not mean much to you but to us they are as strong as marriage — if not stronger."

"That's right," said Maurice. He added, in an attempt to turn the conversation:

"I suppose you'll stay where you are for Christmas. I wish you could spend the day with the rest of us, but —" He looked to Piers for help.

Piers gave it with his usual bluntness. "I'm afraid we can't ask Sarah to Jalna. I'm hoping to get Finch down to dinner."

"Oh, I do hope you can!" said Meg.

Sarah asked — "I wonder what I could send him for Christmas? Can you suggest anything?"

The others looked at her dubiously, then Meg said:

"A cheque is always nice."

"Not in his state," said Piers. "It would mean nothing to him."

Maurice suggested. "Some cheery-looking neckties."

"I have been making a scrapbook," said Sarah, "of notices of his concerts. I take a number of musical papers. There have been some lovely things said. Do you think he might like to see them?"

"It's not a bad idea," said Piers. "Though I doubt if he'd read them."

"What a good wife you are!" declared Meg. "How different to Alayne! Can anyone picture her making a scrapbook for Renny of notices about his horses? Wasn't it marvellous his winning a championship at the New York Show, Sarah?"

"Yes. It was splendid."

"And he hopes to breed some wonderful foals from her."

An enigmatic smile flickered like wintry sunlight over Sarah's face.

Meg said — "I suppose he has paid the interest on his mortgage by now."

The two men were embarrassed. Sarah answered — "Oh, yes. He's paid it all off."

Meg said — "I'm so glad," and turned to Piers. "Has he paid you for the fodder?"

"Yes. He did that after he had sold the ponies. He's got everything pretty well straightened up now. Even the vet."

"I'm so glad."

"If it weren't for him," said Sarah, "Finch and I would be living together. He has turned Finch against me."

"Rot!" said Piers.

"No. It's quite true."

"But why should he?"

"Because he is jealous."

"Then why isn't he jealous of Pheasant?"

"Because Pheasant hasn't taken you away from Jalna. He can't bear to think of Finch living in Europe. Away from his influence. And there's another thing. He dislikes me for myself. He knows he has no power over me and he resents it. Oh, I can't tell you how deeply I think all this out — in my house alone — and how clear it all is to me."

They stared at her, not knowing what to say. They were relieved by the sound of a motor and the entrance of Renny.

After nodding to the men, kissing Patience and gravely greeting Sarah, he said to Meg:

"Christmas beef for you! We've been killing. It's extra good this year." He deposited a precariously wrapped joint in brown paper on the end of the piano.

Meg clasped him. "Oh, how lovely! Your beef is always so good! We shall have it spiced, eh Maurice? My, it does bring Christmas close!"

Renny patted her shoulder, looking half-defiantly across it at Sarah. She rose to go. Piers also said he must leave. Sarah looked rather wistfully at Maurice and Meg.

"Will you two, and Patience of course, come to dinner with me on Christmas night? The dinner at Jalna will be at two, won't it? If you don't come I shall be quite alone."

Maurice looked enquiringly at Meg.

"We shall love to go," she said. "You'll not mind our leaving a bit early, will you, Renny?"

He did mind, but he agreed that he could tolerate it. Patience was delighted at the thought of two Christmas dinners. She danced to the door with Sarah and Piers, he teasing her, pretending to carry her out into the snow. Sarah stood by, with her small impersonal smile. Meg hugged herself in the doorway.

Maurice led Renny toward the dining room.

"Come and have a drink," he said.

He filled two glasses and raised his. "Happy days. Things *are* looking up with us, aren't they?"

With rather a sombre smile Renny lifted his glass. An icy blast from the open front door rushed into the room.

XXI

Christmas

As the summer had been eager to succumb to autumn, so autumn had been all too ready to throw herself at the hoary head of winter. Those first bitter days did not pass, leaving a period of mild weather behind them, but the cold increased week by week till on Christmas morning the mercury sank to twenty degrees below zero.

Long before Finch woke he had been aware of the increasing cold. He had known that he was snuggling closer and closer to himself, wriggling the blankets higher and higher about his ears, and that the bedcoverings could not keep him warm. By degrees he became conscious of the growing brilliance in the room and at last, with a genuine shiver down his spine, he opened his eyes.

The room was radiant. The shapes of ferns and butterflies on the thickly furred windowpane were outlined by ruddy sunlight. The air that came in was as though it swept straight from the North Pole. The snow powdering the sill was dry as down. An excitement, a sensitive quivering thrill as of childhood, stirred through Finch's being. It was Christmas morning!

For a moment the remembrance of the past months was obliterated, he gave himself up to the pure joy of the moment. He listened with ecstasy to the sound of the church bells ringing across the snow. He welcomed the chill of his body. It had been snug and slack too long. He turned flat on his back and drew in the crystal air, cherished its sting in his nostrils.

He remembered Christmases when he was a small boy, those mysterious and beautiful early wakings when Jesus, the church bells, the Christmas tree almost blinded his eyes with their glory! He remembered his fear of Santa Claus, even when he knew that he was really Uncle Nick. Dimly he remembered another Santa Claus whom he had accepted implicitly, his own father. Finch wished he might have remembered him better, known him as a father, though he was sure no father could have been kinder to him than Renny had been.

. He heard the sharp crunch of footsteps on the snow. He heard Renny's voice ordering the dogs to go back. He was off to early service alone Finch felt a sudden pang of pity for him, going off alone. He wished he might have been well enough to go with him. He pictured himself striding with Renny across the fields, stretching their legs as they heard the last notes of the bell. He pictured Noah Binns, the bell-rope in his hands, his arms moving rhythmically up and down, his face raised toward the bell. He remembered the first Christmas morning when he had gone to Early Communion, how he had knelt trembling on the Altar steps between his grandmother and Eden. She had been ninety-six then. It must have been one of the very last times she had gone to an early service. She had kept the little thirteen-year-old lad by her side. He remembered the protecting bulk of her in her black velvet cape and heavy widow's veil thrown back from her face, rising on his right, and on his left Eden's youthful figure with bent head and crossed palms. In his inmost soul he had been conscious of the Christ-child, naked in the cold, of the Christ giving His Body and His Blood to the family kneeling there. Out of the sides of his eyes he had watched Grandmother's hands — the ruby on one of the fingers catching the light as the stained glass of the windows did — stretched eagerly toward the goblet. He saw her bonnet bend, her strongly marked features impassive and noble. He saw her under lip project below the rim of the goblet. Into his own thin hands he took it, placed his mouth where hers had been and felt the beautiful, the terrible liquid pass his lips and enter his body. He covered his face with his hands. Still, while his soul was wrapt, he could not forget those at his side. Between his fingers his glance slid toward Eden, saw him steadily raise the goblet to his lips and his blue eyes beseechingly to Mr. Fennel's face, saw him droop when the Rector passed, as the others did, like blighted flowers....

He lay unconscious of his body and did not hear Rags knock on the door. He came in softly, carrying Finch's breakfast tray, and when he saw that he was awake said with a heartiness that tried to ignore Finch's illness:

"Merry Christmas to you, sir!"

Finch turned his long grey eyes toward him. "Thank you, Rags. The same to you."

Rags set down the tray and hastened to close the window

"Why, you're like a refrigerator in 'ere, sir! It's a Harctic Christmas, and noaw mistake. I've never felt a colder. The pipes in the kitchen were froze solid. The scullery pump was froze. The milk was froze. Everythink was froze but my missus' temper and it was all of a boiling stew, believe me! But it is pretty outside — wot you can see of it." With his finger ends he increased the size of a clear spot on the pane, then peered out through it admiringly. "It's like a Christmas card — the kind that looks just impossible. You ought to get up and see it, Mr. Finch." He looked speculatively toward the bed.

"Yes, I shall, later on."

"Just now it's at its prettiest."

Finch raised himself on his elbow and looked at the tray.

"Scrambled heggs, sir! I knaow you were always fond of them."

"Thanks, Rags. They look nice."

"Do you think you'll perhaps be coming down to dinner, sir? It wouldn't seem right without you."

Finch looked at him suspiciously. "Have you heard anything about my going down?"

"I believe it was mentioned, sir."

"Who mentioned it?"

"Well — I really can't remember."

"I — I'm not going down, Rags. I — couldn't face that tableful of people."

"I suppose not, sir. But it's a pity." He still lingered in the room and Finch realized that he was hoping for a Christmas present. But he had nothing for him — nothing for anybody. But Rags — all those trays — up three flights of stairs! He said, excitedly:

"Look here, Rags, I want to give you something! Open the small left-hand drawer in my bureau. Do you see a pocketbook? Why — it's the one you gave me when I was twenty-one! It had belonged to a German officer, hadn't it? No, no, don't bring it to me! Open it. Take five dollars, Rags! By George, you've earned it — all these blasted trays! Don't thank me…. Just go … I say — go! I want to be left alone…." When the door was closed on Rags he sank back and shut his eyes. He felt exhausted.

He lay there shivering. Even with the window closed the room was very cold. He wished he had asked Rags to find him an extra quilt. Anyway, he had a hot drink…. He sat up and poured himself a cup of tea. The thought that downstairs they were perhaps planning for him to join them at dinner troubled him. He could not eat the scrambled eggs. Yet he could not bear to send them back to the kitchen untouched — not this morning! What should he do with them?

He heard Merlin's deep bark outside his window. That would solve it! He would give the eggs to Merlin! He got out of bed and almost ran to the window, opened it and called — "Merlin! Merlin!"

The spaniel was digging something from under the hard crust of snow. At the sound of his name he raised his kind face toward Finch, waved his plumed tail and opened his mouth wide in a grin. He bowed as though in salutation. Finch tipped the scrambled eggs on to the hard china-whiteness of the snow. Merlin scrambled after them, snuffling. He devoured them in a few gulps, as though he were starving, though he had already had a good breakfast, and licked the snow where they had lain.

"Good boy!" said Finch, relieved.

He stood looking at the glittering world, the silver-dusted trees, the sparkling white brightness flushed pink by the sun, the shadows thrown by the trees a crystal blue. The stableboy, Wilf, was leaving the kitchen door carrying a heavy bucket. A puff of frozen breath hung before his face. He had a plaid scarf round his neck and his ears looked large and beetroot-red. His steps crunched sharply. The air was so clear that it seemed it might shatter. A crackling sound came from the roof above Finch's head. He hastened back to his bed and lay there shivering.

He heard Adeline and Roma joyous in the nursery. They came to his door and thumped on it softly calling "Merry Christmas! Merry Christmas!" His uncles came up together, as though for mutual support, and brought him their good wishes, standing under the sloping ceiling, talking about the coldness of the day. Ernest, pleased to do something for him, went down to his own room and brought back his eiderdown and covered Finch with it. But they were glad to leave him and he was glad to have them go. No one knew what to say to him except, perhaps, Wakefield. He was expected in time for dinner. Renny had written urging this.

Downstairs the house was gay with Christmas wreathing, holly, and a bowl of crimson roses sent by Sarah to Nicholas and Ernest. The Christmas tree stood in the library. Renny and the uncles had decorated it the night before. The trimmings were kept in a huge old bandbox in the attic and brought down year after year. They were of better and more lasting materials than are made today. How many times the gay cornucopias, decorated with gilt paper lace, had been refilled and hung on scented branches! There was a fat pink wax cherub which Renny remembered since early childhood. It always hung at the top of the tree.

The three men and Adeline went to the Christmas Service, she stamping in pride of new overshoes, clutching her first prayer book, one with coloured pictures, which Ernest had given her.

All the family returned to Jalna after Service and were scarcely in the house when Wake arrived looking full-chested and warm-hued in his black cassock.

He was in the highest spirits, delighted to be in the midst of his family again, eager to show them how happy he was, how well he had chosen. The room rang with the laughter of the six children as he romped with them. They tugged at his gown as if they would tear it from his back. He went down on his hands and knees, a steed for Roma.

Piers took Renny aside. "Well," he said, "what are we going to do about Finch? Are we going to bring him down?"

Renny returned his steady look uneasily. "He'll never do it. He'll never consent. I think it's a mistake to urge him. He'll be all right. All he needs is time."

"Time!" repeated Piers scornfully. "Time to go blue-mouldy! Time to go nutty! I tell you, it's now or never! If you won't help, Wake will. Come along, Wake — if he won't come of his own will, we must force him!"

"I agree," said Wakefield. "But I'm sure we can persuade him. And this is the day for it!"

They moved toward the door but Renny stood in their way. "I won't allow it," he said.

"It's now or never," retorted Piers.

"He is not fit to come down."

"He can go back to bed as soon as he is tired."

"He'll never agree."

Wake put in eagerly — "Leave him to me! I'll persuade him."

"Later in the day, then. The dinner would be too much for him."

Piers had been calculating. "Do you want us to sit thirteen at table?"

"Well — h'm, should we really be? That would upset Meg. For myself I don't mind."

"Superstition is abhorrent to me," said Wakefield. "Still — thirteen is not a happy number." He laid his hand on Renny's arm and spoke in the pleading tone of his childhood. "Do let us go! I promise you we shall not bully Finch into anything that will hurt him."

Renny moved aside. "Very well," he said sombrely, "but if this turns out badly you will hear from me."

Piers and Wakefield ran up the stairs like schoolboys, Wake's gown flapping about his knees. They went into Finch's room without knocking and stood on either side of the bed. He lay flat on his back looking up at them with a timid smile.

"Merry Christmas!" said Piers heartily.

"Merry Christmas!" Wakefield bent and kissed him.

"Thanks," said Finch. "Same to you."

Piers considered what he should say next. He half looked forward to, half dreaded Finch's opposition.

Wakefield sat down on the side of the bed and took one of Finch's thin hands in his. He said, in a voice of persuasive sweetness:

"You know, it isn't at all the thing for me to be here today. I ought to be spending a very different sort of day in the monastery. But I wanted so badly to spend my last Christmas — before my final vows — at home, with all of you."

"I'm glad you came," said Finch.

"I couldn't have managed it, if they hadn't known of your illness."

"He's not ill," interrupted Piers. "He only thinks he is."

Wakefield flashed him a look. "He has been in a pretty bad way, I think. But it's almost over. He has an entirely different look in his eyes, hasn't he?"

"He looks all right. Or rather, he will when he gets out of this room."

Wakefield looked steadily into Finch's eyes and said, smiling — "He's coming down to dinner, aren't you, old man?"

"No, no," said Finch, "I can't do that! I'm not up to it."

"Yes, you are," said Piers. "We're here to help you."

Finch gave them a startled look and drew the covers up to his chin. His limbs gave a convulsive twitch.

"You've got to come down." said Piers.

"I can't, I tell you!"

"You must. What will be your end, do you think, if you go on like this?"

"Give me time!"

"You have had time. You have had too much time. That's the trouble. You've got into an unreasoning rut and it's up to us to get you out of it."

"Did you two come up here to torment me? I have been ill, I tell you! If you only knew what I have suffered…. I just wish you had had my head for these past months, Piers."

Piers spoke quietly, almost soothingly. "No need to tell me that you've been ill. I've only to look at you but —"

Finch interrupted violently — "You said only a moment ago that I looked all right!"

"What I meant was that you looked able to get up out of that bed."

"I can't!" He glared up at them like an animal at bay.

Wakefield held his hand close. "Finch, just to please me! Let us help you into some clothes. Let us help you downstairs. Everyone wants you. You shall be as quiet as you please and come upstairs when you like. Don't spoil my Christmas by refusing me this, please, Finch."

"We'll not ask you to dress," said Piers. "Just a dressing gown and slippers. And then a nice little toddle downstairs. You've got to do it, Finch! You may as well make up your mind to it. It's your Christmas present to the family!" He opened a drawer in the bureau. "Socks! Lots of them! And *what* socks! Not like you used to have, eh? You always had holes in them, didn't you? Now then, Wake, heave back the bedclothes.... God — what legs!"

Finch gave himself up to them, his heart pounding heavily, his eyes defensive. He let himself be put into his dressing gown. He leant on Piers's arm and suffered himself to be led to the top of the stairs. The shouts of the children came up from below. He drew back, exclaiming:

"No, no, I can't do it! I must go back!"

"I'll soon stop that row," said Wakefield. He ran down the stairs and stopped in the doorway of the drawing room and held up his hand.

"Finch is coming," he said, in a low peremptory voice. "The kids must be kept quiet. He's awfully weak and shaky. Meggie — Pheasant — will you tell the children to be quiet?"

The children were quieted. They demanded, in hushed tones — "Is Santa Claus coming?"

"No. It's Uncle Finch. He's been very ill."

"Bless the boy!" said Ernest, going to meet him.

"Oh, Finch!" said Pheasant, full of sympathy.

"Dear heart alive, how glad I am!" said Meg and folded him to her bosom.

Finch stood among them half laughing, half crying. It was all so strange, so unexpected. The room seemed new to him. The very house seemed new. And all the faces about him....

Piers steered him toward the fire. Wakefield pulled forward old Adeline's chair. "He shall sit in Gran's chair! A great honour. He's a most important guest. Say Merry Christmas to Uncle Finch, children!"

"Merry Christmas, Uncle Finch," they murmured shyly. All but Adeline, who ran and laid her head on his knees. Really, he could hardly bear it … all this love … this welcome …

Renny was standing by his chair looking down at him with an odd smile.

"Glad you came?" he asked.

"Yes, I'm awfully glad."

Nicholas looked at his large, old-fashioned watch. He said:

"Are we having something soon?"

Rags came in bringing sherry and biscuits.

"Good!" said Piers. "Just what this fellow needs." He brought a glass of sherry and a biscuit to Finch.

Finch sipped the sherry and felt himself warmed and strengthened by the presence of the warm living people about him. He felt that every one of them gave him something — even baby Philip. The very dogs seemed glad to see him. Jock, the bob-tailed sheepdog, came and laid his muzzle on Finch's foot. The spaniels sat shoulder to shoulder, giving soft looks at him. The Cairn puppy scrambled to his knee. They brought Boney on his perch and set him near the chair. He never spoke now but he curved his beak and made chuckling sounds as though in senile mirth. Finch settled himself luxuriously in the depths of grand-mother's chair.

The family talked, but rather quietly, not giving him too much attention — allowing him rather to look on as an outsider, till the first excitement of the reunion was over. Nicholas came and sat close to him and laid his large hand on Finch's knee. Meg talked of the sermon and of how the anthem would have failed utterly had not the Whiteoaks saved it. The children collected in the hall, taking turns at peeping through the keyhole of the library.

Before dinner was announced a savoury odour stole through the room, mingling with the scent of the spruce and balsam boughs that arched the doorways and festooned the pictures. The dogs rose, stretched, yawned, sat down on alert haunches with eyes on the door through which Rags would enter. It was all too lovely, Finch thought, too lovely to be believed in. He was glad he had come down.

At last Rags appeared. There was a shout of joy from the children. Piers came and heaved Finch from his chair. "Now for a dinner as *is* a dinner!" he exclaimed. "Lord, what an appetite you used to have!"

Finch, feeling weak in his legs but strong in his heart, moved with the others to the dining room. They were like a solid wall around him.

When he was in his chair Meg came and ran her hands over his hair. "You might have tidied it, Piers, before you brought him down!"

"I wanted him to look picturesque. The artist, fresh from the throes of composition."

"But his hair is so lank! Not at all like Wake's which always looks charming when it's dishevelled."

"Hm, well, Wake's hair won't look charming much longer."

At this reference to Wake's future, Meg drew a deep sigh and sat down. Nicholas was scowling at her, his eyes almost closed.

"Sorry, Uncle Nick," she said. Patience giggled. Maurice winked at Patience.

Every head was bent. Nicholas muttered:

"For what we are about to receive may the Lord make us truly thankful. For Christ's sake. Amen."

Adeline formed the words of the grace in unison with Nicholas. She said a loud Amen. Renny stood and swept the carving knife along the steel. He cast a swift look about the table. The face of his grandmother, of Eden, of Alayne flashed into his mind.

"It's a pity," he said, "that we're not all here!"

"Yes, yes," agreed Ernest. "How Mamma enjoyed the dark meat of turkey! And that looks like a particularly delicious one."

"*And* the stuffing," added Nicholas. "I'm very fond of it, too."

"She was not the only one," said Renny. "There was Eden. He should be here."

"Please don't remind me of Eden now!" said Meg. "It is too sad."

Piers stared straight in front of him. Pheasant dropped her head and a dark colour dyed her neck.

Mooey said — "I forget Uncle Eden."

"Hush!" said Meg, frowning at him.

"I don't forget him," said Patience. "I often remember him."

"Do you really?" said Renny, smiling at her. "Do you really?"

"That bird will be cold," observed Nicholas, his chin in his hand.

Wakefield put in — "Finch is looking very hungry."

The spell was broken. Renny carved the turkey with expedition. Everyone began to talk. They agreed that Mrs. Wragge had never cooked a better dinner. Her gravy had never been smoother, richer, her cranberry jelly never more perfectly set, her cauliflower whiter or enfolded in a more creamy sauce. The plum pudding was so rich that it could hold itself together and no more. The brandy flared, reflected in the eyes of those about the table. The children all had some. Even baby Philip had his share from Pheasant's spoon. They would have sat long over the dessert, the nuts, and raisins but the children were impatient for the Tree.

As soon as they had left the table Piers mysteriously disappeared and Wakefield announced that Santa Claus would soon be there. Finch was once more established in his chair by the fire, left to smoke a cigarette in quiet while the others trooped into the library. He could hear the resonant tones of Santa Claus calling out the children's names, the joyful cries of the children as they opened their packages. He could hear Wake's laughter, Renny's chaffing of Santa Claus, Meg's and Pheasant's higher tones. It was all as it should be. He went softly to the door of the drawing room from where he could see the tree, starry with lighted candles, powdered with silver-dust. He had a glimpse of Santa Claus's red cap and white beard, of Renny with Philip in his arms. He watched unseen, then went back to his chair. His illness was over, he felt. Every day, from now on, he would come downstairs.

Meg came carrying a large flat book that looked like a scrapbook, and a number of other packages.

"These are all for you," she said, "but I shall give you the book first as it's the most important."

He looked at the packages embarrassed.

"But I haven't a present for anyone," he said.

"As though that mattered! Do look at the book!"

He took it in his hands and opened it.

"Who is it from?" he asked suspiciously.

"Can't you guess?"

His thin cheeks coloured. He laid the book on one side. "I think I'll open the packages first."

He was pleased, he was touched, by their thought for him. The ties, the gloves, the cigarette box, the pullover. They were just what he wanted, he said. His brothers and uncles came in to see him open his presents, except Piers who had again disappeared. Pheasant stayed behind with the children.

"Do look at the book!" urged Meg.

Finch took it up and began to examine the newspaper cuttings pasted in it. The print was blurred before his eyes. He looked up at the faces above him. "I haven't my glasses," he said. "I can't read without them."

"Do run and fetch his glasses, Wake," said Meg.

"No. I'll read it aloud to him. Is it something nice? Is it perhaps something about his playing?" Wake pretended not to know although Meg had already told him about the book. He began to read, in rather a pompous tone, an article on Finch's playing, from a French musical journal. Wakefield read the French carefully. The others listened attentively to take in the sense.

Finch listened quietly at first, with bent head. Then the words and all that they implied began to beat like hammers on his brain. The blood surged to his head. How could Sarah have done this horrible thing to him? How could the others stand about him, tormenting him? He felt that he could scarcely breathe. But he got up steadily and took two strides to Wakefield. He took the book from his hands and laid it on the leaping flames of the fire. He turned to Meg.

"This," he said, "is what I think of it. Tell her."

He sat down in his grandmother's chair and looked defiantly at them.

"Oh no, not that!" cried Meg. "Not after all her trouble!"

She made as though to rescue the book from the fire.

"Let it alone!" said Finch hoarsely. He took the poker from the hearth and poked the book down among the flames. It looked bright and new, as though the fire could not harm it.

Wakefield came and sat on the arm of Finch's chair and said quietly — "All right, old man. Perhaps it's best to burn it. You don't need to be told how you can play. Just put everything, but getting well, out of your mind."

Renny said to Maurice — "Sarah is a stupid woman. No one but a stupid woman would have done such a thing. I stick to that."

"I feel sorry for the poor girl."

"I don't. She simply refuses to be shaken off."

"Well, after all, she loves him."

"Does she! I doubt it. I think she loves only herself."

"She thinks you are against her."

"So she has told me."

Maurice gave him a significant look. "You know it is to your advantage to be friends with her."

He answered grimly — "I know it only too well."

Ernest and Nicholas showed their disapproval of Finch's actions by turning their backs on him and talking in low tones. Nicholas lighted his pipe and settled down to examine all the Christmas cards that had come to the house. He had Rags bring a small table and he spread them out on it. Ernest read the first page of *Lost Horizon*, sent to him by Alayne. He was glad that he had sent her those dainty handkerchiefs.

Meg went back to the children, passing Piers in the doorway.

"Meggie!" called Wakefield sharply and, when she returned, gave her a look that said — "Please don't tell Piers what has just happened!"

She pouted a little, for she had wanted to tell Piers, and passed on. Wakefield went to the wood basket where, among smooth logs of silver birch, a grotesquely shaped pine root lay. He placed it on the burning book and said, smiling at Finch:

"So — that's the end of that!"

Piers came straight to them.

"How do you feel?" he asked Finch.

"Splendid!" answered Wakefield for him. "He'll be a new man in a week."

Finch sat drumming his fingers on the arms of the chair. He felt excited, almost exhilarated. He felt that he had, by his act, cut himself off definitely from Sarah, before them all. The burning of those collected references to his playing gave him a new power of resistance. He watched the flames darting upward about the pine root, fed by the kindling of the book beneath.

Suddenly he saw that the resinous root had been the home of a colony of ants. Out of every crevice they came running in terror. From every spongy chamber their minute black bodies emerged, flying from the terror of fire.

"Look!" he cried. "Look — the ants! Take it off!"

Now the forerunners of the insects discovered a projecting arm of the root which touched the side of the hearth. Along this they led the way, the black army following them in dense columns, their panic subsiding as they realized there was escape.

The surprised grin on Piers's face turned to a frown. He snatched up the hearth brush and began to sweep the ants back onto the glowing coals. Wakefield gave a whistle of dismay.

Finch leapt up and caught Piers's arm.

"You can't do that!" he shouted. "Don't! It's horrible!"

The army of ants, regardless of the fate that had overtaken their first detachment, rushed with all speed from the flames behind them. They began to spread themselves over the hearth and onto the rug.

"You young fool!" said Piers. "Do you want them all over the room?"

"But you can't burn them alive! It's horrible!" Finch struggled to wrench the brush from Piers's hand.

Wakefield exclaimed — "Never mind, Piers! Let them come! Remember St. Francis!"

"What's up?" demanded Renny.

Maurice and Nicholas shouted to Piers to brush back the ants.

"Couldn't we get a dustpan," said Ernest, "and gather them up?"

Piers pushed Finch into his chair. He squatted solidly before the hearth and, as the ants reached it, brushed them back onto the coals. Even though he did, some escaped and hid themselves in the rug or among the birch logs.

Finch's face was distorted. He got up and said, in a shaking voice, to Piers:

"It isn't necessary! It was brutal!" He was ghastly pale.

Wakefield took him by the arm and said soothingly — "Come and lie down for a bit. You're tired."

Finch jerked himself away and swiftly left the room. He almost ran up the first flight of stairs. The din of the children with drums and horns pursued him. He kept repeating to himself — "Ugh! It was disgusting! To see them frizzling — it was horrible!"

In the drawing room Renny said severely — "I knew how it would be! You had no right to drag him down here! He wasn't fit for it."

At the second flight of stairs Finch's strength failed him. He sat down on the bottom step. He heard Wakefield coming after him. "Don't come!" he called out. "I don't want any of you near me!"

He was so weak that he almost crept up the remainder of the steps. He went into his room and bolted the door. He flung himself on the bed, repeating passionately — "The brute! The brute!" It seemed to him that the room was full of ants. They swarmed from every crack, from every smallest crevice. From every direction they came swarming toward the bed. In four black columns they mounted its four legs. They were all over the quilt dancing, writhing, uttering minute cries of agony as the heat of his body destroyed them. Their bodies turned into small black notes, the notes of a dancing, mincing tune of pain. All through his being he heard it. He was the instrument on which it was played....

Maurice and Meg had gone through the ravine to the fox farm, Patience dancing between them through the snow on which the evening shadows lay icy blue. Husband and wife had spent the walk in discussing the question of whether or not Sarah should be told of the fate of her present to Finch. Meg thought she should. Maurice thought not. They compromised by deciding to tell her that Finch had not yet had the quiet necessary for appreciating the scrapbook. Tomorrow Meg would go to her and tell her what had happened.

Piers and Pheasant had stayed to supper and had carried off two sleeping little boys and one very wide awake, excited one.

Roma had been sick and Adeline had a tantrum before they were safe in bed.

Nicholas and Ernest, Renny and Wakefield had sat late about the fire talking. The uncles, mellowed by whiskey and soda, following an indulgence in wine which they allowed themselves only in the festive season, had talked with fluency and wit of their bygone days. They had been equally ready to draw Wakefield on to tell of his life in the monastery, to talk with comforting assurance and faith of his future in the religious life. But at last they were tired out and, after peering out at the snow, consulting the barometer and eating a few sweets as a final challenge to longevity, they went slowly upstairs. It had been a good Christmas, marred only by Finch's hysterical behaviour.

Wakefield did not remain long behind them. The thought of Finch was on his mind, as, on his last visit home, he intended to sleep with him and he wanted to leave an impression of himself for Finch's strengthening in his absence. Before he went upstairs he went over to Renny's chair and kissed him good night. He gave a little laugh.

"What's the joke?"

Wake stood smiling down on Renny's weather-beaten aquiline face. "I was thinking," he said, "that though you're such a horsey chap, you'd make a grand-looking monk."

Renny sat alone now, his long legs stretched before the dying fire, his brown eyes staring meditatively into its embers. The four dogs, as though stirred by one impulse, rose and moved closer to him.

No one had drawn him on to talk. They were all conscious of inner reserves in him, of a certain taciturn aloofness. They all noticed that no gift had come from Alayne to him. She had sent a beautiful book to Adeline. On his part he had chosen Adeline's present to Alayne with great care, a red-and-white plaid silk blouse, quite unsuited to her.... He sat thinking of this, picturing her surprise and pleasure in its unique beauty. He pictured her putting it on for her Christmas dinner with her aunt.... He rose, went to the piano and standing by it picked out with one finger, very softly, the air of "Loch Lomond." It was one that his Scottish mother had sung to him when he was a small boy.

XXII

CLARA

IN SPITE OF the disastrous ending of Finch's first coming downstairs its effect on him was good. In the days following Christmas he began to find the long hours in his room irksome. He found that he wanted to know what was going on below. Added to this his room was on the shady side of the house, tall trees stood outside it. He pictured with longing the sun-flooded living rooms. Wakefield stayed on for two days and on both of them helped Finch to dress and supported him downstairs. Finch clung to him, laughing at his own weakness, looking forward to settling himself in his grandmother's chair by the fire.

His uncles rose late so he was in possession of the big room alone while his nerves were readjusting themselves to their new surroundings. Things began to look not quite so strange to him. His appetite improved and scarcely a day passed when Meg did not send him some delicacy to tempt it.

He liked to sit where he could look out on the two little girls playing with their sleighs in the snow. They had got bright new ones at Christmas and it was strange to see how Roma endured the cold and how a brilliant yet delicate pink came into her cheeks. Adeline was kind to her, careful of her. Up and down the snowy drive she ran with her on her sleigh.

Ernest and Nicholas had already begun to emulate the hibernating of their mother, though at their age she had still been an active woman who feared no weather. They were satisfied to shut themselves in from the still, penetrating cold or the hard-blown, biting particles of snow. When Renny came into the room where these three sat he brought with him the stimulating virility of the winter, the snowy footprints of dogs. His uncles greeted him with the latest news from Europe, according to the fortnight-old London *Times*, Finch with his eager, questioning smile.

Renny was restless in these days. He was irritable and hot-tempered with his men and in the stables they said that, if his wife did not come back to him, it was time he made up to another woman.

In truth he often had in his mind the thought of another woman. He longed to see Clara Lebraux, to have one of his old talks with her. There was no one in his life to whom he could talk as freely as he did to her and he missed this generous companionship.

He suddenly made up his mind that he would go to see her. He told himself that there was no reason on earth why he should not see her, but he took good care that the family should not know of his intentions. He motored to town and from there took a train for the village where she lived with her brother, fifty miles away.

It was a dreary-looking place he thought, as he alighted from the train and captured the one down-at-heel taxi that waited there. It was mid-January. The January thaw had come and there was trampled slush in the station yard. What houses he could see were wooden and of a dingy grey.

Characteristically he had sent no word to Clara of his coming, taking it for granted that, as a woman, she would be at home. He directed the driver to the poultry farm owned by Clara's brother.

As the taxi stood by the gate while the driver enquired at the door for the name, Renny peered through the steaming window for a sight of Clara. If she were about he would go straight to her. He saw a stretch of poultry-houses with wired-in runs, he saw an ugly cinnamon-coloured frame house. Was Clara doomed to live always in ugly houses? The door opened and he saw her standing there. He jumped out of the taxi, paid the driver and presented himself laughing at her astonishment.

It was rather astoundment that Clara felt. She leant against the door, scarcely believing her eyes.

"So you are surprised to see me?" he said.

"Terribly," she answered in a low husky voice.

"Are you going to invite me in?"

She pulled herself together with an effort. "You are the last person I was expecting but I can't tell you" — her face softened to a look of passionate welcome — "but I can't tell you how glad I am to see you!" She put out her hand and he took it in both his. The grip of her strong fingers brought back all their past.

"You're looking well," he said, as they went into the living room together. "This life evidently agrees with you." His eyes took in the conventional ugliness of the room, the bleak view from the window.

"Oh, I am well enough."

"What do you do, Clara? Do you help your brother with the poultry?"

"Not at this season. I shall in the spring. I do the housework — make things home-like for him."

"Hmph! Is he about?"

"No. He's taken some crates of late cockerels to market." And she added, smiling — "Thank goodness."

They sat down facing each other as they so often had. She took one of his cigarettes. "Tell me," she said, "all the news."

"First tell me about Pauline."

She avoided his eyes. "Happy and well. I believe she has done what is best for her. And Wake?"

He answered gloomily — "I can say the same for him. But I can't get used to it. It's a great disappointment."

He went on to tell her of the state of affairs at Jalna but not mentioning Alayne's name. Each time he avoided it Clara scanned his face, trying to discover what was in his heart, what had brought him here. She thanked him for a newspaper cutting he had sent her telling of his success at the New York Show. As he talked of this his face lighted, he drew his chair closer to hers. He laughed as he talked of Mrs. Spindle's performance. They both laughed and the ugliness of the room was dispersed by their vital drawing together. Each poured out to the other the stored-up honey of deep understanding.

He had so much to say. The words poured from him. His plans for breeding, for showing, and the children's prowess, the money he had made which had enabled him to scrape together the interest on the mortgage. Her heart ached with sympathy as she foresaw the future scraping together of that interest, the day when it should not be produced, the falling due of the mortgage, the foreclosure. She distrusted Sarah, fearing her for his sake. When he told her how Sarah had said that if she could not have Finch she would have Jalna, she laughed at Sarah's impudence but she was afraid.

She made tea and over it she said, not able to control her burning desire to hear of his relations with Alayne:

"You have not once mentioned your wife."

He turned his face away and, as often before, she noticed the blackness of his lashes as he lowered them. They gave a softness, she thought, to the hard sweep of his profile, a mystery to his eyes.

"There is nothing to say."

"Do you really mean that? You don't write to each other? But I have no right to ask."

"No, we don't write."

"And you didn't see her when you were in New York?"

"No. She probably didn't even know I was there." He seemed absorbed in the contemplation of some vision.

Clara's heart began to beat heavily. Was it possible, was it possible that all was really over between him and Alayne? That he had come here to tell her so? That they two at last might be everything to each other in freedom? She asked, the words coming huskily:

"Is everything over between you, then?"

He turned toward her startled. Every line of his face was dear to her. She longed to go to him, to take his head in her hands and press it to her breast.

He answered — "No, I can't think that. I can't think that we shan't come together again. I am sure that she still cares for me and knows that I love her."

A sound like the clanging of bells beat in Clara's ears. A mist clouded her vision. He had come then to see her, as a friend! He had never really been her lover. His heart belonged to that cold, hard, shallow woman who had left him and his child....

There was silence between them for a space. The early winter twilight began to draw in. The outlines of the furniture became blurred. There was a grey shapelessness all about them. Clara gathered up her courage and said in her usual curt tone:

"Since you feel as you do about her I think you are wrong in letting this state of affairs go on. You ought to stop it at once."

He asked blankly — "What am I to do?"

"I think you ought to go to her and ask her to come back. I think you ought to force her to say something definite. She never has, has she?"

He gave a little laugh. "Well, she said pretty definitely that she couldn't stand me any longer."

Clara exclaimed almost angrily — "Then why do you think that she still loves you?"

"I can't think otherwise."

"That is because you care so much for her!"

"I suppose so. Our love was too great to come to nothing. We went through too much to get each other. Good God, Clara, she's had my child! She's been more to me than any other woman possibly could be!" The muscles of his upper lip contracted. Again he turned away his face.

Then Clara put all her own love, all her hopes from her. She laid her hand on his knee and said:

"Renny, you must go to her. There is nothing else for it. In a separation like this one of the two must throw pride aside and make the first move to reconciliation. I think you ought to be that one. She went away and left you. Now, I make my guess that she is waiting — hoping for you to go and bring her home. You have told me that Adeline was to go to her. Why don't you take the child yourself? Why don't you take her and say to your wife — 'Here I am with our child! Are you coming back to us or aren't you? Does our past love mean nothing to you?' I think you should make her understand that she's got to come back to you or — give you up forever." On the last words Clara's voice broke and unaccustomed tears filled her eyes.

He laid his hand on hers which still rested on his knee. He was deeply touched by her obvious emotion. He said, with rather a twisted smile:

"You think that would bring her to time?"

"I think you ought to do something and do it right away. It's too miserable, the way you are going on. I can see how unhappy you are. You have enough on your mind — enough to bear — without estrangement from the wife you love, thrown in!"

"And you think I should go without sending her any word? Just as I walked in on you today?"

Oh, this turning of the screw! Clara bit her lip and looked at him dully in her pain.

"Yes," she said, "just as you walked in today. Only with a heart full of love." Now she had done everything for him she could do. Surely she had in a measure repaid the long years of friendship, of comfort and support he had given her — the short months of passion!

"Clara!" he exclaimed. "You can't think how much I care for you! I shall do just as you say. I always have taken your advice, haven't I?"

She squeezed his knee then withdrew her hand. "Good. But I haven't been one to give advice, have I? I'm not that sort of woman. And I'm the last one to give advice in affairs of the heart but — in this case — I feel that I am talking sound sense. If you and Alayne don't watch you are going to have your lives crumbling in ruins about you. And that's an awful thing, believe me."

She got up and went suddenly to the window. He followed and stood close beside her. He said in a muffled voice:

"Don't think I shall ever forget what has been between us. You were beautiful and kind and — I shall never forget."

"Don't!" she exclaimed hoarsely.

A motorcar turned in at the gate and she saw her brother alight from it. She switched on the light and saw Renny's face vivid and expectant beside her. She put out her hand and touched him caressingly on the cheek, then turned to the door which now opened.

Her brother was a small, spare, rather weazened man. He had been brought up in luxury with the expectation of inheriting a fortune. The loss of his father's money had embittered him as misfortune had never embittered Clara. From extravagance he had turned, with the strength of a single-minded nature, to penuriousness. He was constantly worrying over the amount of grain his leghorns demolished in order to produce eggs. They were such fragile little birds and so insatiable!

Now, as he came in, he noticed that only one light was burning and looked pleased. Then he saw Renny and showed his surprise.

"My brother, Duncan," said Clara. "Duncan, this is Mr. Whiteoak. You've heard me speak of him."

Duncan twinkled up at Renny, gripped his hand and said, in a high-pitched voice:

"I am very glad to meet you. My sister and her husband were greatly indebted to you. Well — I'm very glad! It's been a filthy day at the market. And I got very poor prices."

He talked on, scarcely stopping to draw breath. It was delightful, he said, to have someone besides his sister to talk to. With unaffected heartiness he begged Renny to stay to supper. And Renny would have stayed but for something in Clara's eyes. She did not want him to stay, he felt sure of that. Her brother insisted on showing him his poultry. By the light of a lantern they inspected the interior of rows of poultry-houses, where pouting pullets peered down at them from under dangling blood-red combs. Duncan pounced on two eggs hidden in the straw of the nests and railed against the carelessness of the hired man who had left them there to freeze. He confided to Renny that Clara was and always had been an extravagant woman. Yet, in spite of his meanness, Renny liked the little man. And he liked Renny and, though he had driven far that day, insisted on taking him to the station. Under his twinkling eyes Renny and Clara said goodbye.

As he strode along the road to Jalna his heavy soles crushed the nobbles of ice into which the slush had frozen. There was a full, white moon dipping her way through the shining scales of a mackerel sky. The trees about the house stood like pointed black towers touched with silver. There were lights in most of the rooms and a spiral of smoke uncurled itself from each chimney. He felt a new hope in him, a fresh strength. That was what Clara did. She freed him. His gratitude flowed back to her. He thought — "If only I could do something for her! If only she could have a different life!"

But the thought of her was driven from his mind by the sight of a pale figure moving across the lawn toward the silver birch tree. He went quickly to it and discovered Sarah, wrapped in a grey squirrel coat, a fur toque on her head.

She made as though to avoid him but, when she found she could not, she faced him with her enigmatic smile.

"Well," he said, "it's an odd time for you to be prowling about!"

"Prowling!" she repeated softly. "That's a strange word to use. It sounds as though you grudged me a foothold."

He returned, almost complainingly — "How can I help it when I know what is in your mind? You're not like an ordinary person taking the air. I feel that you have unaccountable things in your mind."

At this she looked pleased. "What sort of things?"

"Well — spying on Finch, for one thing."

"That's not unaccountable."

"It is to me. I can't understand how any woman who has pride can so hang on to a man who wants to be free. He's shown you by every means in his power that he does not want to see you."

"But surely I may look in on him!"

"In that room? Were you looking in the window?"

"Yes. He's there. With his uncles. He looks so young and sweet."

"Sarah," said Renny solemnly, "you must never do that again!"

"Very well, I promise…. What else do you think I had in my mind?"

He gave a grim laugh. "We'll not put that into words. All I have to say about that is — the sooner you get it out of your mind the better." He turned on her suddenly, almost savagely. "Finch will never live with you again! You will never own Jalna. Remember that!"

She flinched like a child that is threatened but the smile still flickered over her face. Merlin, inside the house, had heard Renny's voice and had scratched on the door till Rags let him and Floss out. They came racing across the snow, filling the air with their joyful barks. Somewhere from behind the house the sheepdog joined them, adding his deep tones to the welcome. In the stable a stallion neighed. Finch's figure appeared in the window of the drawing room.

"There he is!" exclaimed Sarah and began to run toward the house.

But Renny caught her by her fur coat and held her fast.

"Have you no shame?" he said sternly. "Do you want to go home by the road or through the ravine?"

"Through the ravine," she answered meekly.

"The snow must be deep there."

"I came that way."

He led her through the gate and to the top of the path. The beautiful stark shadows of the trees were penciled against the snow. Sarah's face looked wanly beautiful in the moonlight. As Renny stood supporting her on the slippery path a vibration of hate that was almost akin to love passed between them. He released her and she descended the path slowly, holding to tree after tree as she went, the silver-grey fur of her coat strangely one with the scene.

He returned with his dogs to the house. Inside he looked sharply into Finch's face, discovered that he had seen nothing. He said:

"I'm going down to New York tomorrow. I'm taking Adeline to visit her mother."

"This is news!" said Ernest. "Have you known long that you are going? Alma should have time to get the child ready. I'm not sure that she has appropriate clothes."

"I can buy her something there, if necessary. Alayne will attend to that."

Nicholas said — "This is very good news, Renny. I hope that you will bring Alayne back with you. I don't at all like the way things have been going. You tell her for me that I think she ought to come home."

"It's never been anything more than a temporary separation," said Renny stiffly.

Nicholas's heavy eyebrows went up.

Ernest said — "If you are travelling by day — and I think that would be best for Adeline — you should let Alma know at once. She is such a slack creature that I dare say the poor child doesn't own a clean shift."

Renny went up the stairs to the nursery two steps at a time. The children were asleep. Alma was with the Wragges and Bessie in the basement. Renny took an electric torch from his pocket, opened the door of the clothes cupboard and turned its beam on the small garments hanging there. The dresses were in good condition as Adeline was generally in riding breeches. There was the little fur-trimmed coat she wore on Sundays. He went to the chest of drawers and peered into one after another. What he saw made him scowl. He put out the light, tiptoed from the room, and descended the stairs. This time to the basement. Alma went to bed with red eyes.

XXIII

ADELINE'S FIRST JOURNEY

SHE WAS WOKEN by Alma while it was still dark. She did not know whether it were night or morning and she was almost afraid of Alma's great shadow looming on the ceiling. Without preliminary Alma lifted her, rosy and warm, from the snugness of her cot. She hung limp on Alma's hands like a sleepy puppy.

"Wake up! My goodness, what a sleepyhead! I wish I was you. You're going on the train today."

"Where?" Adeline's eyes flew open.

"To New York to see your Momma."

"Me too! Want to go see my Momma," cried Roma. She had forgotten all her French and now chattered freely in English.

"You can't," said Alma. "Your Momma isn't in New York."

"Where is she?"

"I don't know."

"But I must go too."

"You lie down and keep warm, like a good little girl. I've got my hands full."

Alma was in a state of excitement. She had been up since five, ironing the things she had washed before she went to bed. She had sewn on buttons, polished little shoes. A suitcase was already packed with Adeline's clothes.

She ate her breakfast sitting opposite her father, the light still burning above the table though the sky was growing blue. With the fatalism of childhood she never questioned this upheaval in her life, but behaved as though she had known all along that she was to go to New York. But unlike some children she was not too excited to eat. She munched her way steadily through her breakfast, her eyes scarcely leaving Renny's face. He was preoccupied, nervous. He kept throwing scraps to his dogs, talking to them in endearing terms, as though he were to be long separated from them.

Ernest came down in his dressing gown, carrying his own travelling rug which he insisted Renny must take for Adeline's comfort. He remained to put her into her little hat and coat and draw on her tiny gloves. She was to go upstairs, Nicholas had sent word, to say goodbye to him. The car was at the door.

Renny stood by it looking at his watch. Still Ernest did not return with the child. Rags had gone to the basement, dragging the dogs with him.

"My God!" Renny shouted through the open door, "do you want me to miss my train? Uncle Ernest, bring that child down!"

There was no answer. Merlin, escaped from Rags, came round the outside of the house and climbed into the car. Renny caught him by the tail, took him in his arms and carried him to the top of the basement stairs.

"Rags, you blasted fool!" he shouted, and delivered the dog to him. He returned, swearing along the hall. He looked at his watch.

He bounded up the stairs, met Ernest mildly interrogatory at the top, snatched Adeline from him and ran with her in his arms to the car.

"Now," he said to Wright, "step on it!"

They shot down the drive, through the gate and along the icy road. The sun rose red across the lake which steamed like a glassy caldron. Gulls flew in and out of the rose-tinted mist uttering thin cries. Adeline was in a state of mingled bewilderment and bliss.

This state continued all day, with now one emotion predominant, now the other. She was swept into a new life, into undreamed-of things, into a state of intimacy with her father never before achieved.

But no matter how great her bewilderment she was always mistress of herself. As soon as they had arranged their things in the train and she had found out what was expected of her, she behaved like a seasoned traveller.

Renny was proud of her — of her looks and her behaviour.

He was proudly conscious of the admiring glances she received when he led her through the long rows of carriages to the restaurant car. Many eyes turned toward them as they sat at table there, the small child composed, making animated conversation with him in an almost unchildlike way; the man attentive to her but nothing of the doting father in his aspect. The two were complete in their relation.

She grew very tired as the day wore on, very hot in the overheated carriage. He showed her the pictures in his newspaper. For hours she looked out of the window at the snowy landscape. Then he laid her on the seat with Ernest's rug folded under her head and she fell into a deep sleep. When she woke it was night, a strange night of shifting lights, roaring darkness and changing faces. Her hair clung moistly to her head, her cheeks were blazing. Renny stood her on the seat and put on her coat and hat. She stared bewildered as the negro porter brushed his clothes and dusted his shoes. She had never seen a negro before. All day this one had been nice to her, leant over showing his white teeth, brought her a coloured travelling guide to look at.

"Goodbye!" she called to him over Renny's shoulder. "Goodbye, and good-luck!"

There were more people in the marble station than she had dreamed were in the whole world. She clasped her arms tightly round Renny's neck and wondered however they should find her mother in such a place.

Renny had hoped to go straight to Alayne that night but when he considered how tired the child was and the question of Miss Archer's being able to put them up at such short notice, he decided to go to a hotel.

It was the first time Adeline had ever been in one. She had not known that there were houses larger than Jalna, except, of course, the King's Castle, and she was almost frightened by the innumerable doors opening from the unbelievable length of the corridors. She marched along sturdily, grasping Renny's hand. She thought of food and wondered if ever she would get something more to eat. She thought of milk, and thought — "I could drink a whole cow-full!"

At last a door was thrown open. The porters carried in their bags and they found themselves in a bedroom looking out on a hundred lighted skyscrapers.

She watched Renny attack the radiator, heard him talking to it under his breath, heard its terrible hissing, sizzling retorts, drew in a deep breath of relief when he threw open the window, raised her voice and howled at the top of it as famine implacably attacked her.

He came to her aghast.

"What's the matter? Have you a pain?"

"No!" she howled out of a square mouth.

He caught her by the arm. "Now, look here, no tantrums —"

She gripped her stomach and glared at him out of streaming eyes.

"Hungry?"

She made a gurgling assent.

Oh, the long wait for food! Oh, the unspeakable bliss when it arrived! A glittering damask cloth was spread before her. A waiter disclosed a tureen of soup enough to serve four. There were biscuits and custard and little cakes. She felt that she could go on eating forever, beaming at her father out of grateful eyes.

But quite suddenly she could eat no more and wanted nothing but to go to bed. She felt a revival of excitement at sight of the glaring white bathroom, at sound of the volcanic taps. The water came out raging, steaming. Surely she would be boiled alive!

It was amazing to think that Renny should give her her bath. It was glorious to see the grimy lather on her hands. He bent over her, in shirt and trousers, lathering her well. He rubbed her down, whistling through his teeth as he did so, like a groom.

Oh, how she loved him! Naked she rolled in his arms, hugging him as though she would throttle him, laughing into his face, shrieking with joy when he tickled her.

He had a time of it to quiet her but at last she lay in bed with closed eyes looking remote and touchingly young and weak.

He rang for a maid, asked her to tidy the room and keep an eye on the child. He brushed his own moist hair, put on his coat and went down to dinner.

"I'd call it a day!" he said to himself.

XXIV

THE HOUSE ON THE HUDSON

IT SEEMED TO Alayne the longest winter she had ever known. When she had left Jalna she had pictured a new, active life, a life in which her true self which she felt had been hampered, warped, in the years in that house, might again expand. In the intellectual activity she would free herself from the chains of her life with Renny, heal herself from the galling remembrance of Clara Lebraux. She would mingle with the sort of people she had known before her first marriage, people who read the new books, saw the new plays and discussed them, people who took a broad and detached view of life.

But above all else, above all else she would be far from the sight of the face she had grown to distrust, to shrink from; far from the sound of that voice which now jarred her morbidly sensitive nerves to discord!

Her pregnancy had changed everything. It had complicated everything, given her a different outlook on her surroundings. Else how could all plans she made turn out so futile, so profitless? She found little pleasure in renewing old acquaintances or making new. The people she met seemed, after the highly individual and strong-featured Whiteoaks, stereotyped, colourless. She could no longer become one of them. She was a different person from the one she had been. The harsh contact of Jalna had roughened her. She was neither one thing nor the other, she told herself — at home nowhere.

After the Horse Show, Rosamond Trent insisted on Alayne's going out with her every now and again but she did not recapture even a shadow of the exhilaration she had felt on that night. Now she often wished she had not gone to the Show. Not since had she been able to get the picture of Renny out of her mind. On his stalking mare he kept pace with her thoughts day and night.

She went to meetings of literary clubs and returned in increasing despondency. Then she would go to her room, lie down on her bed and enact over and over the last scenes between her and Renny. She would feel bitter pride in the remembrance of thrusts that had made him wince. She would think of things that she might have said and writhe at the thought that he would never be pierced by their sting. Sometimes she even recalled happy hours and the memory of his infectious laughter made her smile. One by one the faces of all the family would pass smiling before her closed eyes. She would feel that she could almost touch Nook's silky head. She would see the dogs in greedy procession, licking dishes, gnawing bones, scratching fleas. She would see the horses, the pigs, the sheep, the cattle in a fantastic roundabout. But whatever her imaginings were they always ended with the remembrance of her dark descent into the ravine, of finding Renny and Clara there, of the terrible days that followed, and she would roll her head on the pillow and cry till her eyes were red.

By Christmas her condition was obvious and she refused to go anywhere. She and her aunt were invited to spend the day with friends but she refused to go. Her despondency had its effect on Miss Archer, who more than once looked back with longing to the days when she had her house to herself, and her safe income. She was a woman who was ready to enjoy any pleasure that came to hand and she found Alayne's shrinking from society inexplicable.

Alayne made no effort to prepare clothing for the coming child. Little garments could be bought — better than she could make them. But in secret Miss Archer knitted a supply of jackets and bootees, embroidered pillowcases and hemstitched tiny sheets. She gave these, daintily wrapped and ribboned, to Alayne on Christmas morning. Alayne was touched; she put her arms about Miss Archer and said:

"When all this is over, Aunt Harriet, we shall have a happier time. You have been so good to me."

She was touched, too, by the several gifts from Jalna — Ernest's handkerchiefs, Pheasant's scarf, the exquisite lingerie from Sarah. But it was the plaid silk blouse from Adeline that held her. It baffled her. Had he chosen it? But how could he? He would have known it was not her style. Yet there was something mysterious in it, something of his hand in it.... She held it against her and asked:

"Does it become me?"

Miss Archer thought that nothing became her now but she answered:

"I think it brightens you up, dear."

It was at the New Year when Alayne got the letter from her bank informing her that the stocks in which her money was invested had collapsed. The income from them had, overnight, become almost non-existent.

The shock was so great that, at first, she could not take it in. She read and re-read the letter, trying to draw from it a different meaning. But there was only one meaning and that was that she had nothing to live on, there was nothing for her and her old aunt and the child to live on till she was able to take a position — if she could get one!

She felt numb. Almost without emotion she broke the news to her aunt. To Miss Archer it seemed the last straw. She felt her spirit breaking beneath its increasing burdens. She wondered what she had ever done to deserve all this. Surely it was some sort of retribution! With an aching heart she reviewed her gentle past.

Alayne wrote at once to Mr. Cory, her former employer and her friend, put her case before him, and asked for a position as soon as she would be able to take one. He answered at once, telling her that the publishing business had never been worse but offering her a small position at a low salary. However, it would be enough to keep them! By hard work she would be able to keep the three of them.

Now that this livelihood was assured, her mind was able to turn freely to the full significance of her loss. It simply was that the money she had so rigorously guarded, the money she had so implacably protected from Renny, was gone — was dissolved to nothingness. And with it she might have taken the mortgage on Jalna! In a thousand ways she might have eased his struggle. If she had given him her money there would be no mortgage on Jalna. It seemed to her that the mortgage was the beginning of all their troubles. Her bitterness because of it had driven him to the arms of Clara. In this thought she reached a depth of despondency she had not before known. She was sleepless. She could eat next to nothing, yet she refused to see her doctor. Miss Archer began to fear that she would never live through childbirth or that, if she did, she would be unfit to take up any work.

On a morning in mid-January Alayne stood at the window where she had stood when she first broke the news of her pregnancy to Miss Archer, and looked out on the first blizzard of the winter season. From the lowering sky the fine sharp flakes swept in a white cloud past the pane. Alayne pictured great waves shouldering each other in the harbour. Though it was only ten o'clock in the morning it seemed like late afternoon. She had woken so very early, she was so tired and the snow fell as though it would never stop.

She laid her hands on the radiator for warmth and noticed, for the first time, how thin they were and how loose her rings. She wondered at herself for continuing to wear her wedding ring but she had not yet been able to make up her mind to abandon it.

The street was deserted. She listlessly watched the approach of a taxi that looked half smothered in snow. It stopped before the door. A man got out, paid the driver and, turning to the interior lifted out a child. With it in his arms he came toward the house.

She saw the child's face pink in the snow. There was something in the man's walk.... She looked at his face.... She looked more steadily, unbelieving, then believing.... She turned to Miss Archer and gasped:

"He can't! He mustn't! Don't answer the door!" Then she fell in a faint at Miss Archer's feet.

For a moment Harriet Archer was too terrified to move. Then, with a cry of "Alayne, darling!" she knelt beside her and took her head on her arm. Alayne remained white and motionless. What had she seen at the window? What had her words meant? Miss Archer ran to the window and looked out. The taxi had already disappeared, obliterated by the blizzard. The door bell rang loud and clear.

Thank God! Oh, thank God there was someone there to help her…. But what had Alayne said? "Don't open the door!" Again the bell sounded. Miss Archer, almost herself fainting, looked at Alayne. Then she went to the door and attached the chain. She opened the door and peered out.

Renny at once tried to enter through the aperture, powdered with snow, carrying his child.

"I'm Renny Whiteoak," he said. "I do want to get my infant in out of this blizzard. You're Alayne's aunt, aren't you?"

Miss Archer shut the door. She stood leaning against it, the beating of her heart almost choking her. What should she do? Let him in and perhaps kill Alayne with the shock of seeing him? Shut him out and be left to face this crisis alone? She turned back to the living room to see if Alayne were conscious.

The door had not latched and blew open. Renny put his hand through the aperture and adroitly unhooked the chain which was too long. He closed the door behind him and set Adeline on her feet.

Without surprise Miss Archer turned to him.

"You must help me," she said. "I think Alayne is dying."

XXV

Miss Archer and Renny

"Have you brandy?" said Renny.

"Not a drop."

"No spirits?"

"None. But there are smelling salts." Miss Archer fumbled distractedly in a drawer of the sewing table that had been her sister's. She brought out a small dim bottle.

But the stopper was stuck. She kept her eyes away from Alayne's ghastly face and watched him attack it, his lips drawn from his teeth in a savage grimace. He threw it down in despair.

"Get me some water, please!"

Miss Archer ran to the kitchen and brought him water in an enamelled cup. He had thrown open the window and was kneeling with Alayne in his arms. Her eyes were open but they stared straight in front of her. Her mouth hung open and she breathed heavily. He held the water to her lips and Miss Archer saw that his hand shook. More water was spilt than went down Alayne's throat. He raised his eyes to Miss Archer's face.

"Will you send for a doctor?" he said.

She saw accusation, reproach, in his eyes.

She went blindly to the telephone. "I must see the figures," she said to herself. "I must see the figures." But she could not dial the right number though she tried again and again. Adeline came close to her and stood watching, snow melting on her red hair.

Renny carried Alayne to the sofa and sat with her folded close in his arms, waiting.

Miss Archer turned to him. She said humbly — "I can't see the figures."

He made as though to lay Alayne on the sofa but, with a sudden rousing of strength, she clasped his neck in her arms and made a small, moaning sound of dissent. Her eyes turned wonderingly to his face.

"She's better!" he exclaimed. "But we must have the doctor. Haven't you glasses to help you see the figures?"

"Oh, it's not my sight! It is that I am so upset. I'll try again." She went to the telephone and this time was successful. The doctor would come at once. Again Adeline ran to her side. In an access of affection toward Alayne's child she bent and kissed her. "Poor little darling," she breathed.

Adeline whispered — "Take me away. I don't like being with them." Her dark eyes rolled expressively toward her parents.

The appeal went to Miss Archer's heart, flattered her, even while she thought it unnatural. She answered:

"Your mother will soon be well. But till then you shall stay with me." She took the child's firm little hand in her fragile one.

Renny carried Alayne to her room, Miss Archer following with a hot water bottle, Adeline clinging to her. When Alayne's unwieldy body had been covered by an eiderdown, the hot water bottle laid at her feet, Miss Archer took the child and left husband and wife alone together.

Alayne had never unclasped her arms from his neck. She looked unbelievingly, wonderingly into his face.

"Do you know me?" he asked. "It's Renny."

"Renny ..." she repeated. As she said his name the colour returned to her lips.

Seeing this he pressed his own to them. He whispered passionately — "Oh, my darling!"

She lay relaxed in his arms, letting fall from her the weight of the past months, absorbing comfort and strength from him with every nerve in her body.

He asked, in passionate reproach — "How could you hide this from me?"

Almost tranquilly she answered — "I don't know."

"When do you expect it?"

"In about six weeks."

"My God! And to think that I knew nothing! To think that you might have stayed here — had our child here — away from me!" He put her from him and began to pace up and down the small room.

She watched him tranquilly, as though she were lying on a cloud. She felt that nothing could excite her, disturb her. She felt only unutterable surrender, weakness, and peace her lips even formed a faint smile. He looked so strange in that room of hers! It was so strange to see him in that house!

He came and knelt by the bed, took both her hands in his and put them about his neck. He buried his face against her unyielding side. His voice shook as he said:

"Now it is all right between us, isn't it? All the past is over. You have ... forgiven me.... Say that, Alayne — that all is well between us."

"Don't! You are going to make me cry and ... I have cried so much ... I don't want to cry again...."

"Darling, you shall not cry — never again! I just wanted to hear you say that you forgave me...."

All her tranquility was shaken. She said hoarsely — "Forgive you! I am not the only one to forgive! I need forgiveness too. I've been a bad wife to you, I know I have — I feel it now!" She looked up at him tragically.

His face was contorted in his effort not to break down. "You must not say that," he said. "You have always been far too good for me. You know that. You are so good, Alayne!"

She gave a bitter laugh. "*Good?* Yes, *good* — and self-centred and cold and selfish! What do you suppose has happened? All my money is gone — all the money I hoarded — the money I wouldn't let you touch — the money I might have so helped you with! It's gone!"

"Good God!" He stared at her blankly. He rose to his feet and began to question her as to how it had happened. A feverish colour flamed into her cheeks as she tried to explain clearly. She so wanted to be tranquil and relaxed again.

He felt her weakness. The loss of the money seemed nothing. He interrupted her:

"No, no, I don't want to hear about it! Don't tell me. It's nothing. All that matters is that we're together again."

There was a tap on the door and the doctor came in.

Half an hour later Renny came to Miss Archer where she sat in the living room with Adeline on her knee. She looked up eagerly.

"Has the doctor gone? Shouldn't I have seen him?"

"I know what to do. He is sending some soothing medicine. All she needs is complete quiet. She must stay where she is for a fortnight, at least. This has been quite a shock, you understand." Again he looked reproachfully at Miss Archer.

She coloured and said — "I know you think I should have told you how things were with Alayne. But I dared not. She would have been very angry. She was determined to keep everything to herself. Oh, Mr. Whiteoak, she has been in a very strange state! I have been greatly worried."

She looked old, fragile, and appealing. He sat down on the couch beside her and took the heavy child from her lap.

"Won't you please call me Renny?" he said.

She could not have believed it possible for her to entertain such feelings toward him as she now began to feel. She could not believe that the man sitting beside her, his child on his knee, his weather-beaten face ravaged by emotion, his red hair untidy, was the hard-looking horseman she had watched at the Show, the dangerous man who, she felt, had broken Alayne's marriage with Eden, the husband who had broken Alayne's heart. She had never met a man who, by his mere presence, had given her a greater sense of protection, of masculine defence on her behalf.

"I am so glad you have come," she repeated and, after a moment's hesitation, added his Christian name.

"I should think you would be glad," he agreed promptly. "You have had altogether too much on your hands. You should have sent for me."

"But I didn't think — I was afraid that you and Alayne —" She could not go on.

He looked steadily into her eyes. "It's all right. Alayne has —" He interrupted himself to ask — "Did she tell you what the trouble was?"

Possibly never in Miss Archer's life had she experienced a moment of such intense embarrassment. To think that he could face her, look in her eyes and demand whether or not she knew of his shame! Shame for him flooded her face, made her feel dizzy. She bent her head in assent.

"She couldn't understand," he said, "that I still loved her — that, whatever I did, I still thought of her as the most desirable woman in the world…. You can understand that, can't you? A man can love two different women — in quite different ways…."

She broke in — though in a gentle voice — "You don't mean that you still love that other woman!"

"As a friend! Nothing more. For a little while — there was something else but — that's over. Alayne has forgiven me. She's done more. She's even said she was to blame. Of course, that's nonsense. It shows the low ebb she's reached. You can imagine how staggered I was when I saw that she is going to have a baby."

Adeline interrupted, bouncing on his knee — "I said she was! I said she was! Don't you remember? I said she was gone away to get a little baby, just so big!" She measured a space with her palms.

Miss Archer was going from one shock to another. "Oh, no, dear," she said. "Perhaps after a long while the fairies will bring you a little brother or sister."

"Wright found his in the pigsty," Adeline answered. "He told me so. That's why it looks like a little pig…. I'm as hungry as a pig!"

Miss Archer's relief was great. "Poor child! You shall have some of my cookies. Mr. Whiteoak — Renny, could you take coffee? I'm sure Alayne would. She ate no breakfast. I'll arrange a nice little tray and perhaps you will carry it to her."

Renny and Adeline followed her to the kitchen. She felt very much flustered by the two pairs of eyes watching her every movement. Were they going to follow her about wherever she went? How long were they going to stay? Should she suggest their fetching their luggage from the hotel? What food was in the refrigerator? Miss Archer was twice as long as usual in making coffee, heating corn cake.

Renny looked at it approvingly. "How nice!" he said. "I'll stay and feed it to her." As he carried it up the stairs he remembered the night that he and Rags had prepared a tray for Alayne, and how she had refused to touch a morsel.

He had better luck this time. She ate hungrily, taking the food from his fingers like a young child, holding his other hand in hers. She did not speak but lay with closed eyes, only opening them once to give him a deep look mingled of possession and surrender. As she lay with closed eyes he studied her face, which at that moment would have possibly been less attractive to ordinary observers than at any time in all the years of their intimacy, but, for him, she was so set apart by the interweaving of their lives in those years that he saw in her what others could not see — the very lineaments of her face were inviolable to change.

She took the sedative sent by the doctor and fell asleep before Renny left her. He found Adeline seated at a corner of the dining table, eating corn bread with maple syrup and drinking milk.

Miss Archer looked apologetic.

"She said she was very hungry. I do hope I have not given her the wrong thing."

"Don't worry. She has the digestion of a horse."

"How is Alayne?"

"As weak as a newborn foal."

Did he always, Miss Archer wondered, speak of people in terms of the stable? She gave him coffee and again distractedly wondered whether she should ask him how long he would stay. He settled it for her by saying:

"We have two suitcases in the porch. My plans were so unsettled that I thought I had better bring my own along as well as Adeline's. Now, of course, I'll stay to look after Alayne, if you'll have me."

Miss Archer was both frightened and relieved at the thought of having him in the house. She said:

"I am so glad that you can stay. But it is unfortunate that I have no maid. We found it necessary to do without her. I hope you will excuse somewhat haphazard household arrangements."

"I think your arrangements are charming," he returned, speaking rather like his uncle Ernest.

She was gratified. She said, hesitatingly:

"I suppose Alayne will be returning with you."

"Oh yes."

Then she said boldly — "There is no time to spare. I suppose you know that."

"Yes."

Miss Archer wanted to ask him whether or not Alayne had told him of the loss of their money but she could not make up her mind to do so. He had shown no surprise when she told him that they now had no maid. In Alayne's weak state she dared not bring up the subject to her. She must just wait and let him open it himself if so he chose.

He did choose when they two sat together in the evening. Alayne and Adeline were asleep. He had waited on Alayne with a deftness that had surprised Miss Archer, till she remembered of hearing how he had cared for Wakefield during his years of delicacy. She herself had put Adeline to bed. Tired though she was, she had delighted in the splashing of her angelic-looking person in the bath, her still more angelic saying of prayers. She could not understand how Alayne had found it impossible to manage her. The child was docility itself. She beamed up at Miss Archer, waiting to hear her will, running to do as she was bid almost before she was asked. In truth, Adeline was on her best behaviour, which was a mingling of blandishment and a serene enjoyment of a new situation.

With the room cosy in softly shaded electric light, with a dish of salted almonds between them and Renny smoking a cigarette, he almost casually referred to the loss of Alayne's money.

"The poor girl," he said, "feels very badly because she did not do things with it that I wanted her to do. She was determined to save it for the child when it would have been infinitely better to have helped me out of a hole I was in. But, you see, she has never trusted me where money was concerned."

He turned his bright gaze on Miss Archer, who found his frankness terribly embarrassing. She did not know what to say. He, however, went on:

"It's no use crying over spilt milk. The money's gone — at any rate it won't yield anything to speak of for years — and that's that. But I'm not worrying. I have the interest on my mortgage paid up. I've had a fairly good year in my stables. My brother has had a good year on the farm."

She could not help herself. She said — "I saw you ride in New York. It was thrilling. I had never been to a Horse Show before."

He stared astonished.

"Did you really? Where was Alayne?"

"She was there too. Nothing would do but she must see you ride. I have never seen her so excited."

She thought she had never seen anyone so gratified as he now appeared. He beamed at her with the look of Adeline. "How perfectly amazing! And to think I didn't know she was there! To think she wouldn't tell me ... make a sign! Really — in her quiet way — Alayne is a little devil, isn't she, Miss Archer?"

Miss Archer hadn't thought of Alayne in that way. She sat meditating, trying to absorb such an aspect of her. "I think," she said, "she is indeed supersensitive."

"I say she's devilish," he returned tranquilly. "But then, every woman worth her salt is that at times, don't you think so?"

Miss Archer laughed, somehow not ill-pleased by the implication that she herself might on occasion be devilish.

The days that followed were strange to her, probably the strangest she had ever known. The rough wild weather continued. Those four were snow-bound in the house together except when, once a day, Renny took his daughter for a walk, bringing her back covered with the snow she had rolled in, her eyes starry, her lips like cherries. They managed with the work much more easily than Miss Archer could have thought possible. Alayne required little waiting on. She was content to rest on the peace of her reconciliation with Renny, to acquire strength for the journey home. Her mind was so absorbed by her own thoughts that the fact of her aunt's impoverishment passed completely out of it. In her weakness she thought of Miss Archer living on in this house, relieved of the strain of her presence.

But, though Harriet Archer kept a cheerful front during the day, at night she lay awake shrinking in terror from the chasm that opened before her. She tossed on her bed wondering what was to become of her. She shed tears of bitterness to think that Alayne could so easily forget her trouble in her own renewed happiness. Each day she looked more wan, more fragile, than the day before. On the fourth day Renny said to her, after a long, reflective look:

"Something is worrying you, Miss Archer. I'm sure of it. I'm sure that it is something more than being merely overtired. Why, your eyes look as though you had been crying! Can't you tell me what is the matter?"

Oh, there was his devastating frankness again! There was nothing he would not put into words! No wonder that the years at Jalna had changed Alayne.... But, in spite of her shrinking, her reserve, Miss Archer broke down completely.

They were doing the lunch dishes together by the sink. His shirt sleeves were rolled up, his hands gripped a dish-mop. He had used soap enough for the washing of an elephant, Miss Archer thought. But he was a good dishwasher. When the china was rinsed it shone. She held the snowy towel to her eyes and wept into it.

"It isn't as though," she sobbed, "I had been extravagant. I have always been very careful." She controlled herself by a great effort and uncovered her quivering face. "I'd rather not talk about it. I don't wish to trouble you. You have enough worries.... You must not worry about me."

"But I do," he answered gravely. "How can I help when I see you looking so?"

"Have I been such a melancholy sight? I ought to be ashamed!"

"You have been very cheerful, but it's easy to see that you are terribly anxious. I do wish you'd tell me what is on your mind. I might be able to help you. From what you said just now I guess that your trouble is financial. I know a good deal about getting out of tight corners."

"Has Alayne told you nothing of my position?" she asked pitifully.

"Nothing."

"Well — it is just this — I am ruined. The stocks my money is invested in have collapsed.... The income from them has disappeared.... I am practically penniless."

All her proud reticence was gone. She poured out the story of her reverses, her apprehensions, her sleepless nights. It was a relief to unburden herself. She grew comparatively calm as she was relieved of the unhappy tale.

They finished their work methodically, then went into the living room. Adeline was having her afternoon rest, so they were alone. Renny took a turn up and down the little room then faced her, looking down at her domineeringly, as though he would intimidate any opposition.

"I've thought it out," he said. "It's settled! You must come to Jalna to live."

"To Jalna! To live!" The earth seemed to rock beneath Miss Archer. She leant against the back of a chair to steady herself.

"Yes. My aunt's room is waiting for you. We'll love to have you. I've always missed her. You will take her place. It's perfectly simple."

"But — you don't realize what you are proposing to do. You are proposing to take a stranger into your home."

"You are not a stranger. You are Alayne's aunt. You are one of the family. Adeline adores you. You and I get on famously. I need an aunt most terribly. You need a home. It's perfectly plain. Please don't waste your strength in opposing me."

She did not. She went to him and laid her head on his shoulder and wept in relief and gratitude. He put both arms about her and held her close. "Aunt Harriet," he comforted. "Dear little Auntie!"

It was the first time that Miss Archer had cried on a man's shoulder since the day when she had given up her wild young lover at her father's bidding. The young man had justified her father's prediction that he was headed for a bad end but Miss Archer had never quite forgotten him. She gave him a thought now, as she clung to Renny. But it was only a passing thought. He had become a shadow. Renny was a staunch reality.

For some reason she shrank from telling Alayne of his generosity. She asked him to do it. Alayne, when she heard, was ashamed that she had, in her reconciliation with Renny, forgotten her aunt's predicament. She felt overwhelmed by such a magnanimous solution of the problem, but somehow the thought of Aunt Harriet at Jalna did not please her. She could not picture her there. There was also a subtle shrinking from the bringing together under one roof of the two antagonistic spheres of her life. There would always be a note of discord in the harmony she now yearned toward.

The effect on Miss Archer of this assurance of her future was magical. She had a naturally happy nature. She had always had a desire for more excitement, more experience, than had come her way. In her sister's lifetime she had sought always to please her, and her sister had been timid and retiring. Now she saw opening before her a new and thrilling life, among people of strong personality, in a house whose very name had acquired a strange glamour for her. Where she had lain awake at night in terror, she now could not sleep for sheer excitement. She was tired too. It was not restful to have a man and a child in that house, where there had never been man or child, even though the child was as good as gold and the man turned himself into combined nurse and housemaid. He and she did the work together in a sort of devil-may-care agreement that she found immensely stimulating. He talked to her of his stables, of the characteristics of his various horses. He filled the little stucco house with his noise and laughter. He placed the kitchen chairs as hedges and oxers and initiated her into the mysteries of high jumping.

She drank in all he had to tell her, preparing herself for the life in his house. At the same time there rose in her a critical attitude toward Alayne. Why had Alayne dwelt only on the dark side of his nature? After all, he had done no more than many a man. Why had Alayne never invited her to visit her at Jalna? This had always been a faint hurt. Now it rankled in Miss Archer's breast.

As she looked at Renny's thin, muscular form, his red head, and felt her affection for him deepen day by day, she would say to herself in dismay — "And to think that I said aloud, in my own bathroom, that it would serve him right if he cracked his skull!"

She would come behind him where he sat and stroke his hair like a loving aunt. She would exclaim, when he emerged from the cellar after putting coal on the furnace:

"Oh, you naughty boy! Look at your hands! Go straight and wash them!"

It was the first time he had ever been petted and he savoured it to the full. He would stretch out his hand to catch her skirt as she passed where he sat. He would lay his head against her and cajole her into an affectionate passage. He was an enigma, a marvel and a delight to her. When he fell halfway down the stairs with a tray from Alayne's room and

Miss Archer ran terrified to see whether he had broken any bones, he only looked up defensively from where he sat on the floor and exclaimed:

"I haven't cracked a dish!"

Had he expected that she would think of her china at such a time as this? It did not speak very well for Alayne....

Frequently he went into New York and, on one of these occasions, returned with a dachshund puppy under his arm. He set the curious-looking, long-bodied creature on the floor and explained:

"A man in New York has owed me seventy-five dollars for three years. I'd given up all hope of getting it out of him but this morning he gave me this puppy out of a champion-bred litter. It's looking rather seedy because it's just been wormed. But it is a good one and he swears that it will be worth ninety dollars when it is grown. I hope you don't mind my bringing it here. It's a quiet little thing and it can sleep on the foot of my bed."

Harriet Archer's brain reeled. Her world was rocking beneath her but she thought — "Let it rock! This is life! It is real. It is earnest." She said:

"Of course, I shan't mind!" She wished he could have known what a heroine she was being, she so longed, in a measure, to repay him. "Do you think it would like a saucer of milk?"

To him it was the most natural thing in the world that she should take the puppy to her heart. He liked to see her sitting with it in her lap. But to Alayne, when she was first able to come downstairs, it was a sight so amazing as to be comic. Miss Archer resented Alayne's air of levity. She took her relationship to the dachshund and its master seriously, almost aggressively.

Now that Alayne was strong enough they discussed the details of their plans for the future. It had already been arranged that friends of Miss Archer's, a college professor and his wife, were to take her house furnished. It was at rather a low rent but it would pay the rates, keep up the repairs and leave something over for her personal needs.

Though there was so much to be done in preparation she found time to amuse Adeline. She made a scrapbook for her. She made paper dolls for her. She made ginger cookies for her and cut them into the shapes of little animals. Renny thought she was the busiest woman he had ever seen. She never sat down with her hands idle. Before a week had passed she had knitted a beautiful green jumper for Adeline and was at work on a cap and scarf. He thought she was a wonder and told her so.

Alayne's health steadily improved. She recuperated more quickly than the doctor had hoped. At the end of a fortnight she, Renny, Adeline, Miss Archer, and the dachshund pup, with all Miss Archer's personal belongings, set out for Jalna.

XXVI

How They Took the News

Nicholas Whiteoak read and read again Renny's brief letter. Then he pushed his spectacles from the arch of his big nose to the crest of his grey hair and said to his brother:

"Here's a pretty to-do!"

Ernest never liked to hear his brother use their old mother's pet phrases, so to punish him he ignored the remark, though he was burning to know what had caused it. He went on with his embroidery.

Two could play at the game of being stubborn, thought Nicholas. He gripped the letter in his hand, rose rather totteringly because of his bulk and his gout, and began heavily to pace the room. He muttered at intervals:

"Well — well, this beats all!"

Ernest endured this as long as he could, then he spat out:

"Don't act like a fool, Nick! *What* beats all?"

Nicholas halted beside him and threw down the letter on his embroidery frame.

"Read this! Read it aloud. I can't properly take it in."

Ernest read:

Dear Uncle Nick —

I expect you think I have been rather a long time in writing home but you will not wonder when you hear what I have been up against. Alayne has been very ill. When I arrived I found her in a dead faint on the floor. She is going to have a child next month. She is better now and we are coming home Wednesday, on the train arriving at 9.30 a.m. Aunt Harriet is coming with us. I have invited her to make her home at Jalna as she has lost practically everything. She is a very delightful woman and I am sure she will be a nice companion for you and Uncle Ernest. I am very fond of her already. Adeline is in grand fettle. I have acquired a very good dachshund pup in payment for a long-standing debt. Please have Aunt Augusta's room got ready for Aunt Harriet. Tell Finch to get out in the air if he can.

Love to all, Renny.

The brothers stared at each other in mutual astonishment. Yet they were not displeased. They had been finding the winter very long. They were candidly bored by each other. The thought of Alayne's return with Renny, even though in a delicate state, was pleasant. The thought of an addition to the family brought its own pride. The acquisition for their circle of a cultivated woman, such as they knew Alayne's aunt to be, was nothing short of exhilarating. The one thing of which they disapproved was the dachshund.

They wasted no time informing Piers and Meg of the news. That very afternoon there was a gathering of the family to discuss it. Finch alone was not present. He resented the shattering of his privacy by what he thought of as an avalanche of people. Day by day, in the indolent company of his uncles, in the quiet depths of the snowy weather, he had felt himself growing stronger. He could see a change in the looks of his hands and the reflection of his face in the mirror. He began to enjoy reading and, if it had not been for his fear of meeting Sarah, he would have ventured a walk in the brilliant weather. Now everything would be changed. He would have to face the eyes of a stranger.

If Finch was resentful, Meg was furious.

"To think," she exclaimed, "that Alayne would foist her impecunious old relation on us for the rest of her days! And after the way she had behaved to Renny — going off and sulking, as everyone knows she has! She could always wind him round her finger. I think we should rebel. Simply refuse to get Aunt Augusta's room ready for Miss Archer. I think you should write and tell Renny so, Uncle Nick."

Nicholas looked dubious. "Well, Meggie, I don't think I could quite do that. I dare say we'll find her very nice. And — as Renny says — she's lost all her money —"

"That's the awful part!" interrupted Meg. "If she had any money we might tolerate her! I dare say, if the truth were known, we should find that Alayne has little enough of her own left — the money she was so penurious with."

Maurice put in — "Renny always had a foolhardy generosity."

"Well," said Piers, "it's Renny's own house, and if he chooses to make it an asylum for relatives who pay nothing for their keep, it's his own affair, isn't it?"

Nicholas glared at him. "Is there any personal insinuation in your remark?"

"Yes," agreed Ernest nervously, "I should like very much to know."

"Of course there isn't!" exclaimed Pheasant.

Piers looked at his boots and blew out his cheeks. He said slowly:

"Yes, I think there is. As a matter of fact, I've been thinking of this for some time."

Meg looked at him, blinking a little. She did not know what he was going to say, or which side she was going to be on.

He said — "You two uncles have made a long visit here. You're both far from impecunious. It looks to me as though you were staying on indefinitely. Now — what about it?"

"What about it? What about it?" repeated Ernest huffily. "What about your coming in here, young man, and poking your nose into affairs that are none of your business?"

"But they are my business," said Piers. "Maurice speaks of Renny's foolhardy generosity. I quite agree with him. I call it foolhardy to support two well off old gentlemen who own a house in Devonshire, without getting a penny in return for it. I'm damned if I'd do it!"

Nicholas returned, with less temper than might be expected — "Renny would be insulted if we offered him money."

Piers gave a snort. "Try him! Just try him!"

"Everyone is not such a money-grubber as you are, Piers," said Ernest severely. "Renny is a real Whiteoak, a true Court. He has a mind above such pettiness. If you had a better memory you would recall the stories my mother told of her father's house in Ireland and of the relatives who lived there with him — free to come and go as they pleased — free as the air!"

"I have an excellent memory," said Piers. "I remember Gran telling how one of those relatives lived with him because Great-grandfather had won all his money at cards and the poor devil had nowhere to go. I've also heard her tell how, at the day of his death, her father had never paid for her wedding trousseau. Renny Court didn't trouble to pay his debts. Our Renny is a man of honour."

"It is small wonder if my mother's trousseau was not paid for," said Ernest. "It filled seventeen trunks when it was taken to India."

Nicholas said — "Could you expect a woman of her appearance to be satisfied with less?"

"I should expect her father to pay for it," retorted Piers.

"When I think," said Meg, "of the modest trousseau I had when I was married!"

"It was your second," said Piers. "Remember the one you had twenty years earlier. There was nothing modest about that."

Meg gave him a scornful look. "What can you know about it?" she said. "You were a babe in arms."

"I've heard."

Pheasant was scarlet. Maurice stared at the ceiling. With his gaze still on it he said:

"I agree with Piers that Renny would not in the least object to your uncles giving him something regularly. It's surprising what a help paying guests are. If it weren't for them Meg and I should be on the rocks."

Nicholas heaved himself in his chair. "It's intolerable" he said, "that you and Meg should depend on that!"

"What *I* think is intolerable," said Meg, "is that Alayne should force her wretched aunt on us."

"I suppose she considers that one more in such a houseful doesn't matter," said Piers.

Nicholas turned his deep gaze on him. "You seem to forget," he said, "how you and your wife and child lived here for years without responsibility."

"I was working the farm. Paying rent for it."

"And being paid in turn for the feed you raised."

"When Renny would fork over."

"He told me only lately that he had paid you a large bill."

"Yes — poor devil — I hated to take the money."

Meg put in — "I wish I had a close-up of you hating to take money."

Ernest said with dignity — "There is no disgrace in liking money. As a family we like it for what it will bring — not for its own sake."

"What about Gran?" cried Meg. "She hoarded hers for its own sake!"

"She hoarded it for the power it brought her," said Piers. "She knew she had us all on a string."

His sister groaned. "Oh, if only she had divided it among us! Or left it all to Renny — or, perhaps me! *Anything* but what she did do!"

A brooding silence fell on them all. The wind swept shrewdly against the house, carrying bright particles of snow and depositing them wherever there was any roughness of surface. Through the window the turquoise blue of the day showed a new phase in winter's progress. The sunlight brought out the heavy lines in Nicholas's face, the pinkness of Ernest's scalp showing through his hair, the increasing greyness of Meg's and Maurice's heads, Piers's fresh colouring and the length of Pheasant's lashes.

Ernest continued, as though there had been no interruption — "I repeat that we do not care for money for its own sake. I say this specially of my brother and myself. If Renny wants us here — and I know he does want us for he has said so — on a business basis, we shall be only too glad to pay him whatever he demands; isn't that so, Nick?"

"Absolutely. I'll ask him as soon as he comes home."

"He'll never tell you," said Piers. "Or, if he does, he'll name a ridiculously low figure."

"What should you suggest?" asked Ernest, lifting his lip at Piers.

Piers considered. "Well — hm, supposing you give him eighty dollars a month. I think that would be fair."

"You mean between us?" asked Ernest.

"No. I mean apiece."

"My God!" said Nicholas.

"It seems a lot," said Ernest.

"It will make a tremendous difference to Renny," said Piers.

"My P.G.'s paid that," said Meg, "and they hadn't half the comforts you have."

"There's the truth from you for once, Meggie!" said Piers.

"They had all the comfort in the world," said Maurice huffily.

"What I mean is," pursued Meg, "that they hadn't such beautiful furniture in their rooms, or such a variety of food or the run of a wine cellar."

Nicholas filled the room with his sardonic laughter. "The run of a wine cellar! A glass of port after dinner — perhaps thrice a week! A bottle of beer occasionally! Let me tell you, young woman, my father would have never dignified the meagre supply in this basement by the name of *wine cellar*. Added to that, on every special occasion I buy something out of my own purse. The very whiskey and soda Maurice is taking now was bought by me, if you must know."

Maurice looked into his glass. "It's very good," he said.

"As for the furniture in our rooms," said Ernest, "it is our own to do with as we choose. No — eighty dollars is too much. We can't think of it."

"We shall talk it over between ourselves," said Nicholas.

"Well, it's awfully sweet of you," said Meg, "and I'm sure Renny will be delighted." Having patted her uncles on the back she went on — "But you really should object to his bringing that old Miss Archer here. If you both object I'm sure he won't do it. What you say carries so much weight with him."

But though Nicholas and Ernest pretended that they would show opposition to Miss Archer's coming to Jalna, they did nothing of the sort. They were secretly very favourable to it. Like their mother, they enjoyed fresh arrivals and delighted in preparation for them. They had Augusta's room turned out and thoroughly cleaned. They had some of the heavier pieces of furniture carried to the attic, substituting for them less cumbersome ones which would be more likely to please such a woman as they pictured her to be.

They pictured her as the New England spinster of tradition. As Augusta's hair had maintained to the end a purplish-brown colour they endowed Miss Archer's in imagination with the same tinge and thought of it as worn in a Queen Alexandra fringe. They believed she would be rather didactic, rather reserved. It would take some time to get acquainted with her.

They were therefore not at all prepared for the vision of elderly loveliness escorted by Renny into their midst a week later. Harriet Archer had made up her mind to one thing, and that was to look her best before these Whiteoaks. She instinctively felt that the more attractive she looked the warmer would be their welcome. She had the New York woman's instinct for clothes and how to wear them. She was not even aware that the family knew that she was without means. She had yet to understand their intimacy. And she wanted Alayne to be proud of her.

She appeared before Ernest and Nicholas in a pale grey, fur-trimmed *ensemble.* She wore a small, grey velvet hat from beneath which her silvery hair showed in exquisitely finished waves. Renny, obviously proud of her, had just divested her of a handsome mink coat. Her skin was of a fragile fairness and her pastel blue eyes large and appealing. She put a small, soft, ringless hand into each of the brother's in turn.

"I have heard so much about you from Alayne," she said.

Renny returned to the car to help Alayne up the icy steps. The presence of Miss Archer made the meeting between her and the family less embarrassing. She felt as though she were in a dream entering that house again. All was so familiar yet seen as though from an overpowering distance. The tears she had shed here.... What a confused sense of life she had! If only she could straighten things out ... see them clearly ... as she used to before she loved Renny. Now she could feel his arm strong and taut, half-carrying her up the stairs. She was so glad that Aunt Harriet had said that bed was the best place for her.... On the landing they met Finch. He came toward her shyly, holding out his hand. Her eyes filled with tears as she saw how ill he had been. There was something of extreme youth in the gaunt delicacy of his frame.... His lips touched her cheek, then he went down the stairs. Adeline was shouting her excitement in Ernest's arms.

"Do you want a peep at my room?" Renny asked Alayne.

"I'd love to see it."

They went in and her eyes took in the shabby room with its furniture brought incongruously together. She saw the cabinet and china he had bought at Clara's sale.

"If you like," he said, "I'll have those taken out."

"No, no — leave them where they are!"

"I'll tell you what I'll do! I'll give them to Meggie! I'd rather not have them."

"Do that then. Yes — it would be better."

"Should you like to see your aunt's room?"

"No ... I'm so tired."

She lay on her own bed. She lay there marvelling at all that had happened since she had left that room. There, on the desk, lay the blotting pad on which she had written her letter to her aunt, saying that she was going to her. The intimacy of her possessions wrapped her about. Here was the echo of her voice and Renny's, raised loud in their distress. Here were spun the fine filaments of their relationship. Now he moved about the room, doing things to the curtains, laying out the articles from her dressing case. She marvelled at his easy movements, the dexterity of his hands. She felt so heavy.... He bent over her and kissed her. She drew him close.

XXVII

THE NEWCOMERS

"SHE'S A VERY attractive woman," Nicholas said to Renny when he and Ernest had him to themselves. "I expected to see someone much — plainer, less affluent-looking."

"You said in your letter," said Ernest, "that she had lost practically everything."

Renny realized that he had made a mistake in branding Miss Archer as impecunious. He enquired:

"How did Meg take it?"

Nicholas answered — "She was furious. She wanted us to refuse to have a room got ready for her. As though we should interfere!"

"On the contrary," said Ernest, "we went to no end of trouble to make things nice."

"That was decent of you."

"Just what *is* Miss Archer's position?" asked Ernest.

"She looks like a million dollars."

"Well — she owns a very nice house which she has let. But she has had very heavy losses. I didn't inquire into them. You know what Americans are. They cry poverty if they have to do without all their accustomed luxuries."

The minds of his uncles were profoundly relieved. They lost no time in letting the rest of the family know that Miss Archer's losses had still left her affluent. There was nothing to fear from her; possibly something to gain. The family came to see her and their verdict was, in every case, favourable. Meg said that if only Alayne had had the good sense and sympathetic tact of her aunt she would never have brought dissension into Jalna.

Certainly Alayne had never made the individual study of the Whiteoaks which Harriet Archer now began. She had read a good deal of psychoanalysis. Often she had wished for an opportunity to make use of what she knew. Here was a field so virgin, so rich, that it required a mind of dauntless activity such as hers to attack it. The truth was that she had never had nearly enough to occupy her mind and in studying the peculiarities of the Whiteoaks she got rid of some of her own inhibitions.

If she were to live with this family she would leave no stone unturned for the understanding of them. It might be supposed that she would rely on Alayne's judgment. But of that Harriet had a poor opinion since her acquaintance with Renny. From Alayne she had got the impression of a calculating roué. She had found him high-tempered but touchingly affectionate and of a generosity not before equalled in her experience. She had been led to believe that Adeline was a difficult, unloving child, with whom her own mother could do nothing. She had found her over-flowing with love, biddable as an angel. Alayne herself had, on close acquaintance, turned out to be not the perfect niece she had always seemed but a highly irritable and often morose woman, without that larger understanding of life on which Harriet prided herself.

For her future guidance Harriet Archer had bought herself a large notebook in which she made entries of various characteristics as they came to her notice. For instance — "Observe what large and well-shaped hands Nicholas has, with fine nails. Yet his wrist is too small in proportion ... Does his habit of loudly tooting his nose every time he blows it portend anything?... Note how Finch uses his hands and how Ernest sniffs each time before he talks of his old life in England.... Note how Maurice looks at Meg when he is addressing someone else, and Piers's habit of laying his hand on Pheasant's nape.... Notice how frequently the eyes of one or another of the family turn toward the grandmother's portrait."

So, from the first morning of her life at Jalna, Harriet Archer made a study of her new relations and not a day passed but she added to her knowledge. And she did not neglect the old house itself. On that first day she begged Renny to show it her and, if anything were needed to further cement their friendship, her exclamations of delight from attic to cellar accomplished it.

Her pleasure was not affected. She had never seen a house at all like it. Outside a museum she had never seen such beautiful pieces of Chippendale and Sheraton as were in the drawing room. The china used in the basement kitchen was such as she was accustomed to see cherished in a cabinet. On the other hand, there were corners uglier and more stuffy than any she had beheld. She felt a genuine pleasure in these too, partly because of the egotism that allowed them to exist, of the very unconsciousness of their existence. Renny escorted her to the kitchen and she praised the Wragges to their faces — Mrs. Wragge's cooking and his silver-cleaning — even while, after seeing their pantries, she thought drawing and quartering too good for them.

In her Nicholas found a fresh receptacle for his reminiscences. Everyone he knew had long ago heard all he had to tell, over and over again. Now here was a mind fresh as a child's, eagerly interested in his memory of the London of the nineties. He unearthed old photographs to show her. He read old letters to her. At last he unburdened himself of the whole sorry tale of his marriage and divorce. They enjoyed themselves thoroughly.

Ernest told her about his annotation of Shakespeare which he had long ago begun, and still pretended he hoped one day to finish. He was amazed to find that Harriet knew Shakespeare's plays as well as he did, had seen the great actors in them and showed a helpful but not too critical interest in his opinions. He thought her clothes were charming and told her so. She began to dress more especially for him than for the others. Together they talked over the relations between Renny and Alayne and felt a reflected emotion in these discussions. Ernest took one of the watercolours he had long ago done, from the wall of his room and gave it to her for hers. It was the first thing her eyes saw each morning when they opened — a thatched Devon cottage, half smothered in roses and honeysuckle.

She was soon invited by Meg to visit Vaughanlands. She won Meg's heart by her sincere praise of Patience's looks and talents. She praised Meg herself for her unselfishness and strength of character in helping Maurice by taking in paying guests. Meg had an exuberant nature and, when Harriet left, she threw her plump arms about her and told her how glad she was that she had come to Jalna.

Harriet and Alayne went to The Harbour together. Pheasant had invited them to tea so that the little boys might be present. Harriet had brought gifts to each of them. Nook came at once and snuggled close to Alayne. She pressed her lips to his silky head and said:

"You remember how I told you about Nook? Don't you think he's sweet?"

"I think they are all sweet," answered Harriet, and thought — "Alayne is far more tender toward this child than toward her own. A very curious thing. I must take a note of it tonight."

When Harriet Archer looked at Pheasant's childish figure and inno-cent face it was hard for her to believe all that Alayne had told of her. Yet there was a seriousness about her, something withheld in the dark depths of her eyes. It was a look that Mooey seemed to have inherited. Harriet felt herself much drawn to him and, seeing this, Pheasant was drawn to her. When they parted Pheasant whispered to her — "I think you are going to be good for Alayne."

Harriet flushed with pleasure and shook her head but she could not really deny it. Indeed she felt that she was going to be good for all of them.

Wakefield and Finch were the two who baffled her. Wakefield she had not yet seen but from all she heard of him she could make no living figure ... nothing coherent, nothing comprehensible. He was an enigma, a half-malicious spirit. Finch held himself aloof as none of the others had done. He had a way of gliding out of a room when she entered it that she found most disconcerting. He refused to be drawn into talk of the most friendly sort. She felt that he alone resented her presence there. Yet Alayne had always said that Finch was the friendliest, most affectionate of them all.

Harriet Archer studied even the dogs. She learnt their names, their short histories. She went about with tiny biscuits in her pocket which, unnoticed by anyone, she fed to them. The result was that the family soon remarked what a true dog lover she was and how a dog always knew his friends.

The sun put on a new warmth. The deep snow melted and swept in icy runnels through the ditches. Harriet Archer covered her shoes with shiny black galoshes and went with Renny to the stables.

It was the first time in all her life that she had put foot in one. She was amazed by the size of these and by the order everywhere manifest, which contrasted sharply with the haphazard manner of the housekeeping. But the size and order of the stables were as nothing compared to the revelation the horses themselves were to Harriet Archer.

Something in her that had never been awakened, now stirred, reared a strange dream-head, drew a deep breath of the varied smells of the stables. Renny had given her his arm and her delicate fingers clutched it excitedly They walked through the cold alleys, with the open stalls on either hand. The muscular buttocks of the horses caught the light like polished wood. Horse after horse spoke in deep whinnies to Renny as he passed. They curved their thick necks to look at him and at the little stranger by his side. He took her right into the stalls of his two favourites — Cora, an aged mare, with lovely beaming eyes and a white blaze on her face, and a big roan gelding whose mouth he opened to show Harriet his teeth. She shrank inwardly as the great cavern with its huge teeth yawned above her and an iron hoof was lifted as though in protest, but she held her ground. She even moved closer and stroked the barrel-like body. With that touch the something in her rose, shook itself as with a rattling of harness, and said in her own precise voice:

"I'm going to be a real horse lover. I can see that."

They found Adeline grooming the pony that had been Wakefield's, while the stableboy Wilf ran here and there at her bidding. Harriet saw her for the first time in her torn jersey and sagging breeches. She gave her elders no more than a smile but began to show off for Harriet's benefit, lifting the pony's hooves, slapping its flank. "And she is not yet five!" exclaimed Harriet.

They went to the harness room and, in its shadowy quiet, she saw the ranges of saddles, the lines of well-polished leathers — the snaffles, check straps, and pelhams. Harriet let go Renny's arm and touched these things masterfully. She savoured the new bond between her and the master of Jalna.

Delighted with her, he displayed the collection of cups and ribbons. She did not understand one-half of what he said, but she felt that she understood *him* better every hour.

He took her to his office where the little stove was red-hot in her honour. But their breath hung on the air. He put her into his own swivel chair and himself made tea for her in a pot with a chipped spout. As they sipped their tea and he described the careers of the various horses of the lithographs, she felt bolder than ever before in her life. But she knew she was getting chilblains.

When they returned to the house Alayne met them at the door of the sitting room. Her face was flushed and an unnatural glitter was in her eyes. She said:

"I think I'm going to have my baby quite soon. I think you had better send for the doctor."

He turned pale. "First let me put you to bed," he said. But when he touched her she cried out. With her in his arms, his lips on her cheek, he stood hesitating a moment. Then, seeing the door of his grandmother's room open, he carried her in and laid her on the bed.

So it happened that Alayne's son, arriving before his time, was born in the painted leather bed where old Adeline had borne three sons.

XXVIII

SPRING

SPRING CAME QUICKLY that year. The time between melting snow and greening grass seemed shorter to Alayne than ever before. She had seen from her window how the black tracery of branches was veiled in tiny leaves almost before she had realized the buds. Adeline had brought a handful of bloodroot from a sheltered corner of the wood and put their silver stems and drooping flowers into the little brother's hands.

She and Alayne were never so near as when they were drawn together by their love for the infant: though Alayne found the constant "Don't hold him so tightly" or "Don't kiss him on the mouth!" an irritation. Adeline seemed never to remember how fragile the baby was. She wanted to treat him as a puppy and she resented her mother's possessive guarding of him.

Toward this new child of hers Alayne's love flowed in a strong tide, as it had never flowed toward Adeline. She realized this herself and accounted for it by the coincidence of his birth and her return to health and happiness. He had been a smaller child than Adeline, the agony of the birth had been short, and the recuperation gratifying to the doctor and a delight to Renny. In a fortnight Alayne looked like her old self. In a month she was filled with a new energy. The wings of her spirit spread themselves in the new springtime of hope and happiness.

Before the child's birth she had often felt depressed by the lack of maternal yearning in herself. Even after her return to Jalna she had given all her thoughts to Renny — none, except those of foreboding, to the new life within her.

But how different when her son was in her arms! She became aware of a power he was going to have over her life. She felt his little hands take her heart into their keeping.

From her birth Adeline had definitely shown her resemblance to her great-grandmother. In the first weeks all that could be said of this child was that he had his mother's colouring. But one day Harriet Archer, holding him to the light and examining his features critically, exclaimed:

"Why, Alayne, I know who he is like! Why did I never see it before? He is the living image of your dear father!"

Alayne looked earnestly into the tiny face. "I believe you are right, Aunt Harriet. Oh, how wonderful it will be if he really is!"

"There is no doubt about it! He has your father's noble forehead. He has his eyes. Oh, my dear, just wait till I get the photo of him when he was a baby and you'll see the likeness, feature by feature!"

She found the picture and they compared the infant to it in delighted certainty. When Renny returned to the house Alayne told him of their discovery. He looked rueful rather than pleased.

"Do you really think so?" he asked, staring at his son.

"I am sure of it."

"Well, it's to be hoped he doesn't take after him in any other way."

"Why not?" she flashed, at once on the defensive.

He laughed. "What on earth should we do with a Professor of Economics in the house?"

She answered seriously — "It would be the best thing that could happen to us."

He showed chagrin at this. He said — "Then you're glad that the boy isn't like me?"

She drew his face to her and kissed him. "One of you is all I can manage, darling."

But he was not satisfied. "I should think you would have liked your son to be like your husband. This fellow isn't like any of us."

"He is like ..." She hesitated, as she always did, when speaking of her father to Renny.

"A far finer character," he finished for her.

"Surely you can understand how much it means to me that he should resemble my father? Surely you don't feel jealousy of someone you have never even seen!"

He was ashamed. He said eagerly:

"I am glad he looks like your dad, if it pleases you, my sweet! God knows, there are Whiteoaks enough! Perhaps he'll be a go-getter and put the family on its legs again."

Alayne found no allurement in this picture of her baby's future. She frowned and said:

"I hope he will have my father's intellect."

"Look here!" said Renny, "It's time he was christened. And we've never discussed his name. That do you want to call him, eh?" In truth he had thought a good deal about his son's name but had waited for Alayne to say that it should be named for him.

He could scarcely conceal his disappointment when she said:

"I want to call him Archer. You won't mind, will you?"

He repeated — "Archer ... Archer Whiteoak. Hm, it's an odd sort of name!"

"I think it's a lovely name. What a picture it brings to one's mind when you consider the meaning of it! An archer with his bow and arrow, standing beneath a tall oak tree. Don't you see that, Renny?"

"No," he returned perversely, "I see a professor in his cap and gown, riding Mrs. Spindles."

"Oh, you're hopeless!" She pressed the baby close to her and pressed his fingers to her lips.

"May I give him a second name?" he demanded.

"Of course — a dozen if you like!"

"Court, then. Archer Court Whiteoak." Alayne had to be content with Adeline's old perambulator for the baby, when she longed for one of the latest design. A thousand times she thought of what she might do for him, if only her income had not vanished! However, he did have a new crib, of a delicious pale blue enamel, and this stood in the corner of her room, where Adeline's had once been. But what a different child! One might forget he was in the room he slept so sweetly, the little downy silver head just showing above the satin quilt. Week by week Alayne watched his intelligence unfold. She saw that it was of a different order from Adeline's. His grey-blue eyes followed her movements, looked into her face, with what she felt was an almost uncanny understanding. At his age Adeline's gaze had been as remote, as detached as that of some little wild animal peeping from its burrow. Oh, but this boy was near to Alayne's heart! When she woke in the morning he was her first thought. She glided barefoot across the floor to make sure that all was well with him.

Piers remarked to Renny — "It's disgusting, this habit of wives — having a first son with no look of his father or his father's family. Gran did it. Pheasant did it. Now Alayne. My own mother did it."

"Mine didn't," said Renny.

"That's true!" laughed Piers, then asked. "What was your mother like? Neither you nor Meg resemble her."

Renny stared at him incredulously. "You don't mean to tell me that you don't know what my mother looked like?"

"No. How could I? I should scarcely have known what my own looked like — if I hadn't been told that Eden was the image of her."

"Well, all I can say for you is, that you ought to be ashamed. Next Sunday I'll get out the old album and show you their pictures."

These brothers were so much thrown together, they were both so strong-willed and domineering, that quarrels between them were inevitable. Earlier in his life Piers had chafed or been sullen under Renny's tyranny, magnanimous though it was. Now, he not only resisted when he could, but sometimes attempted to tyrannize over Renny himself.

Once Harriet Archer was an unseen witness of one of their quarrels. She had formed the habit of herself walking to the stables every fine morning. The air was becoming fresh and warm. The horses were being schooled for the spring shows. She was often deeply moved by the thought that she was becoming one with the life at Jalna.

She heard raised voices as she approached the paddock. She saw Wright, another man and the boy Wilf standing by holding horses which, attentive and motionless, seemed to listen with dignity to the altercation. Renny and Piers faced each other and Harriet heard from their lips words she had never expected to hear spoken. These were so mixed with the jargon of the stable that nothing was really coherent to her. But she knew that it was all very bad. She was afraid, by the expressions of their faces, that they would come to blows. If they did, she thought, she would cast discretion aside and rush between them. Her heart thumped at the thought of this but she had a faint, a very faint, feeling of disappointment when they turned from each other without violence.

Renny mounted one of the horses and put it at a jump in a manner which suggested that he was ready to fly to pieces with rage. Piers was given a leg up by Wright and galloped down the course after Renny. But his temper affected his mount. It kicked the top bar from the gate, ducked its head and all but threw Piers. Harriet could see how he tugged at the rein, hear how he lathered the horse. Renny galloped back to him. The horses reared. The brothers shouted.

"Now," thought Miss Archer, panting with blood lust, "now Renny will strike him with his crop!"

But Renny did not! Renny was laughing! Extraordinary man! In another minute they were trotting amicably side by side. The boy Wilf looked over his shoulder, saw Miss Archer and grinned at her. She grinned back. She dug her hands into the pockets of her cardigan and stuck out her chest....

Alayne watched this metamorphosis of her aunt with mingled amusement and annoyance. It was funny, it was rather pathetic, but it was most of all annoying. Her aunt was deliberately, calculatingly, making herself over into a Whiteoak. She had almost no material to work with but she was succeeding! She had accomplished in three months what Alayne had not accomplished in ten years. A somewhat chilly rift opened, ever so slightly, between aunt and niece.

During these months Nicholas and Ernest had religiously given Renny seventy-five dollars a month each. His mind had been divided between gratification and shame when his uncles proposed that they should do so. He hated the thought of taking money from anyone under his roof but the temptation was too great, his need too pressing. He looked at the first cheque in bewilderment and delight. It seemed too good to be true. At the same time he was afraid that, if Piers knew of these monthly payments, he would come down on him more severely for repairs and feed bills. He said to his uncles, looking thoughtfully at the cheque:

"I think it would be better if you didn't mention this to Piers. He's a queer dog. If he knew I was getting this every month —"

Nicholas interrupted, rather glumly — "Piers already knows."

Ernest added — "Yes. Piers was there when we first discussed it."

"Well," said Renny, "I'm sorry for that."

Piers did not fail to enquire whether his uncles had toed the line. Renny was able to put him off for several weeks but at last was forced to admit that they had.

"They'd better!" growled Piers.

"What?" Renny turned on him suspiciously. "What?"

The danger of telling him the truth made Piers add — "Well, it is only the decent thing to do." He was very curious to know whether Miss Archer was contributing toward the household expenses. He doubted Renny when he said that her losses were only comparative. But he liked the little woman and he liked her attitude toward the family, toward Renny and Adeline in particular.

He felt that a good deal of sympathy and a little petting were good for old redhead in these days. He saw a troublous time ahead of him. He had Alayne back. Her love for him was obvious. But there was Sarah across the ravine waiting, like a wolf, for the mortgage that in a few months would fall due.

There was one member of the circle whom Harriet Archer had not yet analyzed and that was Sarah. She had already met her in Meg's house. She was not sure how she felt toward her, whether she was attracted or repelled. She was fascinating and yet there was something repellent about her. Harriet was not sure whether it was not the repellant element that fascinated her. There was something cruel in the girl.

~ ~ ~

On a sudden impulse she made up her mind to go to see Sarah. She would drop in, as though casually. Sarah herself had suggested this.

She thought as she walked through the ravine that she had never, even in youth, been more fully conscious of the delights of spring. The iron fist of winter had unclenched. It had half-opened. Now, in its curve, were seen the promised treasures. Soon these would be offered on an extended palm, flung to the winds....

She crossed the bridge and climbed the moist path on the other side. All about was a glossy carpet of wintergreen with its pinkish-white bells. Tiny orchids saved their heads by having stems too short for plucking. An oriole bragged of his beauty and his courtship, in the weeping green fountain of a silver birch. Two red squirrels, halfway up the trunk of a pine, paused in their amorous chase to flaunt their arched tails and upbraid her for her intrusion.

Harriet discovered that she was far less winded by the ascent than she would have been four months ago. Nevertheless she breathed rather quickly as she emerged from the trees and looked across the open space to the fox farm. She wanted terribly to do what she had set out to do, efficiently and yet with caution, and she dreaded interfering in the affairs of other people — something she had never in her life done.

Sarah was bending over a bed of blue hyacinths and she was wearing a pale green dress with long drooping sleeves. The shining convolutions of her massed black braids made her head have the appearance of being carved out of ebony. She turned and faced Harriet Archer with a startled look. In a day of scarlet lips, hers were palely chiselled, folded together in a flower-bud secrecy.

"I hope I have not frightened you," said Harriet. "I was walking this way and I saw you. I couldn't resist coming in."

Sarah smiled palely and held out her hand. "I wasn't frightened," she said, "just excited. When anyone comes on me suddenly I am always hoping it may be Finch."

Harriet, embarrassed by this frankness yet encouraged by it also, answered simply:

"It is very hard for you, living apart from Finch. It is very hard, I am sure."

"It is terrible. And the worst of it is that he would have come to me long ago if it were not for that villainous brother of his."

Harriet blinked. She had barely arrived and here she was in the thick of it! She said:

"Oh, surely, you don't think of Renny as villainous!"

Sarah fronted her. "How else can I think of him? He has deliberately come between two lovers. Isn't that villainous? And it's not only that. You are Alayne's aunt. You know what sort of husband he was to her. He used to come through that ravine — into that wood — to meet the woman who lived in this house. Wasn't that villainous? He drove Alayne from him. Then — when he wanted Alayne — when Clara Lebraux was gone — he went and brought her back. He would like to make us all slaves. But he'll find that I am different. I am not submissive. I'll strike back." A pale radiance brightened her face. She showed her small white teeth.

"Might we sit down?" asked Harriet. "I think we could talk more calmly. That is, if you want to talk to me."

"I want to talk to anyone who will listen!" exclaimed Sarah. "I want to scream his injustice, to the world." She led the way to the verandah and they sat where Clara and Pauline had so often rested.

"How pretty this place is!" Harriet said.

"You should have seen it when I came here. It was hideous. But I have done a good deal to it. It has been something to occupy me, and I like the place. It's secluded and yet not far from the town. I intend to live here always."

"In this house?" asked Harriet, softly.

Sarah gave her a daring look as though to say — "Now go and repeat this to the Whiteoaks!" The words she spoke were:

"No. I intend to live at Jalna."

Harriet felt afraid of her, afraid of her cold, derisive smile. Yet there was something empty, childlike, about her. She was like water on which nothing could be written. Harriet whispered:

"What do you mean — live at Jalna?"

There was never a sweeter voice than Sarah's. She said:

"Don't you know about the mortgage? It falls due in a few weeks. I will not renew it. I'm going to turn all those people out and live there myself. I'll live there alone — unless Finch will live with me."

"Are you firm in this?" asked Harriet.

"As firm as iron."

Harriet Archer said — "Do you know what I think about you? I don't think you love Finch at all."

"Not love Finch! I love him too much. That is the trouble."

"Not the man! You don't love the man. What you love is the excitement of his presence. That's all you care about. It's all you can understand. I haven't known either of you very long but I feel that — know it in my inmost soul. Oh, do try, if it is possible to you — to care for the real man! Then you will know that what you contemplate doing would be the very peak of cruelty to him."

She knew her last words were wasted but she thought — "I must be true to myself. I must give her a chance." She sat contemplating Sarah with her mild, pastel blue gaze. But her soul was seething in protective energy toward Jalna and the family.

Sarah answered, almost indifferently — "I would kill him rather than give him up to that man."

Harriet Archer rose. "I think I had better go," she said. "I can see that there is nothing to be done — that I can do" — then she added, almost inaudibly — "on this side of the ravine."

She returned the way she had come and this time, as she mounted the imposing slope, she felt even less fatigue than before. She felt powerful for good. As she reached the top she looked down at the stream shining below, her eyes took in the fairness of the land. She raised her two hands high above her head and clenched them, as one who declared — "Curfew shall not ring tonight!"

Ernest had just crossed the lawn, a daisy between his finger and thumb. He opened the little white gate at the top of the path for her, and said:

"What a charming gesture! You look the very personification of spring!"

No wonder Harriet wanted to protect this house.

XXIX

HARRIET AND FINCH

FINCH HAD LOCKED the piano and he had the key in his pocket. Several times lately he had been startled by the torturing sound of small children strumming on the keys. He had found Adeline and Roma standing side by side — making the dreadful discords. Their look of exaltation had changed to one of defiance on Adeline's part, fear on Roma's, when he had angrily forbidden them to touch the keys again. They had persisted and this morning he had really frightened them both. They had run away and he had locked the piano and put the key in his pocket. He wondered at himself for not having done this before. It gave him a sense of security, of mastery, not over the children but over the piano itself. He had bound it in silence. Now its voice, appealing, torturing, could not again speak to him.

Curiously, one of the discords made by the children remained with him, not as an irritation but as something strange and suggestive. He hummed it over and over as he went toward the orchard. Lately he had been going there as the most secret place he could find. He would hide himself among the tree trunks in the very midst of the army of trees and lie staring up at the white torrent of bloom. He would listen to the steady murmur of the bees, watch the petals drift down when a bird sprang from a bough.

He could scarcely believe his eyes when he saw how today everything was changed. He was disappointed out of all proportion to what
he had lost. He took it almost as a personal injury. Piers had had his
men at work there. The ground beneath the trees had been ploughed up.
The path Finch had followed was gone. There was nothing there but the
rough brownness of moist earth. And as though this were not enough
Piers himself stood in a wagon with the spraying machine, holding in
his hands the hose from which the poisonous rainbow of the Bordeaux
mixture arched itself against the sky.

Finch's expression was almost comic in dismay. Piers saw him and
called out a genial hello! He waggled the hose and the rainbow writhed
in sinister salute.

Finch waved his hand in reply but it was a limp gesture. He did not
know where to go, what to do with himself. His hand, in his pocket,
fingered the key of the piano.

At this moment Harriet Archer appeared on the path, coming
toward him. He felt that she was coming toward him with purpose and
he was determined to avoid her if he could. But she gave him no chance
of doing so. She fixed her eyes on his face and held him with them as
she drew near.

He had to face her.

She said, rather breathlessly — "I must see you. I have been looking
everywhere for you. Where can we talk alone?"

"Well," he looked about vaguely, "I don't know. I —" A faint colour
flooded his face. "Are you sure it's me you want to see?"

"Oh, quite, quite sure! You are the only one who can help."

He opened his long, large-pupilled eyes in surprise.

"Well — then, of course — I wonder where we had better go." He
looked about him bewildered.

"I should not trouble you. But — you are the only one who can help.
The only one." She looked searchingly into his face. She was afraid she
could not reach him, make him willing to do something desperate to
save Jalna.

"There's a packing shed beyond the orchard," he said. "We might go
there." He thought — If once she gets me alone I may not be able to

escape.... But I'll go with her and — if it's anything I can't listen to — I'll tell her I'm not well.... Perhaps Piers — He said:

"There's Piers. He is much better than I am at ... at helping ... doing the sort of thing.... I'm really no good at all...." He made as though to leave her.

But her small figure blocked the way! "You must listen! You must hear what I have to say!"

He led the way resignedly to an open shed where fruit boxes and crates, left over from the past season, littered the floor. Before them was a stretch of raspberry and blackberry canes in new leaf and the close matted rows of a strawberry bed. They sat down on a bench and Finch took off his glasses and polished them. Harriet had got some of the sandy soil in her shoe. She felt tired and hot. Her strength seemed to have left her. She suddenly felt alone — and alien.

But this weakening of will was the forwarding of her purpose. Finch, looking shyly at her, no longer felt the desire to escape. He said:

"This is a quiet place for talking.... I'm so sorry if you're in trouble."

Impulsively she laid her hand on his. He thought he had never felt a more soothing touch. She said:

"It's not really my trouble — except that I love the place — and the people who live in it."

He looked into her eyes with a deepening interest — with cool intelligence she had not yet seen in his. "Yes?" he said.

She went on desperately — "I suppose you know that — that there is a mortgage on Jalna."

He coloured. "Of course."

"And that it expires this summer?"

"I hadn't thought of that."

Her eyes accused him. "You hadn't thought ..."

His colour deepened. "Well — you see, I've been ill so long.... Nearly a year."

She said, almost sharply — "You don't look ill now. You did when I came here."

"Oh, I'm better. I hadn't remembered.... But, look here, when these things expire they renew them, don't they?"

Harriet Archer rapped out — "Your wife won't! She's going to fore-close. You know what that will mean to Renny — to all of you!"

Finch stared incredulously. "But he'll never let her. Don't imagine that he'll take that lying down!"

"I don't think he knows. She has just told me. I have come straight from her."

"You have come straight from her!" Finch spoke almost dreamily as though to someone who had just returned from an unimagined land.

"Yes. I'm almost out of breath." She felt that perhaps he might resent, for some subtle reason, her agitation. She would therefore give it a physical cause.

He asked — "Why did she tell this to you? Do you think she was using you as a sort of — mediator?"

She saw his hostility to Sarah in the hardening of his lips. She answered:

"Sarah said I might come back and tell him — Renny, I mean."

"And have you?"

"No — I couldn't bear to! Not till I'd seen you."

He asked gravely — "Miss Archer, what do you think I could do?"

"I thought perhaps — oh, how can I put it into words! I thought perhaps you would see her yourself. Plead with her. She's terribly in love with you, you know."

He broke out excitedly — "Tell me the truth! Why is Sarah doing this? I am sure you know."

"She thinks — she blames Renny for your refusing to live with her."

"Then — is she getting even with him? Or trying to force me back to her?"

"Either — or both. I'm not sure that I know."

"Miss Archer, tell me the truth. Did you come to see whether you could persuade me to go back to Sarah?"

Harriet averted her eyes. It took some courage for her to reply.

"I thought perhaps if you knew…. People do come together again — after separation."

"Not after a separation like ours," he said savagely. "I tell you, I wouldn't do that — not to save Jalna — not for Renny's sake — well, it's just unthinkable!"

She looked at him pathetically. "Do you think I ought to go to him — tell him what she has threatened?"

"No. I'll go myself. He's over there now, talking to Piers. I'll go straight to him."

"Do you think he will be able to raise the money?"

"I think he'd move heaven and earth to save Jalna."

He smiled at her. It was the first time she had seen his wide boyish smile and her heart warmed to him. She said:

"He's been so kind to me. No one in all my life has ever been so kind. I can't bear to think ..." She clasped her hands tightly in her lap. "Perhaps after you have talked with him, you will tell me what he said. I'll just sit here and wait."

Finch covered the ground between them and Renny in long strides. Renny turned an approving look on him.

"Well," he said, "I haven't seen you walk like that for a long while."

"Look here, Renny." He took Renny by the sleeve and drew him along the path. The wagon was lumbering away from them, leaving the evil smell of the Bordeaux mixture.

"Renny," said Finch, "I've just been having a talk with Miss Archer."

"I'm glad of that. Nice little woman, isn't she? And fits in surprisingly well."

Finch gave a short laugh. "Yes, surprisingly.... She has just been telling me that the mortgage on Jalna expires this summer. I'd forgotten."

Renny's eyebrows went up. "Why the devil should she tell you that?"

"Because Sarah has just told her that she intends to foreclose."

Renny showed instant alarm but exclaimed:

"She won't do it!"

"You don't know Sarah if you say that. She's absolutely relentless. Hasn't she given you any warning?"

"She's dropped hints. She's said she'd like to own Jalna. She's said she would like to spend the rest of her days here. Of course, the root of it all is, that she wants you." He turned his penetrating gaze on Finch.

Finch bore it and its implications without flinching. He put his hands in his pockets and his fingers closed over the key of the piano. He said.

"And can't have me."

"That's right! Stick to that! She'd ruin your life. I hate the sight of her myself."

"Renny, what shall you do?" There was still in his tone something of the old implicit belief in Renny's power.

The face he looked into was formidable enough at this moment to justify the belief. Its weather-beaten hardness was concentrated into a defensive widening of the nostrils and strengthening of the muscles about the mouth.

"I must raise the money! The witch is mistaken if she thinks she'll ever make her nest in Jalna. If I can't get any of my friends to help me out — and I'm afraid there's not much chance of that — in these days — then I must sell off the horses — some of the land — I'll sell my soul if necessary —" His eyes blazed into Finch's.

Finch caught him by the arm. "Renny — the solution lies with me! It's all as easy as rolling off a log! I have enough money left to pay off the mortgage. You must take it!"

Renny's lips softened to tenderness. "You would do that, Finch? But you mustn't! It isn't fair!"

"But it is fair! It's just — and nothing more."

"God — it will take a load off my mind to have it in your hands instead of hers!"

"No, no, I don't mean that! I don't mean that at all! Renny, I don't want to hold a mortgage on Jalna. I'd loathe it. It's bad enough holding a mortgage on Vaughanlands. You know in your heart that it's only fair you should have a share of Gran's money. This is your share. You are to pay the money to Sarah and tear up the papers. I want nothing out of it — but my freedom! And I'll feel a thousand times freer when she has her clutches off you — her death grip — her mortgage!" He was becoming too excited. His lips trembled. He began to shake all over. Looking at him, realizing what he was doing, Renny too was deeply moved. He could not speak. He just stood staring, his proud face softening more and more till his lips trembled also.

"Shut up!" he said gently. "You're making a fool of yourself — and me too —" He took out a clean handkerchief, neatly folded, shook it and loudly blew his nose.

"It's all right, isn't it? You'll do it straight away?" said Finch.

"Will I? It's the happiest day of my life — I can tell you that. I've been worried over this more than anyone knows. I've been to the bank — I've tried to get a loan from them — but they're being damned careful about loans in these days. As for selling my horses — it would ruin me! But that's all over, thanks to you, Finch. You're the best brother in the world, old man."

"Don't!" said Finch. "Don't thank me, Renny. I can't bear it!"

Abruptly he turned away and began to walk swiftly along the sandy path marked by the wheels of the farm wagon. From it he turned into the narrow bridle path that led through the wood. It was the first time this year that he had gone there. It was a place too pregnant with the memories of his boyhood — all those strange fears and exalted hopes. He had had the dread also of meeting Sarah there, for Piers had told him of seeing her in the very heart of it.

Now he did not give her a thought. He thought of nothing but the new lightness and strength that was pouring into him. His breast ached with the colossal uprising of his spirit. As he strode among the pines he struck his breast with his hand feeling the new power in him. He tried to think what this power was. It rose to him out of the land, as though from the soles of his feet. There was a communion between him and the land such as he had not felt in years. But this was something new because in it was the blending of his childhood, his boyhood, his manhood. All his past, present, and future, all the splendour and misery of his thoughts were one with the land.... He threw himself on the pine needles at the foot of the tall dark trees that shut out the sunlight and buried his face in his arms.

He lay there pressing his body against the life-giving earth. Why am I suddenly so strong, so well, he thought. What has broken the chains that held me to fear and pain? I don't need to ask myself this. It is because I have given away the last of Gran's money. I've given it to Renny who should have had it all.... I've been so selfish, so morbidly wrapped up in my own suffering, that I have forgotten the suffering of others. I was like a swimmer who has been submerged under a great wave, suffocating, cut off from the light and air. But now I can breathe. I can see the light ...

I've given away everything. I've forgotten myself. Now I'm conscious of all that's about me — in a new way. There's no fear in me. It goes through me like music.... like music....

He turned on his side and looked at his sensitive bony hand spread out on the pine needles. His hand had a new meaning. Something apart from himself. His fingers were like five separate beings with individual power of their own. But his wrist bound them to him.

He heard the most minute sounds.... Surely he heard the very rustling of the pine needles as they made room for those that, this moment, fell.... Surely he heard the murmurs of the moss that edged the hump of that strong root.... Was it not possible that he heard the pine roots communing with each other in the warm earth? Heard the faint cry of the bud as it first felt the air?

Something sharp pressed against his hip. He rolled over and thrust his hand in his pocket. He found the key of the piano and took it out. It was warmed by his body. He lay smiling, with it in his hand. The strange, yet rather fascinating discord the children had made on the piano that morning, began to go through his head.

XXX

PAID IN FULL

A CARD WAS stuck above the electric bell stating that it was out of order. But there was a knocker on the door, a man in armour made of brass. Renny knocked on this and the small sharp blows vibrated through the house. Sarah answered the door herself, standing on the threshold with the expectant air she always had now when summoned.

A shadow crossed her face when she saw who it was. Then she smiled a little and gave him a slanting inquisitive look, feeling sure that Miss Archer's message had brought him there. If there was to be a scene between them, she thought, she would summon all the cruelty in her to hurt him as he had hurt her. But she spoke to him gently and they went into a small living room. This was the room where Antoine Lebraux had died, but Sarah had so changed it that it was not recognizable to Renny. It was furnished in green. The lamp was green-shaded and in its light their faces showed pallid, almost sinister. Magazines, boxes of sweets, and cushions were littered about. The air was heavy with the scent of Russian cigarettes. Yet Sarah looked cool and fresh. She glanced inquisitively at the dispatch case he carried in his hand.

He set it on the table and said:

"You may well look at it. There is a good deal of money in it. It's the last of any transaction — business or otherwise — between you and me."

She was mystified. She said:

"You look exactly like an agent of some sort — or a piano tuner. Have you come to tune my piano?"

"No. I've come to pay the piper." He opened the case and showed her that it was filled with bank notes. "There — there is the amount of the mortgage in full!"

"The amount of the mortgage in full?" she repeated faintly.

"Yes. Miss Archer told me that you had made up your mind to foreclose, so I have brought the money. I suppose it's idiotic of me but I couldn't bear to pay it by cheque. I wanted to hand the actual money to you — to see the lump sum pass from my hands to yours. I wish I could have brought it in gold or even silver. But it would have been very inconvenient for you, even if I could have done it. Now, if you will sit down opposite me, I will count out the money on the table. I want you to be sure that it's right."

"Why, yes, if you like —" She sat down beside the table obediently like a child.

But she could not keep her mind on the counting. Her eyes moved from the capable shifting of the notes between his fingers to his face, greenish bronze in the strange light. So all her revenge on him had come to this? He was sitting opposite her unwelding, link by link, the chain by which she had thought to bind Jalna to her....

Curiously, as she watched him, her antagonism faded. It was possible that no heat of anger could survive in the watery-green light of the room. Her glance was almost obsequious as she watched the mound of notes grow beneath his hands, the thousands upon thousands of dollars. She said:

"It was wonderful that you could lay your hands on all that at a moment's notice."

"Ssh!" he returned sharply, and went on counting.

She drooped silent, submissive. When he had laid the last note on the pile he said:

"I couldn't have done it if it hadn't been for Finch."

Her breath was expelled in a sharp exhalation.

"Finch!" she repeated. "Did he lend you all that?"

"He didn't lend it. He gave it."

"But why should he do that?"

A smile flickered across Renny's face.

"Oh," he said, "I think you can guess."

"You mean ... so that I should have to go away from here?"

"Yes. I haven't seen him look so happy in years as when he gave me that money."

Her tone was almost confidential. "Then you think it's absolutely hopeless — his ever coming back to me?"

"I told you that long ago. But you would persist. Now you can see that it's quite useless. You'll have to go away, Sarah."

"But where can I go? What can I do?"

"Good God!" he answered testily. "You have the whole world before you! You're young. You should find another man."

"Finch is the one man I could love. He is the only being in the world who matters to me."

"You should meet other people. It's wrong to shut yourself up here like a hermit. It has made you neurotic."

She was looking at him steadily. He was struck silent by the look of hate in her eyes.

"Why should you look at me like that?" he asked. "I've only done what is natural."

She did not answer. She seemed to draw on all her reserve of power to concentrate her look on him.

He gave a short laugh and said — "Well, I've paid the money ... so that's the end of that."

She shouted, with a vehemence that startled him — "I won't take your money! I won't have it!" She snatched up the mound of banknotes from the table and darted toward the glowing fire.

He sprang after her and caught her by the wrists. She gave a scream so piercing that he turned pale. She tore one hand free and with it struck him again and again. "You devil!" she screamed. "I'll kill you!"

He held her off while he gathered up the notes. He thrust them into a deep drawer of the writing table, locked it, then tossed the key into the glowing coals.

She sank on to the couch and buried her face in her hands.

He asked — "Have you the papers in the house?"

"No," she answered hoarsely. He scarcely knew the voice for Sarah's.

"Well, it doesn't matter. I can get them later. But you must sign this receipt for the money.... If I'd known you'd carry on like this I should certainly have sent a cheque to your lawyer. Now, I want you to behave yourself and sit up." He carried the receipt on a blotting pad to her side.

She sat up rigid and took the pen from his hands.

"Sign here," he said, pointing the place with his finger. She signed. Then she raised her white face, Medusa-like under her black hair, to his: "If it had been you," she said, "if it had been you I'd loved, you would have never cast me off. Oh, I wish it had been you!"

XXXI

UNRAVELLING

THE NEWS THAT Finch had paid the mortgage, that Jalna stood liberated, foursquare to the winds, swept through the house from attic to basement. The house seemed conscious of the good news. It had a prideful air as though it spread its roof with a new assurance above the cherished beings beneath. It drank in the early summer sunshine. It hunched its gables against the beating summer storms. At night its walls re-echoed the cries of the whippoorwills, its windows reflected the lightning. In the mornings its chimneys sent up genial spirals of smoke.

The future master of Jalna thrived. His sister grew handsomer every day. Even Roma's cheeks put on the colour of a wild rose and her spindling legs grew round and firm. Her hair became thick and lay on her head in a golden sheen.

The farmlands showed the promise of rich crops. The blossoms of the orchard trees were set in the seal of fruit. Piers boasted that not a foal, calf, or young pig had died. The hens seemed to delight in hatching large broods. Piers caught Meg in the very act of gliding about his poultry-house with a basket into which she was popping eggs for a setting of his pure-bred stock. She said that she was in a kind of haze from all that had transpired and scarcely knew what she was doing. He let her keep the eggs.

Word came from Wakefield that they might expect him in a few days. Renny had written to him of the paying off of the mortgage and it was understood that Wakefield could not rest till he had had a day with the family. He must join in the jubilation.

It was Nicholas who suggested that they should celebrate by a dinner party, to which all the family must come. This should coincide with Wakefield's visit and should be given in honour of Finch — if Finch felt able to bear that honour.

Finch agreed, but he must not be asked to make a speech, even to this intimate few. He remembered his speech on his twenty-first birthday.

To Renny especially the thought of the dinner came most acceptably. He would be glad of the chance of a little display. The thought that Harriet Archer had known of the distress of his situation, his bitter need of money, had rankled within him. He wanted her to feel that he made no sacrifice in offering her a home. He wanted to impose on her mind the generous well-being of the old days at Jalna. He and Alayne talked over plans for the dinner. She thought he was being extravagant for a family party but delighted in seeing him extravagant. She wrote out as intricate a menu as she thought Mrs. Wragge could cope with. At Renny's wish the best silver and Captain Whiteoak's massive dinner service were brought out. At Finch's wish even old friends were not invited. His confidence was too lately won. He could not face outsiders.

In these days the wonder of each awakening lay in his freedom. Sarah was gone. The fox farm was empty. Now he could wander as far afield as he chose without ever the fear of meeting her. She had said goodbye to none of them. She had gone away without a word the day after her interview with Renny. Removers had come and taken what she owned from the house. It still held the furniture the family had lent her. Already the grass of the lawn was growing long and the house beginning to look desolate. Finch went there one day, his mind full of confused thoughts, and peered in at the windows. He was surprised to see Ernest and Harriet Archer sitting on the couch in the living room in close conversation. Finch, startled, remembered his voyage to England in company with his uncles and how attentive Ernest had been to an American lady on board. Now here he was in obvious admiration of Alayne's aunt. There was something in American women that appealed to him.

Finch went away without having been seen. He could not rest. Nothing he could do satisfied the urge of the new energy that was in him. But he had not found himself. In spite of the happiness, the peace he had given Renny, the sense of tranquility he had been able to give to Jalna, he had not found himself. He longed for the coming of Wakefield.

Two days later Wakefield came. They all had to acknowledge that the life of the monastery agreed with him. He looked healthier than they had ever seen him, and happier too. His eyes glowed with happiness. He could not look at you without smiling.

Alayne had got herself a new dress for the dinner. It was long since she had bought herself anything new — excepting the things for the Horse Show — and she had a woman's instinct to deck her body in her new happiness. She had asked Renny what he thought about it and he had agreed that a new dress would become her. She could have wept when he drew out the last payment he had had from his uncles and pushed it into her hand. She remembered how close she had been with him when she was the one who had money and he had none. But she smiled — took a quarter of what he had offered and gave the rest back. Again she could almost have wept at his look of relief. Was she always to live between smiles and tears?

He was ready first and he came to see her in her new dress, a gay flowered taffeta with a little train. She was standing in front of her pier glass, so that, on opening the door, he discovered two of her. He elongated his face and held up his hands in an excess of admiration.

"A peach!" he breathed. "A perfect peach!"

She faced him. "Do you like it so well?"

"I love it. By George, I have never seen you look so lovely!"

"Never?" she spoke incredulously.

"Never!" he answered with fervour.

She almost agreed as she turned again to her reflection. The new styles suited her and, in the last months, her face had gained something it had lacked.

From behind he clasped her about the middle and they swayed together. He began to laugh.

Her face slanted upward toward his. "What are you laughing at?"

"I was remembering the night I took the money to Sarah."

"Tck — I can't see what there was funny in that!"

"I was remembering how she screamed — really screeched — and hit me on the head."

Alayne was horrified. "Hit you!"

"Didn't I tell you?"

"You never mentioned it! She dared hit you! I always thought she had a violent temper underneath that air of remoteness."

"Yes that's true. And she said something.... What was it, now?... Oh yes — she said that, if it had been me she loved, I should never have cast her off."

"I hope she flattered herself."

"She did indeed. I couldn't have loved that girl — not if she and I were the last two on earth. But I admit I like the thought of her better since she said that."

"Well, thank goodness, she's gone!"

They went downstairs hand in hand.

When Ernest found the opportunity he drew Renny aside and said — "I think it would be better if you did not mention the names of my mother or Eden at dinner tonight. I know you do it out of your great affection but it is saddening and I particularly want everything to pass off happily, without the least shadow."

Renny stared rather aggressively at his uncle. "Do you mean to say it will spoil the party if I mention Gran's name?"

"No, no, no, but — sometimes you have rather a sombre way with you. Do speak of my mother if you like but I really think you had better not refer to Eden ... not tonight, dear boy."

"I'll not mention either of them," returned Renny huffily.

He still looked taciturn when Finch ran into him in the doorway of the dining room. He had slipped in there to look at the table. He had the most extraordinary feeling of extreme youngness and irresponsibility. The thought of seeing the table finely spread was an excitement. He found himself stirred by things which, a few weeks ago, would have left him untouched or shrinking. Now this family party — this close drawing together — this air of festivity — this feeling of being a boy again — younger than any of them — younger than Wake…. He looked eagerly into Renny's face. Would he guess? Renny said:

"Ha, you've been pinching something off the table! Young whelp!"

Rags hardly knew himself in a new coat. No bishop in ceremonial robes could have shown greater dignity than Rags as he waited at table. He was filled with vanity at his own appearance, with pride in his wife's achievement. No one could deny that the dinner was perfect, from the clear soup to the first strawberries of the season served with rich ice cream. Everyone ate well but none so well as Wakefield.

Meg was rather pensive. It was hard to think of Renny and Alayne so miraculously freed from their mortgage while she and Maurice still laboured under theirs — the unpaid interest mounting up and up. But no one enjoyed delicious food more than she did and she put her envy from her and beamed around the table.

Harriet Archer was sitting on Renny's right. She was conscious of the admiring glances he gave at her chiffon dress of pinkish-mauve, at her beautifully waved silver hair. She felt that she and Alayne possessed a style very different from that of Meg and Pheasant. Yet she acknowledged that never had she sat down to a table surrounded by such striking-looking people as these. Her eyes dwelt longest on Ernest's aristocratic aquiline face.

Ernest was rising to his feet. Surely they were not to have speeches! thought Alayne.

Piers exclaimed — "Hear! Hear!"

Nicholas gave his brother an encouraging smile.

"I'm not going to make a speech," said Ernest, rather nervously. "I'm just going to tell you something which I hope will please you. I have all my life had a desire to get married, though you may not have guessed it. But I could never find the one person to whom I felt I was perfectly suited. Now I have found her and, though it's rather late in the day, I think we are going to be very happy. Miss Archer has promised to be my wife."

It was well that the family had had a glass of champagne before this announcement. As it was, they were thrown into a state of excitement.

Renny was frankly delighted. He put his arm about Harriet Archer and kissed her enthusiastically. Nicholas came and kissed her too though the announcement was no surprise to him. The men shook Ernest by the hand. Pheasant hugged him.

Piers exclaimed — "Good for you, Uncle Ernie! Well run! With the odds forty to one against you!"

Meg and Alayne exchanged one of their rare looks of sympathy. This was almost too much. Meg's uncle. Alayne's aunt. He over eighty. Harriet racing toward seventy. But they too achieved smiles of congratulation, though Alayne's was touched with incredulity. In truth she scarcely recognized in this exuberant little woman her retiring New England aunt who had lived up the Hudson.

"We thought," Ernest was saying to Renny, "that we should like to rent the fox farm, if you don't object. It's a nice little house and so convenient to Jalna. I think Harriet can make it look charming. Later on, of course, we'll go to England for a time."

Everyone talked at once. Rags, after ceremoniously offering his good wishes, brought more champagne. Piers and Maurice became a little hilarious. Meg found it necessary to press Maurice's foot under the table as his remarks concerning the approaching alliance showed an inclination toward raciness.

Wakefield alone seemed abstracted. Harriet Archer wondered whether the young monk disapproved. He sat rather in the shadow. Soon Renny noticed this and turned to him.

"Well," he said, "have you nothing to say for yourself?"

"Yes," returned Wakefield gravely, "I have something to say. But perhaps after all this excitement it will scarcely be noticed."

His lips pouted. He was afraid that Uncle Ernest had stolen his thunder.

Renny leant toward him. "What is it?"

"Only this," said Wakefield. He rose from his chair and stood motionless, black in his novice's robe.

All eyes turned to him. The smiles faded from their faces. Renny looked almost apprehensive.

Wakefield fixed his eyes on Renny's and began slowly to unbutton his robe. There was a complete silence as he divested himself of it and laid it carefully across the back of his chair. He now stood before them in a dinner jacket.

A gasp of amazement — even shock — put him at his ease again, gave him the sense of drama that was so strong a part of his life.

He turned to Piers.

"You were right, Piers," he said simply. "You said I'd come back, and I have. But you gave me just six months and it's taken a year. And I haven't left the monastery because I couldn't stick it, but because I knew I had to have the things Renny said a Whiteoak must have. The priests and the brothers have been perfectly splendid about it and — I hope you won't mind having me home again, Renny?" He flashed a smile, in which there was a touch of his boy's impudence, at Renny.

Renny sat silent, motionless as a statue. But though he was so still his eyes devoured Wakefield, noting the shape of his shoulders in the well-fitting jacket, the warm colour in his cheeks. From his eyes blazed his gratification, his relief, his pride.

Piers gave his young brother a thump on the back. "What a young fool you were to waste a year of your life!"

Meg exclaimed — "Pheasant, do come and take my place! I must be beside Wake!" She ran to Wakefield and clasped him to her. "Oh, how happy you've made me! It just seems too good to be true!" She began to cry, looking out of her streaming eyes into her youngest brother's face. "I brought you up, you know, Wake darling.... You must never, never forget that! But for me, you would never have pulled through — I can truthfully say that."

"He's been a mixed blessing," said Piers.

"Tell me, Wakefield, are you still a Catholic?" asked Ernest.

"I was never a better one. Piers says I've wasted a year but I think I'm always going to look back on that year as the best in my life."

Meg was sitting beside him now, clasping his hand. He sat proudly erect. The newly engaged couple were forgotten.

Nicholas growled — "The boy ought to go on the stage — with his looks and his talent."

"Regular movie-star eyelashes, hasn't he," said Pheasant.

"Shut up!" laughed Wakefield. Then he turned to Renny. "Haven't you anything to say to me, Renny?"

Renny answered — "Do you remember that dachshund pup I brought from New York? The chap I got him from said I should be able to sell him for seventy-five dollars when he was grown. Well, I have sold him for one hundred dollars today. What do you think of that?"

"Splendid!" said Wake. If old Renny wanted to talk dog, then dog it should be.

The others fell in with this. The conversation turned to the normal and agreeable channel of stables and kennel. But there was a dreamy undertone to it. Wakefield's return to the fold, Finch's recovery, the advent of Harriet Archer and her engagement to Ernest, Alayne's reconciliation to Renny, the birth of her son; all these changes and readjustments made themselves felt in subtle inflections of the voice, in swift interchange of glances. The dark cords of kinship which bound them inexorably together, vibrated with renewed strength. The continuity was absolute. With purged simplicity they found satisfaction in every detail of each other's expressions and words.

When the others went to the drawing room Renny remained for a little behind. Merlin had lain close to his feet during the dinner. Now he rose, stretched himself and raised his muzzle questioningly to his master. Renny went to the portrait of his grandmother and looked at it reflectively. Then he stepped on the rung of a chair so that his face was on a level with hers. He pressed his lips to the picture and said:

"It's all right, old lady. Everything's going fine."

THE END

THE JALNA NOVELS
BY MAZO DE LA ROCHE

In Order of Year of Publication

Jalna, 1927

Whiteoaks of Jalna, 1929

Finch's Fortune, 1931

The Master of Jalna, 1933

Young Renny, 1935

Whiteoak Harvest, 1936

Whiteoak Heritage, 1940

Wakefield's Course, 1941

The Building of Jalna, 1944

Return to Jalna, 1946

Mary Wakefield, 1949

Renny's Daughter, 1951

The Whiteoak Brothers, 1953

Variable Winds at Jalna, 1954

Centenary at Jalna, 1958

Morning at Jalna, 1960

In Order of Year Story Begins

The Building of Jalna, 1853

Morning at Jalna, 1863

Mary Wakefield, 1894

Young Renny, 1906

Whiteoak Heritage, 1918

The Whiteoak Brothers, 1923

Jalna, 1924

Whiteoaks of Jalna, 1926

Finch's Fortune, 1929

The Master of Jalna, 1931

Whiteoak Harvest, 1934

Wakefield's Course, 1939

Return to Jalna, 1943

Renny's Daughter, 1948

Variable Winds at Jalna, 1950

Centenary at Jalna, 1953

From *Mazo de la Roche: Rich and Famous Writer* by Heather Kirk

International Bestsellers
by Mazo de la Roche
Back in Print!

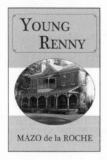

Jalna
978-1-894852-23-4
$24.95

Whiteoaks of Jalna
978-1-894852-24-1
$24.95

Wakefield's Course
978-1-55488-468-1
$24.99

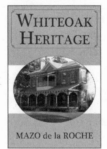

Whiteoak Heritage
978-1-55488-411-7
$24.99

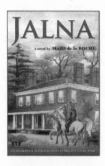

Young Renny
978-1-55488-410-0
$24.99

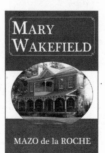

Mary Wakefield
978-1-55002-877-5
$24.99

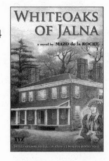

MAZO DE LA ROCHE was once Canada's best-known writer, loved by millions of readers around the world. She created unforgettable characters who come to life for her readers, but she was secretive about her own life. When she died in 1961, her cousin and lifelong companion, Caroline Clement, burned her diaries, adding to the aura of mystery that already surrounded Mazo.

Mazo de la Roche: Rich and Famous Writer
by Heather Kirk
978-1-894852-20-3
$17.95

Available at your favourite bookseller.

Tell us your story!
What did you think of this book?
Join the conversation at www.definingcanada.ca/tell-your-story
by telling us what you think.

 Recycled
Supporting responsible use
of forest resources
FSC www.fsc.org Cert no. SGS-COC-003153
© 1996 Forest Stewardship Council

Marquis imprimeur inc.

Québec, Canada
2010

   This book has been printed on 100% post consumer
waste paper, certified Eco-logo and processed chlorine free.